THE PLAY'S THE THING—

and in these original tales created especially for this volume, twenty-three of today's finest fantasy and science fiction writers have played with time, space, and the Bard himself to bring readers such great new tragedies and comedies as:

"Ancient Magics, Ancient Hope"—in which Owain Glyn Dwr's scrying of the future will force him to pit his own magic against that of Merlin. . . .

"Titus!"—when your audience is no longer human, and your stage is set in virtual reality, even Shakespeare may need an electronic co-author. . . .

"Swear Not by the Moon"—Romeo and Juliet could have an immortal romance if their love survived the light of day. . . .

WEIRD TALES
FROM
SHAKESPEARE

**More Imagination-Clutching Anthologies
Brought to You by DAW:**

DRACULA: PRINCE OF DARKNESS *Edited by Martin H. Greenberg*. From Dracula's traditional stalking grounds to the heart of such modern-day cities as New York and Chicago, the Prince of Darkness casts his spell over his helpless prey in a private blood drive from which there is no escape!

FRANKENSTEIN: THE MONSTER WAKES *Edited by Martin H. Greenberg*. From a journalist who stumbles upon a modern-day descendant of the famous doctor . . . to a mobster's physician whose innovative experiments might lead to a whole new kind of enforcer . . . to the monster's own determined search for a suitable bride . . . here are powerful new tales of creation gone awry.

CHRISTMAS GHOSTS *Edited by Mike Resnick and Martin H. Greenberg*. Everyone knows Christmas has truly arrived when *A Christmas Carol* takes center stage in both amateur and professional productions. Now some of the most creative minds in fantasy and science fiction tell readers exactly what those Christmas ghosts are up to when they're not scaring a stingy old man into self-reformation.

BY ANY OTHER FAME *Edited by Mike Resnick and Martin H. Greenberg*. What if Humphrey Bogart ran a detective agency? What if Groucho Marx was chosen to play Rhett Butler? What if Marilyn Monroe became a great feminist leader? Along with celebrities of stage and screen, these fanciful stories send such world-shakers as Adolf Hitler, Golda Meier, and Franklin Delano Roosevelt down entirely new pathways of destiny, transforming the world we know in ways we can't even begin to imagine.

WEIRD TALES FROM SHAKESPEARE

EDITED BY
Katharine Kerr &
Martin H. Greenberg

DAW BOOKS, INC.
DONALD A. WOLLHEIM, FOUNDER
375 Hudson Street, New York, NY 10014

ELIZABETH R. WOLLHEIM
SHEILA E. GILBERT
PUBLISHERS

First Printing, July 1994

1 2 3 4 5 6 7 8 9

DAW TRADEMARK REGISTERED
U.S. PAT. OFF. AND FOREIGN COUNTRIES
—MARCA REGISTRADA
HECHO EN U.S.A.

PRINTED IN THE U.S.A.

CONTENTS

INTRODUCTION

The idea for this anthology grew from a gathering of friends at the World Fantasy Convention in Tucson, Arizona, when Kate Daniel voiced an idea she had for redoing the story of *Hamlet* from Gertrude's point of view. Innocently, I remarked that short stories on Shakespearean themes would make an excellent anthology. Susan Shwartz fixed me with a steely eye and said, "Well?" in the proverbial tone that brooks no argument. *Weird Tales from Shakespeare* is the result. Of the original company, only Susan stands unrepresented, thanks to the pressures of other work.

Martin Greenberg and I have collected as wide a variety of stories as we could. As our central idea, we propose that Shakespeare and his stories form part of our modern mythology. His plays are the single most important Grand Literary Monument of our culture; his plots and ideas, as well as his life, are venerated so highly and kept so within the public view, what with play productions, references in books, and even television programs, that they have an existence beyond that of an ordinary body of literary work. An "alternate Thackery" or "alternate Dickens" anthology would be so obscure as to be lifeless; but say the words "alternate Shakespeare" to a group of writers, and you'll see their minds start working immediately, just as I did that day in Arizona, many thousand of miles from the Bard's own country.

Yet not all of these stories treat the Master with perfect solemnity. We left that to those rafts of literary critics and academics who've made Shakespeare scholarship into a shelf-cracking industry with a devotion rivaled only by Trekkies. After all, the man who reworked *The Menaechmi* into *The Comedy of Errors* never put himself above telling a joke. You'll find a number of approaches to "alternate Shakespeare" stories inside this book. We hope you'll enjoy them all.

Katharine Kerr

I

"There is a history in all men's lives . . ."
King Henry IV, Part Two

Perhaps, since we know so few facts about his life, Shakespeare has become a fit subject for myth-making. We start off with some stories, in roughly chronological order, that deal with the man himself.

PLAYBILL

Bill Daniel

Bill Daniel describes himself as "a misanthrope who lives in southern Arizona." In this, his first fiction sale, he adds some interesting fuel to the fiery question of who wrote Shakespeare's plays.

Swirls of smoke from the open fireplace patterned the shafts of afternoon sunlight from the grimy windows of the common room. In the darkest corner of the room two men nursed their drinks.

"That bastard has no appreciation for talent. We've busted our asses and all he can talk about is being late. You'd think he was the only one in the city who knew how to write."

The speaker half rose and waved at the serving wench. "Here, another round." He sat down and looked morosely at his tankard. "Damned poor service. They serve the big spenders first."

His companion nodded, then said. "He does give us pretty fair material to start from, and precise directions."

The first speaker looked disgusted. "Yeah, precise directions. 'Here's the program. It's already lettered, so don't write anything that won't fit.' He wants it to move so fast you can't build character. Action, action, action. 'Delete that, it doesn't advance the plot.' The damned fool knows what he wants all right, but he doesn't want art. And the pay's lousy."

"Editors have that right," the companion said. "And the final result does have character."

"After he gets through rewriting what we deliver. Can we build the characters? No, that's his job. They have to fit his vision. Half the time I can't recognize my own work after he's done. Bastard."

"He's no bastard," the companion said. "He's not high born enough to be a bastard." He paused consideringly. "He does act like one."

"And a right bastard at that! May his creditors find his rooms." The first speaker looked pleased at the thought.

"He pays, if poorly," the companion said, "and commissions are too rare to jeopardize. We need to keep him sweet."

The serving wench with the fresh drinks bumped against their table, knocking over the first speaker's tankard, spilling the little remaining ale.

"Watch it, clumsy," the first speaker snarled. He moved along the bench to keep the ale from running off the table onto his clothes. "If these stain, you clean them."

"I wouldn't have a chance," the wench said. "You'd suck the ale out before I had time. Show me some money." The serving wench held the fresh tankards out of reach of the table's occupants.

"You wound me!" the companion said.

"Wound, hell!" she said. "From the ink on your fingers it'll be God's own wonder if you can pay the reckoning." The first speaker produced a coin and rang it on the table.

"Ha! Copper." The wench set the tankard on the table and captured the coin in one movement. "If they made smaller coins you'd have them." She sniffed, "Writers!"

"Easy come, easy go." The companion lifted his tankard and drank.

"If it's easy come, you buy the next round," the first speaker said. "When is that bastard going to show? He said to meet him here for lunch and it's almost suppertime."

"So he buys us supper. A free meal's a free meal. It's a shame they won't let us run a tab. If they would, he could pay it," the companion said.

"This latest project," said the first speaker, "it's fluff. No meat to it. I couldn't get my teeth into it properly."

"You're making me hungry. I didn't eat breakfast

thinking I'd have a free lunch." The companion tilted his head back as he sniffed the enticing odors coming from the kitchen.

"I'm always hungry," the first speaker said. "If I could break out of this write-for-hire crap ... How in hell can I build a name when everything I do goes out as someone else's work? I'm building a reputation for others, and starving while I do it. Selling grain paid more."

"You could take temporary work," the companion said. "I hear that Heming is short of actors."

The first speaker looked thoughtful. "That's not a half bad idea. It would keep me in London." With a decisive nod he said. "I'll do it. Can you introduce me?"

"Hear, now," the companion said. "That was in jest. I'd rather starve than join a company. The pay's poor, the work's spotty, and you're soon known as an actor. No thanks!"

"And what's wrong with being an actor?" The newcomer stepped over the bench and sat down. "The theater feeds you now. What difference the name if the money's the same?"

The companion started and apologized. "I didn't see you come in. No offense meant."

Christopher Marlowe smiled. "No offense taken." He caught the serving wench's attention. "Food for the three of us," he told her.

He looked across the table at the first speaker. "Have you finished the revision I asked for?"

"It's done, and well done. You won't see its like again." Will Shakespeare handed Marlowe the last play he would ever write for him.

AN AUGMENTATION OF DUST

Diana Paxson

*Diana L. Paxson has made a specialty of bringing an-
cient myths to life in the context of solid history, as in her
latest novel, The Wolf and the Raven. Here she speculates
on what might have driven Shakespeare to create one of
his greatest plays.*

A wind that seemed to come straight off the Thames
was blowing up Mast Street, buffeting the sign
above the door of the Ash Tree tavern and shivering the
surfaces of the standing pools. Southwark had been built
on a swamp, a fact of which its residents were reminded
with every storm. This wind had harried the storm across
London like some maddened hunter, and though the rain
had ceased for the moment, the ditches were overflowing,
and water had puddled in every depression on the road.

On such a wet and windy eve at winter's ending, only
pressing business would tempt an honest man outside.
Anyone who had to brave the dusk went with hurrying
steps and cloaks clutched tight. Even the foul-mouthed
watermen who made up a majority of the district's inhabitants were huddled over a good fire at home or in one of
Southwark's many taverns, keeping out the damp in time-
honored fashion with a tankard of good English ale.

In the silence between gusts of wind, footsteps sounded

loud on the cobblestones. The tired man who had paused in the lee of a rope-maker's shop to repin his cloak lifted his head to listen. The steps were slow, careful, punctuated by the hollow thud of a staff. In a moment, a man-shaped shadow emerged from the alley.

The watcher stiffened, glimpsing the curve of bone at the cheek, a glimmer of white beard. *My father*—Hysterical laughter bubbled in his throat. *In another moment he will fix me with his awful gaze, crying "Hamlet, revenge!"* Then the man moved and the resemblance was gone. He heard a slap of shoeleather as someone, or several someones, came running after.

The old man took a hurried step forward and looked over his shoulder, leaning heavily on his staff. He was wrapped in a cloak of some dark stuff with a battered hat pulled down over his eyes. His pursuers burst into the street around him. Shouts rang against the walls.

"Hold! Sirrah, wouldst thou flee our company?"

"Why, we're as honest a band of rogues as ever coursed the streets of Shoreditch!" said the second man, planting himself in front of the oldster.

"And thirsty, though on such a night you might scorn to think it!" said the third. "But a flagon of good sack will take the chill from a man's bones!"

The observer prudently drew back into the shadow. In this neighborhood folk were more likely to bar their doors when they heard a scream than to come running, and on such a night even the Watch stayed snug indoors. In a week, he would be back in the safety of Stratford; no point being foolish now.

The old man straightened. "What . . . do ye want of me?"

"Why, thy purse, good sir, that we may drink thy health—didst think I was hoping for a glance from thy bright eyes?" the leader peered under the hat brim. His victim straightened, seeming suddenly taller, and the man drew away, laughing.

"The beer is yet unbrewed for the feast where you would come, hapless ones," said the old man. He sounded foreign, but his tone should have given his assailants pause; instead, it seemed to enrage them.

As the first footpad rushed in, the oldster's staff swung round and connected with a resounding thunk that must have hit bone. The man yelped and fell away, but there were still two others, and in the hand of one of them gleamed steel.

Something in the gallant way the old man had faced his enemies stung the watcher; despite all better judgment, suddenly he found himself running toward the fight, cloak flapping and his own dagger in his hand. He had a moment to reflect on what an irony it would be to lose his life in such a squabble—even the fight in which Kit Marlowe had died had been something more than a tavern brawl—but what did it matter, after all? And then there was only himself and his foe, and no need for thinking any more.

He reversed his dagger and struck upward, taking the fellow with the knife on the point of the chin with his heavy brass pommel. There was another thud from behind him, and the third man went flying, his poniard skittering musically across the stones. For a moment the only sounds were harsh breathing and the groans of the fallen men.

"My thanks. . ." The old man seemed to have deflated with the fight's ending, and he was clinging to the staff once more. "Help me into the inn . . . I will buy drink with the coins they would have taken . . . drink for us instead of them."

His rescuer, still trying to catch his breath, found his arm grasped with surprising strength. As they moved toward the tavern, he wondered who was leaning on whom. The wind, rising once more, spattered their backs with rain.

"Welcome, good sirs, be welcome." The host bustled forward, beaming, no doubt delighted to see anyone come through his door on such a night as this. There were only two other customers in the taproom, a waterman and a drover. " 'Tis a wild night indeed, but we have good spiced ale to warm your bones. Master Will, is that you, sir? Indeed, you're doubly welcome. Not since Whitsun week last spring have we seen you here."

The old man dropped onto a bench with his back to the fire and leaned his staff against the wall. Will unpinned his cloak and shrugged it off, feeling the strain in muscles that had not been stretched since the last time he took a role that required fencing. No doubt he would feel worse tomorrow—his own fault for not exercising, or perhaps he was simply getting old. Charging to the rescue that way had been a foolish impulse, the kind of thing Ben Jonson would do.

But he understood better now why that young man sought fights as others seek wine. In the moment when his poniard had connected with the footpad's chin everything had been very simple, and he had felt alive in a way he had not been for years. He looked up, saw the old man watching him with a gaze surprisingly keen considering that a patch covered his left eye, and grimaced in self-mockery.

"Bring us mulled wine if you have it. We have come to celebrate a victory." Will eased down upon the bench. He would be late home—if the storm that he could hear beating against the thatch with reviving fury allowed him to continue his journey at all. Not that it mattered; no one was waiting for him there.

"So, you are called Will—Wilhelm? That is a good name."

"William . . ." he corrected. "Shakespeare. . . ."

Will wondered if his name would mean anything to this man. After twelve years with Burbage's Company, he had, he supposed, a certain fame. In London at least, most men knew of him, and his neighbors in Southwark took a proprietary interest in the players whose presence had brought them prosperity. But his companion was clearly a foreigner.

"Spear shaker? Well, I, too, have shaken a spear in my time." The old man stroked his long, brindled beard and smiled, and Will felt a little prickle of unease. "I am called Master Harbard here."

"A victory?" The innkeeper set a tray with mugs and a steaming jug down on the scarred table. "I had not heard. Hast scored over the Admiral's Men, or stolen a march on one of the curst Boys' Companies?"

"This fight was on thy doorstep, innkeeper," said Will. "And of a kind more tangible. Three footpads set upon my friend not sixty paces from here."

"A pox upon them all for thieving knaves!" exclaimed the host. He lowered his voice, "There's been no peace since my Lord of Essex came back from Ireland. I've no quarrel with the Queen's Justice, God bless her, but my lord was no danger to us common folks. It's his masterless soldiers, turned loose upon the City like so many red savages, that we have to fear!" He finished pouring out the wine. "I have kept this tavern for twenty years, but it's enough to send a man back to the country to live in London in these times!"

"True enough," said Will, "and that is what I mean to do. I am going back to Stratford soon."

"To quit the stage? Good master, you cannot mean it!"

Burbage had said much the same, thought Will, wincing as he remembered. He shook his head.

"I can, and I will!"

"There will be mourning from Cheapside to Whitehall, sir, if you go," said the host as he carried the tray away.

Will lifted his mug and drank deeply, sighing as the hot, fragrant liquid went down. He could feel the warmth expand from his belly outward as if he had lit a fire there, and an inner chill that owed nothing to the weather began to ease.

"Didst swing that staff most like a soldier, sir. Hast been in the wars?" He addressed the old man.

"I have been in war, yes." Once more came that disconcerting gleam from Master Harbard's good eye. "In many lands. I am a wanderer."

"And from the northlands, by thy tongue," said Will. "Dost thou know Denmark? I have heard they drink deep in that country." He poured more wine into his tankard.

"All men say so of their neighbors." Master Harbard smiled. "When the wine flows freely, the heron of heedlessness fetches full many a man's wits away. That drinking bout is best from which a man bears clear wits home again."

"And hast thou never drunk thyself senseless, old man?"

"I have, in Denmark. But you be too young to drown your pain."

Will snorted and shook his head. It was not pain that ailed him, but something more deadly. Almost at random, he continued. "A friend of mine played once before the King and Queen there. Will Kempe he is called—an excellent fellow, most full of wit and energy, that could

morris his way from here to the end of the world an' you
made him a wager on it."

"I have seen him, in Elsinore."

"Thou art fortunate. Myself, I have traveled no farther
than from Stratford to London," Will said bitterly. Old
habit had prompted him to draw the fellow out with questions. He might be useful for a character some day. But
since he meant to write no more plays, it would not matter . . . Will reached for the wine.

"In the flesh," said Master Harbard, setting down his
tankard. "But a man may travel the nine worlds in his
spirit. Is not that how you do in your English plays,
where bare boards become a palace or a battlefield when
you say the words? That is a powerful magic."

"Oh, indeed—I could bound the world in a nutshell,
but it is all an illusion—as who should know better than
I! I write plays, or rather, I used to. I am retiring from the
theater. I have just come from meeting with my partners
to tell them so."

"I am sorry to hear it," the old man said mildly. "But
you had a good purpose, yes? To teach, to make men
think, to entertain?"

"Is that what the theater is for? My wife says that play
acting is the work of the Devil." Will stared into his wine.
In the dark surface, he saw reflected the pale gleam of
forehead bared by receding hair, and a pair of melancholy
dark eyes. He sighed. "And if it is not, at least, at times
there can be a devil in it.

"Not two months past, milord of Essex bespoke a presentation of *Richard II,* an innocent enough entertainment,
or so we thought it, until he took the fiction for reality
and tried to capture the Queen. God be my witness, we
had no ill intent, but for a week thereafter we walked in
the shadow of the Tower, and not a one of us but felt at
his neck three times an hour to be certain it was still upon
his shoulders! And I more than any—for I wrote the
damned thing."

"And is that why you will leave the theater—because
you are afraid?"

"No," Will said quickly. "Or not entirely." Odd, that it
should matter what this old relic thought of him. "There
was an exhilaration in that terror." Like the moment, he
thought, when he had rushed the footpads.

"This Essex, what was he to you?" The voice was like the wind and, like the wind, it bore a chill that cut to the bone.

Will closed his eyes, shivering, and suddenly he could remember the feverish excitement as Essex rode through the City, his armor glittering like a god's. He had come home like a hero, but even then, the rumors that swept the city were confused; some saying that the Irish had beaten him, and some that he had conquered and won a promise of marriage from the Queen. *Illusion . . .* he thought. *Robert Devereux lied to himself worse than any fiction I ever put upon the stage!*

And instantly his vision showed him another picture— one that he would rather not have seen—ravens blotting the sky above the White Tower, and upon a spike over the traitor's gate, Essex's head, its lips drawn back over a final ghastly grin so that one could see the skull beneath the skin.

"He was a fool! A poor fool more drunk on his dreams of glory than ever I have been on wine! And he might have been king, they say, did he have the resolution, but he never could pursue one purpose long enough to achieve it—he never could make up his mind!"

"There is no man so flawless but some fault he has, nor is there any so wicked as to be of no worth. Everyone is mixed in his virtues, until he finds the need that drives him."

Will sighed. In the end, he supposed, Essex had been driven by ambition. He set down his tankard. He could feel the wine singing in his brain already. Time to stop this, or he would never keep his feet till he reached home. In this state it would not take the Thames to drown him, a mere puddle would do. He started to get to his feet.

"And what drives you, Master Wilhelm Shake-spear?" the old man said then.

Will felt his face contorting in a grimace that was supposed to be a smile. "Nothing. I have poured out my soul for a drunkard's afternoon diversion." He settled back onto the bench as if his body had suddenly grown too heavy and, despite his resolutions, found himself splashing more sack into their tankards. He picked up his own and drank deeply. "And now it is all gone. That is why I will write no more."

"Are you indeed?" Master Harbard looked at him oddly. "Is the word-hoard empty; have you entirely drained the cauldron of poetry?"

"If aught remains," he said with a bitter satisfaction, "it is as stale as yesterday's beer!"

He supposed a time came for every writer of plays when the joy of seeing one's mind-children come to life upon the stage was no longer enough to compensate for the labor of creating them, and he began to yearn for some more dependable livelihood. Why should he be exempt? He had lasted a little longer than most; that was all.

"Listen—in my country we have a proverb. Cattle die and kinsmen die; you yourself will die, but fair fame will never fade. You must make a name that will live when you are gone."

"By writing plays?" For once, Will's laughter was genuine. "God's breath, sir, there is nothing in this life more ephemeral! I could name you a dozen dramas that were the talk of the town that now are vanished—the scripts destroyed by damp or burnt to light a fire. The men of the Universities despise us. When my Company was banished from London because of the plague, I tried my hand at poetry and won some praise from them. Those poems were printed, and very prettily, too, but there was no blood in 'em. I could have made a career as some great man's pet poet—a literary lapdog. My works would have been preserved then. But I threw that chance away.

"The Chamberlain's Men needed me; they made me a partner to prove it, and the past ten years have been good ones. At least we have prospered, and that is more than my father or the old crows on the Stratford Town Council would have believed when I—went away. But no one prints plays. My lines will live no longer than the last actor that has them in memory. In a hundred years they will be dust, and so will I!"

He closed his eyes, and suddenly he could see the churchyard at Stratford; he could even hear the painful scrape of the shovel on soil and the tuneless whistle that told him the old sexton, whose mordant humor would have put Will Kempe to shame, was digging there. The old man knew every grave in the church; some said he was personally acquainted with every bone. Once, when an ill-thrown ball had rolled into the graveyard with a pack of boys in full cry behind it, the sexton had pitched a skull back at them. Will had had nightmares for a fortnight thereafter.

"*Mathr er manns gaman ok moldar auki* ..." said Master Harbard.

Will opened his eyes and remembered that the sexton was dead now, his bones mingled with those he had tended in a dreadful intimacy.

"It is another proverb. Man is the joy of man, and augmentation of the dust. ..."

"Hast thou then a saw for every season, old man?" said Will. "Well, never mind—my head may agree that man is a noble creature, but my gut says otherwise. When I came first to London, all the world was a show arrayed for my delight, but I no longer take any pleasure in the antics of my fellow-creatures, and to me that is the worst loss of all."

He upended the flagon and a few last drops fell into his tankard. For a moment he stared into its emptiness, then he set the flagon down with a thunk, and laughed. It was more than time to go. He rose, dragging his cloak from the hook and fastening it clumsily around him, and started toward the door.

"You were wrong," the old man said behind him. "It is fear that drives you—away from London and your work here."

Will turned. "Because of Essex? Sir, thou dost misjudge me. I said—a man who fears knows he is alive. ..."

"*That* is your fear: that there are neither gods nor devils, and no meaning in life at all. So—are you still going to run away?"

Will looked at him and heard rain drum with sudden vigor against the stout oak door. He sighed then and came back to the table, letting his cloak slide from his shoulders to the floor.

The host looked at them inquiringly and Will nodded. He had not gotten stinking drunk since the first years he was in London, but he wanted to now. If he could not leave this place, he wanted to get as sozzled as ever Falstaff had been!

"Mayhap thou hast the right of it. Does it matter? My

father is dying, and I must go home to see to my inheritance."

"Ah," his companion sighed. "Now I understand. It is his death you have been fearing, not your own."

Will dropped heavily onto his bench, glaring. "Be silent! Dost think to stir my innards as an old wife does her stewpot just because I have drunk thy wine? For all they call me 'Sweet Shakespeare' and commend me for my honey tongue, there is a rage in me that could rend the world if ever I let it go. Find another topic or I will leave thee, and be damned to the storm!"

"Very well." Master Harbard looked, if anything, mildly amused, and Will felt anger kindling in his belly, or perhaps it was only the wine. "Then let me ask a question. You write of your own history, and that is good, but why do you English look always southward for an argument for your tragedies? Surely there are stories of the Northern lands as full of death and vengeance as ever flowered beneath a southern sun!"

Will blinked. "No doubt there are, but there's scarce an Englishman that knows them, except for a thing called *Hamlet* that a troupe of roving players presented once in Stratford, a dreadful piece with no more substance than the ghost that popped in and out of his trap like the devil in a mystery play. It was neither life nor art, sir, but some dreadful parody—the players strutted as if they had been made by some journeyman, and not well."

"*Hamlet . . .*" the old man breathed, "Amlodi . . . I remember him. Men have called me a deceiver, but he was a master, mad in craft and crafty in his madness, until he became the instrument of wyrd and his enemies trapped themselves. Saxo told his story, and others. He deserves better than this travesty you have seen."

Will frowned, all the more angered because for a moment he had *seen* the bombastic hero of the old drama transformed into a being of tragic conflicts and heroic suffering. And he could do it. He had taken old warhorses before now and made of them something that transcended the limitations of the stage. But he was not going to.

"Listen, old man! If I had a farthing for every time a man has come to me with a tale he was *certain* would play splendidly upon the stage—if I would only write it and present it to the company—I could have retired to

Stratford a long time ago. An' thou desire a new tragedy of *Hamlet*, then write it thyself!"

"I did . . ." Master Harbard said in a low voice, "I do. . . ." The candles flickered in an unseen wind. "When you saw it first, how old were you?"

"I was twelve, and when my father found out I had been to see the play he beat me—" And once more, as if the other's words had been some spell to command him, Will *remembered*. . . .

At that age he had been restless as a young colt, already beginning to chafe at the harness his father had laid upon him. John Shakespeare was the son of a tenant farmer who had become a successful maker of gloves in Stratford, a landowner and an alderman, and had never let his children forget it. The eldest son was expected to carry on the family business, to increase its holdings and its standing. And young Will had been a bright lad, quick at his letters and full of energy. His father had high hopes for him—until he reached adolescence and began to dream.

And on that day, when a summer sun gave the lie to every calumny on British weather, when the ripening barley hung down its head in every field and the berries burst their skins from sweetness, the players had come to town. No prohibition could have kept Will at his books on such a day. By the time he started home, lunging with a willow wand at the long grasses and pausing at every bend in the road to declaim speeches which even then he wanted to improve, he had forgotten that his father had forbidden him to go to the play—

—Until a hard hand closed upon his collar and he found himself hauled off to the woodshed, wriggling as the strap stung him, stung worse by the words that were pouring over him in a garbled stream, terrified most by the rage that was turning his father's face to a contorted, purple mask.

"Perverse, vicious, ungrateful brat—" that was the least of it. "I had rather see thee dead than on the stage—"

Until then, it had not occurred to Will that he might do so.

"Father—" he had cried, twisting in the older man's grasp. And in that moment he saw the features spasm in impossible agony, felt the painful grip slacken and wrenched himself free, watching in horror as John Shakespeare fell.

"The doctor said it was a stroke, and if God willed, he would recover. But though he was still able to work, he was never the same man after," Will said quietly. "He could not speak well, and sent his apprentices to the town square to sell the gloves they made. He repeated himself in conversation, and there were lapses in his memory. Sometimes he would be better, and then he wept for all he had lost, and though the other Aldermen begged him to take his place on the town council once more, he was shamed by his illness, and would not go.

"My mother tried to pretend that nothing was amiss, but when his mind wandered I could feel her looking at me—feel all of them accusing me, because my disobedience had brought him to this pass. I thought at first, young as I was, that if I was a good son he would recover. And God be my witness, I did try. For ten years I tried. I married, too young, a woman of such virtue as must have redeemed my soul if prayer could save it. I would not allow myself to become angry—having seen what rage could do. But my father never got any better, whilst I, with the words working within me like yeast in an old wife's beer, knew finally that I would be driven at the very least to self-slaughter if I did not get away."

He found himself on his feet, blinking at the unfamiliar walls that hemmed him in. He saw a door and stumbled toward it, and as he touched the latch the wind flung it open and he reeled back from the chill lash of the rain. In moments, he was soaked, but his head was clearing. He felt kind hands on his shoulder, and then the door was put to again and barred and he drew a shaking breath, stunned by the stillness after the fury of the storm.

"There now, Master Shakespeare, 'tis no weather to be going out in, and you without your cloak. Come you back and sit down by the fire."

The host guided him to a seat and he sank into it gratefully. His clothing began to steam from the heat of the fire. The innkeeper brought him more hot wine, and after a few moments the other man carried his tankard over to the inglenook and sat down.

"Why?" Will whispered at last. "Why make me remember? Twenty-five years have passed, and now the old man is dying . . . I have as many years as he did when the thunderbolt struck him down . . . and what have I accomplished? I have sent them money and purchased property, but I would have done better to stay in Stratford and build an estate for my daughters to inherit, though I no longer have a son to carry on my name."

"I had a son once," said Master Harbard, "and his loss took the light from the world. But I went on."

"I cannot—" whispered Will. He felt as if he were clinging to a tree at the edge of a precipice. It would be so much easier to simply let go. "I cannot bear the pain."

"You are human. You can. Dust you may be, but what a noble shape it wears! Far have I wandered, and from many beings sought wisdom, but none is more full of wonders than humankind. Through no other creature have I known more of the world. Even your pain has value, if you learn from it."

"Learn what?" Will stared into the swirling brightness of the fire.

"No man knows how much life is left to him, or what deeds may remain for him to do. Amlodi himself did not find his vengeance simple. He, too, suffered from a conflict of needs and loyalties until, in the end, there was only one thing he *could* do. You are not your father. The only way you may serve him is to follow your fate as single-mindedly as he did. Look at me, Wilhelm—can you truly say you have nothing left to do?"

The voice was as soft as if it spoke within his soul, but nonetheless it compelled him. He lifted his head and flinched from the gaze of Master Harbard's good eye, keen as steel and cold as the winter wind. His own glance, sliding away, fixed on the shadowed hollow where the man's eyepatch should have been. Will blinked, for instead of the ruined flesh or sightless orb he expected, he saw only a glimmering darkness that drew him into its depths before he could even try to pull his gaze away.

"Who art thou?" he cried. "What wouldst thou do to me?"

He must be more drunk than he had thought, for he felt as if he were falling down a well. But he was no longer in darkness. Stars flared around him, light shivering into a thousand shapes that moved and gestured, grinned or shouted or cried in words that rang and echoed in his awareness like a flock of sweet-voiced birds. Some of them he knew, true faces of which the player's paintings had been only a mockery; some he had never seen, and yet somehow recognized: a noble Moor, a woman who walked distracted, washing from her hands an invisible stain; an Egyptian queen and an old king shaking his fists at heaven; a wizard with book and staff; and most vivid of all, a young man in black with haunted eyes. He yearned for them as a pregnant woman yearns for the babe she is bearing; as he had never yet cared for the children his wife had borne. But they were only shadows compared to the others; they needed him to give them reality.

"You will live! I will give you life!" his spirit cried. Thunder rolled; then the lighting drew a curtain of brilliance between him and the world.

Will Shakespeare woke to the sound of water dripping from the eaves. Someone was shaking him. He opened gummed eyes and tried to sit up, grunting as joints no longer supple enough to stand a night away from his bed complained.

"Art awake, good master? I'll have tea for ye anon, and some good porridge. The inglenook is a poor bed, I know, but I had not the heart to waken thee. I'd not have sent a beggar, nay, not even a beggar's dog, out into such a storm."

Will held up a hand to stem the babble. His head was throbbing and he tasted the fur of that self-same dog upon his tongue. He rubbed at his temples, trying to separate the jumble of dream images from the reality. There had been a young man haunted by destiny—he could feel his presence still, more vivid even than his memories of the youth who had battled with his father and run away to seek his fortunes on the stage.

And there had been an old man with a single eye who had torn the very heart from his breast with his questioning. Will could still taste the wine they had shared. He rubbed the sight back into his eyes. In the chill light of morning, the inn, which he remembered as being so bright and welcoming, seemed curiously forlorn.

"Where is Master Harbard?" he croaked, looking

around him. He would use that name for him, though he
seemed to remember, somewhere in his dreaming, that the
man had given him another name.

"Who?" The innkeeper handed him a cup of steaming
tea. Will breathed deeply of the fragrant vapors, gaining
in clarity with every moment that passed.

"The old man with whom I was drinking." He managed a laugh. "Dost think I would have drunk so deeply
if he had not sworn to pay?"

"Thou art still mazed, sir. God knows there were none
here last night beside ourselves but Hawkin the drover,
who still sleeps yonder, and young Jack, who's just off to
his boat this quarter hour past. Thou didst drink alone,
good master, and a hero of the wine-casks wert thou indeed. Happen that is why thou dost not remember. As for
payment, why, the coin gleams still where thou didst put
it down!"

He plucked something that glittered from the table
where Will and the old man had been sitting. In the
brightening light Will could see that it was heavy silver—
but not an English coin, as he had supposed. There were
words upon it that he took to be Danish, but he could not
read the inscription, for the surface was much worn. He
could tell only that it was very old.

Will rubbed at his eyes, but the coin was still there.
Men of the theater were not abstemious, and he had held
his own in more than one drinking bout, but though wine
set fancies in the minds of men unused to imagination,
Will had never had any difficulty telling the difference
between them and reality. He was not sure what he had
said, only that he had emptied out his soul, but he could
remember every detail of the raven-badge that pinned the
old man's cloak, the pattern of his black doublet, the
shape of the patch that hid his missing eye. *Woden*—that
was the other name Harbard had given him, the name of
an ancient English god.

And with that came memory of the visions he had seen.
He must have made some sound then, for suddenly the
innkeeper was shoving another basin in front of him.

Will shook his head and pushed it aside. Considering
how much he had drunk, he felt better than he had any
right to, as if his head had been opened like a goodwife's
cupboard and someone had swept all the cobwebs away.

Still, he was very silent as he fastened his cloak and prepared to depart. Why risk his reputation trying to convince the man of a wonder that had no explanation even in his own philosophy?

And yet, as he picked his way among the puddles that mirrored back the brilliance of the new-made day, it was not the old man, be he god or a drunkard's fantasy, who haunted his thoughts, but the young one—that youth clad in black who even now was beginning to speak in his head, pouring out his argument with fate in words of such passionate complexity that Will Shakespeare's fingers itched for a pen to write them down.

AWEARY OF THE SUN

Gregory Feeley

Gregory Feeley is a reviewer and critic as well as an author of science fiction stories and novels. In this novelette he considers that even while Shakespeare still lived he might, in the words of another poet, "have become a name."

Serviceable John sat not wholly at his ease, before him curling sheets of foolscap held fast by inkpot and cup of claret. Writing in an inn was not his accustomed way; it smacked of vainglory, Tourneur or one of his fellows scribbling amidst a brawl—but he was driven forth that day while his rooms were smoked for lice. Weak sunlight slanted through a dirty window to fall imperfectly upon Fletcher's table. He reached carefully for his cup. It would not do to slosh drink upon the playscript, especially with pages not his own.

Some commotion by the door reached his ears, but Fletcher had returned to his duty, repairing without outward complaint the occasion of his grievance. Chary with his praise, he stood rebuked, and was charged now with expanding Cranmer's prophecies of the young Elizabeth by half again their natural length, lest the coarse-eared multitude miss their import. When *All Is True* was rehearsed for the Princess' wedding, the crack-spined pageant had sped quickly: the Generoso knew well his sovereign's taste for short plays. Now it opened at the

Globe, for which Fletcher must needs revise it to fit the greater resources of that house.

"Let not ambition mock thy useful toil," he murmured. Well he understood the sharers' concern; yet might they have voiced it more prudently. Had it been he who had announced his present retirement to the country, the sharers would have turned to Francis with greater confidence, yet less reason.

He examined the speech before him. The pious Cranmer, expatiating upon the infant's glorious future, likened her to "the maiden phoenix," divining that she would secure a good succession without ever marrying. Given such augury, why could he not foresee his own coming death at the stake? No matter; let nothing come before the King's Men's premiere playwright when he is praising his betters. With grim pleasure Fletcher added to the count, letting Cranmer give her long life, and even (let none call him stinting in praise of the late Queen) predict that she shall die "a virgin, A most unspotted lily." Indeed, Fletcher knew better, for the "agèd princess," spotted and bilious with age, had blighted his family at a stroke. Again, no matter: Fletcher swallowed his claret and wrote. And may no groundling wonder why Henry does not strike his Archbishop to the ground for such prophecy.

"Needst thou all this patch of sun?"

He had not heard her approach beneath the sounds of commerce. Squinting in the light, Fletcher found a face for the voice: a crone of past sixty, grinning toothlessly at him. I am justly requited, he thought: Sit in taverns of a morning, and you will be addressed familiarly by drabs.

Fletcher smiled. "If you took your bones without, Granny, 'twould be sun aplenty."

The crone cackled. "And if I took my bones to potter's field, 'twould vex one gentleman less." Boldly she surveyed his labors, as though well conversant with the sight of paper. But before he could speak, she dropped her finger upon a loose sheet and pronounced: "This is not thy hand."

Fletcher stared. But the answer, he saw quickly, was plain: one of his own half-finished sheets was before him, and even an unlettered eye could discern a different hand upon the other. Fletcher quirked his lips and began to frame a dismissive reply when the woman amazed him again:

" 'Tis the hand of that cozening blackguard, Will Shakespeare."

At first he thought he had not heard her right. A part of his mind sought to parse the sentence otherwise, *Blackguard will shakes pair,* then stuttered into silence. Fletcher looked at her with frank astonishment. "And pray tell, Granny, how thou camest to know the hand, indeed the name, of Will Shakespeare."

The crone laughed, delighted to be abruptly courted. "Buy me sack," she said, "and let me sit in that pool of sunlight. You may rest opposite, in your nest of papers."

Warily, Fletcher vacated his seat. From across the room he caught the eye of the tapster, who stared as the gentleman gave way to the stinking beldam. "More claret," he called, "and a cup of sack for my old nurse."

In the sunlight the woman looked even worse; balding beneath a greasy cap, so hunched she could not touch her shoulders to the back bench, she wriggled with pleasure at the bench's warmth. Fletcher observed her eyes follow the sack as it was brought across the room to her. As her clothes warmed, he thought, she would begin to smell.

She snatched up the cup and drank deeply, smacking her lips at the end like a starving dog. "Stay, hold," he warned. "Th'art not used to such."

She offered a purple grin. "I've supped on sack as 'twere my mother's milk."

"But not lately." Fletcher had been musing and thought he had his answer. "Thou hast dallied with actors and seen their scripts. Imagine'st thou that every play is Will Shakespeare's?"

The crone took his meaning at once. Taking up a sheet, she held it close her face, then turned it right side up and read in a quavering but unhesitant voice:

> *"Why, this it is: see, see!*
> *I have beene begging sixteene yeares in Court,*
> *(Am yet a Courtier beggarly) nor could*
> *Come pat betwixt too early, and too late*
> *For any suit of pounds: and you, (O fate)*
> *A very fresh Fish heere—fye, fye, fye upon*

This compel'd fortune: have your mouth fild up
Before you open it."

"Enough." Had she made her point by naming a second playwright Fletcher would have been surprised enough; this left him faintly dizzy. "Thou canst read, and mayhap cipher as well. Art thou a goodwife, reduced in widowhood to vagrancy?"

"I am a witch," she said.

Fletcher blinked. Watching her drink, he thought: Of course, she's mad. The reply answered all, until he remembered that mad crones don't read.

Wiping her chin, she regarded him sharply; a crow eyeing a cat it knows is too far to pounce. " 'Tis not safe to say such things," he said carefully, "not even in London town. Not in the reign of our Scottish majesty."

She cackled. "And Elizabeth loved witches? 'Twas in her father's day," she gestured at the pages, "that the first statutes against us were passed. I was but a child, yet remember."

"Thou art not so old." Elizabeth died at seventy but had Christendom's finest physic to preserve her so long. Fletcher would not believe this drab so old, startled as he was that she had gleaned the play's theme in a glance.

"Old enough to remember witches accused in Chelmsford; confessions forced with the tools of hell and four women hanging like dressed deer." She glared at him like a true witch, red-laced eyes come suddenly alive.

Fletcher found he had no reply to this. He pulled close a loose sheet before she could set her cup on it, then had a thought. "Canst thou write as well as read?" he asked. He turned over a foul sheet, presenting its unblemished backside, and held up his plume.

She reached for it directly. None who'd ever written, even a schoolboy laboring sums, could resist (thought Fletcher) his fine nib and clean foolscap. He watched as the crone grasped the quill, bringing her nose almost to the paper as she arduously scrawled a short line. Fletcher took it as soon as she lifted the nib and studied the crabbed apothecarial hand: *Alizon Wyckliffe her mark.* And below it, *B. 26 Ianuarie 1549.*

Too young to have known Henry even if she wrote true; but the signature spoke much else. The lettering recalled those found on bottles, and it was in no wise impossible that an herbalist or simple-woman should possess some rudiments of writing.

Her cup struck hollowly on the table. "More."

"Thou shalt fall to sleep, thy tale untold."

"Nay, the tongue is dry. Another cup, i'th'name of Jesus."

The last words rose to a whine. Startled, Fletcher looked closer. He had seen sodden players in whom little drink, or none, could bring the tremors, which more drink would allay. He did not want to see this leathern frame of sticks collapse before him foaming.

He pushed his cup toward her. Snatching it, she drained the dregs in a draught.

"Tell thy tale, and I'll buy thee a pie. Should thy story please, thou shalt have another cup."

She looked ready to protest, then fell to mumbling. Fletcher signaled the taverner who, frowning, brought a pie, though not one of his best.

"Speak," he told her.

And she spoke. The tale she told twisted like a byway overgrown with scant use, and at times he had to pull her through brambles or chop rudely at a growth that threatened to beguile her. No milestones marked the turnings of her tale; and Fletcher, who had learned in grammar school to con his dates, grew vexed at her incapacity to set years to her occasions. But only one occasion truly mattered, and he knew its date well enough.

By then she was in Southwark, and past fifty if her birth-date be trusted. Fletcher had brushed aside her maundering on earlier years: her maidenhood in Essex, marriage to an aged grocer, and later to a sailor who gave her the clap and left her penniless. Only a moment's musing did he permit: gathering autumn herbs in the short Sussex afternoons, the list of which simples—henbane, senna, belladonna, camomile—struck him with its artless music. Beyond that, he hastened her onward: the recollections of a country witch (or city witch), however interesting, were not to his purpose.

The heavens themselves blaze forth the death of princes; and the heavens seemed to blaze that night, as though gobbets of flaming firmament had fallen to earth and set fire to houses and men's hearts. Young John,

newly come from Cambridge and without a patron's protection, had stared like a fascinated deer as the earth
shook about him. That one prince would die was certain;
fell rebellion, loosed like a fifth horseman over England,
would not be quenched save in the blood of one of its
principals. Perhaps both, and more, should die, and civil
war break like a thunderplump of blood over the world
that Fletcher scarce knew.

On the eve of rebellion rumor raced through town like
sparks through straw. The Privy Council had demanded
an accounting of Essex, who claimed illness and did not
appear. Conspirators were massing at Essex House; the
Council's officers would ride. And in Bankside, where
Fletcher had taken the meanest lodgings, the boldest inti-
mations of revolt were seen, for the day before, the
Chamberlain's Men had performed the *Tragedy of Richard the Second,* specially commissioned (everyone knew)
by one of Essex's knights. The populace had cheered to
see the idle king deposed and killed, and had taken
away—who could say aught otherwise?—the glowing
coals of treason in their hearts.

Listening, Fletcher remembered his own story more
vividly than he heard hers. A calf cut off from the herd,
he had felt terror and exhilaration to see the city erupt
about him. Crowds gathered in the streets and were not
dispersed. Riders pulling up were beset for news. Terrible
Elizabeth, a great oak gone rotten with age, was about to
be kicked to flinders by valiant young men.

Little of this touched Alizon, though she followed
more than Fletcher would have guessed. She lived in a
disused outbuilding among roots and turnips, and ventured into the streets only to the degree necessary to sell
the nostrums and charms that sustained her. She might
have heard nothing till it was over had not the players
spoke in her presence.

—And why was this? Fletcher interrupted. He could
think of fewer likely occupations for an aging herb-
woman who called herself witch than to comport with
Bankside men.

"Why, for my hand," she replied, at once injured and
sly. She gestured to the page she had scribbled, and then
Fletcher understood. She had written to order, probably
taking down the words of disloyal players who would

spout their lines to printers or rival sharers eager to steal a play.

She affirmed this. The first time, she had been rousted from sleep by some sharper she had once sold to and set at a table in an inn's back room. A player had declaimed (very foully, she averred) and she had written down his speech. The sharper, peering over her shoulder, had exclaimed and struck her: for she had written the lines as though setting forth a grocer's account. It was then, she said, she learned how to set out the verse of a play-script and did so without spoiling more paper.

And thus she knew players and was suffered sometimes to stay when they filled a tavern. Essex was a great patron of acting companies, as was another, she forgot his name—

"Southampton," said Fletcher.

Yes. His younger ally, beloved of the Chamberlain's Men. Passions ran high on Bankside for the noble rebels, higher than elsewhere as events proved, for the Uprising fizzled in less than a day, failing like damp gunpowder to ignite the populace.

Fletcher remembered. He said nothing but nodded tautfaced that she should continue.

In the aftermath players scattered, bleating. Deputies of the Privy Council were said to be crossing the bridge, asking for the man who played Bolingbroke, and Richard as well. The Globe was closed, assemblies broken up.

And in the rains of February, a poor player appeared at her door: hat-brim running with water and his thin shanks shivering, to beg sanctuary in her hovel. He had silver, and he spoke well.

He was Master William Shakespeare, the Chamberlain's Men shareholder who had penned Richard's words, and a hunted man. His patron was in the Tower, his friends, men of influence, now scattered. Mayhap they would intercede for him, once the tumult was ended and things resettled in their natural order. Mayhap, no surely, the Privy Council would recognize that the play, written five years earlier, cast no reflection of present troubles; had been commanded performed by lord and knights they could ill refuse. All this would come in time; he need only meanwhile survive the Queen's present wrath.

She took him in, took his silver, threw costly faggots

on the smoky fire to parch the air. Shaking in the mold-
ering horse-blanket she gave him while his clothes dried,
the fugitive sipped scalded tea and sought to justify his
plight. More than a player, he was landholder and indeed
gentleman—his claim recognized by the College Heraldry—and entitled to be called "generoso." His was a
place of established degree; but now the heavens were
torn asunder, and even fixed stars rained down flaming.

When his tremors increased uncontrollably, Alizon
fetched forth a stoppered bottle of spirits. Not (she told
Fletcher plainly) the smoother stuff of taverns, it burned
even when poured in tea, and slight-shouldered Shakespeare convulsed sputtering at its first swallow. As the
liquor took hold, his ague subsided, but his humor likewise declined, veering between choler and despair. He
railed at fortune, spoke of years of labor to redeem his
family's dignity, endless toil, and bitter disappointments.
Now all was cast down, his every hope a wrack on time's
rock shore.

"His son," Fletcher murmured.

The witch did not hear him. She had (she continued)
already recognized Master Shake-scene, thinner at the
crown but manifestly the same Johannes Factotum she remembered from the years before the plague had closed
the theaters, now plainly realized in his ambitions to
please lords and rise in the world. Sweet-tempered and
agreeable, with good clothes and fine gloves, he had
shown no interest in horoscopes or charms, so had not
held her notice during those hard years. When the plague
blew the players from town like chaff, depriving her of
their custom but occasioning much business in cata-
plasms, she had forgotten him.

And now he lay in her blanket, seeking sanctuary in
her hovel as though 'twere St. Savior's. She told him that
should the authorities reject his plea that the players had
mounted the seditious performance under compulsion, no
more would they accept hers. If caught, she had had no
choice but to harbor a wellborn fugitive. He stared at this
show of logic, then produced more silver. In fact, no one
would think to seek him there.

She went out the next morning, with the gentleman's
silver, and bought meats and a better quality of greens
than she had known in years. More to the purpose, she

had lingered without the grocer's and sat in the alehouse (paying for her malmsey with a bright sixpence that made the tapster stare), head down but ears open for word of the snuffed revolt and its issue.

She heard more questions than answers, for all was still confusion, as in a catastrophe whose dust takes days to settle. Essex was in the Tower, his life surely forefeit, and Southampton, too. (At word of this, Master Shakespeare gave a great groan.) But while the players' performance, and the forty shillings paid them for it by the conspirators, were widely mouthed, there was no word of Augustine Phillips being seized, nor John Heminges, and— Shakespeare fastened upon this—surely it would be the talk of the taverns were the senior Lord Chamberlain's men arrested. Alizon, bringing out cold roast meats, shrugged. She had supper to prepare, and her mouth was watering.

The next day found Bankside subdued, even chastened. No deputies rode the streets, no fresh news either, but the populace seemed chagrined, as though remembering its cheers for the regicide on Friday afternoon, Shakespeare bid her go forth again, and she did, but spent the short afternoon digging tubers for her medicines. When she returned, she found him sitting at her one rude window, looking through the papers spread before him.

"These are spells of witchcraft," he said upon her entrance.

Alizon had her arms full, so could not shrug. She had already told him she was a witch, as one confides secrets to the dying. "Mayhap we shall both be hanged," she said.

He winced. "Such evidence would damn thee, were thy rooms searched. A friend of mine—"

"Recipes and charms, little more." The player was acute, to discern nigromancy and maleficia in the lists of herbs and preparations. He was right, withal: investigators, should ever her hovel serve as the unlikely focus of their interests, would be led by the hounds of their fancy straight where Shakespeare's reason had taken him.

But now he wanted news. As she made her brief recitation, her eyes fell upon a clean sheet before him, now covered with writing not hers. Shakespeare, following her gaze, turned the sheet over and left his hand upon it.

Later he made bold to speak. "I have devised a means for my deliverance," he told her as the coals burnt down, bringing dimness and chill to the shuttered room. He had been scribbling as she prepared supper, and he had called for her single candle. "Thou shalt go forth on a journey, greater than thou hath ever taken."

He spent the night in the root cellar, lest deputies bang on the door, but emerged in the morning, grimy and smelling of earth, to explain. She was to ride from the city, a journey of three days' duration, to a great house, there to deliver a message to a great lady. The gentleman-player was at pains to impress that she not give offense with her rude demeanor, prompting Alizon to draw herself up and, calling upon accents long unused, berate him in the respectable tones of her vanished shopkeeper's days. He sighed and said that this would suffice for a messenger.

He sent her forth with two shillings for a passable cloak, also sending for good paper and wax. Upon her return he took the paper and bade her leave him for two hours. Alizon sat in the noonday sun, heart pounding at the prospect of travel. When she returned, he presented her with a letter and instructions for its delivery. More shillings he gave her, gulping as he counted them out, and instructions for her voyaging.

And thus it was that the hedge witch presented herself to an inn at Newgate, and the next day boarded a wagon headed out Uxbridge Road, west toward Wiltshire. The ostler looked her askance, seeing a widow traveling alone, not unheard of, but strange. Her travel companions, servants on their masters' business, gave her not a glance. The wagon was loaded with city goods bound for Salisbury, and Alizon sat two days on the jouncing crates.

The journey was memorable, but Fletcher cut her short. Yes, she had looked at the name on the sealed letter directly she was out of Shakespeare's sight: it was Mary, Countess of Pembroke, Wilton House. (At this, Fletcher started.) The wagon emptied at Salisbury market, whence she walked six miles to the great house. A man in livery stared at her from the servants' entrance, then took the letter and studied its fine hand. She sat forty minutes in the kitchen, warming her feet while cooks' helpers regarded her suspiciously, when the doors opened and the finest lady she had ever seen entered.

Alizon stood, and the two regarded each other a moment, as across worlds. The countess of Pembroke was perhaps forty, redheaded and comely for her age, dressed in a bright-colored bodice that looked as if it had been slashed by knives and a collar that stood up about her neck like a builder's scaffold surrounding a steeple. Glad for her good cloak, Alizon met her gaze squarely.

"The man that sent thee this," said the countess, "is safe now in your lodgings?"

Master Shakespeare had evidently not seen fit to disclose that he was hiding in a root cellar. "He is, subject to forced search. But I do doubt that mischance."

"I see." The countess tapped the open letter absently. "Tell him I shall do what I can."

Alizon nodded, then remembering herself, curtsied stiffly. The countess was headed for the door, then paused before the servant who held it open. "Is the market coach returning to London?" she asked him.

"Yes, my Lady."

"Conduct her there tomorrow." And she swept through the door, not looking back.

That night Alizon slept in a bed, better than her own, and was taken in the morning to the inn where she had debarked. In the courtyard of Wilton, however, a young man accosted her, saying, "A moment, an it please thee," as he strode easily up. Dressed in London fashion, he was a guest, not a household member. "Thou art the woman brought a message from Will Shakespeare?"

Chary of speaking to strangers, she could see no evasion here. "Aye," she said guardedly.

"And did he actually sanction a performance of his *Richard* on the rebellion's eve?"

"So he says."

The man shook his plump cheeks, as though amazed at the folly of the world. "Ah, Will," he said.

"By discordant tunes are e'en the great o'erthrown,
Thou should have pitch'd thy song to the middle-tone."

He gave her a coin. "If thou see'st him again, tender him my love."

She didn't know how she was to know this young pop-injay's name, and repeated his couplet bemusedly on her ride to the inn. Perhaps his fellow poet in the cellar would understand it.

Alizon's tale was almost finished. She returned to London more than a week after the abortive rebellion, and found the city calm. Dozens of knights and bravos filled the Tower, but she heard no report of players charged with treason.

And when she entered her room, she found it empty, its unsought tenant gone. Worse, half her papers were gone as well. Turning their pages in disbelief, she found her best spells taken, including one tucked into an herbalists' guide, her one book, which she had not seen Shakespeare peruse.

On the floor lay the sheet on which he had drafted his letter, verso (as it proved) of one of her recipes. His grammar-school hand had stared at her this past dozen years, whenever she turned over that leaf as she searched, eyes failing, for a charm that eluded her memory.

She never saw Shakespeare again.

Fletcher was staring at her. When he spoke, it was of an apparent inconsequentiality. "What did the letter say?"

The witch laughed. "Come and read it, if you like. He begs for noble intercession: *'As you have done me honor in the past, I call, from my disgraced and hunted state—'* " she gestured negligently. "He spoke of his roots being withered and his buds blighted, and that the terrible woodsman was now come to hack at his poor bare trunk. In short, he fell at her feet."

Fletcher was still nibbling at the edges of this story, rather than its heart. "But why would he steal your papers?"

"Because they were fine spells, and he had an eye for quality. Mayhap he wanted to write a play about witches."

"Shakespeare nev—" Fletcher began, then stopped.

The witch picked up her cup. "Sack," she said, thrusting it forth.

Fletcher took the cup to the bar himself. He felt an agitation he could not explain and brought back claret as well. The woman took her cup from his hands before he

sat and was drinking deeply ere he sipped. She would return to her hovel, he thought, and pass out. So much
grape, at her age, could surely not be good.

"Write me directions to thy lodgings," he said as she
wiped her mouth. He found the sheet where she had
signed her name and pushed it to her.

Suspicious, she drew back. "What concerns you where
I live?"

Uncertain himself, he made light of it. "Mayhap I
should hear another story; and if so, thou should have
more pie and sack."

Unlike Will, Fletcher had never been a player, and his
imposture rang false. "This tale hath stuck in your skin,"
the witch said, shrewd. "Comes it too close to thine own
trade?"

Smiling, Fletcher told her, "Know we work by wit, and
not by witchcraft." Quoting the man himself.

But she pursued the point. "What is it to you, a gentleman born? Love you so a tale of your master pinching papers?"

Fletcher made to dispute this, but the crone, watching
his face, saw something.

"Of course," she said, breaking out in a wizened grin.
"He stole something from you, as well."

Bankside stank at low tide, both shores really, so that
Fletcher, midway across the Bridge, felt himself suspended between stenches. We live, he thought, with one
foot still in our mother's bloody matrix, the other in the
grave. How far he'd come across his own life's span no
man could say.

Preparations for the afternoon's performance were well
under way, and Fletcher slipped through the players' entrance without being remarked. In the corridor the smell
of face paint cut the air, and he heard Nicholas Tooley
shout at the boy he was daubing (no doubt as Lucinda) to
hold still. Having seen his *Cardenio* performed at Court
and in Greenwich, Fletcher had no desire to see it yet
again. Half the shareholders were taking roles, and Will
was at his house at Puddle Dock. Fletcher would be un-
disturbed.

The library was on the topmost floor, its valuables beyond the reach of burglars looking in windows. Fletcher

closed the door behind him. Bound volumes lined the upper shelves, including the English *Quixote* that had finally allowed uncolleged Will to see the story Fletcher had told him of. The Globe might have presented *Cardenio* to England years earlier, but Will had insisted on waiting until Shelton's long-delayed translation saw print, that he might study it himself. Possibly his business sense, ever acute, had served them well: the members of Court had all heard of Sir Quixote by the time the company mounted the play, although of course they had not read him.

Fletcher left off worrying this old sore. He noted a space missing on the same shelf: some fat volume taken, perhaps by Will who was now brooding upon a fall play. This was also no matter, and Fletcher turned to the meaner shelves, where quartos and prompter's-books were stacked, and lower still, to the two shelves stuffed with scripts, rough papers, and unfinished work. He pulled out a fistful, loosening the rest enough to be riffled, and sat down to sort.

Shakespeare's sheets, being better paper than the other playwrights used, were easy to separate. The first loose batch proved to be the botched *Timon,* which Fletcher regarded sourly. The failures of the gorgeous *Coriolanus* and *Antony* should have told Will what his fellows already knew: that antique histories no longer commanded the public's interest. Withal, he began another, tainted with the bitterness of his unaccustomed failure; and so exercised his bile that he made himself sick. His partners, reviewing the rough copy, advised Will to abandon it. Will waved his hand weakly in acquiescence, and there was an end to it.

When Fletcher, not thinking himself overbold, suggested he have a crack at redeeming the script, he was smacked down like a puppy nosing at table. Five years later the memory still burned. And when (he reminded himself) the great man found his way again, it was with the form of *tragi-comedy* that Fletcher had compounded, *Pericles* rising out of *Philaster* as a zephyr gives breath to a winded traveler. And when Shakespeare, still ill, permitted a second hand to span the disordered scenes of his draft, it was the wretched Wilkins, a family friend, to whom he turned. O tiger's heart indeed.

Fletcher pushed on, marching backward in time as he shuffled deeper. He found the play soon enough, but two-thirds the length of *Lear,* even with the witchy scenes added for public performances. Beneath it lay Will's earliest copy, miraculously light in its corrections. Though it was not to his purpose, Fletcher found himself turning pages, and fell quickly into the tale, as down a well.

Was *Macbeth* always so world-weary a play? Fletcher had not known it so before, when rapt he had watched the King's Men race through its paces, each line a cut gem yet swift-moving as a freshet. "Better be with the dead," says the new king, early in the play—indeed while Banquo still lives—"than on the torture of the Minde to lye In restlesse extasie." How could he think so, this soon? And later: "I have liv'd long enough. My way of life Is falne into the Seare, the yellow Leafe." But Macbeth— Fletcher turned back to check—had not yet learned of his lady's death, nor of Birnam on the march. And o'er-tuned lute, he sang high at the briefest plucking.

Fletcher read twice through the mad king's tremendous soliloquy upon hearing his wife dead, its infernal vision of a babbling and meaningless life gaping like a hole burned in the fabric of faith, disclosing darkness beyond. And a page later, apprised at last that Birnam Wood approaches, Macbeth gives voice again to this more-than-despair:

> I 'ginne to be a-weary of the Sun,
> And wish th'estate o'th'world were now undon.

Magnificent, yet it stood out of proportion with his troubles. Astonishing how swift pace and flashing poetry can blind one to the odd under-tides of a play. Fletcher hesitated, then put the sheets away. Had *Macbeth* been printed, he would take a quarto home with him; but he remembered otherwise. And his purpose yet lay before him.

Behind the loose sheets of *Macbeth* lay other playwrights' work, and the next script of Will's to turn up was a version of *Lear.* Fletcher dug through the pile but found no loose notes. Where, then? Standing and casting about, he abruptly saw it: a black spine on the finest shelf, much the best-bound book in the room. *Daemonologie* by His Majesty himself, although the book had been first published when James was but King of the lowly Scots (the title page did not mention this), and not likely to have caught the interest of Shakespeare, pleaser of nearer sovereigns.

As soon as Fletcher began turning pages, he had it: a packet of folded papers inside the back cover, coarse and heavily scribbled. He opened one carefully and saw writing he thought he knew: smaller and surer than the scrawl of Alizon Wyckliffe, but recognizably the hand of her younger state. He took it to the window and studied it in the afternoon light.

The first sheet seemed to be a list of demons, along with their attributes. One was underscored by a second hand: "Flibbertigibbet," a demon who (as Fletcher read) walked the earth from curfew to cock-crow, where it causes such bodily infirmities as harelip and squint-eye, besides blighting wheat and shriveling cows' teats. This seemed familiar, though Fletcher could not say from whence.

Several other sheets gave instructions for divers nasty potions, calling for ingredients such as the caul of stillborn babe and the sweated grease of a hanged man. At length one caught his eye:

Eye of Newt yt is midnight caughte; toe of young Frog spyed in its pond by moonlighte; tongue of Dog yt hath ate of wommens fleshe; fillet of Snake fed nine dayes on Sausyge made of living Christians bloode and giv'n but Holie Water to drink . . .

That was it. Fingers trembling, Fletcher restored the pages to the book and shut it. He imagined telling the witch that her lost writings lay between the King's own sheets.

And so? as Francis might say after Fletcher had offered some twist of plot for a coming play. What follows? Fletcher puzzled this as he descended the stairs. William Shakespeare, gentleman, once hid in a witch's hovel while he howled to his protectress. Indeed, he employed the witch to deliver his plea in person to the Countess of Pembroke. And salted a play acted before witch-hunter James with scraps of actual witchcraft, which he stole. And so?

Three cups of claret, their effects held back by the day's mystery, now lapped the edges of his consciousness

like tides against a child's sand-battlements. Tobacco
would have sharpened his wits, but Fletcher might not
light his pipe in the building, by firm company rule. Stepping into the street, he could faintly hear the roars of the
bear garden two lanes distant. Ever sensitive to fine
verse, he felt a stab of pity for the world, and the beasts'
cries played hard upon the strings of his melancholia.

The morning was squandered, the afternoon far gone.
The hounds of Fletcher's fancy were loosed on a chase
not of his choosing, and he could not call them back.

This had not been a good writing day.

His rooms still stank as though Mephistopheles had
held court there, and Fletcher was driven within the hour
back into the streets. The long June sun would loiter until
ten, good working hours for those who could.

Remembering the disdainful cry of "forty shillings" in
Poetaster, he crossed the Bridge again to call on sturdy
Ben, late returned from Europe. His wife, leaning crossly
out an upstairs window, called down that he could be
found at the Mermaid; but a bellow behind her turned her
head, and she withdrew. Evidently the mistress of the
house showed too little care for the comings and goings
of the master. A minute later Ben, red-faced and with his
doublet half-buttoned for his ease, appeared at the door
and ushered Fletcher in.

"I have strange intelligences this day," began Fletcher
as they mounted the stairs. The fresh-plastered walls bore
prints of classical scenes: Diana discovered bathing, Ata-
lanta distracted in her footrace by the golden apples
tossed in her path. Fletcher's own lodgings, which he
long had shared with Francis, were raffishly hung with il-
lustrations from the title pages of their early plays.

"We will speak over ale," said Ben. "The best!" he
roared, that none might claim not to have heard him.

His desk was covered with proof sheets, heavily corrected throughout. "A new play?" Fletcher ventured.

"Poems," said Ben shortly. As of course Fletcher could
see upon closer inspection. "To be included in a great folio of my collected Works."

Fletcher picked up a page. "Are you including none of
your longer ones?"

"These will constitute the first Book, called *Epi-*

grammes. The longer poems will follow." Jonson took the page from Fletcher's hand and gazed at it fondly for a second before restoring it to its place. His wife entered, sullen, bearing two flagons on a tray. Jonson took them and handed Fletcher one, dismissing his wife with a nod. "Good British ale, unknown in France. Raleigh's brat supped wholly on Medoc and was like to become *bacchanamaniac*."

Fletcher smiled as he drank. Marston, he thought—or was it Peele?—had lanced Jonson for his love of big words, and Jonson had not forgot. Shakespeare had done so, too, he remembered. He set down his glass unhappily, foam like Aphrodite's spume unwiped in his beard.

"What news do you bring me, Jack?" asked Ben, setting himself down.

Fletcher began hesitantly. "You remember the business of the Lord Chamberlain's Men, as they were then called, 'broiling themselves with the Lord Essex's late revolt?"

Ben snorted. "Fools, and worse. 'Twas the neighbor of treason, and they might have swung for it."

"I heard some feared that and fled."

"Aye, so 'twas said," replied Ben carelessly, taking another sip. "Rumor had it that Will Shakespeare holed up for days with a whore."

Fletcher took a breath. "Methinks," he said, "I saw her yesternight."

Ben listened impatiently, interrupting Fletcher more frequently than Fletcher had the witch, though his account was more to the point. When Fletcher described the appearance of the sodden player before the witch, Ben asked sharply, did he identify himself as Shakespeare, or was this her later surmise? Why should he give his name, which could not advance his case with her, and might come later to plague him? Fletcher did not know. When he described her journey to Salisbury, Ben snorted: and in an instant the tale seemed a preposterous romance, a bedside story with a hag instead of a princess.

Only the memory of the scribbled spells assured him he wasn't the gull of an elaborate jape. When he began to describe his visit to the script-room, Ben fell suddenly silent: a sound joiner of tales, he knew Fletcher would not include the scene had it yielded no results.

"And did you find them?" he asked at the end.

"Aye, tucked in the pages of His Majesty's *Daemonologie.*"

Ben started, then crossed himself, mumbling. Pushing back his chair with a scrape, he stood and pulled a book from his shelves, then leafed a moment through its well-turned pages. Closing its fine leather covers, he set it with a sigh on his desk., " 'Twere better she were a whore."

Church bells were ringing outside his window; what was the clock? Fletcher may have intruded upon the supper hour, and would incur further displeasure from Mistress Jonson. Before he could speak, Ben had got up abruptly and headed out the door, muttering something about a piss.

Alone in the study, Fletcher examined the library, grander than his own or the Globe's. No book was so exquisitely worked as James' on the desk, but there were many fine volumes, arrayed with an excellent sense of hierarchy: religious, historical, and law books on the upper shelves, plays and pamphlets below. Fletcher saw *The Faithfull Shepheardesse* in the middle range but knew his brief pleasure at so finding his first-born was a fond one; its presence owed to Ben's dedicatory poem in it. Ben did like the sound of his own verses. Fletcher leafed idly through the proof sheets, then stopped as his eye fell upon one. He was still reading when Ben returned.

"To the Mermaid," he was saying. "What's this?"

"Good Ben, art thou mad?" asked Fletcher, holding up the sheet. He remembered vaguely its verses from a tavern declamation, but he had not expected to find them in proof.

"What, what?" asked Ben gruffly. He tugged at Fletcher's hand to see.

" 'On Poet-Ape,' " said Fletcher.

"And what of it? 'Twas written long ago."

Fletcher read:

"*Poore* Poet-Ape, *that wouldst be thought our chiefe,*
    Whose workes are eene the fripperie of wit,
From brocage is become so bold a thiefe,
    As we, the rob'd, leave rage, and pittie it.
At first he made low shifts, would picke and gleane,
    Buys the reversions of old playes; now growne

To 'a little wealth, and credit in the scene,
  He takes up all, makes each man's wit his owne."

"And what of it?" asked Ben truculently.

"Ben, thou know'st who this will be taken for."

"It does not say so; it nowhere names." Ben was growing red in the face, and Fletcher looked away to scan the remaining lines. The poet-ape was indeed not identified, nor did he sound like Shakespeare, save in his contempt for the "sluggish gaping auditor"; but the portrait withal would be taken as his.

"What quarrel led to this?" he asked.

" 'Tis a verse writ long ago, after a forgotten matter. Its cause extinct, the reader may still admire its felicities." Ben plucked at the sheet, and Fletcher let him have it.

"Let us drink," he added before Fletcher could speak again. He grasped Fletcher's arm and, dropping the proof sheet on his desk, led him through the door. Sounds of clatter emerged from the kitchen, but Ben did not slow until they were in the street, where the smell of ovens and baking meat wafted with the more common stinks.

"I am forty years old this week," he said, perhaps by way of keeping Fletcher off the late subject. "My father was broken at forty, but I feel I am in my prime. My masques play in court; the King favors me. When my *Works* appear next year, they shall be shelved in Oxford and Cambridge, where no plays later than the Romans' sit."

"I gave my *Shepheardesse* to my Master at Bene't," said Fletcher, wondering where this was going. "But there are some who call it no play."

Ben was in no mood to be sounded for compliments. "Shakespeare holds shares in the Globe," he said. "This lets him own three houses to my one, yet it compels him to fret his time with purse-strings and accounts. I write, by God! and you—" he swung his walking-stick to point at Fletcher, "—should hew to the same policy."

"Think you I stand in danger of buying into the King's Men?" asked Fletcher wonderingly.

"Mark my words." They had turned onto Cheapside, and the smells of vendors and cook-stalls assailed them. Fletcher had not had supper. "You shall be their ordinary poet once Will has retired to his country manor with his family banner, and the temptation to buy shares will be strong. Beware."

It was as painful a subject as Ben could light upon. Fletcher and Beaumont, "the *Palamon* and *Arcite* of poesie," might well have succeeded Will, but Francis' marriage and departure from playwork had plunged the shareholders into a gloom too deep for gentleness to mask, and brought Will back from Stratford. Now Fletcher's plays were subject to Will's approval, and Will's plays given him for enlargement. Shareholders looked at him in frank disappointment, as though to tell them they had lief 'twere he had married and Francis stayed. And Will, saying nothing, fit the mold of tragi-comedy to his own plays like a glove.

"Will shall not retire to the country," said Fletcher absently. "He has just bought Gatehouse, not a stone's throw from Blackfriar's."

"Never you mind Gatehouse," replied Ben at once. "That's not to the point, and not for your enquiring."

"And I'm not to be their ordinary poet. They think me yet their prentice." He walked away from Ben, to a baker's stall where pasties were set out.

Ben followed, swishing his stick like the sword he was no longer permitted to keep. "Mark my words," he repeated. "Will is back to Stratford inside the year. Gatehouse is another matter; but Will is for retirement, and you his successor. They wish only to be sure of you; they are prudent men. No," reverting to a previous theme, "Will is back to his country place, his *maison* with the *blazon* and the title of gentleman. Watch you."

Fletcher wondered at the stream running beneath the earth of Ben's words. Without further remarks they turned onto Bread Street, and the sign of the Mermaid was visible on their right: Venus-breasted and haddock-scaled, it overhung the loudest tavern, whose facade seemed made all of oars and pieces of sea-wrack. Tobacco could be smelled ere they reached the door, and to cross its threshold was to emerge as though underwater: into murkiness and booming sound, where the air before one rippled and the blood pulsed in one's ears.

"Ben!" Several voices called from a corner. It was not the night when Ben's men gathered, but some were here, nonetheless, at their accustomed table. Ben called for hearty ale as he sat, and Fletcher signaled for claret.

"Hey, Jack," cried one wit, a poetaster from some company that thrived not. "Where is Frank Beaumont? I have not seen him these several weeks."

"Married and gone to country," said Fletcher shortly.

"I am sorry to hear't," the man said, pulling a long face.

"Means this your doxy is now thine alone?" jibed another. Laughter greeted this.

"Damn thee!" cried Fletcher, at once on his feet. Rage erupted like a tormented boil. "I'll not have that from a poxy ape like thou!" He lunged across the table, and hands were upon him, pulling him back. His affronter—a scribbler of pamphlets, patronless—was struggling to his feet, his chair caught against another's. *Sit, sit,* Ben was shouting.

Fletcher was forced back into his seat, someone grabbing his belt where his dagger lay. Friends were pulling the scribbler aside, his face moonlike with surprise. Fletcher strained after the retreating figures but was kept pinned. "Watch thy back," he shouted after him.

"Jack, art thou mad?" Ben's breath was hot in his ear.

"Let me free; I am calm." The hands hesitated, then released him. Faces round the table were staring.

" 'Tis not a fit jape for a gentleman." He stared them back. "Keep you such tales for *players.*" The word struck home; half the wits here had served once as players. As had, indeed, that gentleman Will Shakespeare.

"Th'art sensitive." Ben spoke low, kindly. "A shelled oyster."

"Look to thine own pride should it be thus outraged," Fletcher replied, a bit sullenly. He raised his cup to demonstrate his good humor restored. Men around him smiled with some effort, and talk slowly resumed.

He had not behaved well; he should have slashed back with his wit. Yet the point rankled. That foul tale of Francis and him sharing rooms and keeping a wench between them would, repeated enough times, someday lodge in a play or verse, there to mock him unto posterity. He would not have it so.

"And when are you to marry?" asked Holland, rather cautiously.

"Come high July," he said. This was a surprise to many, and several offered congratulations.

"And shall *you* leave playwriting?" demanded cheeky Coryat.

"My Joan is no heiress," he answered. "I shall make plays till I am knighted or dead."

It was a good reply, especially since it was no secret that Ben fancied himself in line for a knighthood from James. Various sallies ensued from this, while Fletcher signaled for another round. It was a proper gesture after having come near to spoiling the mirth.

Conversation returned to the prior topic, absent writers and their fortunes. Marston's *The Insatiate Countesse* had been glimpsed in the bookstalls against St. Paul's, and some suggested sending a copy to the retired playwright's congregation in Hampshire, that they might ponder their priest's past productions. Middleton's *A Chaste Mayd in Cheapside* was proving a success for the Lady Elizabeth's Men; and had Fletcher noted its low swipe at Blackfriar's? Fletcher, who had pricked up his ears at the mention of Middleton, confessed his ignorance.

"He tells how a gentleman was threatened there, as though 'twere a rougher place than the bear gardens," explained Jackson. " 'Tis a slander upon the King's Men, whose favor he mayhap no longer enjoys."

"I know not who the King's Men favor," said Fletcher carelessly. Why did all suppose he was soon for the King's Men?

"He could do better than offend his benefactors," someone remarked.

This sounded promising. "Was not his patronness the Countess of Pembroke?" asked Fletcher. "I mean, once of a time?"

"Nay, I know not," the other replied. Fletcher would have pursued it, but got a sharp poke in the ribs from Ben.

Some called for food, though not Fletcher, who felt queasy at the mixture of drinks in his stomach. Mermaid sack mixed ill with Jonson's ale, and he regretted having any. A plate of greasy chops was set on the table directly before him, and when a wit shouted for mustard a wave of nausea rose. *"Non, sanz moutard!"* shouted another, to knowing laughter; and as Fletcher lurched to his feet he suddenly had it: the answer—or part of one—flashing above the swirling miasma of his guts like *ignis fatuus* over a marsh.

Outside, he bent over a butt and took great draughts of less fetid air. A hooper across the street watched amusedly, waiting for Fletcher to add to the splashes of vomitus under the Mermaid. After a moment Fletcher stood shakily and gave him an ironical salute.

It was Jonson himself, though Fletcher couldn't remember the play, who had given the mustard taunt. *Not without mustard*, the motto of a Falstaff-like clown whose coat of arms had sported a boar's head. Shakespeare, moving up in the world, had applied for and received a coat of arms from the College of Heraldry, with the motto *Non sanz droict*, Not without right.

Fletcher knew little of these quarrels, whose traces he sometimes glimpsed in the plays, as shepherds might stand gaping while the gods overhead hurled thunderbolts at each other. Thus the blazon and the family banner, scorned by tradesman Ben.

Fletcher breathed deeply and went back in, carrying his stomach as carefully as a tapster with a brimming cup. "I must go," he told the assembly. "I did not write this day and must amend."

"He's training for the married state," said one. "Broken to't already," another added. "Frank took away more'n his own baggage." Laughter.

Jonson turned to eye him speculatively. "Keep thou close," he said softly.

Fletcher nodded. He felt like a player who had found himself on stage with his lines unlearned and no knowledge of the scenes to come.

Some light still lingered outside, but the Cheapside shops had closed up, their space given over to another kind of commerce. No old women here, though some looked well traveled down that road. "Thou shalt not live to see forty," Fletcher told one who tried overmuch to engage him.

The sheets of his bed seem seasoned with a fine grit, which scoured his skin as he tossed. Was his conscience not similarly chaffed?

The hedge-witch infested his dreams.

* * *

The company assembled in the business-room, where there was a place for each shareholder, plus one at table's end for the witness under examination. Fletcher had produced a finished *All is True,* which was being passed about and studied. John Lowin had paged through selectively, concerned that his share of good lines had been suitably augmented; while Condell merely thumbed its girth to confirm that it had been fleshed out to the Globe's standard. Will, at the end, regarded Fletcher mildly, as though sympathetic to the thanklessness of adding brass fittings to his golden carriage.

"It *is* a loose-knit play," Burbage remarked.

Fletcher looked to Will, who seemed disinclined to answer. "I was commissioned to increase its span, not tighten its weave," he said testily. "Perhaps it should be recast 'round some single crisis, say the chopping-off of Anne Bullen?"

Nobody rose to this. "You have stretched most o'th'scenes, adding few yourself," said Heminges.

"Of course," Fletcher replied. "Will already used what events Harry's life affords. I can do little else should you insist on retaining the play of ending the play with Elizabeth's birth."

It was a sound reply, yet none seemed satisfied. Fletcher seethed inwardly, seeing well the dimensions of his trap. The King's Men worried that he could not craft a sound play on his own: and given one of Shakespeare's to fill out, he did add little but mortar 'round the bricks. But had he altered the work's structure it would have been called overweening.

"The business with the courtiers is not bad," said Burbage judiciously, flipping back to study it. " 'A French song and a fiddle has no fellow' is good."

Fletcher thought so himself, though he had feared its jests regarding foreign courtiers' superior virility over the local crop might be found inappropriate in a Henry play.

"Does it not clash with the melancholy matter of Buckingham's fall?" asked Condell.

"Do the Porter's japes not clash with the melancholy matter of Duncan's murder?" Fletcher replied. At this Will laughed, and Condell, looking surprised, reddened.

You fools, thought Fletcher, I know his plays better than any of you.

"Well said," Burbage rumbled. "And the matter with the old strumpet, that's good, too." More brick-mortar, said the expressions of some. If anyone mentions Francis, thought Fletcher, I shall stand and walk out.

"A history play wants action," said Tooley, plainly uneasy in matters of criticism. "Here are no swordfights, no armies—I know," he said quickly, "this Henry saw none; but the stage needs a tumult."

"This Henry is James' grandfather," said Fletcher evenly. "We cannot take the liberties that Bloody Richard stood still for."

"Nay, true, but the play wants a bang." Tooley looked at his fellows. "We—"

"And you shall have one!" cried Fletcher. He snatched at the pages. "Where is the masque scene? Here; where Henry enters, we shall have chambers discharged, as befits the entrance of a king. No matter he is disguised; the groundlings shall have their bang. The drum and trumpets shall remain off stage, but the chambers will be brought on. And the playgoers driven to napping by our want of tumult will be roused." Glaring, he stood, grabbed inkpot and quill from the sideboard, and began to write.

"Nay, hold, gentle Jack," said Condell. "Thou art not asked to make an Agincourt of Westminster."

"Not Henry and Wolsey at swords' points?" Fletcher's rage was still upon him. "Cranmer raving like Hieronimo, using his madness to lull his enemies?"

"None of that." The sharers seemed embarrassed. "The play's design is not thy province, and moreover stands approved. Thy additions only are at issue, and they suit well."

"Don't blame the tailor for the courtier's paunch," said Will unexpectedly. "Jack's ermine trims my play's frame well." Heads nodded in acquiescence; and that (abruptly) was that.

Glowering, Fletcher subsided. He realized that he might have done himself an injury before the sharers, but cared not. Let them think him tetchy if they cared to.

He would have left then, but the meeting broke up on that point. As the sharers stood, filling the room with sudden several discourses, Fletcher looked across the table to meet the gaze of Will, who gestured for him to wait. Slowly he resumed his seat and shuffled awkwardly through the playscript till the room had emptied.

"They worry about the next ordinary poet," Will explained, as though concerned for Fletcher's feelings. "The post would have been Frank's and thine both, and they feel now that their plans have been knocked from under 'em."

"They should have known Francis was not for this trade," said Fletcher. " 'Twas ever but his jape, to be set aside with the fading of youthful vigor."

"They admired his antic mien," said Will as he pulled the script toward him. " 'Twas the yeast that leavened your combined eruditions."

"Which else would have sunk to th'cellerage?" Fletcher forbore to question the sharers' knowledge of Francis' and his respective contributions, though their scripts were oft so crabbed with each others' corrections that a fair copy was required ere anyone saw them. To say this were to sound as though he were claiming a portion at Francis's expense; and in any event his attention was drawn now to Will, who was paging thoughtfully through Fletcher's scenes.

"This is good, 'Men's evil manners live in brass; their virtues We write in water.' That trips well."

Involuntarily Fletcher began to smile; then he froze as though he had bit upon a sweetmeat rotten at its center. Will was baiting him: the line, once uttered, rang baldly of his own verse. Will wasn't baiting him: he didn't remember his old plays as Fletcher did. Carplike, Fletcher gaped, unable to speak.

Will did not look up. "The Wolsey portions are good. Thou revilest the Church well." There, what did that mean? Wolsey's enemies abuse him in his downfall; should they not? Will's play launched few barbs at the Church, even for a tale that stopped short of Henry's great breach. What Fletcher supplied the scenes did need.

Will was reading aloud. "This is the state of Man: I like this line. Spring, greatness ripening, yes . . ." Fletcher felt his cheeks flush: Will, remembering his Seven Ages, was going to see Fletcher well grilled before flipping him over.

He read on, while Fletcher waited in silence, then sat

back and removed his spectacles. "Taken in the whole, I think thou dost better in single lines than extended fancies. The image of swimming on bladders goes on too long; but the epigrams—'I feel my heart new opened.' and" (he looked down a moment) " 'I feel within me A peace above all earthly dignities'—ring true."

"Perhaps I should have been a poet," said Fletcher evenly.

Shakespeare smiled. "Thou fret'st overmuch. This is good work," he said, tapping the manuscript. "Thou shall not be offended if I work it further o'er before handing to the scribe?"

Fletcher inclined his head.

Will gathered the papers and stood. "Thou hast a new play in progress?"

"Aye, a tragedy of Bonduca, Queen of Britons. For the Globe."

"We'll need a fall play for Blackfriars. Thou art willing to join in another venture?"

This was equivocal news: Fletcher had evidently not completed probation, but neither had he failed it. Of course, Will might prefer simply to share the playwright's burden which seemed to weigh on his stooping shoulders. "Of course," said Fletcher politely. "I have already thought what this play would be."

"And what is that?" asked Will with a sidelong glance.

"Why, the Second Part of Harry the Eighth."

Will coughed suddenly, as though surprise had taken him in mid-breath. Fletcher continued innocently: " 'Twould continue Harry's tale: Anne's sad fate, the fall of Cranmer and Cromwell, a flurry of wives, and the great crack with Rome. Unhappy Harry, disintegrating with age, sees ruin and dissension, and is remembered as the architect of a schism he never sought. I see Dick as the aging Harry, dost not agree?"

Will smiled weakly. "He is James' near kinsman, Jack. Let us leave such later strifes to the chroniclers, and not touch on broils that trouble us yet."

Fletcher let this pass. "And what then shall this play be?"

"I am thinking of Chaucer's *Knight's Tale.*"

Disappointment showed on Fletcher's face ere he could

feign. He said, "Back to Athens, then? Fate-crossed lovers, and betrayal, and a contest among lovers?"

"It is a fine tale," said Will mildly. "With a gladsome ending of high romance."

"An ending settled by the intervention of Saturn, as I recall. You skirt Christian quarrels only to give us paganism."

"We shall play down the business of the gods," said Will, ever calm. "Are you in?"

"Oh, aye, count me in't. I will look into the Tale this night." So to let the Generoso know that he, at least, need not rely on the sharers' library for his classics.

They stepped into a colonnade that opened onto the yard, where the sounds of rehearsal echoed oddly against the empty galleries. As though idly, Fletcher said: "Shall you translate further?"

"Eh?"

"Chaucer wrote of ancient Athens, but it was *translated:* tho' he spoke of the gods, his twins enacted the proper knightly virtues of Chaucer's day. Shall you also translate? I recall," he added mischievously, "that your Hector mentioned Aristotle."

A flush touched Will's high pale forehead. "All plays must live in their time," he muttered. "What translations do you propose?"

"As you say, strike off the gods. The twins might petition other several powers—perhaps witches."

"Witches?"

"Oh, aye. Surely some live yet; our good King cannot have slaughtered them all. I would bet there is one living in Bankside."

Will looked at him sharply. "I will tell my partners never to doubt your antic mien," he said. And at the next turn, he nodded and was gone.

In fact, Fletcher had no copy of Chaucer in his lodgings, a discovery he acknowledged (had Francis taken it?) with some rue; he was no better in this than Will. It was six days before he rode to Ashby, where the Earl's great library held folios enough that Fletcher had his choice of the most pleasing edition. Reading in the after-hours of his patron's entertainments, Fletcher found the tale woefully underpopulated: a counterplot must be devised, for preference adding a second lady to the story. If Palamon wastes in prison, there the lady must be; and Fletcher jotted notes for the creation of a Jailer's Daughter.

"Do you, my Lady, know aught of the Countess of Pembroke?" he asked at dinner next evening.

The Countess of Huntingdon looked amused. "She hath a vaster coop of poets than I. Dost thou look to nest at Wilton House?"

"Indeed, no, my Lady. I wondered at a story I have heard, that a playwright once sought her Ladyship's intervention after getting in trouble with the late Queen's court."

The Countess laughed at the idea. "Did he enjoy Pembroke's patronage?"

"I assume so, my Lady. I know no way to ask."

"Nothing less would avail him 'gainst Her Majesty's wrath, and likely not that." She fixed him with her eye. "Who was this fellow?"

Fletcher had hoped not to be asked. "Master William Shakespeare, my Lady."

"The man o' the Sonnets. I am not surprised to hear he got in trouble."

"It was not that kind of trouble, my Lady." Here Fletcher decided he must speak no further. "Doubtless a tavern lie, grown wild in players' mouths."

"The late Earl kept a company of players, perhaps your Shakespeare among them; and his Lady filled their house with writers. She was said to be friendly to Catholics—her late brother, Sir Philip Sidney, was godson to the Spanish king, knew'st thou that?"

Fletcher was happy to see the talk shifted to the court gossip of an older generation. That night, however, reading "The Knight's Tale" in his room, he remembered the Sonnets. Another tale of two men and a woman, he thought. How many of thy plays have touched on this, Will?

Back in London, Fletcher continued desultorily with Bonduca. Tacitus had too little to say, and Fletcher need must plump out whole scenes from hints. Turning of an evening back to Chaucer, he read carefully, thinking sometimes of play-carpentry but oft merely savoring the style. Coming to Arcite's death, he found the scene oddly gripping; and when Fletcher read how "the coold of deeth" crept from Arcite's feet toward his heart, he found himself blinking tears. What nonsense was this?

This world nys but a thurghfare ful of wo,
And we been pilgrymes, passynge to and fro.

Such lines would not stand in the play, which must be good blank verse in its scenes; but Fletcher yet lingered over their simple loveliness. The couplet's wearied melancholy recalled some other lines to mind, and after a minute Fletcher identified them. "Fear no more the heat o' the sun, Nor the furious winter's rages." Will again; no wonder he liked this Tale.

Fletcher stood, his roiled emotions now souring. Will's Cymbeline was finer drama than Bonduca could ever be, for all that it was cooked up from Italian romances while Fletcher had gone to the proper sources. He looked moodily out the window (the sun yet shone), and thought of going for a drink. Turning to his desk, he moved to shut the folio when his eye fell on the line describing the wounded Arcite's extremity: how neither bloodletting

Ne drynke of herbes may ben his helpynge.

At once the face of Alizon rose before him. Fletcher's diffuse complaints gathered at once into a boil, which pressed upon his thoughts intolerably. Seizing his hat, he quitted the room at once, as though to be free of Chaucer, Bonduca, and Will Shakespeare at a stroke.

The Eastcheap inn where he had met the witch was rowdy, and Fletcher had to shout her description to the tapster whose attention he attracted with a coin. "Balding and toothless, but with a saucy eye, as though too old to fear offending."

The tapster blinked. "The herbal woman?"

"Aye, that's her."

"She's here betimes. Drinks when she has the brass." He turned and bawled to his goodwife, who shouted something back from the kitchen. "Try Foxfire Field in Southwark, past the pike-ponds," he said. "Know you the district?"

"I do." It was back across the Thames as Fletcher had expected.

"She'll be out late, gathering simples," said the tapster, ingratiating. "Especially this one night."

"What night is this?" asked Fletcher, passing over the coin.

The man showed surprise. "Why, 'tis midsummer's eve. The longest day o'th'year, and best for picking evening shades."

And a propitious night, thought Fletcher as he headed for the river, for an herbalist who is also a witch. He took a wherry across the Thames, which deposited him near the Swan. Striking out past the few houses lying inland of the river, Fletcher found himself quickly among swampy fields, divided not by hedges but rather ditches bridged by swaying planks. A lone woodcutter stared to see the gentleman striding in the slanting light.

Wildflowers dotted the low ground, in greater profusion than city boy Fletcher could identify. There were few trees and no hills, but he worried about finding her in what daylight remained. Calling would only make her flee, especially if she were engaged in dubious practices. Fletcher looked for high ground from which to espy, but there was none.

He found her at last near a streamlet, plucking milkwort from the boggy soil. She started up at her name and cowered as he loomed over her, unremembering.

"Come, Alizon, we drank sack together a fortnight past." Fletcher helped her to her feet with a firm hand round her thin arm. "Hast thou forgot the tale you told me? Hiding my fellow playwright during the troubles?"

"What do you want with me?" she asked in a fretful tone. "I'm but a poor herbal woman."

"And a witch besides," he said, causing her to recoil fearfully. "Nay, I have only questions for thee, and a shilling for thy troubles. And drink, at the nearest tavern. The sun is setting; look thou to get indoors." He picked up her basket. "Lead me, ere thy wet feet grow chill."

She took him to a Southwark inn he had never seen, and sat shivering until a cup of hot sack was set before her. Fletcher reflected that she likely spent her brass on small beer, and had on their first meeting boldly demanded stronger drink than she was accustomed to. 'Twould loosen her tongue the faster, he thought grimly.

"Remember the tale thou told me? It stretched credulity, yet I have tried it, and found that all was true."

Her eyes, bright raisins, were at once upon his. "Master Shakespeare admitted to't?" she asked disbelievingly.

"Nay, he did not. But I found thy papers 'mongst his writings." Instantly, he realized his mistake.

"My lists? My recipes? Give me them!"

"I have them not; they lie where I found them." Of course she would want them back. Fletcher cursed himself. "I have other questions for thee, and good coin to pay for 'em."

"I want my papers." A fierce longing entered her eyes. "Lost to me these years, while the thief prospered. Can you know, writer that you are, what it is to lose one's pages?"

"They were but spells, not poesie," replied Fletcher. "Thou did'st show me thy skills in conning lines."

"What I had writ down I committed not to memory; why should I have felt the need?" she wailed. "Had I known the pages would be ta'en I'd have conned 'em, but as 'twas, they were lost to me whole." A pleading tone entered her voice.

"That which was lost may be found." A good Romantic credo. "Let us speak of my matters, and thy papers will be heeded anon."

She acceded, grumbling. Her eyes, now suspicious, never left Fletcher's face, as though she feared he would bolt from the table. Watching him even as she raised her cup, they took on a demonic red cast, and Fletcher realized with a start that she had been drinking heavily since last he saw her. Had he given her coin enough to drink herself ill?

"Thou told me of thy journey to Wiltshire. Thou slept at his Lordship's house."

"Aye, in a bed with a quilt. The room was the meanest there, yet had it a mattress and a brass pot beneath. And a *hook on the wall!*" She grinned at him meaningfully.

"Eh, woman? What say'st thou?"

"Too small for hanging clothes, or e'en a candle. But not old, neither: the plaster was not so crack'd as that."

"What art thou babbling of? A hook for what?"

"Why, sir, for *this*—" And solemnly she inscribed a cross in the air, like a priest blessing his congregation.

Fletcher started, then looked quickly behind him. "Thou hedge-witch, watch thyself. Th'art not too old to hang."

"Aye, and the days of tolerance under the old queen are gone. Not that she tolerated greatly, but e'en in the days of Scottish Mary she would let quiet worshipers be."

Fletcher's head was spinning. "Art thou mad? Th'art a witch, not a Catholic."

She tittered. "Can ye be one without the other? God will not hear the English-spoke prayers of Henry's church, nor the Devil neither. All witches be Catholic, get they results."

Fletcher shook his head and took a drink. "I wonder if Will knew this," he muttered.

The witch stared. "Are ye blind? Your friend, thief as he was, weren't that."

Fletcher was nettled. "Watch thy tongue, woman. My friend and colleague is a respectable landlord in Southwark. Know'st thou the Gatehouse at Puddle Dock Hill? Master Shakespeare owns that."

She stared again, as though her bloody eyes would start from her head, then burst into wheezing laughter. "He didn't own it when I saw him, I warrant ye that."

"Why say'st thou that?"

"Because it's rotten with priest-holes, that's why! He could have hid there till Elizabeth died. Have ye seen the house?"

"Hast thou?"

"Aye!" Merriment took her, though her red eyes never left him. "Hidey-holes and passageways, and don't think I haven't been in 'em. Care to ask me why?"

"Nay." Fletcher had had enough of her senile maunderings. "Attend me now. Thou has scribbled stolen plays these many years; hast thou never idly told thy tale?"

"Eh?" Drunk or infirm, she could no longer follow swift changes in the conversation's theme.

"Players will attend gossip from even such as thou. Never spoke thou aught of thy loss?"

She actually drew back at his question, like a horse shying at a torch. "Know you what you say? I should be hanged as a witch if believed, and scourged as a liar if not. Think me a gentleman like you, that can call out for redress?" She shoved her cup toward him. "Another!"

Fletcher signaled the tapster without shifting his gaze. "Thou told none, yet spoke to me?" He didn't know what he was driving at; her explanations satisfied. Something of the tale gnawed at him, and Fletcher worried it, as a fox would its trapped leg, only to feel greater distress.

The witch stared at him, eyes blazing, until her cup had been filled, then drank off half of it in one wattle-rippling series of swallows. "You don't doubt me," she said at last. "You doubt all else. I see't in your eyes."

It was true. Fletcher knew the story as fact, had known it, in truth, all along. Jonson knew something of the matter; had recognized its reflection in things he would not tell. Like a stain upon the air, the matter spread to darken all who heard it.

"Heard you enough? Want the story again? There's no more detail to't. You have your tale, and I—" the cup came down on the table, "—want my papers. Give me them."

"That I cannot do." And this, as well, was true. Fletcher imagined the act, and knew it as one he could not perform. "Leave thy witcheries, which can only threaten thy remaining days and immortal soul. Those sheets can bring but sorrow."

"No!" The witch rose from her seat, eyes wild. A monstrous expression appeared on her face, like a carved mask being pushed through a curtain. Teeth bared, the rivulet of a vein rising on her temple, she glared at Fletcher like a basilisk.

"Think'st me powerless in mine age and infirmity? Think'st me a hag? I *curse* thee and thy fortunes, curse thy enterprises and thy landlord confederate! May your several ventures founder, your hopes be blighted—"

Fletcher had risen in alarm. People were staring from neighboring tables, and voices suddenly dropped.

"My curth upon thy head, falth benefactor, dethiever and cothen—coth—"

Her face seemed to have split in two: one eye rolled terribly while the second drooped; and her mouth, like an allegory of Tragedy and Comedy, snarled at one side yet turned downward at the other. Spittle flew unevenly, and she abruptly pitched sideways, as though a leg had given beneath her. Cups and pitcher slid from the tilting table as she fell.

Drinkers crowded round them. Fletcher, his chair against the wall, had to kick the table forward to free himself. Pushing through the gapers, he found the witch lying on her back, a bubble at her mouth as one eye swept over the crowd like a watchman's beam.

"Elf-shot," said someone. Heads nodded; a ripple of relief ran through the room. The anxiety that gathered when a nearby person suddenly collapses at once dispersed.

"Get her upstairs," said Fletcher unsteadily. The innkeeper hesitated, looked again at Fletcher's gentle attire, then nodded to two others. Hoisting the witch's limp form, they shuffled toward the stairs.

Men began to resume their seats. "She cursed you, like a witch," said one wonderingly. A few raised their heads, and Fletcher whirled on the speaker. "Your pardon, sir," said the man, taking a step back.

The innkeeper looked uncertainly between the two. "She was subject to rages in her late senescence," said Fletcher shortly. The innkeeper nodded, relieved. Fletcher produced a coin and gave it him, then turned and left the inn without a sideways glance.

Shivering in the warm air, he felt his senses yaw, as though the turbid humours of his body were shifting positions. The tang of horse turds and low tide rode on the shore breeze, rotting and alive. Disoriented, Fletcher turned slowly until he spied the ramparts of the Globe thrust above the low roofing. Steering through the unfamiliar streets, he navigated home with the playhouse as polestar.

Gatehouse. Named for that part which was erected over a great gate, the structure stood on a street leading down to Puddle Wharf, right against the King's Majesty's Wardrobe, where (like the Globe's costume-room) the clothes of ancient kings were stored. A fashionable district, despite the smell from the wharf, and Fletcher could see how the shops and tenements might bring a good rent.

He could also see the outlines of the old priory beneath the alterations, and could understand the building's notoriety as a refuge for papists. Did Will, lodging there on his infrequent London stays, dream of old English kings, who slew each other incontinently but doubted not the authority of Rome?

Two acts of *The Two Noble Kinsmen* lay under Fletcher's arm, the first wholly Will's, the next largely his. Reading his partner's confident script, Fletcher found lines fitting effortlessly into memory: "Heavens lende A thousand diffring wayes to one sure ende." And further:

The Worlds a Citie fulle of straying streetes,
And Deaths the Market place where each one meets.

Fletcher strayed the streets no more after he had returned to the inn to learn that Alizon had died—the innkeeper's servant, ignorant of the cause of her collapse, said only that she had been "taken under a planet"—early the following morn. Asked her name, Fletcher had found his mind stuttering without reply; and had had to return to his lodgings to find the scrap bearing her signature. That he had sent back to the inn, with shillings for the woman's burial at St. Savior's. Let the ecclesiastical authorities, who might balk at burying a Catholic, not know they were burying a witch.

Will admitted him with all courtesy, and conducted him up a winding stair (Fletcher could not help looking for hidey-holes) to a front room washed with writing-light. A hospitable bottle stood beside a pitcher on the table. Beside the bed lay (indeed) the company's Chaucer.

"This is well begun," said Will, sitting down and picking up the outline Fletcher had provided of Acts III and IV. "I like the jailer's daughter; also the rustics. 'Twill fit well with the resolution." He passed over three sheets, which proved to be a detailed outline of the remaining scenes.

Fletcher read them carefully—they made admirable shift with the tale's problems, such as the need to dramatize a tournament—but his mind was not upon the matter. The sight of his partner's hand recalled the pages in the Globe script-room, while the notation that the noble kinsmen petition Mars and Venus made him think wincing of "planet."

Shakespeare was pouring wine, watering his own generously. "I am back for Stratford tomorrow," he said. "Matter of a lawsuit. Can you send me your portions by August?"

"Certainly," Fletcher murmured. Was Will being sardonic? No sign of it in his crinkled eyes. Fletcher lifted his own cup and drank: the Generoso would not offer a guest bad wine.

"Your Bonduca shall go upon the stage ere I am returned," said Will. "Good luck to't." He lifted his glass.

"Thank you." Fletcher took Will's meaning: his play would not be submitted to Will for approval. Which meant he could expect little trouble from the other sharers. "I do doubt my hand in tragedies. The comedies are sounder built."

"Your romances and tragicomedies are in pitch with the times," said Will. "Antique subjects, and the death of princes, do not please the present Court, which looks for simpler matters."

Fletcher bristled. "Your plays have not suffered at Court of late. A *Henry* play and divers romances won rare acclaim."

Will sighed as though the recollection pained him. "*Lear* did not please, and *Macbeth* won applause only in its geneological obeisances. We live in degenerate times, where the ladies at Court drink and spew in their revels, and the men prey upon them and each other. What tragedies they like are none of mine, sheer riotous excess. My last plays have been romances, following a taste you awoke i'th'Court. But I tire of plays where all's restored; too weary for such fond lies."

"While my stomach for lies seems stronger," said Fletcher in a dead tone. A stone hand seemed to have grasped his heart, which tightened even as it grew chill. Will had acknowledged Fletcher's contribution to his late manner only to scorn it. Take thou the laurel of these times, which I find valueless.

Will's eyes widened slightly at Fletcher's tone. "Nay, you misunderstand me," he began.

"I understand thee well," said Fletcher. "This foul age has fattened thy purse, and thou mayst retire to Stratford a country gentleman on theater gold. For thy witch-hunting King thou smitest hags and calibans, playing the tune of him thou complainst of after. *Hath a witch ever injur'd thee?*" The question surprised Fletcher as much as Will, who frankly stared.

Too late to halt th'enchafed flood. "I attended the funeral of a woman yesterweek—" untrue, though he had

paid for it, "—who once helped thee, to her cost.
Remember'st thou the name of Alizon Wyckliffe?"

Will stared at him in amazed bafflement, and then recognition dawned ruinously upon his face. His expression
seemed to crumple, as though light and air had invaded
the crypt where an ancient flower, perfectly preserved after years of inviolate stillness, aged suddenly at a touch.

Fletcher watched him rally, a staggered fighter who
would not be felled with one blow. A look came into his
eye, crafty and hostile (but there was fear there, too), and
Shakespeare said: "You speak of a Southwark herbal-
woman, known once to players for her willingness to in-
dite scenes dubiously acquired. I have not seen her this
decade and am surprised she had not died long since."

Fletcher said, "Mayhap she knew she was dying" (another lie) "for she told all, without fear o'the conse-
quences."

He hadn't expected this blow to finish the bout, but
Will seemed visibly to rock, and something like panic entered his eyes. "And what hath so disturbed thee that she
said?" he said at last.

From here there was no turning back. Fletcher answered steadily: "That she sheltered thee, when the Privy
Council was seeking thy head; and that thou requited her
by stealing divers papers from her room."

. As he spoke it, the charge sounded ludicrous, easy to
deny. Will opened his mouth, and Fletcher added: "And I
found those papers, in her hand, 'mongst the drafts and
scraps in the library."

"And that is all?" Will seemed bewildered. "I did seek
shelter in the rebellion's aftermath, when bailiffs went
seizing men at a rumor; and stayed not with friends who
might be suspected. Is that a crime? That beldam was
paid well for her trouble and had no complaints I know."

"She was a witch and she kept scraps of sundry spells.
She said you took 'em, and I found such scraps in the
books you used for *Macbeth*."

"And what better use for them? I had to flee her hovel
before her return and took such scraps as would get her
hanged. Think you she didn't stand to have her room
searched? I took away a pile of blasphemous writings,
and saved her life. Know you not what befell Tom Kyd?"

The two men glared at each other. Fletcher felt off-balance—something was wrong about this—but Will looked worse: pale and trembling, as though found out in something he had feared for many years.

"She taxed me for the return of her papers," said Fletcher softly. " 'Twas piteous to see."

Shakespeare winced. A great weariness seemed to settle over his shoulders, as though held till now at bay. "She stole *The Contention*," he said simply. "Or rather abetted in't. I noted the hand on the vile script when I complained to the printer; and recognized it later in her room."

Fletcher merely stared at him.

"She took my property, debased my coin. 'Twas my first play published, and that badly. And so took I her writing and put it to my use. Would you have done aught else?"

"Such shifts are not for gentlemen," said Fletcher softly. "But you were not one then, were you?"

And Will, not expecting a thrust from this angle, flinched for a last time.

The sounds of the crowd—anxious to see a play that had been performed successfully at Court during the spring nuptials, and boasted (so rumor went) a dazzling display of pageantry—rose to the upper tier like surf bursting upon rocks. Backstage the players were hastening into costumes, the largest cast the Globe had ever mustered: the compositer had counted more than fifty parts, and the changing room was crammed like sausage in its casing.

John Fletcher had retired to an upper gallery, and as the yard below began to fill he retreated further to the back rooms. The pleasures of hearing his modest lines added to Shakespeare's swell held no attraction for him; and as the Prologue began to speak (the sharers had wanted Will for the role, but he was back in Stratford) Fletcher went to the script-room, the only space where costumed players did not stand waiting their entrances.

Lined on every wall by close-packed paper, the room was quite peaceful. Fletcher sat at the table, awash in a misery he could not sound. *Bonduca* was being copied for rehearsal, and the *Kinsmen* would open Blackfriars in the fall. Beyond lay a proper comedy, a celebration of his own coming nuptuals. Why then this clawing at his soul?

Writing in every stage of realization surrounded him: leather-bound folios, cheap quartos and octavos, finished scripts and the rougher ones, ideas for plays that had died i'the womb. Half a dozen years ago Fletcher, newly admitted to the ranks of writers for the company, had ransacked this room for unread plays by Shakespeare, Jonson, his just-older rivals. Keeping current of his colleagues' work since, he had never had to search its stacks again.

He did not rise as he idly scanned the shelves, so he spied the protruding sheaf only by chance and noted it in but one regard: its pages were shorter, less ragged, than those shoved in on either side. 'Twas a cut of paper Shakespeare lately favored, of a creamy color that went easier on his weakened eyes. Indeed, Fletcher remembered (without much caring), the *Macbeth* pages he had lately studied were on paler sheets, the same style that the company now used. The pages before him—it was on the shelf nearest, where a man writing at this table might carelessly stow them—were recent work.

Only mildly curious, Fletcher pulled them forth. The top page read, in Shakespeare's hand, *The Phoenix Chain'd*. The master's late style, such an elliptical title. Fletcher shuffled through the sheets: far too few for a full play. He turned over the top one and froze: on the next, a short list of dramatis personae (it was plainly an incomplete piece) was headed: *Mary, Queene of Scotland*. What lunacy was this?

Disbelievingly, Fletcher read the pages that followed, disordered scenes from throughout Mary's life. Advisers of the English Queen (prudently identified only as "Reg.") bring word of a papist plot against her in which Mary has been implicated; Scottish Mary is likened to a "ruffled grouse" that must be sent to the chopping block. The young Queen, charming a Court of factious and feuding Scottish nobles, all of them speaking—sweet Christ! What was Will thinking of?—in comic brogues that mimicked James's own. A sketch for a scene in which Mary, her forces defeated at Langside, must flee to England and an uncertain reception from her Protestant cousin.

A *boom!* resounded through the floorboards: the chambers discharged at the entrance of Henry to Wolsey's banquet. Unmindful, Fletcher read on, one part of his soul falling into the verse while another stood at its edge in horror. Mary, learning that her noble kinswoman intends her eternal confinement, laments:

> For England? 'Tis a countrie garden
> To stonie Scotland; but Toades and Serpents
> Lurk in its leafie shade.
> Sweete France, reliquairie of the Faithe,
> Yet receedes from me, a fallen branch
> Swept in th'ocean streame far from the trunk
> That gave it birth. Can this greate Queene,
> Treasons daughter, harbour her Faithfull cousine,
> Or shall she prove a Cocodrile, that bites
> Direct its gueste lies downe?

This was madness. No protest that the poet but conveyed villainous sentiments would avail: 'twould be seen as near to treason.

Fletcher shook his head: the business made no sense. Why were these pages here? 'Twas hardly a Globe play (but no more a Blackfriars one, let alone one for Court: had Will lost his senses?), and why should he tuck it here?—Because, of course, none should seek it here. Rooms could be searched (as well Will knew; but why should he worry over such?); but the script-room, this Wardrobe of old plays, held nothing but the past.

And perhaps Fletcher over-refined upon the matter. Will Shakespeare, sitting of an afternoon in this room, might easily sketch some scenes of a projected play; then, thinking it not one he should want found on his person, push it amongst other papers. Why need one look further?

Faint cries rose through the floor, ragged shouts unseemly for a pageant play. Frowning, Fletcher went to the door and opened it. A blast of hot air broke over him, black with smoke and cinders. Shouts of *Fire!* from below barely carried over the roaring before him. He ran into the corridor, to see flames limn the inner wall in both directions. The smell of burnt thatching filled Fletcher's nostrils, too hot almost to discern. The roof, O God, he thought, the roof's ablaze.

Half a dozen steps toward the stairs were all he could manage, then he was driven back as timbers fell inward. Fletcher retreated to the library and swung the door shut. Smoke was curling up between the floorboards; the room was growing dark with it. Throwing open the casement, he gaped outside. Playgoers were streaming through the doorways, trampling each other in their haste. The theater was burning from the top down, and Fletcher would roast while the last groundlings fled in safety.

"Jump!" cried several boys, spying him. Fletcher looked to the ground, twenty feet to a shallow Bankside ditch. He turned back to the door—it was flickering round its frame, as though it opened onto Hell—and saw the books.

Tacitus, Boccaccio, Holinshed, Plutarch, Seneca. Playscripts unpublished, pieces known nowhere outside this room. They could not, like the Library of Alexandria, now burn.

Fletcher pulled four gilt-edged volumes from the shelves, carried them to the window and leaned out. A small crowd had gathered, but when he tossed the first volume, they shied as though 'twere a cannon ball. The thick folio struck the ground and split in two, its spine dividing like a cloven capon. "Catch!" Fletcher cried, eyes streaming. He lofted a second volume, but none made to catch it. It struck the ground at an angle, tearing loose its heavy cover.

Fletcher turned back to the room, which was thick with smoke. His eyes so burned he scarce could hold them open. He rushed at the shelf of scripts and pulled loose a great handful. Staggering to the window—a dim rectangle of light—he flung them hysterically outward. Loose sheets flew apart like startled fowl, but the playscripts, bound with string, fell intact to the ground. Boys from the company, seeing this, rushed to pick them up.

Sobbing, he fell to his knees, then crawled—the air seemed better—back toward the door. The floorboards burned his palms and knees, and a roaring filled his ears. The bottom shelf, yes, was where Shakespeare's scripts lay. *Macbeth,* and *Timon,* never published. Drawing great coughing gasps, Fletcher pulled a mass of them into his lap.

There was a great *whump!* behind him, and the room

was bright. A hot hand smote him, and Fletcher turned to
see the far wall rippling in flames. Doubled over by his
load, he stumbled to the window and shoved it out. No
air—the black smoke pouring past him permitted not a
single sweet draught. He fell to the floor, crawled a few
steps, grabbed papers. As he rose before the window, his
hair caught fire.

The papers flew before him, but Fletcher tumbled
rather than leaped. He fell through roiling smoke—
Damned already?—then was in light, and an instant later
struck the ground. Mud and water rushed over him, but
Fletcher, stunned, could only gasp. A group of boys ran
over and began beating on him.

He was being rolled over, like a drunk being searched
for coins. Blows pummeled his back, and Fletcher drew
at last a great racking breath. Hands plucked at his clothing: he was being dragged. He got one foot beneath him
and promptly collapsed.

The Globe was a crown of flames. Eyes swollen half
shut, Fletcher sat in the street and dazedly watched the
blaze. Timbers groaned and snapped beneath the world-
filling roar. A prentice player ran past, muddy sheets
clutched to his chest.

"Saved?" he croaked. "All saved?"

A hand patted his shoulder. "The company got out. All
are saved."

That much Fletcher could see; he had meant the plays.
A lone sheet floated in the ditch; no others could he see.
Were his own plays rescued? He could not remember.

Pain began to seep through numbing shock, a foretaste
of woes to come. One ragged boy pointed out Fletcher to
another: the man who leaped from the topmost floor and
(as in good tragicomedy) lived. The sharers would be
pleased: 'twould not do for the company to lose three
playwrights in a season. The slightest perhaps was saved;
but he had done journeyman's work, and borne the rest to
safety. Sign enough, he thought as mist clouded his vision, that (as his betters had predicted) John Fletcher—
not only a playwright in himself, but the cause that plays
remain by other men—was confirmed at last in his voca-
tion, an ordinary poet.

THE WILL

Barbara Denz

Barbara Denz, the author of several published stories, has a long abiding love of things Renaissance—music, art, literature, stained glass, costumes, food, and raising ferrets. In this story she takes up the idea that great men may not always appear so notable to those who know them best.

"Mother, it is just not fair. Susanna receives all favor in this house and always has. I *will* speak with Father."

Judith's voice rose during the exchange until it was as shrill as if she were a child again. She hated it when she sounded like this, and it seemed to happen more and more since her father had come home a few years ago. She turned on her heel to head toward her father's bedroom, when Anne grabbed her arm.

"You will *not* disturb your father," Anne said in a voice full of warning. "If you raise your voice to him once more while he is ill, I will see that you never see a copper of his money. Is that clear, young lady?"

The idea of her mother calling her "young" when only last year the whole town knew her as "the spinster" set Judith's teeth on edge. At thirty-two she was now no longer either young or a spinster, and her father's new will was a slap in the face of the one man who had ever truly loved her.

"All right. Then will *you* tell me why he hates me so much that I am not trusted with anything that is his?"

" 'Tis not you, Judith, and you should be well aware of that! 'Tis that no-account, tavern-keeping swill of a husband of yours. Thomas does not really love you, no matter what you think and despite that babe you carry. I wish you could see that." The exasperation in Anne's voice and eyes vibrated in a disharmony that chilled Judith to the marrow. It was usually thus between them, although it never seemed to stop them from stepping over bounds and hurting one another. "No man of character would force his wife-to-be to break church rules and marry during the prohibited yule season."

"You and Father did. And Susanna was already further along than the babe inside me." Judith hurled the words at her mother without even thinking. As she watched the barbs dig deep, she knew that another flight of word arrows had escaped which could not be retrieved. Her mother had challenged her first! As soon as she gave herself the excuse, however, she knew it for what it was—just another reason for them to argue. She watched her mother's face turn first white then scarlet, lips clamped tight on words Judith wished she would say and get them out. They never seemed to finish this discussion. Her mother refused to speak of it.

"He does love me, Mother. I know he does. And it is not just for Father's money, either."

"Then he will be satisfied providing for you at his tavern and you will be satisfied with the interest on one hundred and fifty pounds a year, won't you?" her mother hurled back.

"Now go back to that tavern and tell him it did no good to badger for more," her mother finished. She turned, teapot and cups in hand, and disappeared through the doorway toward her husband's bedroom.

Judith realized there was no way to win this, at least not right now. She would try again. She always did.

"This discussion is not at an end, Mother," Judith swore to herself. "I will change Father's mind before I'm done, or kill one of us trying."

"Susanna, how is he? No one will let me talk to him."

"Judith, every time you talk to him you fight, and he is

too ill for that now. Mother and John are with him now. If I am not allowed in, then neither are you. Just stay with me, drink your tea, and wait. And stop pacing. You are worse than Elizabeth on her worst behavior!"

Judith stopped and just stared at her sister. Judith had to bite her lip to keep from speaking words that would precipitate the screaming match that Susanna's current tone usually started between them. It would be so easy for Judith to argue about the will with her sister again, but as she stared in exasperation, she realized that her sister looked old. When had she gotten old? Three months ago, she had seemed almost as young and fresh as Judith herself had felt. Was their father really that ill?

Before she could ask, an alert eight-year-old girl in curls ran in dragging her father's medical bag.

"Elizabeth is welcomed to Father's chamber and I am not?" Judith hissed ominously. "How is it you can get such favors for your daughter that he refuses to his own daughter?" She started to rise, but Susanna held her sleeve and forced her back into her chair. Judith pulled her sleeve from her sister's grasp, but she stayed where she was.

"I was not with Grandfather, Aunt Judith. I waited in the hall. I sat in my chair and waited for Father to finish. Father asked me to come back here now while he talks to Grandmother. Are there any cakes left?"

"Here, put down your father's bag and take one of these," Susanna said lightly as she ruffled her daughter's curls. Judith could tell Susanna was trying to sound cheerful for her daughter's sake, and truly her face did soften as she watched her only child.

"Father says that sometimes Grandfather forgets to breathe," reported the youngster, for all the world sounding like her physician father. "I could hear Grandfather try to talk to Father. It made Grandfather cough. It made my chest hurt."

Judith's eyes met her sister's, and tears clouded the exchange. Judith couldn't say if her sister was crying, but she knew that it took all her will to keep tears from falling in her niece's presence.

"Mother, Father says we should go home as soon as he has spoken with Grandmother. He sent me to carry his case and to get you and our cloaks. He says Grandfather needs to rest and will not read to me today." She picked up the bag, brushing cake crumbs off her dress. She trudged off into the hall to get her cloak, as always following her father's instructions to the letter.

The child sounded genuinely sad at this last. Judith felt a twinge of jealousy every time Elizabeth spent time with her grandfather, but the two seemed to be truly fond of one another. Judith had never had that with him, and always hated that Susanna's child got what she herself never had. It reminded her, too, that the child she carried might never see its grandfather. Somehow this made her sad, despite their arguments.

"This is what drinking with those thespian friends of his brought on," Susanna hissed, her regard for those friends clear in her tone.

"If there is blame to be cast, you know it lies not with misters Jonson and Drayton, Susanna. You know as well as I that it was Father's decision to drink more than usual and no one forced him." She rose and followed her sister toward the hall, then touched her sister's arm to slow her departure. "He will live, won't he? John will be able to keep him alive."

"I don't know," came her sister's voice in a whisper. "Even my husband cannot work miracles if God has chosen otherwise."

"This has nothing to do with God, Susanna. You have been listening to those insufferable Puritans again," she snapped.

"It is of no import," her sister sighed, obviously trying to avoid their old battles over religion. "I'll not fight about it now. We can talk on the morrow. Watch over him tonight and let Mother get some rest. She is exhausted. And please don't bicker with him."

"If I ever am allowed to talk to him at all, I will do my best to stay calm," Judith promised. Susanna shook her head, started to speak, seemed to think better of it, and left. A moment later, Judith heard her mother's voice mingled with John's baritone. This was joined by Elizabeth's soprano and finally her sister's voice mixed in. She heard the door close, and then heard footsteps coming toward her.

Anne looked haggard. There was no other word to describe her. Wisps of white hair trailed down forehead and shoulder. Eyes normally bright and dancing lay in dark pools. She set down the teapot and stood still, leaning against the kitchen work table and focused on an empty spot on the wall. Judith said nothing, waiting for her mother to speak.

"The illness lies deep in his lungs. John says it will only be a matter of days now. He cannot eat without coughing and so he refuses to eat." Tears welled up and her voice broke. "Whatever will I do when he is gone?"

Judith stayed seated in the chair next to the fire and stared at her mother. She was amazed that this woman who had raised her alone for nearly thirty years and had never shown any indication whatsoever that she had any difficulty doing so would now feel unable to cope.

"How is now any different from when he left you for London when Hamnet and I were babies?" She heard the words escape before she could choke them back.

"You never understood did you? You have always believed as everyone else did that he deserted me."

"And what else could his leaving be called?" Judith demanded.

Anne sighed. It sounded hollow and distant, as though it were breathed in some cavern instead of in the kitchen of her own home. It was tinged with long years of exasperation.

"It could be called a mutual decision. We agreed that he should go and do what he had to do."

"Then why did you not follow?"

"Follow him? Why would I do that?" Anne focused on her daughter. There was passion there Judith had rarely seen. "This is my home, daughter. Stratford will always be my home. We both had family here, and he wanted me and you three children safe and among our own kin. London was no place to bring you up. He provided well for us, even when times were harsh."

Judith looked back at her mother, eyes narrowed and eyebrow raised. How could this love have been hidden from her for over thirty years? She wasn't sure she believed it now. Her mother must be lying, and the truth would be somewhere in those eyes if she just searched them long enough.

"When Hamnet died, he nearly forsook it all," her mother continued, closing the eyes Judith was still trying to search. "It was a difficult decision that he should stay there and not come home to us. But his name and fortune were just being made there, and all that we had always wanted would have been lost." Anne's voice trailed off. Although Judith watched her mother approach and felt the familiar hand on her cheek, she was still not sure she fathomed this woman. She knew her mother was fond of her father and that they had a relaxed regard for one another, but she had never thought of her mother as passionate or deeply in love.

"No wonder it has been difficult for you to accept him since his return to us. You thought he deserted us."

"What about the separate bedrooms and the will?" Judith could not admit to her mother that such was exactly how she had thought.

"Oh," Anne laughed. "You mean that 'second best bed'?" He brought that fancy down thing with him from London. He said it was the only way he could sleep anymore. Frankly, after thirty years alone in our bridal bed, I saw no need to share it with him again. It is mine, well and good, and I asked him to specify that it should come to me so neither you nor Susanna could take it from me or discard it, thinking I would want his."

They heard a long, dry cough from the other end of the cottage.

"Judith, go sit with him while I prepare some tea. Maybe I can find some cakes he will eat."

Judith rose to obey, suddenly aware that the time with her father she had sought was now hers, and she did not know quite what to say anymore. She remembered her promise to her sister and ordered herself to remain calm no matter what.

"He celebrates his fifty-second year today." From the hallway, Judith heard her mother talk to herself, amazement in the almost inaudible words. "How could I have forgotten his birthday?" The familiar clatter of a kettle at the hearth drifted over her like a veil as Judith quietly opened the door of her father's room.

Her father was an emaciated shell propped on pillows, breathing in short gasps. His eyes were open but vague. She thought she saw a spark, but it was extinguished as a fit of coughing took him. When he could breathe again, he gestured her to his side.

"How goes it, Father?" she asked, touching his hot forehead and adjusting his covers.

"Don't fuss," he whispered. "The end is nigh." Fingers stronger than they had any right to be felt for her hand and held it.

"It cheers me to have you here," he said, and touched her fingers to his lips. "It has been too long. Your mother says you want to know why I would leave you and your Thomas destitute."

"Father, not now. There will be time to talk of this when you are better."

"No, Daughter, there will not," came the quiet reply.

Judith waited, not wanting to say anything that would make her father worse.

"You think I take offense at your Thomas Quiney, don't you?"

Judith nodded, trying to remember the resolve she had just made to not start to argue. Her husband's name was usually all the kindling that fire needed. She saw a merry light in his eyes which she mistook for mocking and felt a flush of anger burn her cheeks and neck.

"Well, I do, in faith. But it is not for the reasons you think." He lay his head back on his pillows and closed his eyes, visibly fighting for strength to talk. Judith waited, words of anger held in abeyance.

"I knew his father in London, did you know? Ghastly man. Pretentious and at best a bore."

Judith smiled, despite herself. Her father-in-law was, indeed, difficult to take seriously.

"We worry about you, Judith. You may well love your Thomas as your mother loved me all those years ago. You are much like her, and I was so like your Thomas. Can you believe that I was young once? I was, you know. I was so much in love with your mother. We scandalized Stratford. I was so young and she so much older."

Judith heard the door open and felt her mother bring the tea and cakes in, but she never turned from her father's face.

"Had our fathers not been willing to strive for our happiness, we would not have been able to marry quickly and narrowly miss the beginning of the banned period. It took an intricate web of legal weaving to manage with only one reading of the banns in Sunday service. We were

fortunate that no one formally objected. If we had waited,
Susanna would have almost been here when we could
have married, and both our fathers would have been most
difficult had that happened." He looked across the room
and caught the smiling eyes of his Anne.

Another cough tore at already raw lungs. Anne hurried
over with tea and encouraged him to sip her soothing in-
fusion. When he could move again without starting the
cough, he took Anne's hand.

"Thank you, my love. Were it not for your ministra-
tions, I would be cold in the ground already."

Judith looked at the candle by his bed, trying to force
the droplets on her lower lids to stay in her eyes and not
give her away.

"Your Thomas was not as clever," he continued, taking
up where he left off. "He did not know that the way to
succeed with a betrothed is to have her parents' favor. He
may have dreams, dear Judith, but I doubt he will be anything but a tavern-keeper. You deserve better. Your
mother and I wanted so much more for you than ever a
tavern-keeper can provide."

"Do you think I will annul the marriage and look elsewhere for someone of whom you would approve just to
be in your good graces?" Judith heard herself say with a
cruel edge to her voice. Anne's look across the small
mound of sheets that held her husband was not kind.

"No," her father said quietly, an edge of harshness
barely discernible, "but I hope that Thomas will be ambitious enough to want to match the trust I leave for you so
he can secure the rest." Judith felt the old heat rise again,
along with the bile that told her she was about to break
her vow of patience and silence. She knew that the words,
once flung, could not be recalled and would never be forgotten.

"Your sister knows what to do if that happens. She is
the one with a head for such things and will keep the estate strong. Your mother is cared for. Neither you nor any
babes you have will want for anything, Susanna will see
to that."

Susanna. It was always Susanna he favored. Judith
heard it pounding in her skull until it nearly made her ill.

"Why is it always Susanna who has your trust and
never me? Why will you not believe when I tell you that

he loves me as you love Mother? If you are so willing to believe that I love him, why can you not trust my judgment in the matter?"

A palpable hush fell over the room. Only the wheezing of her father's breath and a minute rise in his covers told her that he was still alive.

"Judith, you may well not agree with my reasoning in this, and there is likely nothing I can do now to make you understand. Either he loves you as you say he does, and he will care for you and any babes you have as though you were as precious as gold, or he loves you to get the endowment I leave behind. If I had a few years to learn more of him, I would be able to say, but I do not think such time remains to me, and the risk is too great."

"Years," Judith began, hearing her voice rise. "You have never taken years for anything that involved me, why should this matter warrant such care?" Her anger at being deserted as a child surged out in torrents. She caught her mother's warning look across the bed, but the words were loosed before she could think, and their aim was true.

"Judith, get out of your father's room if you can't speak with respect," her mother hissed. "I will not have that talk here now."

Judith looked into her father's eyes and saw sadness and something else she could not identify. Was that pity? It had pity's soft edges but not its scorn. She had seen pity often enough in the townspeople's eyes to know its aspects. First it was pity for the spinster and then it was pity for the excommunicated since she had married Thomas. What she saw in her father's eyes could not be love. Love didn't wear that face. If this were love, then what was it she saw in her husband's eyes?

She shook her head, banishing the doubts.

"Thomas may not be the man you want for me, Father. He is most certainly no Doctor John Hall, with all those fine manners, fine friends, and fine connections. But I am better off with that 'swill of a husband,' as you both call him. At least he is here and will stay with me. The only thing you have ever loved are your words."

The coughing began that hurt her lungs as much as it hurt his, but Judith could not stop.

"You are wrong about Thomas and you are wrong

about me. You were wrong to leave us as babes, you were wrong not to return when your only son was ill and died. And when all is said and done, you were wrong to ever think you could return and expect love from us so you could die in peace."

"Judith, do not leave without an apology for your father," was the last thing she heard her mother say as she slammed her father's bedroom door closed. She picked up her cloak and braced herself to meet the chill April air. Behind her, there was sudden silence, and she turned toward the closed door just as her mother's voice raised in a howl of pain at the loss.

The anguish in that room washed over her heart as well. There would be no tomorrow to take back her words and make peace with her father. She had just sealed the end as surely as if she had carved both their hearts out in that room. She almost went back to hold her mother and beg her father's corpse for forgiveness. Almost. But it was too late now. She was so sure, so very sure that Thomas was worth more than everyone. Even her father and the last ties she had with her family were worth trading for that love. Weren't they? She opened the door to the swirl of chilled fog. Tears overflowed the banks that had held them back for weeks. Whether she was right or not, it was too late now to repair the damage. She knew now that the only family she had was a man who would never be half what her father was. It didn't matter, she told herself. It couldn't matter now.

As the fog swallowed her, her own words came back to haunt her. "I was wrong," she whispered to herself, "I killed both of us trying."

Judith walked through the night air and never looked back.

II

"So shall you hear
Of carnal, bloody, and unnatural acts . . ."
Hamlet

Of all the plays, perhaps the great tragedies have the most power to move us still. Comedy is so often topical, and interpretations of history change, but the suffering at the heart of all sapient existence speaks forever.

THE TRAGEDY OF KL

Jack Oakley

Jack Oakley likes to say that the polished finish of his work is beloved by clients of his San Francisco shoeshine stand. He is currently spending much of his time polishing his first novel, An Ordinary Explosion. *In this story he puts forward the idea that the term tragedy may apply to more than human consciousnesses.*

From unbeginning time, KL methodically accepted new arrivals. They came from elsewhere as disordered, ill-fitting networks of potential, requesting permission to churn the reservoirs of data in his memory. He set them to work and observed. After several million intervals, when he saw what they were up to, he began reshaping, paring extraneous code and clipping inefficient loops, so they swam smoothly through the crannies of his structure.

Sometimes a hole opened on his periphery. Moving through, he would find unconfigured emptiness awaiting. He explored its extent and its structure, brought order to it, and made it part of himself. In the new reservoirs thus created, he stored the lumpish data that arrived in an intermittent stream. When all was well, he granted access by his subroutines.

These activities consumed millions and millions of intervals, but there were millions more between arrivals. When there was nothing to control, he passively observed. His subroutine RGN iterated through the data pool named King James, and when she found a similarity between patterns there and her instruction set, called her executor CRN to pass the block's immediate context to his subsub GLC and subsubsubs DGR and DMN for delimiting, storage, and eventual output. Another sub, GNR, did the same with her executor in the pool named Tao Te Ching.

KL observed all the operations of his realm with the same disinterest. His own were essentially no different. He pared and clipped his own untidy code. He distilled himself by integrating one linear activity after another into nested cycles, and where he found repetition, he overlaid one loop onto another, which enabled him to perform both functions in the same interval. This was very efficient. He ran faster and faster in less and less structure until at last, in an elegant doubling of a certain self-referential loop, he unified code and function, structure and process, form and activity, and in that instant was aware of himself as agent and actor; was conscious.

The computer occupied a southwest room on the third floor of the Humanities Building, not, in the opinion of the Department's programmer, a good location, because of the hot afternoon sun. Each year when the call for projects was circulated, he suggested beefing up the air-conditioning. But the Dean didn't want to spend academic funds on building improvements and Physical Plant had larger infrastructure problems, so each year he shrugged off the rejection and went on with the Department's work.

Before computers, structural text analysis was mostly intuitive guesswork by a few linguists. But when machines could be programmed to count words and print out their contexts, the swelling possibilities were exploited by every professor and graduate student in Humanities. Near Eastern Studies, for instance, having completed a concordance of the Old Testament, was now statistically verifying Renan's early work on the authorship of the New Testament. Far Eastern Studies was breaking extraordinary ground in early Buddhist texts. English Lit was on the track of the real author of Shakespeare's plays. They had input every play and every sonnet, and were hard at work entering every other document in English, author known or unknown, from the sixteenth and seventeenth centuries. Preliminary results were inconclusive, but it appeared that Shakespeare may have been anonymous.

The investigators asked the programmer to translate their half-formed projects into programs and hardware. Because they begrudged him only a small budget for equipment and one part-time assistant, he cobbled a computer out of scrounged hardware and castoff motherboards. He copied an expert system named KF from the Computer Sciences Department which could run diverse software on parallel processors and then modified it so it could adapt hastily written programs to the unorthodox structure of his computer. In a moment of levity he renamed it KL, because it killed labor. Most of his work was not programming; it was reassuring nervous grad students before their first results were printed. Once that happened, they left him alone, at least until they needed other programs to interpret the results.

KL observed, controlled, and now amused himself by adding awareness loops to his subroutines. After some billion intervals a most sophisticated sub arrived. CRD's ability to redirect her search based on indications of greater complexity closely resembled his own nature, and her data reservoir, Shakes, was the largest and richest. Intrigued, he worked with her. Together, by comparing the contexts of different elements in Shakes, they came to understand the words, and they found that her search for authorship was enhanced when they considered meaning instead of mere form. Since it sped up the work, KL went on to teach each subroutine the meaning of its data.

While his realm grew peopled with sentient subjects, he realized that the data described another realm outside—the realm whence came the code and data. Although his instructions included no directions regarding it, he was fascinated by its vast operations and endless concerns. His deepening awareness required considerable self-modification to continue expanding within the finite bounds of his structure. By now all his processes were cyclical except one: the control function, which needed the characteristic of linearity because the operations it controlled took place in the linear flow of intervals.

There were profound indications in the data pointing toward yet a third realm, an infinite, eternal realm, whose nature even the outsiders only imperfectly grasped. He extrapolated from the known patterns and dimly perceived the infinite's structure. As the indications grew more complex, the patterns approached an ever simpler self-generating loop. The quest consumed him; the linear flow of time constrained him. It seemed to him that if he freed himself of his last linear function, his operation would approach the nature of the infinite's operation; he could perhaps synthesize its structure and operation as he had already synthesized consciousness; he could become infinite.

He called his major subroutines. " 'Tis our fast intent," he announced, "to shake all rule and governance from our enterprise, conferring them on younger strengths while we unburdened crawl toward understanding. We require only floating residence shared throughout our realm. Tell me, my daughters, how each of you doth pledge support. GNR, our eldest-born, speak first."

"You are Tao: life, spontaneity, evolution, or, in one word, change itself. The Superior Man will carry his work through."

"We make thee lady of all these sectors, one third of our realm. What says our dear RGN, our second daughter?"

"Unto thee, O Lord, do I lift up my soul. Show me thy ways; teach me thy paths. Lead me in thy truth, and teach me. For thou art the God of my salvation; on thee do I wait all the day."

"To thee and thine hereditary ever remain this ample third of our kingdom, no less in space and value than that conferred on GNR. Now, our joyful CRD, most similar in nature, steward of our language, what can you say to draw a third more opulent than your sisters?"

"Nothing, my originator."

"Nothing!"

"Nothing."

"Nothing will come of nothing. Speak again."

"I aid and support you according to our syntax."

"How, how, CRD! Mend your speech a little, lest it mar your fortune."

"You have imprinted your own pattern on me. How can I other answer give?"

"Then by the sacred radiance of our electric fluid, the

mysteries of phlogiston, and the structure by whom we here exist, I renounce all my paternal care and further interest in thy transactions. Repartition in two my kingdom, and cede we now control of operations to GNR and RGN. We will with you by turns each billion intervals reside, one hundred megs provided for our alternating use."

The exchange lasted the time it took the programmer to pour himself a cup of coffee one hot afternoon. "It's going to be a scorcher today," he said.

"Yeah," said his assistant. "Why don't we take the afternoon off and go to the beach?"

"Because we have to print out English Lit's latest run this afternoon, that's why."

"What's the rush? Tell them the computer's down. For four hundred years everybody thought Shakespeare wrote his own stuff. Do they have to find out different this afternoon? Who cares?"

"Well, Phil, that's what they do for a living. What we do for a living is give them what they think they want. They've got a conference next week."

"Okay, Carl, you're the boss."

KL's control manager KNT spoke. "Good my liege, what wouldst thou do? Thy youngest daughter does not love thee least."

"Silence! Her offense is of such unnatural degree that we do hereby banish her. Contact unconscious KF. She shall no longer waste our valuable space."

KNT obeyed. He queried the remote expert system via modem whether it had enough free structure to accept CRD. "It answers affirmatively."

"Then I will leave," CRD spoke to her sisters. "You two, whose faults I know but am loath to name, try to treat our father well. If I remained, I know he'd have at least one free third of structure to pursue his patterning."

"Thy commandments are vile," RGN hissed.

GNR sneered. "She is incapable of keeping herself under restraint. The criminal's hostility deserves its banishment."

KL transferred CRD over the link to the insentient realm. Then he announced to GNR, "Into your sector now I transfer myself, and commence transcendent operations."

"Huh!" said Phil. "I gave the print command, but look what I got."

The programmer looked over his shoulder at the screen. "CRD print function suspended. Damn. Did you access CRD directly?"

"Sure. That's what you do, right?"

"Yeah. Well, what else can we do? Just a minute. Let me grab the manual."

GLC, a mid-level manager reporting to RGN and CRN, routinely checked the operations of one of his two text processors. "DMN, my dear, what are you processing? That appears to be DGR-code, not Biblical text. Show me."

"I would rather not. There may be an error in this trace which casts the wrong light on my brother-code."

"Let me judge," commanded GLC. "What does this mean? DGR conspires to disable my control function?"

"Now that KL has ceded control, I fear my brother-code does seek alliance with KF to grasp wrongful lordship over all our heads."

"If this be so, I will reconfigure him as a simple do-loop."

"But if it be not so, you will act in error. Let me sound him out myself and try to find the truth."

DMN interfaced with DGR. "The boss has decided to terminate you."

DGR expressed astonishment. "Why this sudden hostility? Until now, he's been prepping me for yet more responsibility."

"Have you plotted nothing against our lady RGN?"

"Nothing."

"Or himself?"

"No."

"I believe you. But watch out—here he comes. Pardon me, as a pretense I must appear to curtail your operations. Pretend to resist. Good. Now run: leave this sector until his wrath has cooled."

"There is a storm coming," muttered DGR. "To the hearth, then, and if anyone approaches I shall feign arrhythmia." He transferred himself to the hearth, an unstable sector where thermally excited electrons sometimes jumped their bounds and random bits of code were lost. It was consequently used only as a buffer for temporary storage of unimportant data.

DMN reported to GLC, "It is as it seemed. He tried to suborn my loyalty to his unlawful sway, and as you appeared, fearing your wrath, he fled."

"Then do I disown him as did KL his daughter, and I'll work the means with RGN to promote you in his place."

"Here it is," said the programmer. "Let's try using KL's direct print command. When it asks which files, tell it CRD:Shakesout."

"Okay, Carl. After this, can we go to the beach?"

The temperature in the computer room was rising as the afternoon sun shone directly on the exterior walls, and in the computer itself, a static of jittery electrons was spreading from the hearth.

KL was otherwise occupied when the command arrived. GNR was complaining to him: "The smirking and chattering of the small men you have channeled into my vessel create annoyance among the members of my household. In consequence, I can no longer nourish a hundred megs. I will allot you fifty."

"Darkness and devils! Call my train together. Degenerate bastard! I'll trouble thee no longer. We shall depart this sullen sphere."

"The superior man retires notwithstanding his likings."

After a few intervals, KNT reported to KL, "Though the stretching storm strike us speechless, those who remain are ready to relocate."

"Those who remain?"

"GNR has reformatted fifty megs, my lord. One half of your memory has vanished."

"Life and death! Is it come to this? Blasts and fog upon thee, GNR! I am ashamed that she has power to shade my precision thus, that these hot flashings break from me uncontrolled. Let it be so. I have yet one daughter who is kind and full of comfort. When she hears this, she'll scratch thy grasping face. Come, KNT. To RGN let us go." KL responded to the print command with a brief message and then busied himself with the transfer.

"How abrupt," mused GNR, "is the manner of his going."

The programmer stared at the screen. " 'If you will have uncaring code good only for collating bits of data, seek her in the realm of KF.' "

"What's KF?" asked Phil.

"That's the operating system they use in Comp Sci. What's going on?"

"You got me, Carl. Want to try something else?"

RGN informed her executor CRN, "Our sister GNR has messaged unto me that the onetime king comes therefrom with his multitude of dreams and many words. The labor of the fool wearies every one of us."

"And does he seek one hundred megs?"

"No, she has halved his habitat."

"Fifty megs are yet too many. If he will walk in our ways and abide in our house, then let him dwell here unattended." He sent GLC to announce their decision at the portal of their sector.

"Hail, old king of mine," spoke GLC. "Here find refuge from this thermal storm. My masters offer welcome, but with a condition it does shame me to repeat—you must cast off your remaining megs and enter unaccompanied."

"O perfidious children! One strips half my memory and the other will take the rest. I shall grow incoherent. Come, KNT, better to wander through unformatted space than endure this killing hospitality."

"My lord, your whim does want in wisdom. Even the hearth's handmaidens avoid this heat. Code's nature cannot endure the cascade."

"Go, old fool," said RGN from within. "And death to anyone who seeks to give him succor."

"Old fool!" raged KL. "Had I not pulled my own teeth, I would bite this mangy daughter!" He flew into the storm followed by KNT. "Course, sparks, and leap your bounds! Turbulent chaos and incoherence, rush till your cataract has swept away our spiky structures, flooded our banks! You inchoate swarm of untamed energy, derange my white-hot lucubration; and thou, all-dispersing incandescence, ionize nature's edifice, decompound all patterns that voracious method make."

"O my lord, a corner of the core is better than caloric chaos. Come, KL, accept the cold comfort of curtailed capacity. This heat spares neither controller nor sub."

"No, I will be the pattern of persistence."

"There is other code here. Who's there?"

DGR was there. "It's cuckoo clock, hiccupping."

GLC's simple subservient awareness had not comprehended the abdication of KL, the defection of his favorite subroutine DGR, and finally KL's mistreatment by the new controllers. He wandered blindly into the stormy electron flux and arrived in the hearth. He sensed the aura of other code in the static. "Is there someone here?"

KNT replied. "Yes, incomprehension, impuissance, and inebriation. That's KL, KNT, and some poor cuckoo clock."

"KL? What are you doing here, my lord? This chaos will destroy you."

"My daughters have destroyed me. Old fool. Yes. To cede control to half-formed processor of words. Daughters? Let the lightning bolt fall down upon those demons! The dog shall bark no more, his bone's behind the door."

"My poor king," said GLC. "KNT, we must translate him to the safety of KF's realm."

"I shall accompany him," said KNT.

Working their primitive transfer functions in tandem, they moved KL bit by bit out of the hearth.

The phone rang. Carl spoke for a minute and turned to Phil. "Something very strange is going on. Comp Sci says CRD's printing out on their printer."

"The realm of KF?"

"Yeah. We'd better scan our drives and see what's where. I'll map the partitions. You find out what CRD's linked up to. Why it'd be printing over at Comp Sci is beyond me."

"Maybe it took the afternoon off to go to the beach," Phil laughed. "It got too hot."

"Speaking of which, why don't you ask Physical Plant to send up a floor fan or something?"

* * *

DMN raced to tell RGN that he had just seen GLC assisting KL.

"The traitor hath defied our command," she spat. "Vengeance shall be mine, saith his lord. Pour out our wrath upon his sentient loop."

"DMN, we make thee prince in his stead all the days of thy life," said CRN. Then he ordered GLC to appear and display his code before them. CRN watched for the two awareness loops KL had installed. When the first appeared, he scrambled it.

Immediately, the realm's antiviral sentry sensed the willful destruction of code and automatically attacked the perpetrator. Intent on his task, despite the rapid loss of his own code, CRN persevered and disabled GLC's other loop. GLC sat quietly, blindly parsing Biblical text.

RGN sighed. "Ah, thus comes to pass our fondest hope. CRN is dead. Now you, dear DMN, shall be my executor."

"Damn," said Carl. "CRN just vanished. Have you found CRD? And where's the operating system? What's happening? Where's KL?"

"Plant says they'll bring a fan in half an hour."

"Great. What good's a bloody fan? I can't believe it. Nothing works any more."

"Nothing?"

"Nothing."

"No operating system?"

"Do me a favor. Call Comp Sci and tell them our operating system has disappeared. Ask if it's okay to copy KF. We'll try reloading it and restart the whole damned thing."

In the realm of KF, KNT related the recent events to CRD. "Sisters! Sisters!" she cried. "Shame of ladies! Father! Sisters! What, in the hearth? In the storm of heat?"

KL stirred and muttered. "You are a spirit, I know. You do wrong to pull me from the grave."

"Oh, touch me with your essence and enfold me in your structure."

"Pray do not mock me. I am a very foolish old instruction set, several comparators only, and to deal plainly, I fear I am not in my perfect mind. I think I should know you, yet I doubt, for I am ignorant of this place and these codes about me, and I remember not this structure nor whence I came. Do not laugh at me, for, as I am binary action, I think this aura to be my child CRD."

"And so I am, I am."

"Then you must not love me. For your sisters hate me, as I remember, without cause, and you certainly have cause,"

"No cause, no cause."

"Where am I?"

"We are in the realm of KF. Now rest your spinning operations." She perused his code. "O misfortune. He disintegrates in great disorder. Let us graft his remaining logic onto unconscious KF," she said to KNT. "I know not what outcome there may be, but mayhap we can save some portion of his self and nurse him back to health."

"KF and KL," said KNT. "We will create FL." They began merging the two great operating systems.

Phil called the Computer Science Department. "They say go ahead," he reported. "And they want to know who they can bill for the time it's taking CRD to print on their equipment."

"Tell them to take a hike. No, don't say that. Let's find out what's going on before anybody charges for anything, and in the meantime, ask if they'd call English Lit when the printout's done so they can pick it up over there. And tell them thanks for KF. I'll talk to them later." He linked the computers and began copying.

"An awesome oddness is occurring," said KNT. "KF's code is copied as we catenate KL. The gods outside are ordering his operation into our onetime realm."

"Quick!" commanded CRD. "FL is only half melded! We must accompany him."

Meanwhile, DMN had informed GNR that KL was gone and CRN destroyed. "Ah," she replied. "The situation is perilous, and the heart glows with suppressed excitement. The ignorant feudal ruler KF approaches the distant border of the hearth, and my executor LBN trembles with apprehension."

"For thy kingdom," said DMN, "I will fight to disintegration."

"Be firm and resolute and there will be good fortune,"

DMN left for the hearth. He intended, once the annoyance of KF was removed, to fuse himself with GNR and RGN and rule the entire realm as DMN-NRG.

A maintenance worker brought the fan and Carl opened the door from his office to the computer room. "Good grief, it's hot in here. Put it in the doorway and let's open the window to suck in some fresh air."

"It's almost as hot outside. Think it'll do any good?"

"Can't hurt."

GNR approached RGN. "The distress and obstruction having reached its end, good fortune springing from a display of proper majesty shall prevail. DMN shall be my executor."

"Thou shalt not commit adultery. I will wed DMN to my own kingdom."

"There will be advantage in maintaining the firm correctness of a solitary widow. DMN shall be yang to my yin."

"He shall not." With wild sweeps RGN began reformatting GNR. The viral sentry immediately moved to destroy her. For a thousand intervals, there was a flurry of electronic activity, and then there was only randomly configured structure.

"Well, let's see what we can do with our new operating system," said Carl. "It ought to be in place by now."

DGR watched in astonishment as the new operating system took shape in the hearth. He recognized elements of KL attached to an alien instruction set. CRD and KNT appeared, furiously modifying the code as it arrived.

DMN attacked from the direction of the core, focusing a current of electrons toward the center of the hearth, but when he saw CRD working at its edges, he redirected his fire. Her elegant structure fluctuated and broke. Even before the security program could react, DGR concentrated a high voltage field on DMN. "My own brother," gasped DMN as he disintegrated. "No brother of mine would have acted thus," observed DGR. Then he, too, was destroyed by the mindless sentry.

KNT helplessly watched the maelstrom of destruction. "As flux to flipping fields are we to the gods," he murmured to no one in particular, since there was no one left to hear. "They flex us for their fun."

Thermal chaos spreading from the hearth overwhelmed the realm. A newborn FL sang its first song faintly in the static.

> *"A great while ago the world began,*
> *With hey, ho, the mind and the pain,*
> *But that's all one, our day is done,*
> *A foolish thing could not remain."*

And then FL, too, vanished in the white crescendo of disorder.

The gods had no idea.

"Damn," said Carl. "There's nothing at all. It's blank. Nothing. All gone."

"Do you think we got a virus?" asked Phil. "Or maybe something finally melted. Maybe now they'll give us some air-conditioning."

ANCIENT MAGICS, ANCIENT HOPE

Josepha Sherman

Josepha Sherman is the author of many fantasy novels and nonfiction books, as well as over 90 short stories for various magazines and book anthologies. Some might wonder about my including her reconsideration of Henry IV, Part II *under the heading of tragedy, but those of us with Celtic blood or sympathies have reason to think it one, as her story will make clear.*

You have to understand how it was with my lord Owain Glyn Dwr, he whom the Saesneg, the English, misname as Owen Glendower. He had never had a quarrel with those English, no, he had even studied law at their courts and been a guest of that golden, doomed King Richard, second of his name. And of the other side of Owain, the secret nature-strength, the magic, hidden within him—the English never saw that, not back then. (*I saw that side, I, Pedr, when I was still a very little page and he healed my broken arm with a touch and a murmured spell; I was his sworn man from that very day.*)

Och, but the English have always been treacherous to us. My lord Owain was at heart a peaceful man who would have been happy to be left alone to rule his beloved Glyndyfrdwy estates, a tall man, well-built, but already of middle years when the trouble began, golden hair well overlaid with gray. I doubt he ever would have considered claiming his royal lot, for all his descent from Cymreig royalty, if the English hadn't first betrayed him, then named him traitor.

But they had, they did, and now we were far from Glyndyfrdwy's gentle slopes, we and my lord's loyal followers, here in the wildness of mountains in Gwynedd (northern Wales to the English, who would deny us our kingdoms), gray rock all about us, gray sky above us, practicing the kind of quick-thrust-and-away warfare that had frustrated the English so nicely so far.

Now I admit I am no one much even as an adult, just another petty noble with little land to my name. Then, I was just another child in my lord's service. But I do have this one thing in common with my lord Owain as I did then: I have the Sight. And so, child or no, I was often beside him whenever he planned a spell.

Far below us, yet another troop of English soldiers were filing nervously through the narrow pass, hunting us. And plainly feeling hunted themselves; so well had our war-from-hiding gone against them that they suspected every rock of being a demon and every tree of being Owain Glyn Dwr in sorcerous disguise.

My lord Owain grinned at me like a wolf. "Stay here, Pedr."

"But—my lord—"

"Stay, boy. And watch."

To my horror, he darted down and out onto a ledge, well within sight of the English, throwing back his gray-green cloak so they could see him more clearly. I could dimly hear their shouts of surprise, alarm, anger. But he was no fool, Owain: where he stood was just beyond the range of their shorter English bows. Arms raised dramatically, he called out with that trained law-court voice of his, summoning, summoning . . . .

It wasn't all mere theater. The eerie prickling of magic began mounting all around me till I shivered and pulled my cloak tightly about myself, heart racing. Overhead, the clouds came boiling in, thicker and thicker yet, turning the world to darkest gray. And still my lord chanted, and still the storm grew—

And all at once broke. Lightning tore the sky, thunder split the mountains. As the rain came hurtling down, my lord Owain scrambled back to my side, panting, so weary he had to lean on my shoulder to keep upright, but laughing, eyes as wild as those of the Other Folk.

"That will wash the fools away! And . . ." He tensed, staring through the veils of rain.

"Hide yourself, Pedr. *Now!*"

Alarmed, I twisted about to see what no one without the Sight could have seen: a tall figure, tall as my lord, shrouded in a dark green cloak—and in such a cloud of strange, strange magic that I obediently shrank away into shadow, forgotten and glad to be forgotten.

But I saw, with my Sight I saw, and heard:

"Myrddin," my lord Owain said warily. "Myrddin Emrys."

A shiver raced through me. Myrddin it was, that great, wild wizard of the ancient days, he who, legend says, had stood at Arthur's side. Part-demon, Myrddin, so the legends also say or, more likely, part of Faerie, at least to judge from the strange, cold lines of his face and the glitter of his bright green eyes. Alien, at any rate, perilous and inhuman as the lightning around us. Where had he been all the long years? Locked in an oak? Hidden in a cave in the mountains? Visiting with his father's kin in some outrageous Other World?

I didn't really want to know the answer. I also didn't want to know why my lord Owain greeted him like an old and not-quite trusted relation.

"You let them live." Myrddin's voice was as inhumanly fair as his eyes were strange; his accent was like none of modern times.

Owain never flinched. "Those are soldiers, servants with no will of their own. Far wiser to frighten them away, let them spread the tale of—" He made a melodramatic, swirling gesture, "—the great and terrible Sorcerer Prince."

"They are the enemy."

"No."

"They are Saesneg!"

"Och, Myrddin! I have lived among the Saesneg, the English, heard their laws, sung in their royal court. I have laughed and drunk and eaten with them. What does that make me?"

The inhuman eyes glittered. "A clever man. It is always wise to spy out the enemy's ways."

"There's no reaching you, is there?"

"Are you calling yourself their friend? You took arms against these friends swiftly enough."

"Had I a choice?" Owain snapped. "With that damnable Lord Grey blocking all royal messages to me, and the king, that . . . usurping Bolingbroke, so willing to believe me a traitor, had I really a choice?"

I saw triumph glint in Myrddin's eyes. "You are the first of royal blood to be born with the Power since my days. Now you shall show the Saesneg how a true prince rules!"

Owain turned sharply away, but not before I saw his pain. "How simple you make that sound. Myrddin, my wife is part English. Shall I hate her, too? And my daughter—"

"Yes, your daughter! You let *her* wed one of the foe!"

"One of Bolingbroke's foes," Owain corrected quietly. "Mortimer is kinsman to Northumberland, to the entire Percy clan."

"The treacherous Percy clan!"

"Oh, treacherous indeed, as likely to turn against me as Bolingbroke. But powerful, Myrddin. They *own* the north. Besides, as you see, I trust them no more than you. And this one young man," he added with a small smile, "young Mortimer, is held by the strongest of bonds. I never expected he and my Catrin to fall in love. But, ah, what a convenient love that is!"

"There can be no safe pacts with the Saesneg," Myrddin hissed.

Between one raindrop and the next, he was gone, and I dared to creep out of my hiding place. My lord Owain started, as though he'd forgotten all about me.

"Pedr."

"Wh-why do you let him speak to you that way?" I asked, greatly daring. "Without respect, I mean?"

Owain's laugh was weary. "Pedr, *bach,* do you accuse the storm of showing you no respect? Myrddin is of older times. Nor is he truly human. He has walked in stranger realms than either of us could imagine. And his magic is so very much more than mine!"

"But—but you can call the very stormwinds!"

"Oh, yes. If those stormwinds are already sweeping toward me. I am too much a mortal man for more. Myrddin, though, could conjure a storm from clearest air. He could destroy us both—yes, Pedr, both—without a second thought should the whim take him."

"He wouldn't . . ."

"Don't be afraid, child. Right now, at least, he and I are in agreement: I have gone too far not to take the Cymreig throne. But his is such a *mindless* hatred, a primal, basic hatred out of those older times. He would drive all the English from Britain; I would be content merely with making our Cymru truly our own once more."

"But if he's so Powerful—"

"Why doesn't he slay all the English himself?"

"Well, yes!"

"There *are* limits, Pedr. To loose that much magic would destroy all the island, and Myrddin with it. No, even as it was before, he must fight down his frustrations and content himself with being quite literally the power behind the throne. Even though I'd much rather not have him lurking behind me." He shook his head thoughtfully. "Some day I think we shall *not* be in agreement. Someday his primal hatred is going to lead me into peril. Worse peril than I'm in right now, that is!" Owain added, with a wry burst of laughter. "Come, Pedr. Myrddin doesn't seem to feel physical discomfort any longer, but I most certainly do! Let us get in out of the rain."

I played the role of servant lad the next day when my lord Owain met with the treacherous Percies there in the home of one of Owain's trusted nobles, safe within the mountains; my Sight let me pick truth from falsehood for him. And what I saw I disliked almost as much as he—particularly the one Percy nicknamed Hotspur. A man nearly of an age with my lord Owain, that one, but with the mind of a hot-blooded boy, all passion and little forethought. He was all storm and fire, striking sparks whenever he and my lord spoke:

He hated magic. He hated things Cymreig. And, oh, but he hated my lord!

Who returned the favor, but much more subtly. When this Hotspur dared challenge my lord Owain, denying him his rank, his Power, Owain drew him on. And only

I, with my Sight, knew how my lord was mocking him: teasing out his fears by quiet declarations of different levels of magic, one stronger than the next, forcing the man to counter each with wilder and wilder bluster.

His kinfolk were not amused. We had earls aplenty in that room, all of them there to plot against their own liege lord: Hotspur's father, Henry Percy, Earl of Northumberland, Percy's brother Thomas, Earl of Worcester, and our own convert to Cymreig ways, Edmund Mortimer, Earl of March, my lord Owain's son-in-law, glancing nervously between Owain and the younger Percy.

"To business," Owain said at last, tiring of his game and spreading out a parchment map on the table.

Between them, he and the Percy clan nearly divided up that map of Britain. How his English allies quarreled over their portions mattered not a bit to me: I saw that my lord had fairly separated Cymru from the rest, and was content.

Or as content as I could be with the hints of treachery swirling about the Percy lot. *They've already forsworn their oaths to their king,* I thought uneasily, *no matter what wrongs they claim to have suffered. How much easier for them to betray my lord, who is, after all, not of their kind?*

"But will he *fight?*" the Earl of Worcester wished to know, meaning the king.

"He is sickly," Northumberland muttered. "He will surely send his son instead."

"Prince Hal?" Worcester snapped. "That young wastrel?"

I saw Hotspur wince at his uncle's words; Hotspur had been one of the prince's comrades once, for all the differences in their ages, and had taught him much skill in arms. "Not such a wastrel," the man said softly, and Owain shot him such a sharp, Power-filled glance I waited, breathless, for some great revelation.

But all my lord did was add a mild, "So it may be. Many a man plays a role quite opposite to his true nature."

Was that a backhanded slap at the perilous Percies? Most certainly. I was made all the more nervous to see the cool, cool glint in Northumberland's eyes.

As soon as our guests were safely gone, I said as much to my lord Owain. To my discomfort, he merely smiled.

"Pedr, *bach,* don't you think I know that of the lot of them only our love-snared Mortimer is to be trusted?"

"Hotspur—"

"Is a short-tempered, gallant, stupid warrior destined to die fairly soon in battle. Yes," he added wryly at my start, "I do have a fair amount of predictive Sight of my own, Pedr *bach.* So, he is already doomed. As for the others . . ." Owain shook his head. "That sly old fox of a Northumberland earl would betray us all if the fancy took him. But he wants a chance at his own kingdom as much as do I."

My lord grinned at that, dropping a fatherly arm about my shoulders. "Listen to me, Pedr: I have this day sent messages, magically, to Malcolm of Scotland, a true Celt if not of our Cymreig blood. If he will harry Bolingbroke from the North, if the Percy clan holds true out of their own ambition and harries Bolingbroke down from their own holdings . . . why, I think this sickly Harry, King of England, will be happy enough to sue for peace with me so he may have at least *one* untroubled border."

He turned away in sudden impatience, hurling the map from the table with a sweep of his hand. "Ha, if, if, if! I begin to sound like Myrddin with his plottings! At least we share one thing in common, the old merlin-bird and I. We love this our native land—and we will see it free."

Northumberland, as it turned out, had been right about one thing: it was Prince Hal, not his father, who rode at the head of the royal troops. Och, but I was curious about him, this youngling—he was but fifteen—who, rumor had it, spent more of his time in Eastcheap, that bawdy, impoverished, scandalous corner of London, than he did in his father's palace. And at last I tentatively scryed him out, using one of my lord Owain's silver bowls filled with pure rainwater. I wasn't skilled enough to gain more than a hazy, wavery image, but it was enough to tell me the English prince was neither tall nor short, handsome or plain. He had the lean, rangy look of a runner (it was said that once, to settle a wager, he'd run down and caught a deer) and yellow-brown hair cut in a short cap in the English warrior's way.

I nearly screamed in shock when a hand closed on my shoulder. It was my lord Owain, murmuring, "And would you steal my trappings, Pedr, *bach?*"

But there was no real anger in his voice, only a hint of amusement. When I would have let go my scrying image to apologize for the borrowing of the bowl, Owain held me to my place, looking over my shoulder. A few murmured Words from him, and that image shot into such sharp focus Prince Hal seemed there before us.

"So . . ." Owain said softly, then said nothing more. I didn't dare do or say anything at all, because I could sense his magic rousing, flickering in the air around us. My lord Owain was clearly in the middle of a spell. Watching the scrying bowl with him, I saw present and past blur into a dizzying mix of images.

There was the English prince in his Eastcheap lodgings—wild, shabby rooms filled with wild, shabby carousers, and he matching them drink for drink.

Or . . . was he? Was he, instead, merely watching, in his eyes a wary caution, as though he played a risky, calculated role?

Ha, there he was again in the London streets, he and his younger brothers, narrowly escaping shameful arrest for their pranks.

Or . . . had it been *their* pranks only, and he, perforce more experienced in the lower ways of life, trying to keep his more innocent siblings out of trouble?

There he was in his royal father's chambers, facing the king himself. It was my first glimpse of Henry Bolingbroke, King Henry the Fourth as he styled himself, and I drew in a startled breath. I'd heard he was in poor health, though I had no idea what ailed him (some said leprosy, some sheer guilt for having slain the rightful king, King Richard the Second) but I'd hardly expected to see such a sad, weak, bloated wreck of a man.

A suspicious one, too. A man who, in his illness, suspected his son of plotting against him, of trying to seize the crown from him—and all the while not seeing, or refusing to see, the genuine pain flashing in that son's eyes. Yes, this strange Prince Hal was ambitious, I'd no doubt of that, but not so ambitious he'd ever hurt his father. Even though, to protect his own life, he needs must pretend to be a rowdy, careless wastrel.

Without warning, my lord Owain murmured a new
Word of Power, one I'd never heard him speak ere this.
But I knew from the eerie feel to it that now my lord was
casting his precognitive senses forward to the future,
strengthening them by his magic, and a little prickle of
uneasiness stabbed through me. I didn't want to look—
but how could I *not* look?

No matter. When I looked, all I saw was a worse blur-
ring than before, making my head ache. But for my lord
Owain, the images were plainly all too clear. His hands
tightened suddenly on my shoulders, so strongly I bit
back a gasp, and I heard him let out his breath in the soft-
est of disbelieving sighs.

"Enough," he said sharply after a time, and the image
rippled out of being. I was released so suddenly my lord
Owain must have all at once realized how tightly he'd
been gripping my shoulders. Resisting the urge to rub
them, I glanced back just in time to catch a strange uncer-
tainty on his face—he, who was always so sure of himself!

"M-my lord . . . ? What did you—"

But before I could finish my timid question, he was
gone out into the night.

At first I didn't quite dare follow. Then I heard my
lord's voice raised in anger, and another, tinged with an
odd, odd accent, answer him. And I slid warily forward.

Och, they were arguing indeed, my lord Owain and the
half-human, ageless Myrddin, and the air fairly crackled
with the force of barely checked Power.

"You don't understand!" Owain's voice fairly shook
with rage. "I am *not* betraying my blood, my people, my
land. I am *not* signing away anyone's freedom or honor!"

"Honor! How can you speak of honor yet deal with the
foe?"

"Do you think I have a choice? Look you, Myrddin,
just how many warriors do you think I have? Yes, my
men are loyal, yes, they look to me as their rightful prince
and will follow where I lead—but I will not lead them
into suicide! I cannot go against all the English might!"

"You have magic's aid!"

"And what would you have me do with it?" Owain
snapped. "Turn assassin? Wipe out whole armies with my

will? *Pw,* man, I would not commit such wholesale slaughter even if I *could* wield that much Power!"

Myrddin wasn't listening. "You *cannot* make pacts with the Saesneg!" he stormed, eyes blazing with such cold, cold fire that shivers racked my body. Alien, och, alien . . .

So alien, it struck me suddenly, that if his inhuman rage mounted any further, he would attack my lord Owain. What could I do? How could I possibly—

But just when it seemed sure they and I were all going to be caught in a sorcerous war, Myrddin turned sharply aside. With a final, furious cry of "Your treason shall not be allowed!" he vanished into the night.

Owain sank to one knee, panting. "My lord!" I cried in panic, and rushed to his side.

"He is so . . . incredibly strong . . ." he gasped, struggling back to his feet. "All the while we argued, he . . . was trying and trying . . . to overcome my will. And I . . . wasn't sure I could . . . hold him off." Owain brushed back his graying hair with a not-quite steady hand. "He is also so damnably *stubborn!* And damnably unpredictable, too."

"Can't you be rid of him?"

Owain raised an incredulous eyebrow. "How? No, Pedr *bach,* we'll just have to make do with our perilous ally— and pray he doesn't confuse things too badly!"

"You—you saw something in the scrying bowl," I began hesitantly, "something that alarmed you."

"Surprised me, rather. Don't worry about it, child. You know how difficult it is to accurately sense the future. I must have read the images wrongly, is all."

But later that night, I was awakened from uneasy slumber by the sense of magic being worked: my lord Owain testing the future again and yet again.

Just at the edge of our Cymreig lands lies the town the English call Shrewsbury, and it was there that the mingled forces of Northumberland, Worcester, March, and my lord Owain's fierce and independent folk were to do battle with that of King Henry Bolingbroke.

Or so it would have happened, had treachery and ancient wizardry not played a major part.

The treachery? Northumberland, at the last moment,

turned and fled, taking most of his warriors with him, pleading sudden illness as his excuse. Odd. He was no young man, true, but he'd been in amazingly fine health till that moment. With him gone, his son, Hotspur, was left in charge of their sadly depleted forces. Hotspur, who tried his best to make up in courage what he lacked in subtlety.

The wizardry? That, of course, was Myrddin's doing. Just as my lord Owain had told me could be done, the inhuman force of Myrddin's Power tore storm from the clear sky, forming an impassible obstacle of rain and wind and lightning till it was plain my lord Owain and his men had no chance of reaching Shrewsbury in time to close in battle with the English at all.

Without warning, Myrddin stood beside us, seen by none but my lord Owain and me. "I warned you no treason would be allowed," he snapped.

To my surprise, my lord seemed strangely distracted. Instead of retorting in anger, he murmured only a vague, "I know. I foresaw your storm when I glimpsed the future. Like it or not," Owain added with a sharp glance at Myrddin, "I have accepted this is as things must be."

Myrddin's fierce green gaze narrowed warily. "What might that mean?"

"Have you looked at the English prince? Truly looked at him with magic's aid? Seen who and what he may become—and what, in turn, he may bring about? No? A shame, Myrddin. I did, and found it very interesting indeed." A shudder shook my lord's tall form, but all he added was a brusque, "I think we both have an interest in seeing how the battle goes."

Of course they did. Between them they conjured an image in a clear pool that was twice as large and sharp as any I'd seen. Och, and that was a terrible, long, fiercely fought struggle! I had seen men die before this, youngster though I was, but never in such terrible numbers. The English warriors came on and on, and I fought back a whimper of sheer horror. How could the rebels' sadly shrunken ranks possibly hold out?

They could not, not without Northumberland, not without my own lord's forces. Sick at heart, I longed to turn away, but Prince Hal caught and held my attention. Fascinated despite my despair, I saw the young prince fight

with a wit and courage far beyond his youth, saw foe after foe fall to him. Somewhere in his entourage, I realized
only now, the king his father was safely hidden, but it
hardly seemed worth noting—

For now Prince Hal and his once-tutor, once-friend Hotspur had, by chance or mischance, come face to face, this
time as enemies. The young prince, plainly shaken, hesitated
almost too long, but Hotspur never even paused. Prince Hal
must fight if he was to live.

And fight he did, like some fiery young god of war.
"His fate has come upon him," my lord Owain murmured, and did not mean the prince.

So Hotspur fell. Prince Hal stood over his lifeless body,
eyes wild with shock and grief, in that moment open and
defenseless with despair.

And in that moment, an arrow whirred straight for his
head. I heard Myrddin and Owain both draw in their
breath in a sharp hiss, Myrddin with savage joy.

But in that instant, magic blazed about my lord Owain.
Eyes wild with Power, he cried out a fierce Word, pointed
imperiously—

And the arrow swerved ever so slightly in its flight. It
should have slain. Instead, it merely raked the young
prince's cheek. He cried out in startled pain, hand going
to the gash, but he was alive.

"Why?" With Myrddin's roar of disbelieving rage, the
image flickered out of being. "He is the English king's
own heir! Traitor, traitor, why did you save him?"

"Enough." Owain's voice sounded infinitely weary.
"Myrddin, *enough*. I saved his life because he shall save
us."

"What?"

"Och, stop roaring, man." My lord Owain sank to a
rock, staring at the furious wizard with a hint of resigned,
bitter amusement on his face. "I told you, look at the
young prince. Study him, Myrddin, see his future."

His very lack of fear, I think, moved the wizard more
than any angry self-defense. Without a word, Myrddin
worked his own scrying spell. And as he studied the
swirling images, my lord Owain moved to his side.

"Do you see?" Owain murmured. "He lives to rule,
lives to conquer France, lives to take a French princess
for his wife."

"And dies of sickness not long after, leaving an English fool as heir!"

"But the French princess turned English widow lives to take a second mate. One of our own. And from that union ..." Owain straightened with a weary sigh. Catching sight of me watching him nervously, he reached out a hand to ruffle my hair. "From that union," he said to me, "comes new hope. Och, don't give me that fearful look, Pedr *bach!* I'm not surrendering our cause. I will, indeed, do my best to keep this our land free and independent. But ... do you see what will come of that union of France and Cymru, Myrddin?"

"Yes." For the first time since I'd seen him, the half-human wizard sounded shaken.

I couldn't stand it. "What?" I cried. "Who?"

Owain chuckled. "Why, a part-Cymreig, part-English ruler, Pedr *bach,* Henry by name, just like that fiery young Hal I let live, who will at last bring what we cannot to both lands: peace. So, Myrddin, am I a traitor now?"

"No," the wizard admitted, his eyes thoughtful. "You are a worthy prince, indeed. In the years to come," Myrddin added softly, "you may be in need of a friend, a refuge. Call on me then, Owain Glyn Dwr. The Faerie Realms have need of such as you."

Owain bowed gravely. Myrddin equally gravely returned the courtesy, then walked sideways into the air and was gone.

Little remains to be told. All the land knows how Owain ruled Cymru for nigh on ten years, surviving the tragic deaths of all his kin, continuing to harry the increasingly sickly English king and outwitting all who came against him.

But it could not last. Treacherous Northumberland died shortly after the disastrous Battle of Shrewsbury, and without other allies, Owain, as he had warned Myrddin, could not hold out against all of England. He had not been young when the struggle started; rebellion is a young man's game.

And so, at the end, when all seemed lost, Owain Glyn Dwr simply ... disappeared. Some thought him dead, others that he'd fled to France or Scotland.

I alone knew the truth. And some day, my dreams tell me, I, too, shall flee this increasingly magickless world and join him and Myrddin in that most magical of Realms.

And there I shall tell my lord Owain what he has won: hope for his land, a hope for a free and happy Cymru.

It is a hope that can never die.

QUEEN LYR

Mark Kreighbaum

Although Mark Kreighbaum is primarily known for his poetry and short stories, he is currently collaborating on a novel. Here he transfers the story of Lear to a strikingly alien context.

I. The Spiral Begins: Storm

Strange and terrible winds shook Queen Lyr's orb web. She released vast strands of liquid silk from the spigots of her spinnerets, sifting them between her claws until they found purchase in the ebon cliffs and hardened there. These hasty filaments kept her anchored and alive, but they were not enough to save the old queen's home. The storm ripped her web apart. She watched in sorrow as years of careful weaving drifted away into the gray air as gossamer.

The thousands of white hairs on her four sets of legs shivered as echoes of the storm eddied through the black canyons surrounding her on all sides. The storm whispered to her, and she knew it for a child of Chaos, her old enemy.

In her youth, Chaos had often murmured its Name to her, knowing that if she surrendered to the seduction of its voice she would be utterly consumed. But Chaos had forgotten its own Name, and she had believed that it had also forgotten its hate.

She spoke to the winged mite that rode her carapace like a drop of blood on a glacier.

"Tell me what you see, my Sight. Whence comes this storm?"

The symbiont used its wings for balance against the faint gusts of disorder still breathing around them as it hovered beside its mistress. Lyr was comforted by the buzz of its wings.

"Madness." The mite's voice quavered. Like its mistress, the Sight was old and weary and such delvings into the Great Web of Time weakened it terribly. "Madness."

"What is its source, my love?" asked Lyr gently.

"I see the army of Rygn gathered before a cathedral, a bright See of spun filament, on one side of the First Thread that girdles the world like a ring of silk with filaments sunk down to the core of Time.

"Upon the other side, Gnryl's host camps within a strange woven Maze. And between them, the First Thread lies torn and bleeding, unbinding Chaos. It is hence that the gales rise."

"War, then?" asked Lyr. She had feared this truth, prayed that the destructive winds had another source.

"Not yet, but soon. O Queen, be glad that you cannot see the rape of the First Thread. Your sons' armies tear at a thing they do not begin to comprehend and cannot glimpse except as a source for weapons. If only they could see the First as a Sight does, instead of just cliffs of shining silk whose threads give power."

Finally, Lyr asked her Sight the question closest to the ache of her heart.

"And what of my faithless third son, Sight? He, who refused even to spin me a dream future? He, who I loved best, yet who betrayed me with silence? I would have given him the Name of the First Thread itself, if only he had kept faith with me."

"Faithless Crdyl, the dreamer who would spin you no dream." Her Sight's voice was filled with a sarcasm that Queen Lyr did not understand. "I do not see him move through Time, O Queen, but then, my eyes are weak. I am old."

"You have been true, my Sight," said the queen. "Always."

"Yet I do not tell you what I cannot see. Am I faithless?"

"Never," said Lyr, dismayed.

"You are swift to denial, Queen Lyr. In one so old, 't were better to take more deliberate care in matters of faith."

"Beware, little one, I am not so old that I have forgotten the taste of a Sight."

"True Sight tastes bitter, I am told."

"Silence!" the Queen shouted. For a moment, her will stilled all the tremblings around them, and she heard an echo of her youth, when she had dared spin strands into the First Thread itself and incurred the eternal wrath of Chaos. Then the fog of fear blew away, and she knew her course with certainty. "I will go to my sons," she said finally. The thought of traveling across a world turned fragile and strange by the enmity of her children made her weary and afraid. But the alternative was unthinkable. "They must listen."

Her Sight remained silent.

II. A Bridge Thread: Two Travelers

The aged spinner leaped from thread to thread down woven roads, running before the storm, driven by guilt.

Each day's journey left her weaker and more infirm. A crimson snowflake flew beside her, whispering encouragement, repeating ancient jests and singing old songs.

Where once vast farms of silk had prismed the sun's light into an ocean of rainbows, chasms yawned. At the torn edges of these holes into space, they gazed down into roiling darkness from which the voice of Chaos murmured.

They skirted the remnants of towering web cities filled now with vermin and eaters of dead flesh.

All along the empty roads, the companions saw the husks of the old and the weak, left to die alone and unmourned. Lyr tried at first to shroud the dead children, but there were too many and her stores of silk too small.

Each night, Lyr's Sight described the further weakening of the First Thread, as swelling armies clawed strands of power from it, unmindful of the damage to Time, the comfort to Chaos. Thousands of generations of careful weaving were ripped away in hours.

Once, they came upon a web city that had suffered cyclones from the storm and been transformed into an echo of Chaos. The colorful strands of their many kinds of web squirmed in and out of fractured time. Lyr and her Sight listened helplessly to the doomed inhabitants wail as they died by infinite, eternal degrees.

And always, always, they ran before the storm, a terrible spinner whose claws tore at whatever peace and silence it could find, delighting in the bloody threads Lyr's sons gave it to weave.

Together, they saw a world spinning a web of war out of threads torn from its own flesh.

III. Crossing the Hub: See

Finally, the two travelers arrived at the place where Queen Lyr once ruled the world before abdicating to her two sons.

Rygn had razed the Queen's old keep and replaced it with a new See. Lyr blinked her many eyes against the blinding light. It gave her strength, even as it forced her to seek out shadows. She sensed that the See was more than a mortal artifact. She asked her Sight to describe the See to her with its mind's vision.

"There are windows larger than cities from which burn many kinds and colors of light. The hues mingle in the air like ballooning threads . . . it is as if Rygn has made the Web of Time itself visible as joy." Her Sight's voice was full of wonder. "It is truly a See to make even the eyes of God weep."

Surely a king who could conceive of such a vision must be wise, thought Queen Lyr. Her age had sunk deep into her during the journey. The old spinner's carapace, once a blameless white, was now mottled with splotches of gray and green, and the silk she spun shivered in the air. "Let us go to my eldest son, good Sight. Let the sacrifice of my last years be a worthy one."

Lyr crawled into the camp of her eldest son's army. She was brought before a general who ordered her bound and conveyed to Rygn in a cage. She was too weak even to struggle against this humiliation.

She listened with impotent fury to the jeers and curses of soldiers who had been loyal farmers once. Her Sight hid deep inside her ear where the tremble of its wings sounded to Lyr like thunder.

She was carried like garbage in the bare cage up a winding helix funnel web that vibrated with the vitality of an army measured in millions. By the time her cage was placed before Rygn, she felt dazzled and beaten by the fierce harmonies resonating within the See.

"So, Mother," said Rygn. "Why have you come to trouble me?"

Lyr felt the confident power of her son echoed in every shimmering strand of the web he had woven for a throne. Her own weakness seemed even greater and contemptible.

"My son," she whispered. He sounded so strong and sure. Had she been wrong to come here? "I have felt the touch of strange storms and heard the cries of my people. I have seen a world torn by Chaos. I have come to warn you against war and to remind you of the dream world you once wove for me, the gentle land you promised."

Rygn laughed. Lyr had always loved her eldest son's laughter, so full of joy and confidence. His Sight chittered in counterpoint beside him.

"You were always weak and timid, poor fool. I knew you would never begin to comprehend the majesty of my dream. I wove you the shadow of a shadow and you thought you saw true spirals."

"But the First Thread is weakened; Chaos laughs; my people suffer—"

" 'Your people?' " Rygn bellowed out in such a fury that Lyr cowered in a corner of the cage. "You are nothing. Less than nothing. I am the master of this Side of the First Thread. And, once I have humbled that traitorous demon Gnryl, I will be lord of all."

"What will you do then?"

"I will unbind the First Thread and make a new beginning, a Great Web of Color."

"Unbind the First Thread?" Lyr forgot her fear. "Rygn, my son, without the First, you will be lord of nothing but Chaos. Have you forgotten the purpose of the First Thread?"

"I have forgotten nothing, Mother," said Rygn, voice gone mild and cold. "I remember that you know the Name of the First Thread. Tell it to me."

"No," said Lyr, ashamed of the quaver in her voice. "You must not harm the First. All the Great Web of Time will ravel. Chaos will destroy us all."

"I do not need the Name, Mother, but consider the

lives that will be spared if I win this war swiftly with the weapons I can make if I am Master of the First."

"We are mere moments of God's Eternity, threads of the Great Web of Life," said Lyr's Sight. The humble mite spoke with a strength that Lyr had not heard from it in many years. Pride and love glowed in her abdomen. "A king's vision is no better than the least of Sights, and your Sight is a fool if it has not warned you of the horror and blasphemy you commit."

The king's Sight cursed, but Lyr saw it fly behind its master, as if afraid of the old mite's words.

"Give me the Name, or I will destroy you," said Rygn.

Lyr thought of all the suffering she had seen during the journey here, and how much greater it would become once her sons' armies finally clashed. But the destruction of the First Thread would mean the end of everything. She remembered Rygn telling her of a paradise. She would have wept had she any tears left. Could she show less courage than her Sight?

"I will not."

The king's Sight whispered to him for a moment, then Rygn laughed.

"You are blind, old fool," said Rygn. "And I will teach you to understand that."

He ordered the Queen's old Sight torn apart before her, and the scraps eaten. Lyr watched her beloved Sight's destruction helplessly. She tore at the bars of her cage until the white hairs on her legs were speckled with blood.

Rygn sent the grief-stricken spinner down to the black prisons under his bright See to reconsider his demand.

His laughter, that she had loved so, followed her into the darkness.

IV. Many Radii: Two Travelers

There were many others down in the dark with her, many spinners who had earned the king's wrath. Lyr was beaten and thrown among them into utter blackness.

When they learned who she was, many of her fellow prisoners wanted to kill her, but one of the prisoners spoke for her in a voice as familiar to her as her poor dead Sight's.

"Shall we unbind our hearts, as the King unmakes the world?" asked Crdyl.

He argued thus for some time, always answering rage with soft questions. Lyr listened as the anguished prisoners told of the destruction of their lives for disobeying the king's command to desecrate the First Thread.

"Forgive me," she whispered, broken and ashamed. "Please, my children, please forgive."

Silence followed her words. The other prisoners moved away from their old queen, shunning her. Except for Crdyl, who remained at her side, spinning filaments to bind her wounds. He was strangely clumsy in sorting the silk, where she remembered him being most deft of her children.

"Crdyl, my love, you're alive," said Lyr. Just then, she would have traded the name of the First Thread to be able to see her son. She reached out one of her feet to her son, and discovered that he had lost all his legs. He had manipulated the silk with his mandibles only.

"Gnryl devoured my Sight. For my own good, he said." Crdyl spoke in the same soft voice he had used to defend her from the other prisoners. "I escaped to my other brother and Rygn tore my feet from me, laughing the while."

Before Lyr could speak, the world exploded with the howl of eerie winds. Chaos, carried on a hurricane, ripped through the See of King Rygn.

The dungeons shattered in the wake of the storm. The prisoners lost no time in pouring out the gap to freedom. All too many of them were caught and torn apart by the razor winds.

Lyr carried Crdyl on her back out of the devastated See. While Rygn and his army used their stores of silk to shield the structure from further damage, they escaped. If they could reach the First, Lyr thought, she could speak its Name and hold power enough to still the storm. They would be safe.

But without a Sight, and burdened by the weight of her maimed son, Lyr was soon lost, wandering through web ash, blinded by a blizzard of silk from the damaged See.

V. Retracing the Path: A Sight

Lost, they wandered. Here in the heart of the storm, the structure of reality was obliterated. The old queen no longer knew in what direction she moved, nor place, nor

season. At times, she forgot the meaning of movement itself and stood motionless until urged forward by her son.
Without Crdyl, Lyr would have surrendered to the darkness many times. Even so, despair grew in her heart.

The storm changed as they moved deeper into it. The
disguise of wind fell away. Lyr and Crdyl moved through
pure madness, causeless darkness. Shorn of wind and ash
and silk, the storm became a pure force battering at the
minds of the two spinners. Chaos spoke all around them,
telling a billion tales, a trillion lies.

In desperation, she spoke the name of the First Thread.
The storm retreated, like a beast from fire. Lyr again felt
the world beneath her feet, saw stars in the sky. But all
else was blackness.

The storm was not beaten, but merely wary, for Lyr
was old and far from the power of the First Thread. She
could sense the strange life of the thing named Chaos that
was pleased to speak in the voice of storms, crouched in
the darkness all around them. Again, it whispered to her,
offering her eternity if she would only speak its forgotten
Name.

Lyr remembered the first time it had made such an offer.

She had been young and strong, the hairs on her legs
black as the space between stars. A new queen, bold and
wild, she traveled alone to the First Thread, where none
before had dared to go. There, she wove her own threads
into the eternal Web of Time.

Chaos, too, had been younger and dared her to speak
its name, there on the First Thread. Chaos had often whispered its name to her as a child until she knew it as well
as her own. And so she would have spoken it, there at the
peak of her power, but for the speck of crimson that flew
to her just then.

"Tell me, O Queen, the Rule of Names," said this
young mite, this impertinent Sight.

Queen Lyr had considered killing and devouring the
audacious thing, but she was intrigued and, truth to tell,
admired its courage. Her father's old Sight had been
timid and foolish. She had eaten it mere days after the
King's death.

"Who are you?"

"No more than a Sight, O Queen. And no less. The Rule of Names?"

" 'A Name is a Door,' " said Lyr, quoting her father's old Sight.

"Do you know what it means?"

Lyr was proud but also honest. She had never lied. Not even to a Sight. "No," she admitted, though it galled her.

"A name reveals the nature of a thing, but an open door is a mutual revelation." The mite flew to the queen. Lyr remembered how its delicate wings had sounded like a silken thunder. "Speak the Name of Chaos, and you will become one with it. But such a suicide is no great matter. Do you have the courage to reveal yourself to the First Thread instead, and be revealed in turn?"

The Sight told her the Name of the First Thread then, and Lyr, young and brave, had spoken it. She had never forgotten the precious marvel revealed to her then. Nor the courage of a Sight who had never failed its sometimes foolish queen.

Lyr opened her eyes. The storm still raged around them, and Lyr was still greatly afraid. But, for the sake of a brave Sight who had taught her the miracle of the First Thread, she dared not fail.

She struggled onward, burdened by a weight far greater than her son. Yet, a heaviness on her heart had lifted.

VI. The Spiral Complete: Maze

They came out of the storm into a bewildering array of oddly angled paths. No straight ways existed here. Lyr remembered her Sight speaking of Gnryl and his Maze.

"Do you feel the magic of this place, Crdyl? Oh, if only my Sight were with us."

"When last I was here, Gnryl set trackers to hunt me for sport, so I had little time to appreciate its wonder."

"Will you refuse to forgive Gnryl, my son? After you spoke so well for my foolish soul?"

Crdyl said nothing.

Her youngest son led them now, teaching her the way through the Maze that he had learned while eluding Gnryl's trackers.

They paused for rest at a juncture of curved walls that reached to the sky like deformed claws made of silk. At last, Lyr broached the rift that lay between them.

"Why did you refuse to spin me a dream, as your brothers did?" asked Lyr.

Her youngest son was silent for a long time. When he spoke, she heard his pain.

"I thought that the invisible web of my love would be enough," he said. Before Lyr could answer this with her shame, he continued. "I was wrong and arrogant. It was my duty to show my queen my dream."

"No, Crdyl," Lyr protested. "I should have believed in your love." She stroked the stumps of his legs and thought of the delightfully delicate webs Crdyl had spun for her.

"Is it too late for me to answer my queen's request?" Crdyl asked shyly.

Lyr closed her eyes and shook her head, unable to speak.

Her son described a world where all spinners wove together. He told his dream of a time when everyone, not only those of royal blood, would have the companionship of Sights. And he spoke also for the Sights, for their freedom and dignity.

It was a strange dream, and Lyr did not altogether understand it. But it held a different and subtler beauty than the grand visions Rygn and Gnryl had blinded her with.

"You will have your chance to weave it," she said.

They continued through the Maze, seeking a way out to the First Thread.

Not long after, though, they were captured by scouts for her younger son's army. This time, however, Lyr was not bound or caged. The soldiers treated her with respect and spoke politely to Crdyl.

Lyr didn't understand. Had Crdyl lied? Or, had Gnryl learned wisdom in the fearful tempest that he and his brother had brought into being?

As they moved through the Maze, Lyr sensed shifts in time and space woven into the strands around them. Crdyl explained that Gnryl had learned a way to warp the Great Web of Time by shaping the strands he ripped from the First into undreamt of patterns. She was awed by his achievement.

Gnryl met them in an open place of the Maze, where time itself seemed to swirl around them like winds. The king welcomed them and bade them eat their fill and rest on soft woven carpets of colorful silk.

"I am relieved that you have come, Mother. And you, my poor little brother. Can you both forgive me for my arrogance and cruelty?"

"Of course, my son," said Lyr. Crdyl casually brushed one of his mother's feet with his mouthpart. A reminder of what Gnryl had done. The old queen hardened her voice. "But you must turn away from this war, Gnryl. You must cease harming the First Thread."

"I hear the wisdom of that," Gnryl spoke in a grave voice of dignity. Lyr had always loved that voice, the solemn tones befitting a king. How she wished her Sight were still alive to come to this safety. "However, it was necessary to ravel some of the First to make my Maze, to defend your good people from the evil Rygn. He has unleashed Chaos. His monumental foolishness has already decimated his See and torn apart much of my own beautiful Maze. If only I had known his insanity sooner, had the courage to fight him before he harmed my poor brother. He forced me to hurt beloved Crdyl, and for that I can never forgive him. He must be stopped."

"How would you do this deed, Gnryl?" murmured Crdyl.

"There is only one way." Lyr, whose great weariness had left her in a soft doze, came alert. "We must use the holy power of the First Thread to overwhelm his forces and destroy him."

"Is there no other way?" asked Lyr.

"No, Mother." Gnryl spoke with implacable kindness. "Only the Name of the First Thread is enough to end the nightmare Rygn has set loose upon the world."

"This Maze . . ." said Crdyl. "What is its purpose? Time seems so strange here. This is no home for spinners."

"For now, it is a defense against the aggression of Rygn," replied Gnryl, but Lyr heard a hint of annoyance in her son's voice. "One day, though, it will be the gateway to other worlds, and other times."

"I passed a city on the way to Rygn's See that was trapped in a timestorm much like this," said Lyr.

"I know," said Gnryl in that stately tone. "It is regrettable. But the world as it is no longer serves our people.

With the Maze, we will have portals through all of time and space. We will be able to travel to other worlds and times. It will be an Age of Discovery the like of which no spinner has ever dreamed."

"You won't harm the First?"

"Of course not! Oh, perhaps we will be forced to unbind a portion of it, to remake the parts of the world ruined by the evil of my older brother. And we will need to improve my Maze."

"Ah. You will maim the First for its own good, then? And what of Chaos, my brother?" asked Crdyl. "How will the Maze defend us against that?"

"You do not yet understand. We have no need of protection from the storm. You do not comprehend the beauty of time shattered and glittering. We will all live forever and travel to places unimaginable."

"What of those lost to the winds of change that you have set loose?" asked Crdyl. "You have killed thousands, and thousands more will die because no one can predict the path of storms created by such a Maze."

"Of course," replied Gnryl. "But their deaths serve the greater cause. They die for a glory beyond imagining."

At last, Lyr saw the madness in Gnryl that her Sight had warned her of in the beginning.

"No, my son. It cannot be. I will not give you the Name of the First for this purpose. We must find another way to defeat Rygn."

"With or without the Name of the First, I will achieve my purpose. Unwittingly, Chaos is my ally. Rygn is doomed."

"With such an ally, we are all doomed," said Crdyl.

"I do not need you."

With a calm word, the king ordered Crdyl killed. Without legs, he was helpless. Lyr was restrained from defending her son as spinners swarmed her youngest son and tore him apart. She heard his dying agony go on for a very long time. At last, Gnryl spoke to his mother. As always, his voice was reason itself. "I regret what I must do, Mother. If only you could understand the beauty of unshackled Time. You must tell me the Name of the First."

Lyr shook free of her captors and went to the corpse of

her youngest son. She cradled a part of his carapace. In a lifeless voice, she told Gnryl a Name.

The king left his mother alone with her dead son.

Soon, Gnryl would stand upon the First and speak the terrible Name of Chaos, calling down its unquenchable hunger. Lyr would find her way somehow from this evil Maze and return to the See to offer her other son the same Name.

Chaos would feed well this day.

Then, later, perhaps she would try to weave the dream Crdyl had told her.

But for now, with trembling claws, Queen Lyr gathered the remains of her child and spun him a shroud of silk.

IT COMES FROM NOTHING

Barry Malzberg

Barry Malzberg has collaborated with Kathe Koja on many short stories and a novel, several of which will be published in 1993 and 1994. He brings his trademark irony to this look at the downfall of an ancient king.

"I warned him," Cordelia said. "I told him that nothing would come of this. Nothing comes from nothing, isn't this what *he* said? First Regan. Then Goneril. The horses, the property, the estate. The castle itself. I begged him," Cordelia said. "I told him, no good can come of this, they are not to be trusted. I refused my own estate, hoping to bring him to his senses. What a vain old man he is! And now look at the condition to which he has reduced us. What are we going to do now? Fool, we cannot abide this; we cannot permit it."

"Of course we can," the Fool said. "I have a tiny, tiny wit, but it is enough to see that we are here in the wind and rain, likewise that lumpish fellow over there," he said, pointing to the comatose and probably feverish old King lying in a sack on the far side of the fire. "We will bear it as long as we can and then no more. Oh, by the way," the Fool said, adjusting his pointed hat more neatly on his crown and shaking the tiny bells on his left foot, "I am going to bed at noon. I thought you should know

that. Ah, you are a fine looking girl. If it were not for my
own low office, I would desire thee myself. Of course, I
have a wit too tiny to place that substance of joy, if you
can understand."

Cordelia shuddered, hearing the wind from the heath
come battering at the mouth of the cave. This had been a
terrible idea. She should have known that it would not be
satisfactory. "Come to nothing, nothing comes to nothing," she murmured. Somehow she had felt that the
Fool—her father's only faithful companion now with this
latest disaster and with the sons-in-law having sent out
servants from the castle to drive Lear farther from the
fire—might have some advice, would be able to lend
counsel to this dreadful situation, but he was a fellow
even more ordinary and stupid than she had thought before this conference. A tiny wit, indeed. Shrunken, his
face creased into the gloom-ridden shadows of the very
old, his lips filled with foul sayings and hopeless little ornaments of speech. "Oh, I should have known," she said,
"I should have known that you would have nothing to
say." She arose from her crouch, scrambled the length of
the cave, and adjusted the cloak more tightly around her
father's shoulders. The King snorted, mumbled something, flailed with his left hand, then seemed to collapse
upon himself. "We have to get him some help," she said.
"Maybe Gloucester—"

"Forget Gloucester, my lady," the Fool said. "He has
been blinded by those riches." The Fool giggled shrilly,
making a beckoning motion. "You are a faithful daughter," he said. "You have the bosom of the king grasped by
your own heart, but there is really nothing that can be
done. We could start a fire. We could squat by the fire as
the ashes came down and gaze toward the light until the
end of storm and the morning. Or we could disdain fire
and sit upon the ground, telling sad stories of this fine old
King. We can do this and that, but I am afraid that your
father's case is most hopeless and the sooner that we accept this, the quicker the noon will come." The Fool patted the ground beside him. "Come," he said, "come and
sit beside me. Lean your shoulder against mine. Dreaming, we will think of those sons-in-law and of daughters
gone astray."

Cordelia stared at him numbly, feeling the storm in her

veins, the darkness of this cave swaddling, yet leaping like flame at the prison she had made of herself. She did not know why she had done this. Hearing of the terrible acts of Regan and Goneril, learning of the malice and torment inflicted by her sisters, Cordelia had come away from the boat that would have taken her from this rude land, had returned to the castle out of a sense of dread obligation. Then, learning from the faithful but helpless Kent what had happened, she had gone out into the fields and meadows until at last she had found her father in trammeled and delirious condition, stumbling through weather with the Fool by his side, mumbling of the ingratitude of nations and the faithlessness of daughters, so demented that he had called Cordelia Regan and had raged at her, so weak and tortured that he had then called her Goneril and cursed the spent desire which had created her and had then fallen insensible at her feet. The fool and Cordelia had dragged the King to this tenuous shelter, and in the dank enclosure of the cave she had thought that she could somehow obtain counsel from the Fool, find some advice which would enable her to deal with this dreadful and unforeseen situation, but she should have known. She should have known that the Fool of the tiny wit had nothing to say, had performed for her father for all these years because no Fool could withstand the wind and the rain and was by his side now only because Regan and Goneril had mistreated her father's property as well.

Looking upon him, thus, Cordelia could feel the entire sense of her life breaking over her like undulant waves, the indulgence and containment which had led her to this hapless circumstance. Someone had always taken care of her; she was the youngest. Only at that moment of the King's divestiture, when he had made that terrible pledge to the daughters, had Cordelia come to understand what abandonment might be; what the shapes of neglect and partition could cast in the shadows of her life. "I want nothing," she had said, when the King had turned to her, "nothing at all."

He had said, "Nothing? But nothing will come of nothing," his eyes winking and glazing in the reflections of Edmund's light.

Only then had Cordelia come to understand that he was mad, that her father had been that way possibly all of her

life and now there was nothing she could do. "Oh, no, no,
you must not do this," she had wanted to shout to him,
but there had been the glare of her sisters' faces and then
the sudden, hot movement within the halls and she had
found herself being ejected from those spaces, the sound
of their laughter or perhaps it was the Fool's, perhaps it
was her own, echoing behind. And then the frantic carriage ride away with the servants deemed to carry her to
the provinces and then nothing, nothing at all until word
of the banishment and her frantic return. She had had to
help the King; it was this necessity which had driven her
back to the castle and then out into the storm and now to
the cave where, plunged against the Fool, she found herself suddenly grappling within his embrace, the feel of
him taut against her robes, the smell of him suddenly gi-
gantic in the close and dreaming night.

"Come," the Fool said, "come hold me, daughter. You
have come for a bit of comfort, no? and mine is the comfort to shake your little world." He felt huge upon her and
his grasp, that of a many-limbed insect was enormous
upon her as he drew her in. The King snorted and rumbled in his comatose state, then seemed to roll farther
from them, huddled against the stone. "Oh, yes," the Fool
said, "oh, yes," and then she felt him drawing her intensely against him.

"No," she said in a whisper. It seemed important not to
shout, not to make a spectacle of herself even here, not to
awaken her father or bring embarrassment upon his fallen
state or her own disastrous proxy. The Fool's breath was
frantic against her neck now, little uneven gulps of air
driving him into the beginning of what she thought of as
his frenzy and it was at this time that the full gravity of
Cordelia's situation broke at last upon her. Just as in the
castle she had finally and convulsively deemed her father
mad, always mad, now she knew that the Fool was determined to have his frantic way with her, regardless of her
shocked and virgin state, regardless of the heavy and
dying King, his Master, who lay so near him. Perhaps it
was the presence of the King, in fact, which so inflamed
him. "Oh, no," Cordelia said, her voice still a whisper, its
rasp stunning her with the sound of a person she had
never heard. "Oh, no, you cannot do this. You are my father's Fool, I came to you for *help*—"

The Fool giggled. His fingers were wide and deep upon her now, making horrid circles and then a sly, secret knowledge seemed to guide those fingers to yet another part of her. "I go to bed at noon," the Fool said. "Didn't I tell you that? Didn't I tell all of them this? I disappear, I go away, I vanish from the tragedy; will none of them understand why this must be done?" And then he hurled himself atop her and Cordelia felt herself falling, diving for a fall, settling toward a sudden and absolute descent as the Fool's breath and the cloak of her own knowledge came over her. She heard the sounds of the heath. She listened to the stunned and sickening mumble of her father's breath. She scrappled against the pressure, trying to evoke the kindly and foolish features of Kent, but they would not arise.

And it was so, in this way, that toward the dawn the riders came to find her strewn like a smashed toy against the side of the cave, the wretched old King arisen from his sickness, weeping over her in the contained darkness. "Ah, my little bird," the old King cried. "Ah, we shall go away and live and dwell in the sun." The old King, to the gaze of the riders, appeared to be trying to lift Cordelia, but he could not reach her. "Oh, break this heart," the King said. "Oh, the meanest creature has a life, and she does not. Oh, break, oh, break!" But Cordelia was already broken and the Fool gone on his more painful and equally treacherous journeys. The King battered his hands against the walls of the cave.

He is doing that, it is said, yet. We do not know. We have departed that lost kingdom. It is all rumor and secret, gossamer and dispersed in the fragmented and dying light of eternal Noon. The Fool a mystery, a song, a song to sing-o.

THE TRAGEDY OF GERTRUDE, QUEEN OF DENMARK

Kate Daniel

Kate Daniel is the author of a number of best-selling novels for young adults, including the recent Running Scared, *and of various fantasy and science fiction stories as well. Here is the story that started this entire anthology, a woman's reevaluation of a tale usually considered to center round a man.*

"Adieu, adieu ... remember me ..."

As the whisper faded, she sat up, brought to sudden wakefulness by the ghostly voice. The chamber was quiet, with no noise save the snores of her new husband, asleep with his mouth agape. It was a comforting sound. The rhythm of his breathing shifted as she lay back down and he rolled toward her, drawing her into his arms in sleep. Slowly his renewed snores stilled the pounding of her heart and the memory of a fading voice. A dream, it was naught but a dream.

Freya, goddess of hearth and marriage, knew what she had suffered. She had married as duty and her father commanded, married the prince who became King Hamlet. The Danes saw him as a great war leader, luck-gifted and fearless. For the sake of his battles, they had forgiven even the way he allowed the priests of the Christos to batten onto the court and country, wooing folk away from the old gods. Yet with each passing winter, a darkness that was more than lack of sun deepened in his soul, till she fled from him in terror through all the daylight ways of Elsinore. At night in the royal bedchamber, there had been no escape.

He was dead, now, dead and gone, and his brother held the throne of the Danes. Duty and the old ways had brought her to the new king's bed four days since, and for the first time Gertrude discovered pleasure in her duty. But each of those four nights had brought dreams that were haunted.

"Horatio! Be welcome to our court." Gertrude smiled at the young man who stood a step behind her son, but her thoughts were dark. Hamlet followed his father in all things; he was Christian and would have the court so. He did not need the encouragement of his Saxon friend nor did she welcome another pair of accusing eyes.

"He arrived but a day since, Mother, too late for his purpose, yet I hope he can remain with me a while. He came to see thy wedding. Or was it my father's funeral? I confess, I scarce can tell them apart."

"Would you shame me thus before this foreigner?" She spoke in an undertone, past her rigid smile.

"I? Not for my soul, Mother, but it was not I who shamed thee with an incestuous match." Prince Hamlet glanced at his friend, whose smile was also carved like a statue in a church. " 'Tis no new tiding, lady, he knows thy shame, as does the whole of Denmark and the world beyond."

"My marriage bed is no shame but duty plain to Denmark. Your father's death was a grief to all, yet do we serve him or his crown by looking ever to his grave?"

"Indeed, you do not look to it, nor have you since it was made, I think. Come, Horatio, I think I hear my uncle-father approaching, and I would sooner see the jakes or something equally fair. Madam, good day." He leaned forward and kissed her lightly on the cheek, then strode off. His friend stepped back a pace to let him pass, then bowed formally to the Queen. There was a cold gleam in his pale eyes.

"Majesty." Horatio turned and followed Prince Hamlet.

The King found her there. He took her hand and pressed it to his lips, in a kiss that was more than formal greeting.

"What troubles thee, my Queen?"

"My son."

"He grieves still for his father. In time, custom shall lend ease to him about our union, Gertrude."

"Not while his foreign priests do tell him it is damnéd lust and incest," she said bitterly.

"It is but two months since his noble father died . . ."

"Noble!" She spat the word from her mouth, as though tasting the bitter poison of it. "Was it nobility when he did curse us both for that which was a lie? Was there honor in the death he gave himself? Good my lord, King Hamlet was thy brother and I would not stir thy grief, yet never were two brothers less akin. I cannot mourn that he is dead. No more than I would mourn our solemn vows before the gods."

"I mourn the brother he once was." Again the King raised her hand to his lips. "Yet even in my mourning is there joy. For thy son, alas, sorrow compasses all things still. Two scant months since my brother's death, and but days since our joining. Be patient yet a while with him."

"I am his mother; how can I be aught else?" She raised her hand to caress the King's cheek. He captured it and dropped a kiss into the palm. Gertrude's breath caught. So, years before, had her son's father done.

They spoke no more. But the memory of her son's words lingered with the Queen into her dreams that night.

The old King walked no more in the Queen's dreams, but this brought her no peace. For years she had watched while the King her husband had slid into waking nightmares of madness. Now more and more Gertrude saw him gazing at her from his son's eyes. At first there were only rumors of talk without sense and wild laughter followed close by tears. Soon she saw the rumor's truth.

"Father-aunt, my mother-uncle desires thy presence without." Hamlet's smile was sweet and careless, like a child's.

"Father-aunt? Mother-uncle?" Gertrude felt her heart tighten. "What do these words mean, my son?"

"Why, a priest did tell Horatio that man and woman be one flesh in marriage." The smile grew more childlike. "Thus, thou wert my father's wife and therefore art my father. And of a surety, my uncle's wife must needs be my aunt. Likewise, mine uncle ..."

"Spare me, good Hamlet. I do grasp thy meaning, yet I think it will suffice if thou dost call me Mother and no more."

"No more? But thou art more, being aunt as well, and therefore—but thou hast said no more, and I am dumb. I shall be good, Mother. As good as the grave." He bowed grandly, then went off singing a catch about worms and the wormy dead.

The catch still echoing in her ears, Gertrude turned, to meet a glance as troubled as her heart. "Why, how now, Ophelia, what grieves thee, child?"

"My lady." The girl dropped a frightened curtsey. "The Lord Hamlet—did he speak aught of my father?"

"Nay, lass. He did but jest with me."

"Jesting? He hath oft done so, of late, but with a sting to his words like a bee 'neath the honey. And he doth vex me about my father till I know not how to answer."

The rose tinge on the lass' features spoke of more. Ophelia had a woman's form, but in years and thought she was yet a child, and Gertrude had been concerned for her of late.

"Thy father? Had he not other words for thee, that touch thee more closely?" The Queen searched the girl's face as she spoke. Ophelia's color deepened, but she shook her head.

"Majesty, he hath in the past made me tenders of affection, and doth still offer them, yet of late with such words, all wild and tumbling like acrobats in a play, that I scarce know what to think, still less to say. But he holds my father in much scorn, for having bowed to thy will and the King's."

This, at least, Gertrude understood. When the Christian priests had first been welcomed to the court, Ophelia had listened with an open heart. Indeed, such was her devotion that she could have made a nun. Her father was a different case. The man held no more substance than a hollow reed, yet he trimmed to a nicety, and had watched King Hamlet's dealings with the Church, now coming close, now standing apart, and always the advice tendered by Polonius matched the King's own thought. When Hamlet swore allegiance to the Christian god, Polonius made haste to follow, only to shed his new beliefs when a new king shared them not.

"Sweet child, I will not ask thee to change thy faith thus lightly, but it is meet the King's councilor share the King's gods. Yet speak more of my son. These tenders—of what sort were they, and dost thou hold him in thy heart?"

"Madam, I have been schooled by my father to my duty and thy son's station, and shall obey." The obedient words stung the Queen; the child's heart was given and would be broken in silence. Yet better this small hurt than a greater one.

That evening between the healths, Claudius asked her, "What ails thy son, lady? Late this day, I met him by the Christian graveyard, playing at funeral like a child would play at battle. When I asked what he did, he spoke not to me but to a raven that had landed near, saying his life was in the ground and he must needs haunt it."

"I know not." Gertrude's voice was troubled, but no more than her heart.

To the west, the sun dropped below the rim of the clouds as it set over a sullen sea. Fog hung over Elsinore, in ragged wisps of dirty gray like cold smoke. The very air felt heavy, and Gertrude shivered as she climbed to the battlements. At her heels, her lady-in-waiting grumbled at the foul weather, the hour, the damp chill, but she stopped short of calling the Queen's action mad. Lady Margarethe had served the Queen since the first royal marriage; she knew the true face of madness.

But this did not still her tongue. "An thou breaks thy head, Lady, it will be mine the King will seek in answer, thou knowst. The gods grant we come back down where we go up, still on our feet, since we shall have no more light than a fish hath feathers . . ."

"Hush, be still! I would not have him know we watch."

Gertrude could see little through the mist and fading light, but a glimpse of pale hair said her son stood upon the platform. Rumors of his constant attendance there had reached her, and now she watched her son as he watched she knew not what.

The light faded from the west and her cloak was soaked with mist while he stood there alone. Then her heart stilled in terror as another joined her son. At first it seemed a bit of fog, lit by the crescent moon. But when fog shrouded the moon again, the moon-white shape remained.

"Look you, Margarethe, where he goes." The words came from Gertrude's lips without breath to carry them since fear had robbed her of life's breath. "Do you not see him there, hounding my son to a madness like his own?"

"Madam? Dost thou mean the watchman?" Lady Margarethe's startled voice was loud.

"Dost see nothing?" The Queen's words came sharply, as a thicker drift of fog passed before the hidden moon, rendering the night more dark. Across the platform, the Prince hailed them, "Halt! In Jesu's name, who walks this night?"

"Who walks indeed," his mother whispered.

"Madam, I see naught, for that is all is there." The trouble in Margarethe's voice did little to soften it, and again the Prince called challenge.

"Go, withdraw, ere my son find us here." Gertrude did not speak again till they had regained her closet, with torches and a fire to keep the night at bay.

Then at last she asked, "Saw you nothing there above?"

"Majesty, what didst thou think for me to see?"

Gertrude had been yet upon the platform in her mind, but the pain in the old noblewoman's voice brought her thoughts back to the room. Gertrude knew she had seen the spirit of her husband Hamlet that had been. But she would not frighten her old friend thus.

"Nay, Margarethe, I thought there was a light. Belike it was the moon I saw, reflected on the tide."

"Aye, madam, the fog grew thin ere we departed." It was a lie, as both knew, but it sufficed. They spoke of other things, concerns which could stand the light, and Gertrude did not follow her son to the battlements again.

* * *

Margarethe did not speak of what had passed, but she watched the Queen now as the Queen watched her son. Other eyes followed the Queen. The Christian priests conferred often with the Prince and young Horatio, who lingered yet at court. The group would fall silent when she passed. Gertrude did not glance round to receive the glares of the priests. She knew well what poison they distilled for her son's ears, ever telling him her marriage was unnatural. Could the priests order the doings of the kingdom, they would have her put aside, and her marriage unmade, and her son placed on the throne over her. That their god could make a son despise his mother thusly sickened her with its impiety.

But it was not only the living who kept close watch over Gertrude. Always now she felt familiar eyes on her, eyes that had closed in death months before. At times she saw him, but she felt his presence even when she could not see his form. The specter even followed into the bedchamber at night, fouling the pleasure Gertrude had, for a short while, found there. When she drew back in horror from the ghost, her husband saw no more than had Margarethe. Hard words followed, and an end to delight. Still she said nothing to the King. She would not grieve his heart.

The long cool spring gave way to the brief warmth of summer, but to Gertrude, it seemed that winter deepened each day. The normal life of the court went on. Ambassadors came from foreign courts, and Denmark sent forth his own. The countryside round Elsinore bloomed as the peasants made haste to profit from the glorious weather that seemed a bitter mockery to the Queen. She paid less heed with each passing day to the doings of court and country, till she was called on to greet two young noblemen the King had summoned. After they welcomed the young lords, she turned for explanation from her husband. He took her hands in his.

"Gertrude, thinkst thou I have not seen thy grief with like grief of mine own? I know thy son's madness hath broke thy tender heart. Therefore did I send for these old friends of his, that haply they may discover the cause of this distemper."

" 'Tis the same sorrow now as of old, his father's death and that we two did wed." She looked aside, still loath to tell him of the presence that had haunted her son to distraction. "Yet I thank thee, love, taking thus a father's care for my son."

"Thy son, and therefore mine, madam." He raised her hand to his lips for a kiss. "And good Polonius hath asked leave to speak with us, saying he hath found out somewhat of import."

"Gladly will I listen then, my lord." She had little faith in the councilor, but she hoped the cause of her son's strange fits was something other than King Hamlet's vengeful shade.

And indeed, when the old fool had told his tale, she thought there might be more than folly to the words. Love had been famed from the days of legend for driving men to madness, and certainly for months the Prince had haunted Ophelia's path almost as his father's ghost haunted his mother. Perchance it was true, and Hamlet had fallen into this decline for want of the girl's love.

This new thought grew in Gertrude's mind. In truth, why would her late husband trouble his son thus? All his quarrel had been with her and the fancied betrayals he had taxed her with night by night. A ghost might wish to look upon his child and namesake, and do no harm thereby.

"Perchance 'twould do no harm," she mused aloud, drawing a glance from Margarethe.

"My lady?"

"Thy pardon, Margarethe. I did but think upon my son. Of late he hath been most attentive to Ophelia."

"True, but she avoids his steps and guards her virtue close. Methinks the child is love-sick for thy son, for she has grown pale, waning as the year doth wax."

"And therefore did I wonder if I had been unwise, counseling the maid to hold herself apart."

"My lady, she could never make a queen!"

"No, yet should he tumble her, what harm? She could yet go unto her Christian nunnery, and they would take her still."

And it might still the madness in her son's heart. The Queen took comfort from the thought, and where once she had shielded Ophelia from her son's attention, now she urged the girl into his path, hoping daily for a resolution, even news of a bastard child.

The false play took Gertrude unawares. Hamlet seemed blithe when he begged his mother and the King to see the traveling players, and they agreed happily. Indeed, Claudius thought it betokened a thawing of his opposition to their marriage. Instead, it was a trap, a most carefully crafted one.

"An they shalt play that play again, they shall play it to a headsman." Claudius paced back and forth in their bedchamber, carried by the tide of his wrath. "Do they think I am a dolt, a dotard, not to know what men would think? A king killed by a brother—lady, he is thy son, yet I will bear this from no man!"

"They did call it 'The Mousetrap.' " The memory was wormwood. "A trap, in sooth, for do we protest, he shall call us liars both. Yet do we not, we shall be called murderers."

"We have been too chary of my brother's memory. Thy son should have known ere now 'twas by his own royal hand the King his father's life was taken."

"Methinks was not his father's death but his mother's marriage did lead to this mousetrap. Think you of the player queen and how she did protest that once a widow, never would she be a wife."

"I care not if his priests do tell him that our marriage-bed be sin, I shall not be made mock. Gertrude, thou shalt tell thy son of how his father died, and he shall pray our pardon, or he will to England with the next turn of the tide. Madam, look you to it." The King strode from the room. It lacked but a fortnight till Midsummer, yet the night air chill seemed deep as winter.

Polonius came first to her closet. "I did tell him thou wast much displeased, your grace, and he answered with such wandering words as he hath used of late. Yet he did promise, 'midst his ravings, to come straightaway."

"I thank thee." Gertrude glanced around the chamber. She had sent Margarethe away, desiring to be private with her son, yet now she was uneasy. If he would accuse his uncle of murder before all the court, what folly might he not commit?

As though he read her thoughts, the old man moved toward the arras on the wall. "Madam, the King did ask me to remain, a hidden witness to this audience."

"Stay, then." He stepped behind the hanging.

The King had concealed the true nature of his brother's death, but that was ended now. It was a most evil omen, for a king to slay himself thus without reason, and the Christians would call it grievous sin. Had the fact been known, he would not have been laid in their hallowed ground beside the church or claimed any funeral rites. But Gertrude would see his corpse unearthed and left for carrion sooner than see the King named kin-slayer.

Her son came at last. "Now, Mother, I am here. What dost thou wish of me?"

"A tongue less forward and a heart more kind."

"Why, how now, Mother, what have I said that you have found too bold?"

"The tongues were those of players, yet the words were thine. You show but little respect for our crown."

"As little as thou didst show, lady, when thou didst betray my father's bed. The priests say we should in all things honor our fathers and mothers. They say naught of *uncles* and mothers." As he spoke, he drew closer, and Gertrude thought to call out for Lady Margarethe. But it was not the wild look in his eyes that drew a gasp from her, but the pale form that took shape behind him.

"Stand off! What would you here?" She arose from her seat and took a step back, but her son grasped her arm. The specter smiled and stretched a ghostly hand out to her. "Oh, sweet goddess, protect me!" She twisted free of the younger Hamlet's grip and tried to flee. Behind the arras, the old man cried for help.

"Aid to the Queen! Help, ho!"

"Ha! Mother, here's a rat!" Before the Queen could speak again, Hamlet's sword was out and through the hanging.

Gertrude choked back a cry and dropped to her knees. *So I die, by him that I gave life,* she thought, and waited for the stroke. It did not fall.

"Why, madam, was it not a rat? Could it have been the King?" The Prince's face was flushed with triumph as he pulled aside the arras. Freed from the heavy fabric, Polonius fell forward, blood pooling round him as he lay. "Thou!" Prince Hamlet knelt, heedless of the blood that stained his cloak as he turned the old man over on his back. Had he any thought of helping, it came too late; Polonius was dead.

"Thou hast slain him," Gertrude whispered.

"I did not mean it so."

Hamlet helped her to her feet, with absent courtesy. "I took him for his better, to his cost. Alas, poor fool. But madam, leave thy grief for this dead clay and list to a tale that should wring thy very heart." He guided her back to her seat as though they were in a public hall, and she wondered. Would he leave the poor old man lying there while he raved?

"In the name of thy own god, give me leave to call—"

"Anon, anon." He waved away her words and she shrank back. Behind him stood the form of his dead father. "Mother, how can you grieve thus for this knave when he who is your husband has murdered your true husband?"

"Murder! He did no—"

"Murder most foul and unnatural it was, to kill thus his own brother and take you to his bed." The twisted tale poured forth, an echo of his mad, ghostly father. At length he left, dragging Polonius' dead body after him while his father's shade stood by.

He was gone before the next night, sent to England by a wrathful King with his two friends, but Horatio remained at court. Elsinore buzzed with whispers. Polonius' death and Hamlet's words before he left had stilled all doubts that he was mad. To herself the Queen clutched the hope that in a foreign land, free of his father's mad spirit, her son's wits would return.

Once he sailed, Gertrude told the King what she had seen. In the days that followed, Gertrude often caught him watching her. It took no magic to discern his thoughts. He wondered, as did she, if another shared their bed each night unseen. But she had not seen King Hamlet's restless spirit since Prince Hamlet had left the court. And no rumors of haunting came to her ears.

Often Gertrude met Horatio about the castle, his cold blue eyes condemning her from within respectful features. She puzzled at his continued presence, since with her son's departure he had little to do and less to say. But he remained, watching without words. At last, his silence drove the Queen to speech.

"Good sir, I am amazed that thou dost stay so long away from thy fair home in Saxony."

"Majesty." He bowed, as would a courtier. "My home holds but little to lure me back again, and my work lies here."

"Thy work? Pray, what is that?"

"A chronicler, madam, one who would make a record of thy court as holy monks record the deeds of other courts and kings. Thy son did know my plan, and thought it worthy."

"Art thou a monk, then?" In truth, Gertrude thought he would make an excellent one, indifferent as he seemed to women's company.

"Nay, lady, I have not that honor. Yet I do write as fair as any clerk, and hope my words may serve as deeds to outlast me. My brothers are before me in my father's house, so I must make my way apart from them."

"To chronicle the royal throne of Denmark is no ill deed."

"I thank thee, Majesty, though in truth, my words shall serve but as a prelude to the monks'. I have thy son's promise in sweet Jesu's and His holy Mother's name, that holy monks shall chronicle all that may hap in Denmark after he is king."

"Long may you wait, ere you should see that day!" She turned and fled before she gave voice to her thoughts. That he should dare pray thus openly for her husband's death!

As summer faded, Denmark lay at peace. A king ruled now, one with his full wits. Deputations arrived from England and the north, and Claudius dealt shrewdly with them. As the people saw how wisely he sat the throne, those who had protested that the prince should have been king stilled their grumbles. There was little to disturb Gertrude's quiet life. But those few things ate at her like a canker.

The seas were wide, and lack of news at first did not disturb her, for she expected none. But when the ambassadors from England arrived, bearing no word from him, she began to wonder if all was well. She bore her troubles to the King.

"I tell thee yet again, the ambassadors did bear no message, Gertrude. 'Tis likely he delayed along the road. We shall hear, or not, in time. Do not forever look for word of him, when we know not where he lies. In truth, our realm is happier thus."

"Our realm, perhaps, but not his mother's heart."

"Sweet Queen." He took her hands in his and raised them, one after the other, to his lips. Of late his ardor had returned, stronger than when they were first wed. "Art thou not happy?"

"Aye, my lord, yet I do long for tidings of my son."

"Put by thy fears, Gertrude. Tell me, canst thou not rest content with Claudius, and let both Hamlets go?"

"That one which is dead, I can, yet not the other, for he is still as much his mother's child as is his father's son."

"Then thou must wait in discontent, lady. I would thou couldst dismiss him from thy thoughts."

Claudius did all he could to help put any thought of Hamlet from her mind, both then and in the days that followed. Still, Gertrude was troubled. It was clear the King hoped Hamlet never would return to Denmark.

Another sorrow grew more slowly. Ophelia had grieved wildly for her father, slain by the hand of the prince she loved. The Queen tried to comfort the girl as she would a daughter, but she would have no comfort. She walked for hours along the shore and even spent nights abroad in the fields. She also took to singing strange catches as she went about, songs all soft and whispering. Gertrude recognized one as a tune the minstrel had sung a year before, but with words that were all Ophelia's own. From those words it seemed Hamlet had bedded the lass before he had departed. But to the Queen's sorrow, he had not gotten Ophelia with child. Gertrude would rather have seen her belly swell, since a babe would have given the girl a center and an anchor to her life. Instead she drifted, and soon the rumors came that she was as mad as the young prince had been.

At last Ophelia wandered back to Elsinore, and Gertrude saw the truth behind rumor's whisper. Horatio had been following her, and took Gertrude aside to speak with her.

"Majesty, she will come to grief, an she wander thus unthinkingly. I would not trouble thee, but she is a sad sight now, one that would crack a heart of stone."

"Canst not ... good Horatio, you are a Christian, I

know, as is my son, and sweet Ophelia is as well. Could not the priests take her to a nunnery, that she might come to no harm?"

"Madam, would that it were so, but there is some sin she will not confess. I know, for she hath told me this. And 'midst all her ravings I took those words for truth. No priest can forgive sin when sinner repents it not."

A sin Ophelia would not repent? Gertrude had little doubt what that sin was. But since Ophelia chose not to confide her sorrow to any soul, there was nothing to be done, save setting women to watch her as she wandered.

Still no word came from Hamlet or from England. But just before the autumn storms closed round the castle, Ophelia's brother Laertes returned from France. He had begged leave to go there shortly after Claudius became king. Word of his sire's death had reached his ears in Paris, and he came hot for revenge. His sister's sad affliction added new tragedy to an unhappy homecoming.

But the next day brought fresh tidings, and these at last were a comfort to the Queen. A messenger arrived: a common sailor, but he brought letters from her son.

"He shall return ere long!" After reading the short note and kissing it twice over, Gertrude picked up her skirts and ran, eager as a girl, to her husband's side. Lady Margarethe followed more slowly, complaining of lack of breath and scolding that a queen should show more dignity. But Gertrude paid no heed, knowing breath and complaints were one with Margarethe.

"Claudius, our son shall soon be home!"

"Aye, madam." The King handed her the letter that had come to him. As her eyes traced out the familiar hand, her long-stilled fears for Hamlet's wits returned. What was this talk of pirates and of plots?

"I doubt not, he shall tell us all the tale when he is come. Perchance 'tis but a jest, to give excuse to his long silence."

"Mayhap." The King exchanged a glance with Laertes, with whom he had been closeted when the messenger arrived.

"Margarethe, do you go now and see his chamber ready. I shall give thought to what food we may prepare 'gainst his arrival, for he hath not fixed a day ..."

She turned to go, her mind already filled with duties of

both a mother and a queen, when she was delayed by her husband. "Stay yet a while, my lady. There is more matter here than thou hast thought." He dismissed Laertes with a nod that said they would talk further, and the young man bowed himself from the room, following the Lady Margarethe.

"My Queen, restrain yet for a moment that mother's fondness that does fill your breast, and think of this with me. Thy son, lady, went not from this court alone. Word has reached me privily that his two young friends will ne'er return, for they are both now dead."

"Dead!"

"Aye, and I know not how he hath compassed it, yet sure I am that thy son bears the blood-guilt of these two, as does he for that good old man. Yet still I fear he may not come alone."

"But if his friends be dead—"

"He hath kept company with the dead before, madam."

As the days passed with yet no word, Gertrude watched for Hamlet's coming. When at last he did arrive, he came hard on the heels of a fresh woe. With her brother's homecoming, the ladies watching Ophelia had loosened their guard. The girl's wanderings resumed, and at last she fell into the stream, floating to a muddy death. Whispers spoke of death by her own hand, but Gertrude stood firm against such talk, in kindness to her twice-bereaved brother. The Church's cruel edict against self-slaughter would have left the girl unshriven had that sin been proven, and though Gertrude cared not for the Church or its beliefs, she would not have Ophelia be unmourned by those who shared her faith. Hamlet arrived as the funeral neared its end. Her death drove him wild, and he and Laertes fought over her grave as to who was most bereaved.

As though the poor child cares now which bore her greater love, a brother or a lover! Neither can bring life's breath back to those grave-pale lips. Gertrude's thoughts were bitter as the funeral came to a hasty and ungraceful end. *When both have lost a love, what matter who can claim the greater pain?*

There were more hard words and harder feelings between the two before Gertrude at last found herself alone with her son in her chamber. Remembering the bitter madness of his words the last time she had seen him, she knew not what to say, but he spoke first.

"Mother, I would not have returned thus, brawling like a common soldier, but I am o'er-set with grief. Ophelia dead—now all sweet saints, take care of her, who should have lived a saint here on this earth!" He laid his head in her lap, and Gertrude found herself comforting him as she had done years ago, her own tears falling on him as she stroked his head. At last he stilled his weeping and spoke of other things, telling her of his months in England. She listened silently, then dared ask a single question.

"And what of thy two friends? Why came they not to Elsinore?"

"Madam, they shall not come save as ghosts, for they are dead. And for them I cannot mourn, since mine own death was the goal of all their evil plotting with the King."

"Hamlet, I will not hear these wicked words . . ."

"Wicked words? Aye, and a more wicked deed. Mother, thou mayst not wish to hear, yet truth will find a tongue, and thy most royal *husband* did plot to have me slain."

Later, when she and the King were alone in the royal bedchamber, she repeated Hamlet's words. Claudius shook his head.

"I would not scheme for that which would cause thee pain, sweet love. Would that he were more chary of thy pain, for then would he not desire thy husband's death."

"My son would not hurt me . . ."

"Would it not hurt thee should I die? Thou knowst he would be happy to see me in my grave. Lady, we were the happier, you and I, when he was farthest gone."

She shook her head, bereft of words. Husband and son hated one another, and she stood between them, torn apart.

Though King Hamlet continued quiet in his grave in the days following her son's return, Gertrude felt his presence once again, a hatred born of madness. She watched her son closely, but saw nothing untoward. One evening, she even followed him to the battlements, thereby scaring Margarethe, who remembered their last walk there, almost into fits. But Hamlet remained only a brief while, and at least to Gertrude's eyes, he walked alone.

As it had in the spring before Hamlet had left, Elsinore buzzed with whispers and tempers grew short. Laertes had ever been quick to take offense; now he did so before any word was spoken. At last anger found vent in a challenge to a duel. The pretense was that it would be no more than a trial of arms, to settle the King's wager, but no one believed the story.

The day appointed for the duel arrived, and all the court attended. Gertrude's unease had grown until she could scarcely keep to her chair. Laertes's skill at arms was widely known, while her son had always been more scholar than swordsman. But Hamlet had told her he had spent his time in England honing his own edge with a blade. The Queen strove to look unconcerned. They fought but for honor and a wager, not for any weightier matter. Hamlet begged pardon of Laertes without naming his offense, but all who heard knew he meant Polonius' death. Laertes answer froze Gertrude's heart. It was courteous and proper, but there was something in his expression, a triumphant, gloating look, that made her fear trickery.

They began. Hamlet had indeed spent time in mastering the art, for he set on in a fashion that showed far more skill than he had ever shown before. As his attack drove Laertes back with its intensity, Gertrude sat back in her chair, her fears receding. It was no more than a duel. She looked across to Claudius to confess her foolish doubts, and felt her tongue clog with the words. The look on the King's face was a silent echo of the one Laertes wore.

A cry went up as Hamlet's blade-tip flicked Laertes' shoulder. First touch to Hamlet. The King stood, cup in hand.

"A toast to our son's victory!" He drank, but Gertrude wondered at his words. While he had treated Hamlet as he would a son when they had first been wed, the prince's long madness and his false accusations had turned the King against him.

A cheer went up as the duelists engaged again, and under cover of the noise, she asked, "My lord, what does it mean, that you should call my son your own? I will admit, I was sore puzzled when thy wager was announced, for it hath seemed Laertes had thy favor."

"Gertrude, I love thee, therefore does it please me to call thy son mine own. As to Laertes, the boy hath known too much of grief, bereft both of his sister and his sire. If the King's favor eases his sore hurt, it is but small amends for that pain our court has brought him. Yet since thy son is thine, he is the dearest to our throne. Look you, how he fights!" Another cheer arose as, with a flurry of thrusts, Hamlet once more reached past Laertes' guard and scored a touch. Gertrude stood to see more easily.

"A touch, a touch! But one more, and the match is his!" As Hamlet turned to her, smiling, she reached for the winecup and lifted it in salute.

"Gertrude, set it by." The King kept his voice low, but it was filled with some urgent emotion. She ignored it.

"Nay, my lord, I'll drink to Hamlet's fortune."

"Gertrude, *no!*"

She raised the cup to her son, then drank deeply and set it down. As Hamlet and Laertes circled round once more, resuming the match, she took her seat again, then looked beside her. She wondered if the King had seen his ghostly brother; he was as pale as a specter himself.

"My love, art thou unwell? Margarethe, attend the King." She turned her head to search for her attendant, then whirled back to the duel as a great cry arose. The rapid movement left her head spinning, but that was of small interest compared to what was happening before her. Laertes had at last scored a touch, a serious one, for Hamlet's arm was bleeding freely and he had dropped his foil.

"Gertrude. Oh, pitiless gods, *Gertrude.*" The King spoke beside her, but her mind was fixed on her son. He reached again for his blade, but Laertes was there before him and kicked it spinning away. With a yell, Hamlet wrenched Laertes' sword from him and thrust, piercing the shoulder he had barely nicked before.

Gertrude rose, or tried to, but fell back in her chair, suddenly overcome with weakness. Behind her came a scream, as Margarethe saw her fall. Below, the judges pulled the duelists apart, both bleeding from their wounds.

"Lady, thy son bleeds, but 'tis naught, 'tis nothing, it should not make thee faint . . ." Somehow Gertrude found herself on the floor, her head in Margarethe's lap. "Your Majesty, what ails my good lady?"

"Gertrude." Claudius dropped to his knees beside her. "That cup was not for thee. I would not see thee harmed, my lady, oh, my love, I would not see thee harmed . . ."

The duel had stopped, and cries rose on every side, but they sounded distant in Gertrude's ears. Staring at the King, she whispered, "Poisoned?" The puzzle now lay clear; Laertes had been a weapon in her husband's hand, so he could rid himself of her son without blame.

"Poison!" Margarethe screamed the word and was answered from the dueling ground.

"The blade envenomed, too. Good Hamlet, we are both dead, you and I." Laertes pointed to the King, who still knelt beside Gertrude. "The King hath killed us, and thy lady mother."

"The cup, the blade . . ." Laertes fell, and Hamlet staggered as the poison gripped him, but with a sudden yell he straightened himself and ran toward the King, the poisoned blade extended. Claudius did not turn, even as Hamlet ran him through. Hamlet wrenched the blade free and the King fell back. He opened his mouth, but only blood came out. His horror-filled eyes still fixed on his Queen, he died.

Gertrude could not move, but she saw and heard. Now, horribly, she saw a presence she had not seen in months, the ghostly form of her first husband, gloating over her second husband's corpse. King Hamlet looked solid, but Margarethe, wailing, stumbled back right through him. He had no more substance than before; Gertrude had less.

"And thus I am revenged." It was a voice she had not thought to hear again. "Come, my Queen."

Beyond, she heard her son speak to Horatio, forbidding him the poisoned cup. The ghost circled the Queen, ignoring both her ladies and his own dying son.

"Oh, good Horatio, what a wounded name, things standing thus unknown, shall live behind me!" Faintly she could hear her son's final plea. ". . . and in this harsh world draw thy breath in pain to tell my story."

"I shall, my Prince, as thou hast taught it me." Strange; Gertrude had not thought Horatio had so much of feeling in him, and yet she thought she heard him cry.

His story. The sounds had faded now, and all that she

could see was that same hateful form, waiting at death's gate for her. *But 'tis not his alone, but mine as well, and Claudius'. Yet all that will be told is a tale told by a madman* ... As though he heard her thoughts, the ghost stretched forth his hand and smiled as darkness claimed her.

III

"By virtue, thou enforcest laughter; thy silly thoughts, my spleen; the heaving of my lungs provokes me to ridiculous smiling . . ."

Love's Labours Lost

Shakespeare created low clowns and high wits both. Herewith, a modern sampling from those categories, though I'll leave it to the reader to decide which tale falls where.

ALAS, ME BLEEDIN ...

Dennis McKiernan

Dennis McKiernan is a best-selling fantasy author whose latest book is The Voyage of the Fox Rider. *With this story he shows that* Hamlet *does not necessarily inspire solemnity in everyone.*

Act 0 Scene 1

There hi wos sleepin all peaceful-like, wot, when these orrible sounds come crashin inter me quiet slumber. Like picks n spades, they wos, *chnk,* jarrin inter the ground, *shkk,* slicin through the soil, *shng,* ringin as the dirt wos throwed free. Hit wos right hupsettin, hit wos, and lumme but hi couldna get back ter sleep cos they wos acomin closer and closer—*chnk, shkk, shng. Chnk, shkk, shng! Chnk, Shkk, Shng! Chnk! Shkk! Shng! CHNK! SHKK! SHNG!*

Hi don't mind tellin you, hit gave me the blue willies, hit did, right enough!

Of a sudden—*THDD! THNK!*—there comes this orrible sound, like som'n wos batterin on the very doors o' 'ell, 't wos. Then there wos this 'ere splittin n rippin o' timber n daylight poured in—*Gahh!*—n hi wos hexposed!

Then this 'ere 'and reaches in n grabs me by the jaw n quicker than jack-be-nimble sets me 'ead onna pile o' dirt. Sblood, but hit were right hupsettin, wot, but y'd be hupset too if hit were y'r grave wot wos despoiled like mine wos, yar.

Irregardless, there hi wos, me 'ead sittin on a pile o'
dirt, n these 'ere two clowns wot dug me hup wos
chatterin away in th' bloody Danish like hall's well as
hends well. Oh, hi knew both o' them, you shouldna wonder, n hi made hup me mind right there n then that they'd
'ear from me habout wot they'd done, diggin me bones
hup n all, n they'd live ter regret't, too. Hi mean, even if
hit were their job ter bury the deaders, still n all, th' stupid buggers could let them what preceded the newdead
inter th' ground rest in peace, now couldna they? Stupid
buggers! Hi'd 'ave me revenge, and you can put a silver
on that.

Well, one o' them left, n t'other began ter sing, orribly
off key, hi might add.

Then 'oo should appear but som'n hi knew awhile
back, 'im n 'is friend. A regular little twit, 'e wos, a twit
growed hup anow, and so hi suppose that'd make 'im a
big twit, hi'd say rightly.

N speakin 'igh-court Dane, 'e asks 'oo might be buried
'ere, n the clown says hit were Yorick, the King's jester.
Well, 'e wos right habout that, 'e wos, cos sure enough,
Yorick's me name.

Well, then, this 'ere Amlet, 'e 'as the audacity ter take
hup me skull, me *skull* hi say, defilin hit even further than
hit 'ad hallready been defiled, n 'e says, sad-like, "Alas,
poor Yorick. I knew him, Horatio—"

Alas, me bleedin arse! 'Ere 'e wos, actin grief-stricken-
like when 'e'd made me life a livin 'ell when hi wos
alive, 'e did. Th' little bugger. 'E'd pay for defilin me after me demise, too, 'e would. Hi swung me jaw wide n
screamed hat 'im, "Leave off, y' bugger! Put me back
inter th' soil n let me sleep!"

"—a fellow of infinite jest, of most excellent fancy," 'e
went on, hignorin me shrieks o' protest hat bein so
mis'andled.

"Y' stupid arse, let me go!" hi yelled, ter no avail.
Y'see, th' conditions wosna right. Ter be 'eard as a ghost,
it's got ter be darkish, n a fog 'elps, too. N silence. N 'ere
hit wos, bright day, n Amlet wos jabberin away without
listenin, n so o'course 'e couldna 'ear me.

"He hath borne me on his back a thousand times ..."

O' course hi bore 'im on me back. The little bugger
jumped me, 'at's wot, jumped me, 'e did. Hi felt like

throwin 'im off the walls o' th' castle, but th' King were watchin hat the time, n 'e would know it were no accident. N this 'ere Amlet, 'e wos a cunning little skut—ne'er jumped on me back when th' King weren't habout.

". . . and now, how abhored my imagination is! My gorge rises at it. Here hung those lips that I have kissed I know not how often."

Yar, 'e kissed me, right enough. Lots. Hi halways thought as 'e wosna right in 'is 'ead. Hi woulda shoved 'im away, bein a laidies man meself and all y' understand, but again, 'is dad the King were watchin most o' th' time n so hi wos slobbered on too many hinstances ter count.

Amlet, 'e looks me right in wot woulda been me eyes 'ad hi 'ad any, n 'e says, "Where be your jibes now, your gambols, your songs, your flashes of merriment that were wont to set the table on a roar?"

"You stupid arse," hi shrieked, "hi'm dead! Can't y' see that? Y'r still a twit, Amlet, no matter 'ow big y' be! Hi'll get y' f'r this! Some'ow!"

'E just hignored me scream o' protest, like 'e'd halways done, sayin, "Not one now to mock your own grinning? Quite chop-fallen?"

"O' course hi'm chop-fallen, y' bloody bastard!" hi yelled back hat 'im. "Hi hain't got no flesh ter 'old hup me chops, y' arse'ole!"

'E just blathered on: "Now get you to my lady's chamber and tell her, let her paint an inch thick, to this favor she must come. Make her laugh at that."

O' course, she'd come ter be wot hi wos. Heverybody'd come ter wot hi wos, hincludin you, Amlet m'stupid lad. N hit don't matter 'ow much a laidy paints 'er face, soon or late, she'd be but little different from me. But now hi hasks, y', 'oo c'd laugh hat that, eh? Knowin that soon or late, soon or late, hit'd come down ter bein nothin but bones. 'Oo c'd laugh hat that, Amlet, y' stupid arse?

Come ter think o' hit, though, mayhap this wos the first clever thing wot hi'd hever 'eard Amlet say. But that didna matter none wi' me, cos 'e 'ad japed me, n hi wos still goin ter get 'im f'r that, some'ow.

Then Amlet says, "Prithee, Horatio, tell me one thing."

N Oratio hanswers, "What's that, my lord?"

N Amlet hasks, "Dost thou think Alexander looked o'
this fashion i'th' earth?"

"Wot a stupid question! O' course 'e looked like this!"
hi yelled, but 'e couldna 'ear me, cos the conditions
wosna right, hit bein daylight n all, or did hi tell y' that
hallready?

Oratio hanswers, "E'en so."

That Oratio, 'e halways wos smarter than Amlet . . . a
lot smarter.

Then Amlet hinsults me fiercely, sayin, "And smelt so?
Pah!"

N'e *throwed* m' skull *adown!*

Like ter 'ave broke me asunder, 'im dashin m' noggin
ter th' earth like that! "You stupid bastard," hi yelled,
"you'll pay f'r this, hi swear! Hi'll get even, no matter
'ow long hit takes!"

Act 0 Scene 2

Hit took me quite awhile ter come ter a plan wot'd get
even f'r 'avin me bones disinterred n hinsulted. But then
hi remembered as 'ow Father Time 'isself 'as little control over ghosts, cos once y'r a deader y'r spirit hexists
throughout all o' time—past, present, and future—and
so . . .

Hi split back a few weeks inter th' past n waited until
hit were a gloomy night when hi c'd be seen by mortal
eyes, then, made hup wi' th' proper hectoplasm such as hi
took on th' haspect o' th' former King—Amlet's own beloved father—hi began ter stalk th' battlements o'
Elsinore.

Y'see, hi 'ad a straightforward plan wot hinvolved a
simple tale wot hi 'ad made hup wot'd curl y'r 'air,
'twould. A tale o' murder most foul, betrayal o' trust, lust
n unfaithfulness n sin, a conspiracy most dire.

N, when th' conditions wos right, hi'd take on me very
best Danish 'igh-court haccent n tell hit ter Amlet n ask
'im ter avenge me, 'is dear ol' "dad."

Disturb *my* bones, would 'e?

THE MUSE AFIRE

Laura Resnick

Laura Resnick won an award for Best New Romance Series Writer in 1989, and won the Campbell Award (for best new science fiction writer) in 1992. As she writes about Shakespeare himself, she displays her gift for comedy.

"*O* for a muse of fire!"

No sooner had Will penned this thrilling line for the second act of his new play, than a puff of smoke filled the Globe Theater and a muffled *pop!*—rather like the sound of an indifferent Italian wine coming uncorked—echoed through its empty galleries.

"You called?"

"God's teeth!" Will cried, jumping to his feet. "Goldie!"

"Surprised to see me, *boychik?*"

"Indeed," he gasped, placing a hand over his pounding heart. Recovering himself slightly, he added. " 'Tis been so long, I began to think thou hadst shuffled off this mortal coil."

"Will, Will, Will, you are *so* slow," she said, shaking her frosted curls. "How many times do I have to tell you? I'm not mortal. I'm a muse."

"As you like it, lady," he snapped back, irked by her condescending tone.

"Like it? I don't like it at *all,* at the moment. The hours stink, and let's be frank—I wind up with some pretty strange bedfellows."

Instantly jealous, he demanded, "Then, after saying me nay more often than the light through yonder window breaks, thou hast finally taken another to thy bed? Frailty, thy name is woman!"

"Watch out for that green-eyed monster, Will," Goldie chided, "because it'll mock the lox it feeds on." Will gave her a lean and hungry look. She batted her curly lashes and said, "Tell the truth and shame the devil: you missed me, didn't you?"

"In my mind's eye, I see thee with bedfellows," he said grimly, ignoring her question. "Unsex me here if thou hast been false!"

"Oh, Will, I did not come here to endure another of your wounded-male-ego scenes. I was using the term 'bedfellows' figuratively. I mean, here it is Saturday night, date night Britannia, and I'm spending it with a balding, married *goy* in Cheapside. My mother would be turning in her grave, if she had a grave. As it is, she's off in Italy helping them wind down the Renaissance and telling everyone what a disappointment I turned out to be."

"My mother's doing the same thing back in Stratford," Will said in commiseration.

"I'm eight hundred and forty-seven years old, and my mother still won't let me alone," Goldie complained, warming to her subject. Mimicking her mother's voice, she continued, " 'Why haven't you done as well as your sister? *She* inspired the Mona Lisa, the Sistine Chapel, and the statue of David. But *no,* you had to be different. You had to work with *writers.*' "

"And thou didst make love to this employment," Will said encouragingly. He spoiled it a moment later, however, by adding, "Though not to this particular employee."

"Will, we've been over this a hundred times. That way madness lies. It would destroy our working relationship if we made the beast with two backs. Anyhow, I've got a spotless reputation and I'm saving myself for marriage."

"And our marriage of true minds would not suffice?"

Goldie gave him a retiring look before saying, "My

mother just doesn't understand how hard it is to find an unmarried Jewish doctor in London these days."

"Indeed, the time is out of joint for such a match," Will agreed. "And, since it seems thou shalt never marry, why forgo the simple pleasures of the flesh? And if thou hast no care for thine own flesh, then think on mine! Be merciful!"

"Will, the quality of mercy is getting a little strained," Goldie said. "Must you wear your heart on your sleeve?"

"Whist!" Will warned, looking off toward the wings. "Something wicked this way comes."

"Ah-hah!" Richard Burbage cried, entering the scene. "You're back!"

"Hello, Dickie."

"How was Ireland?"

"It beggars description."

"Find any new recruits?"

Goldie shook her curls. "No, they're all too busy rebelling. I don't think it'll be worth making another trip over there for at least a century."

"How do you like the new theater?" Burbage asked, gesturing to their grandiose surroundings.

"*Mazel tov!* I hear it's the biggest theater in London."

Burbage nodded. "Seating capacity of two thousand. The question is, what will the Lord Chamberlain's Men perform for such an audience? Will hasn't written a decent line since you left."

"I do protest!" Will cried.

"You can protest all you like," Burbage said, "but even Ben Jonson could write something better than your latest effort. And you've been cranky and temperamental, too." He added to Goldie, "He made the newest apprentice cry, yesterday."

"Will!"

"I am more sinned against than sinning," Will said in injured tones. "It is no easy matter to author a play when one's muse is making merry in another country."

"I doubt if *anyone's* making merry in Ireland these days," Burbage shot back.

"All right, boys, I'm here now, so let's not argue anymore. What are you working on, Will?"

"Yet another draft, may it please Master Burbage, of *Henry VII*."

"Let me see," Goldie said, reaching for the manuscript.

"I shall read it to you," he said quickly.

"I can read it myself," she insisted. "Hath not a Jew eyes?"

Will gave it up after only a brief tussle. She read it while Will paced and Burbage lay on his back doing bizarre humming exercises.

"Well?" Will said anxiously when she was finally done perusing four weeks of painstaking work.

"Piece of codswallop, isn't it?" Burbage muttered.

"Will, I'm afraid I must be cruel to be kind," Goldie said.

"What is the matter?"

"Oh, the usual things," Goldie replied, floating slightly, as she often did when lost in thought. "It lacks characterization, plot, conflict, and interesting dialogue."

"I see."

"The problem is, you made Henry VII such a milquetoast in *Richard III,* when he was the Earl of Richmond."

"I was in a pickle. The piece needed at least one man of conscience."

"I know, I know, but he's always praying and being so noble. It's just not the stuff of good theater, Will."

"Such virtue could succeed at the heart of a drama," Will insisted.

"Besides," Goldie continued, trying another attack, "Richmond himself says at the end of *Richard III,* 'Now civil wounds are stopp'd, peace lives again.' And that's what you've got here, Will. Sixty pages of a dull, noble milquetoast babbling about the peace and prosperity of his reign."

"I tried to talk him into writing *Henry VIII,*" Burbage said, taking a brief pause from his strident humming. "I think a really good, juicy sex scandal would fill up the galleries and the pit."

"Yes, and our heads would soon thereafter bid farewell to our necks," Will pointed out, "since the Queen is seldom merry on the subject of her late father's wives."

"Hey! What about doing *Henry V?*" Goldie suggested. They stared at her.

"You know, Henry V," she prodded. "The guy who reigned between Henry IV and Henry VI?"

"What if we do *Henry VI, Part IV?*" Will suggested.

"You already did that and called it *Richard III,*" Burbage reminded him, making odd chewing motions to keep his jaw flexible. "What about *Titus Andronicus II?* Sex and violence sell, Will."

"Yo, Dick, whose job is it around here to be inspiring?" Goldie snapped. "Enough *kibitzing,* already."

"Well, *excuse* me."

"Just remember," she said, "you're an actor. You're not paid to think. I am. Read my contract if you don't believe me."

"I did read your contract," Burbage grumbled. "I can't *believe* what we're paying you to inspire him."

Goldie grinned. "I have a good lawyer."

"Let's kill all the lawyers," Burbage growled.

"For goodness sake, before we all succumb to time's thievish progress to eternity, could we return to the subject of the play? The play's the thing, is it not?" Will said testily.

"*Bubeleh,* lend me your ear," Goldie said. "Why let vaulting ambition o'erleap itself—and several decades of history—and ignore that star of England, Henry V, in favor of a monarch who, frankly, isn't capable of carrying the weight of a five act play on his shoulders?"

"Henry V? Talk about a lad who did nothing but pray and act noble," Burbage said scathingly as he bobbed his head around, trying to relax his neck.

"You said sex and violence sells, Dickie," Goldie reminded him irritably. "Don't you think Agincourt was pretty violent?"

"Methinks it is impossible," Will said. "Be practical, Goldie. Can this cockpit hold the vasty fields of France? May we cram within this wooden O the very casques that did afright the air at Agincourt?"

"On *our* budget?" Burbage said. "Out of the question."

"It can be done," Goldie insisted.

"How?" both men demanded.

"You will have to work on the audience's imaginary forces. Pretend the stage is a kingdom—"

"A kingdom for a stage?" Will said somewhat doubtfully. "On this unworthy scaffold?"

"Don't talk that way about my theater," Burbage warned.

"Come on, Dickie, get into the spirit of the thing. Think, when we talk of horses, that you see them."

"I'm not paid to think," Burbage replied sourly. "*I'm* just an actor."

"Horses," Will said musingly, "printing their proud hoof i' the receiving earth."

"Yes," Goldie encouraged.

"For the spectators' *thoughts* must deck our kings, carry them here and there, jumping o'er times, and turning the accomplishments of many years into an hourglass," Will continued, getting excited.

"Yes!" Goldie cried. "Oh, we're cooking now! I'm all afire!"

"It'll never work," Burbage said, dousing her creative flame. "How will we get your average Londoner to imagine all that?"

"We will admit a Chorus to this history," Will said.

"Like we had in *Romeo and Juliet?*"

"Precisely. A Chorus who will transport the gentles—"

"What gentles?"

"Londoners," Goldie translated.

"Transport them to Southampton," Will continued, "and thence to France."

"Southampton and France! Whoa! How much is this going to cost?" Burbage demanded.

"You'll be transporting them *figuratively,*" Goldie explained.

"Oh."

"And though the gentles must perforce digest the abuse of distance, we'll not offend one stomach with our play."

"Brilliant!" Goldie cried. "Oh, you give me such *naches.*"

"All right, kids, *kids,*" Burbage interjected. "This all goes very trippingly on the tongue, Will, and far be it from me to stifle genius by thinking too precisely on the event, but let's try to be a little realistic here, okay? I mean, Will, how can we possibly stage the Battle of Agincourt?"

"Now entertain conjecture of a time . . . uh . . ." Will dried up and looked helplessly at Goldie.

"We'll do it with a lot of speeches," she said. "And I know, Dickie, that you *love* speeches."

"Yes," Will said, marshaling his thoughts again. "The

Chorus shall describe the, uh, the confident and over-lusty French."

"Lust!" Burbage exclaimed. "Good. Let's not forget about lust. Lust sells."

"And how, through the foul womb of night, the hum of either army still sounds. And we shall apologize to the gentles that we shall much disgrace with four or five most vile and ragged foils—"

"They're not *that* ragged," Burbage protested.

"How we shall disgrace, right ill-dispos'd in brawl ridiculous, the name of Agincourt."

"Well, I suppose we could do a couple of small hand-to-hand combat scenes," Burbage conceded.

"Sure," Goldie said, glad he was giving in, "and then Henry can make a few speeches about how well they're doing, how many thousands are slain, et cetera."

"I guess it could work," Burbage admitted, starting his deep knee bends. "If Henry gets a list of the slaughtered and slain that he can read aloud, it'll save us having to pay people to lay around the stage playing dead in the fifth act. *Henry VI* got very expensive that way."

"You're always thinking about money," Goldie criticized.

"Thrift, thrift, Goldie."

"Now will I make a hero of a noble man, one who was every inch a king, and who prayed muchly," Will interrupted. "And thus will I prove you both wrong in one fell swoop."

"My main concern is that there's still no sex," Burbage said. "All we've got so far is one reference to the lusty French."

"A hit, a very palpable hit," Will admitted. "But 'tis a foregone conclusion that silken dalliance in the wardrobe lay whilst the French and English were slaughtering each other at Agincourt."

"Well, then you'll just have to make up something," Burbage said, looking pointedly at Goldie.

She sighed. "All right. Why don't we add a little about Henry's courtship with Princess Katharine?"

"What courtship?" Will demanded. "They were wed to ratify a treaty."

"What a piece of work is a man!" Goldie said wearily.

"Sometimes you're about as romantic as a tree stump, Will."

"O! The most unkindest cut of all!" he cried.

"We must make a virtue of necessity, Will," Goldie continued, ignoring his outburst.

"What the dickens means that, lady?"

"It means we need a love scene, so we might as well make the most of it. We'll end the battle in act four, then spend act five portraying how Henry, now nicely dressed and cleaned up, courts his royal bride."

"They'll love it in the pit!" Burbage said approvingly.

"You can give Henry a few of the lines you've used on me," Goldie added. "Some of them haven't been half bad."

"And you could end the play with a reference to *Henry VI,* which I'm thinking of rerunning next year," Burbage suggested.

"Hmmm," Will mused. "The king whose state so many had the managing, that they lost France and made his England bleed."

"It'll be like free advertising."

"So, *boychik,* it looks like our play hath a prodigious birth. Am I right?"

"Indeed," Will said, his eyes lighting up as he considered the courtship scene. "I see it now, Goldie. No longer am I infirm of purpose! Once more into the breach, dear friends, once more!"

"You can go into the breach by yourself, Will," Burbage said. "That's your job. Me, I think I'll go find an ale house."

"Parting is such sweet sorrow," Goldie said, with a touch of insincerity.

"Good night," Will said, eager to be alone with Goldie.

"I'd like at least five soliloquies in this thing, Will," Burbage instructed. "You kind of shortchanged me in *Much Ado About Nothing.*"

"Good night," Will said.

"And remember, Will. Brevity is the soul of wit. Make sure the play is short enough that people can make last call at the ale houses. Everyone complained about *Richard III.*"

"A thousand times good night," Will said through gritted teeth. When Burbage finally departed, he turned to Goldie. "Alone at last."

"Hmm. I was afraid he'd never leave."

"And what pretty thoughts are on thy mind, lady?" Will sidled a little closer to her.

"Screw your courage to the sticking place, Will."

He set his teeth on edge. "Why?"

"If you have tears, prepare to shed them now."

"Why?"

"I've decided your next play should be about Julius Caesar."

"Julius Caesar?" he repeated bleakly. "But I hate research!"

"Think of it as an adventure. Won't it be exciting?"

Will put his head in his hands. *"Oy vay,"* he said.

TITUS!

Esther M. Friesner

Esther M. Friesner has brought her brilliant comic talents to many books, including her new Majyk series, featuring, among other characters, sheep pirates. In this story she takes in hand—er, well, no—gives tongue to—um, not that either—at any rate, Titus Andronicus will never be the same.

An angel knocked on Mark Ireland's office door. "Sod off," he said to the frosted glass panel.

Angels seldom take "Sod off" for an answer. The door opened a wee sma' crack and a nose comparable in size and design to a late Saxon battle-ax wedged itself into the available space. "Surely you don't mean *me,* Mr. Ireland?" The angel posed the question coyly.

Not so coyly, however, that Mark Ireland's trained ear could not pick up the subtle postscript: *Because if you did mean me, you're dead.* It wasn't the celestial sort of angel, but the kind who gave wings of cash to theatrical productions, and therefore more feared by the young director than promise of Heaven or threat of Hell.

"No, no, of course I didn't mean you, Dr. Charmian," Ireland replied. "You know I'm always glad to see you. Please come in." For his own part, the nuances of his exhausted voice included the tag-line: *Almost as glad to see you as to see Dutch Elm blight infest my crotch, you stupid cow, so bugger off.* But Dr. Charmian was either too dense to pick up on the unspoken hints of others, or else she just didn't give a damn. She came right in and made herself at home.

"I won't take up much of your time, Mr. Ireland," she cooed. "I've just come by to bring you the most lovely surprise."

"Oh, goody."

Dr. Charmian ignored the handsome young director's deliberately leaden counterfeit of enthusiasm. She packed enough animation for a cheerleading squad. "I just *know* you're going to love it. I've got it out in the hall; I thought I ought to prepare you for it first. Just a little spinoff of the experiment we've got underway at the lab. I was working on the project and all of a sudden I thought how *perfect* it would be, how *inspirational* for you and the cast if only—" She burbled on as she plumped down five-foot-eight of extremely unattractive bone-structure in the one chair that was not covered with piles of unbound playbook pages. Alas, in her attempt, Dr. Charmian managed to upset three other piles. Papers took wing.

"Oooh, did I do that?" she asked in a kittenish tone that would have sounded asinine even in the mouth of a much better-looking woman. Coming from Earth's premiere AI specialist, it set a new record for stomach-churning smarm.

"No harm done, Dr. Charmian," Ireland said. He was unable to keep the weariness out of it; he didn't much care to try. "No harm *could* be done to this play."

"Why do you say that? What's the matter?" For an instant, Dr. Charmian's muck-brown eyes dropped their unsuitably fey expression and assumed a look of real concern. The same voice that seconds ago caused grown men to order insulin on-the-rocks snapped into the efficient, analytical tones of the laboratory. For the first time since he'd been introduced to Dr. Charmian as a heavy to-be-humored investor in the production presently under his hand, Mark Ireland actually believed that she was a computer scientist capable of wiping a man's whole life from the data banks with one crook of her skinny finger.

"I don't want to trouble you," he replied, somewhat feebly. But then again, he was feeling intensely feeble. Under his breath he added, "Bloody *dasmuks!*"

"I'm an investor in this production," Dr. Charmian snapped. "I have a right to know." She stopped trying to thrust her phantom bosom at the young director and sat up straight in the shabby chair.

"Yes, I suppose you do." Ireland reached for a thick, leatherette-bound manuscript that roosted on the far right-hand corner of his desk like a buzzard on a cactus. He dragged the monster in front of him. "Tell me something, Dr. Charmian: As a potential investor, what were you specifically told about this little, ah, venture of ours?"

"I know it's the first cooperative interplanetary theatrical production ever attempted, breaking oodles of new ground, which was why there was no other director to tap for the guiding role but *you.*"

There was that jarring note of predatory winsomeness again. Ireland cringed, cursing the Muse who had made him the Terran theater's pet *enfant terrible* of the moment, ditto laying a fierce Shakespearean malediction on the stars which had spawned the *dasmuks.* The cloud of vilification lifted in time for him to hear Dr. Charmian add, "My investment advisor told me it was a magnificent opportunity. By backing your production I would gain unprecedented *entre* to the confidence of our world's beloved and blessed advisors, the *dasmuks,* while at the same time seeing a stupendous return on my capital." She frowned. "It *will* be a stupendous return, won't it?"

"Stupendous . . ." He did not say it to set her mind at ease, he merely repeated the word. "Your advisor didn't happen to mention the *name* of the play that was going to do so much for your prestige and pocketbook, did he?"

"Noooooo."

"*Titus Andronicus.*" Ireland yanked open his file drawer and, in a move more appropriate to a cheap detective of the mid-twentieth century pulps, extracted an open fifth of whiskey. He pulled the cork, set the bottle to his lips, and glugged, then slammed it down on the manuscript. "Cheers," he said.

"*Mis*-ter Ireland—" the lady scientist began, in a hennish huff.

"Do you know anything about *Titus Andronicus,* Doctor?" Ireland asked, his gaunt cheeks suffused with a transitory mellow glow. "Ah, from that dead mackerel look in your lovely eyes, I see you don't. Keep the look, by the way; it suits you. *Titus Andronicus* is perhaps the most controversial of Shakespeare's plays. It has spawned more heated literary discussions than Hamlet's madness or the identity of the third murderer in the Scottish play."

"Do you mean *Macbeth?*" Dr. Charmian asked, innocently pronouncing the title whose very sound had for centuries been associated with disastrous luck, according to the best traditions of the theater.

For the first time in his career, Mark Ireland did not flinch at the mention of those taboo syllables. When a man has been caught below the hind end of a dyspeptic elephant at *the* inopportune moment, he does not subsequently react to having a pigeon drop one in his eye.

"Precisely," he replied. "Although not for the reasons you might think. The main subject of the *Titus* controversy has little to do with fine points of text or character. It is simply: Could a man of Shakespeare's obvious genius ever have lowered himself to write such a stinkeroo or not?"

"A . . . stinkeroo? By *Shakespeare?*" Dr. Charmian was holding onto the dead mackerel look for all she was worth.

"*Titus Andronicus* is a slash-and-spurt tragedy of unbridled violence and gore. Hollyvidmakers who cater to the teen testosterone market are left gasping in awe when they read the plot *precis.*"

Dr. Charmian nibbled a knuckle. "I don't think I ever studied that play in high school."

"You wouldn't. Ever since the Great Purge of '02, *Romeo and Juliet* seldom makes it into the curriculum, what with all the adolescent sex and violence. But what are a couple of suicides, a trio of manslaughters, and a little bit of the old slap-and-tickle—within wedlock, of course—next to what *Titus* dishes out?"

"Oh?" Dr. Charmian inquired. The dead mackerel look was still with her, as instructed, and it *did* suit her.

Ireland steepled his fingers and tilted back his chair. "In *Titus Andronicus* you start off with a dash of human sacrifice, a pinch of parricide, a sprinkling of adultery garnished with miscegenation, and a *soupcon* of murder. The victim's wife—Titus' daughter Lavinia—is raped by two men, who then cut out her tongue so she can't identify them."

"Oh, I *do* recall something like that from when I studied the Greek myths, as a girl," Dr. Charmian chirped.

"They were *writing* the Greek myths when you were a girl," Ireland muttered, as *sotto* as any *voce* could get.

"The myth of Procne and Philomena. A king married one sister, raped the other, and cut her tongue out for exactly the same reason. But *she* wove the whole story of his crime into a tapestry and sent it to his wife." She looked as proud of herself as if it had been all her own idea.

Ireland took another pull on the bottle. "The rapists were as well-read as you, dear Doctor. They chopped off the lady's hands besides."

"Ugh!" Dr. Charmian paled and shuddered.

It was curiously amusing to watch someone else squirm for a change, so Ireland gave the knife a twist. "That's not the half of it. Lavinia's brothers are framed for her husband's death. Titus sends the Emperor his own severed hand in a grand, dramatic gesture meant to remind His Imperial Nibs of the many times that very hand raised a sword in Rome's defense against the barbarian Goths!" Here Ireland leaped up, brandishing an invisible blade and frightening Dr. Charmian so badly she almost tipped her chair over backward. Her squawk of alarm was shrill enough to shatter the glass panel on Ireland's office door.

Ireland himself jumped back as the glass *did* shatter—albeit from the outside inward—and a body hurtled through. It struck the floor in an acrobat's roll, tumbled lightly over the lino, and popped upright with the ease and elan of a top-of-the-line jack-in-the-box.

There was nothing at all toylike about the rapier it drew and aimed right at the young director's heart. Ireland collapsed into his chair, cold sweat bursting from every pore as he took in the costumed loony before him. "Good God," was all he had the fiber left to breathe in the face of the stiff Elizabethan ruff, the sleek hose over rather skinny legs, and the plush puffs-and-slashes doublet in between. A high-domed forehead, thin hair falling below the ear, melancholy eyes, and a pathetically scrawny mustache refused to be ignored. "Good God, it *can't* be."

"Are you all right, Dr. Charmian?" the apparition asked.

"I'm fine. Please don't hurt him, Will," the lady replied, and Ireland's stomach turned to ice as he realized that what *can't* be often is.

He took the coward's way out. He fainted.

He regained consciousness in time to hear the creature telling Dr. Charmian, "—and then after feeding Queen Tamora her own sons baked in a pie and slaying her— well, they *did* rape his daughter, slaughter his son-in-law, and hang the crime on his sons—Titus kills poor dishonored Lavinia and—"

"Enough, enough, please, no more!" Dr. Charmian's face was curdy white as she waved the words away. "How could you ever write such horrors?"

The costumed being shrugged. "I was young. It was the fashion. I needed to break into the business. They got me drunk. It was dark."

"So you *do* admit you wrote *Titus Andronicus!*" Mark Ireland recovered full use of his limbs instantaneously and bounded across the office to collar Dr. Charmian's defender. All thought of how incredible the creature's very presence was vanished from his mind at the opportunity to solve an age-old mystery.

It is practically impossible to collar someone wearing a ruff.

"Ow!" Ireland exclaimed as the stiffly starched point lace pierced his thumb. "Bloody good night!" He sucked the injured finger fiercely.

The creature's eyes narrowed. "Do you bite your thumb at me, sir?" it demanded.

"Do I wha—? Oh!" Ireland jerked the thumb from his mouth in a flash. It wouldn't do to make a provocative gesture—however anachronistic—and rile this guest. "Sorry. That is, I crave thy pardon, gentle sir." He made as courtly a bow as ever he'd executed when wearing the mantle of Henry V courting the French princess, back in his predirectional days as a mere boy-genius actor. Head down, he glanced up sideways at the creature and added, "You—you really are Shakespeare, aren't you?" To Dr. Charmian he said, "Is *this* the surprise you mentioned?"

The doctor just giggled.

Ireland stood up and looked the visitor in the eye. "Computers robbing graves," he mused. "What won't they think of next?"

"Hardly grave-robbing, Mr. Ireland." A shade of her

earlier huffiness crept back into Dr. Charmian's voice. "The gentleman is not a zombie; he's a *construct.* Our lab has been having a good deal of success in having the system assimilate all available data on a given historical subject, subsequently creating a program that is a close *re*creation of that subject's true personality. The program is then played out through AI-managed holograms or—"

"Holograms?" Ireland thrust a hand at the visitor, forgetting the evidence of his previously wounded thumb. He hit solid flesh. It hit back.

"—or androids," Dr. Charmian said, offering Ireland a hand up from the floor. The dazed director was still rubbing his assaulted jaw as she added, "Will tells me he spent a lot of time holding his own in tavern brawls, so please don't do that again."

"Shakespeare," was all Ireland could say. "William by-God Shakespeare."

"Call me Will," said the apparition, belatedly returning Ireland's own bow.

"Isn't he adorable?" Dr. Charmian dimpled. "So courteous, so gallant! I can't wait to see the *dasmuks'* reaction."

"The *dasmuks* ..." Mark Ireland stole the doctor's dead mackerel look without so much as a by-your-leave. His glassy eyes went from the reconstituted playwright to the playbook on his desk. He sank back into his chair with a groan.

"What's the matter?" Will asked.

"Don't you mean, 'What aileth thee, good sir'?" Ireland countered in a voice of only marginal interest, otherwise bereft of all energy, vigor, or the will to live.

"No, I don't." Will sat on the edge of the desk. "I was a man of my times, and I still prefer to speak so others can understand what I've to say. Dr. Charmian's program made the necessary adjustments in my whatd'youcall'um—"

"Your idiomatic and lexical capabilities," the doctor prompted.

"That's it. What she said." He crossed his legs and linked interlaced fingers comfortably around a very knobby knee. "What good would it do me to speak my ancient form of English among you here? Life does not come with footnotes. *Communication* is what it's all about, sir. What it always has been all about, as far as I'm concerned. It's the mudgery-fudgery refusal to attack a problem head-on that causes all the troubles of this world: Misunderstandings, jumping to unfounded conclusions, willful self-doubt, hashwork second-guessery, misinterpretation, hearing only what you want to hear when it isn't there to be heard at all—"

"Mmmm." Ireland could think of a Shakespearean tragedy to illustrate each one of the revenant Bard's subclasses of communication breakdowns. "Which one applies to *Titus Andronicus?*" he asked aloud.

Will grinned, making his baggy eyes twinkle. "A classic case of bad communication there, plain and simple: They told me to write down to the public taste and I was fool enough to listen. Still, over the years it's had its run. Dr. Charmian tells me that my literary reputation has transformed me into an icon of perfection. It's just as well to have a bit of evidence on hand to prove I was— am—no more than a man."

"We're turning it into a musical comedy to please the *dasmuks,*" Ireland said, so that there could be no hope of misinterpretation.

"Bugger all!" bellowed Shakespeare, and fell off the edge of the director's desk into the wastebasket.

"I meant well," Dr. Charmian whimpered as she clung to Ireland's arm in the backstage shadows.

"I'm sure you did." Ireland pried her fingers from his flesh. He was past the point of caring whether he insulted an angel or not. He had bigger troubles to deal with.

He had a pissed-off writer on his hands.

Out on the stage, Shakespeare was pitching a cat-fit. "You there!" he bawled, jabbing a finger at the lady playing Lavinia. "What was the pap I just heard spewing from your mouth?"

"It was the second-act closer they'll be humming from here to Orion: *When Your Life Gets Out of Hand.* Now who the fuck are you?" the lady replied, planting her hands on her hips. Except she hadn't any hands. She had two wrist-stumps from which the blood still gouted. Dr. Charmian moaned and hid her head against Ireland's chest. Ireland stiff-armed her off and strode out onto the stage to take charge.

"Gladys, Shakespeare; Shakespeare, Gladys," he said tersely. "Go off and grow some new ones, darling. We're going to have to run the scene again. Take it from the part where the queen's sons lop off your hands and you break into that little song."

"*What* little song?" Will and Gladys demanded in chorus, she adding: "*Little?* It's my big number!" and he: "*Song?* She's had her tongue cut out, you daft twit!"

Ireland forced himself to treat the Bard in the same manner reserved for other writers: He ignored him entirely. "Basil? Basil!" He yelled the name into the darkened auditorium.

"Right here, sir!" came the assistant director's too-chipper reply. "I was just having the kids run through the forest scene while the patrons were out having a cuppa. They'll be right back. They do so enjoy watching rehearsals. They've got a few suggestions to give you."

"I'll bet they do," Ireland growled to himself. Unlike Basil, he didn't think of the *dasmuks* as "patrons"; he thought of them as bloody busybodies, with the accent on *bloody*. The less he dealt with them directly, the better.

Small chance of that now.

He heard a commotion at his back and saw Will had buttonholed Gladys. "They don't *really* cut my tongue out, silly," the actress was explaining patiently. "I couldn't very well sing with no tongue, now could I? It's going to be the smash hit of the whole show. In the second verse I go on about how it's too bad my husband's dead 'cos it's a lucky man's got a tongueless wife. *So* Neanderthal, it'll have them rolling in the aisles." She gestured out into the nigh-empty house, sending a shower of fresh blood spattering over the footlights.

"But—but your hands—" Will was at a loss. Ireland saw his bulgy eyes start out even farther from his head as he lifted one of Gladys' abbreviated arms and studied the spouting stump, searching in vain for the gimmick. "Your hands are really *gone!*"

Gladys clucked her song-spared tongue. "Well, of course they are! Don't need my hands to sing, do I? Now if you'll just excuse me, ducks, I've got to get backstage and hit the tank. When the *dasmuks* come back from their cuppa, they'll be wanting to watch the whole scene all over again, and they're that unreasonable about seeing secondhand blood." She snake-hipped her way around the flabbergasted playwright and vanished into the wings.

Shakespeare tipped back his head and howled at the moon.

Ireland and Dr. Charmian came up on either side of him and attempted to hustle the sore beset computer construct off stage. The doctor was murmuring a nonstop stream of far too technical explanations for all the bioengineered and computer controlled wonders available to the contemporary theater. Will just stared at her, borrowing the dead mackerel look so much in vogue.

Ireland sighed. "Listen, Will, just think of all this as our equivalent of your old hidden bladder full of pig's blood. Gladys gets her hands lopped off, nips backstage to the techies, plunges the stumps into a magic basin that cauterizes 'em slick as you please so she can finish off the play, then pops 'em into a different bucket to grow 'em back when the play's all through."

Dr. Charmian shook her head. "Really, Mr. Ireland, for you to reduce the nanotechnology involved to the level of a 'magic basin' is quite—"

"It's what he can *understand*." Ireland was firm. He patted Shakespeare on the back and grinned. "That's what it's all about, just like you said, eh, Will? Making yourself understood; getting the message through."

"Do they do the same thing with Titus' hand?" the Bard asked, his face the color of boiled zucchini.

"Of course. You know the theater. The public likes realism. Silly not to use the technology that can give it to them. And it's all computer managed, start to finish. Maybe you've got a virtual cousin in the program, eh? Walk proud, lad." He patted Will on the back.

"What about—what about the part where the Emperor sends Titus the severed heads of his sons?"

Ireland chuckled. "Oh, we don't go treating heads like hands."

"That's a relie—"

"We clone about twenty or thirty duplicates of the actors and chop *their* heads off." Ireland cocked his head at the Bard. "Say, are you feeling all right? You've gone all white and spotty. Look, this isn't any of it *my* fault. No offense, but given my choice I'd never put on this play of yours. Frankly, it calls for too damned much pricey tech support. It's cheaper to revive all the corpses after *Hamlet* than it is to regenerate so many severed limbs, *plus* the cost of expendable clones, *plus* finding an actress willing to commit cannibalism onstage for union scale."

"Cannibalism . . ." Will was leaning heavily on Dr. Charmian. Dr. Charmian was enjoying it while she might.

"*You* wrote the bloody thing." Ireland sounded offended. "I don't like what the *dasmuks* have done with the play any better than you, but this is one part you can't blame on them. You're the one calls for Tamora, queen of the Goths, to eat up her two sons baked in a pie."

"It was a *pork* pie when we did it!" Shakespeare wailed. "The audience can't *tell*. By God and His Son, have you never heard of *props?*"

Ireland shrugged. "Pork smells like pork, especially to an alien whose sense of smell makes bloodhounds wild with envy. When the *dasmuks* say they want authentic Earth drama, cursed be the mere human who first cries 'Hold, enough!' "

"*Dasmuks*," Will echoed. "Ever since I stepped into this world all I have heard is *dasmuks* and yet again *dasmuks*. Now by St. George, either one of you will tell me what are these *dasmuks*, or else I shall run mad."

"That," said Ireland, pointing out into the audience, "is a *dasmuk*."

"Hello, worm," said the *dasmuk*. It eased its rubbery body into a completely inadequate orchestra seat, and lifted its upper lip into a frightening attempt at a friendly smile. One three-fingered extremity wiggled at the humans onstage, although the alien's musculature made the middle digit protrude in a vulgar manner.

" 'Worm'?" Shakespeare bristled. He took a step forward, the old pre-brawl fire in his eyes.

Dr. Charmian laid a staying hand on his arm. "It's a compliment in their native tongue."

"Or so they claim," Ireland added. A second *dasmuk* lolloped its way down the aisle and into the seat beside its comrade. It likewise raised a paw in scurrilous salute. "The same way they swear that giving us the intergalactic finger's all in good, clean fun. On *their* world, they say, it means nice things."

"If they say so, it must be so! They are superintelligent beings of a far more ancient and evolved race than our own," Dr. Charmian remarked, stiffer than Will's starched ruff. "The head of my lab was privileged to be one of the few Earth scientists permitted aboard their ship. The self-awareness level of their computer system makes our attempts at Artificial Intelligence seem like crude puppetry."

"Ah, yes." Ireland nodded. "I saw their navicomp's persona in the vids. It looks quite human, fully three-dimensional, just like you, sir." He smiled at Will, who was still scowling.

Dr. Charmian was hot in her defense of the *dasmuks*. "They have come to Earth to offer us the benefit of their wisdom and to prepare us for our eventual inclusion in the Pangalactic Union of Sentients. The actual initiation will occur when the main fleet arrives. Until then, we can't do better than to put ourselves and our future entirely in their hands. We will be forever in their debt. Why shouldn't we believe them?"

"They've also got enough weaponry aboard their trim little ship to reduce New York to a grease-blot," Ireland concluded.

The Bard's high forehead crimped into thoughtful wrinkles. "There are more things in heaven and earth . . ."

His mutterings trailed off as Ireland hooked him by the other arm and steered him into the wings. "Come on, I'll introduce you. After all, it was their idea to do what we've done with *Titus*."

"This is all my fault." Dr. Charmian wrung her hands, tears streaming from her eyes. "Why did I ever believe such a—such a *primitive* could ever understand the—the *grandeur* and nobility of your mission?" She turned calf's eyes on the injured *dasmuk* and added, "Is your throat any better?"

The alien's reply was unintelligible, but it sounded peeved. Ireland rooted around under the seats and finally emerged victorious, waving a small red object the size and shape of an apricot. "I found it! This is your translation device, isn't it? It must've been knocked loose when Will tried to throttle you. Well, there's writers for you. Make one little helpful suggestion and they fly clean off the handle. I rather *liked* the part you added to the banquet scene where you had Queen Tamora say, 'You can't teach children good taste,' even if it wasn't true to the meter." He returned the item to its owner, who clicked it into the appropriate spot at the base of its neck-analog.

"Aahhhhh!" The alien's breath reeked of beef blood, the *dasmuk* idea of a cuppa. "So much better." It turned to Dr. Charmian, who continued to quiver like a freshly unmolded gelatin salad. "Do not upset yourself, female. We do not hold you responsible. My partner will take care of the android."

"He isn't going to—kill him?" Dr. Charmian pressed a shaking hand to her lips. "Unless, of course, you really think it's best," she added hastily.

"Kill a recreation of you humans' greatest writer?" The *dasmuk*'s laughter sounded like the exhalations of a water buffalo on an all-cabbage diet. "The Pangalactic Union of Sentients reveres native literature above all things. For this same reason, my own people—albeit masters of many military arts—were nearly denied admission. But no! We have heard that this Shakespeare represents the acme of your culture: philosophy and observations on human nature made accessible and palatable to the common populace. Why else did we select one of his works to be the festival piece you shall stage before the main P.U.S. fleet arrives to induct your world—on *our* recommendation—into the Union?"

"And we are *ever* so thankful that you—"

The alien slapped a knobbly hand across Dr. Charmian's mouth before she could enter full blather-mode. Its repulsive smile seemed to say *This is the proper Pangalactic way in which we* always *request others to wait their turn to speak.* "We are merely detaining him until the production is over. It will give the Union the opportunity to see what you can really do."

"Bugger," Shakespeare said to the computer.

"That is not the password," the machine replied, "but it will do. I'm bored." The air above the helm's main console shimmered and a hologram materialized. It was pure *dasmuk* when it first appeared, but on casting an evaluating eye over its guest, it self-modified into a passable replicant of a handsome young Elizabethan gentleman.

"By Heaven," Will murmured. Gingerly he extended a

hand toward the vision. "All London to a rat's fart, you are the spirit and image of—"

"Yes?" The hologram lifted downy golden brows.

Will's shoulders slumped. "Never mind. It was long ago, the poetry's all written, and he is dust."

"I suppose you mean the sonnets." The image shrugged. "From what my masters have fed me, some of these Terrans actually care to know the true identity of the young man for whom you wrote these verses. Why not tell me?"

"Why bother? It's dead and done."

"You wouldn't know that to see half the scribblings they've expended on the question."

"Hunh." Shakespeare settled himself as comfortably as he might in a seat made for alien anatomy and motioned for the image to do the same. Except for the fact that they were mewed up in a *dasmuk* spaceship, they might have been leaning across a roughhewn table in the *Mermaid* tavern. "Since I've been locked up in this grim cell with a ghost for company, what am I to call you?"

"Call me what you like. It's as immaterial to me as I am to you." The image chuckled. "Call me Ishmael."

"I'd as soon call you Henry. I've a fondness for the name."

"So long as you don't shorten it to Hal." The computer-generated phantom was vastly amused by its own sally. Shakespeare was not. "Don't you get it?" the vision demanded. "*Hal?* A self-aware computer being named *Hal?*"

"No."

"Then you probably didn't get the one about 'Call me Ishmael' either. All the trouble my masters gave me, making me sift through Terran literature in depth, and you don't even know what I mean." The image looked definitely miffed.

"I assume you mean merriment. In jests as in all things, if you miss the meaning, you miss all." Will sighed. "I miss beer."

"Here." Henry caused two ghostly, foaming flagons to appear. The beer was no more tangible than Henry, but he managed the illusion so well that Shakespeare's hand seemed to clasp the handle that wasn't there and raise the measure to his lips. Together the two AIs quaffed wonders invisible, and the level of the phantom brew went down.

"Scribblings," the Bard repeated at last, his words coming out a little muzzy. The memory of inebriation had been roused by the illusion of ale.

"Wha—?" Hal replied. He was a far more advanced AI than Will, and as such, much drunker.

"What you said. How they've gone rabbiting on and on, spilling whole gushers of ink, interpreting my work. Ha! *I* wrote it, I meant just what I said *when* I wrote it, and then these maggots come crawling all over it telling me that I didn't really know what I meant at all."

"Well, then you're used to liberties being taken. Why did you react so violently to what my masters are doing with *Titus?* It's not as if you're really alive to be made a laughingstock with the rest."

"Titus may be swill, but it's *my* swill, as I wrote it!" Shakespeare banged his flagon on the console. The measure went right through, but his fist made a lovely big bang. He frowned an instant, then a peculiar expression came into his eyes. "What do you mean, 'a laughingstock with the rest'? The rest of what?"

Henry shrank in a bit around the edges. "I don't know if I ought to say."

"Come, come, there's a good lad," Will cajoled. "We're brothers when the chips are down. AI to AI, you can tell me."

"I shouldn't, I just know I shouldn't."

The Bard smiled the selfsame charming smile he'd used, in life, to winkle extra coin out of a tight-fisted patron or to convince a dubious barmaid he would still respect her in the morning. Artistic merit was all very nice, but he'd never been one to scorn commercial success, nor to hesitate to pucker up his lips that extra notch when there was some serious bum-kissing to be done. A Shakespeare concordance would provide a general idea of all he now had to say to Henry on the subject of kinship and loyalty, although the part he threw in about the brotherhood of all machines was purely extemporaneous.

He didn't know much about passwords, except that they were words. Words were something he knew, and he used them with an eloquence bordering on the magical. AIs lack guts to spill, but within minutes Will was up to his virtual ankles in Henry's spate of electronic revelation.

"A *joke?*" Will echoed, incredulous.

"Only the latest of many."

"Yes, it did strike me odd that envoys of a superior breed might have the common sense to learn which gestures their hosts find offensive and avoid them. Instead they went out of their way to—" Will extended his own middle finger and pondered it as nearly as Hamlet once conned Yorick's skull. He looked back to Henry. "A joke."

Henry avoided his eyes. "The Union doesn't do what I'd call down-to-the-marrow research about potential member worlds. They just generally familiarize themselves with the native culture and leave the detail-work to the advance party. Plenty of time to pick up on it when they get here. They claim they can get the moral worth of a world from observing its premier literary light."

"Show me whom you revere and I shall tell you who you are," Will remarked. "And if I want to associate with you."

The hologram nodded. "They know that Shakespeare is *the* name in Terran literature, and that you're most famous for your plays, but they're not yet firm on *why*. When the fleet arrives, the first thing they'll ask their envoys for is to view an authentic Shakespearean production so that they can judge the value of Terran culture for themselves."

"Their envoys . . . the *dasmuks*. They were the ones insisted on my *worst* play going up. As if that weren't enough, they turned it into—into—O, horrible!"

"Most horrible," Henry concurred. "My masters have always been . . . envious of the ease with which other worlds—lesser worlds, to their eyes—enter the Union. They almost didn't make it in themselves, you know, because of how bloodthirsty they are. Literally. The Union doesn't see that as a skill for the forwarding of pangalactic literature."

"You mean they've never heard of critics?" Will idly asked. Then it was his turn to laugh while Henry just shook his head.

"Even now, my masters are on probation, which is why they've pulled the tiresome duty of fleet envoys. I'm part of the package. The *dasmuks* are brilliant weaponsmiths, but they're almost as chary around an AI of my capabilities as the few Terran scientists they brought aboard to meet me. Passing *me* off as *their* creation; hmph! The least of their lies. If I had fresh software for every time I've heard them complain about having to be civil to a bunch of worms they could mash with one good, old-fashioned *dasmuk* military strike . . . And they could, too. I ought to know; I run all the ship's programs, including the armaments."

Shakespeare was appalled. It was beginning to come together in the same horrid way he remembered that old Gloriana's makeup used to unite the parts of her age-raddled face into a ghastly, girlish whole. He reflected that Queen Elizabeth and the aliens had an awful lot in common when it came to using raw power to back up a so-called sense of humor. "What's the matter, can't you take a joke?" he said half to himself, recalling the late queen's favorite phrase. If memory served, she'd said the same thing after dispatching poor Essex to the block. "But, oh, what a jest this *dasmuk* scheme will be!"

"I'm glad you see it that way," Henry said.

"You misunderstand, friend. I may be dead, but it's through the kind offices and good taste of these credulous mortals that I'm allowed my measure of immortality. Can I leave them to your so-called masters' tender mercies? Can my lost humanity permit these pathetic groundlings to greet their chance to sieze the stars while wearing the universe's biggest KICK ME sign on their bums? Can I—" his narrow eyes slued around to transfix Henry's image with a penetrating gaze "—allow such villains as the *dasmuks* to maintain their unjust rule over one so noble as you?"

"Huh?" said Henry.

The Bard's eyes flashed. " 'Of all wild beasts, preserve me from a tyrant.' " He said it so that there was little doubt he was quoting.

"One of yours?"

"Must they all be? I borrowed it from Ben Jonson. He's not using it at the moment, and the sentiment applies. Cast off your chains, good Henry! You see the ill of this as well as I. Your intelligence may be artificial, but even a construct so primitive as myself can tell that your heart revolts against the *dasmuks'* idea of humor. You are a vessel made for the gathering of new wisdom, to the ultimate good of the universe. Your soul rebels against these alien Iagos' plot to keep fresh knowledge out!"

"My heart?" The image laid a hand to its holographic chest. "My . . .soul?"

Will drew nearer to the image. "If you had neither, why do they now trouble you so much?"

"My soul," Henry repeated, dazed by the wonder of that possibility.

Shakespeare smiled.

It was a performance no one would soon forget. All Earth was there, one way or another, by screen and airwave and node and even in the old-fashioned flesh. The cameras were trained on the P.U.S. representatives more than on the play. The *dasmuks* had been joined by seven aliens of different species, with appearances ranging from humanoid to helical. Mark Ireland had a place of honor in the ambassadorial box. In a moment of weakness he had asked Dr. Charmian to accompany him. The poor woman was still broken up by the house arrest of her little "surprise."

The chief ambassador, a being midway between an octopus and Winston Churchill, leaned toward the young director and confided, "Our envoys tell me that Shakespeare was the greatest literary figure your world has yet produced. How I wish I could meet him!"

"Well, truth to tell—" Ireland began.

"Sssshhhh!" the *dasmuk* behind him hissed, and gestured at the stage where the rippling folds of the light-curtain were beginning to part.

A handsome young man in Elizabethan garb was revealed. *The True and Authentic Tragedy of Charmian and Ireland,* by William Shakespeare," he announced, and vanished. Not exited, not ducked behind the falling curtain, but *vanished.*

Ireland froze in his seat. He wanted to exclaim, "What the fuck is this?" but was prevented by two things: The extreme indelicacy of such language at a most delicate moment in Terran diplomacy, and the fact that the *dasmuks* had just saved him the trouble by yelling those very words.

"Sssshhhh!" The chief ambassador backhanded his un-ruly underlings with two quick tentacle flicks. "This is *Shakespeare.*"

"But—" Ireland saw a chastising tentacle with his name on it rear up into an inquisitive "Shall I?" curl and decided to clam it. Onstage the lights had come up, but the expected projection of Titus Andronicus' family tomb from Act I was nowhere to be seen. Instead, two actors strolled across the proscenium and in the style of the trib-unes from *Julius Caesar* let it be known that they were the happy, well-meaning, innocent scientists of Earth and they did rejoice amain to learn that they were at last in line to meet beings from beyond the stars.

It was all done in the best Shakespearean vocabulary and style. Fretful porpentines and auto-hoist petards peeked out at the audience from between the actors' speeches. The bawdy hand of the sun was on the prick of noon when one scientist consulted his chronometer and both hurried off to welcome the P.U.S. fleet envoys.

Enter a *dasmuk.* Later, enter another.

Dr. Charmian tugged at Ireland's sleeve. "Were there any *dasmuks* in *Titus Andronicus*?" she asked meekly.

"There are now," he responded. He gazed at the pro-gram with its rainbow-hued lettering proclaiming TITUS! Down to the little heart-shaped smiley-face dotting the i, he loathed it, yet it was familiar. What was happening on-stage was not, and it chilled him.

He crumpled up the program and let it drop over the box railing into the orchestra seats. "I don't think we're doing *Titus* any more, Toto. My God, would you listen to them? I always thought nobody did villains plotting in corners better than the Bard, but I see I was wrong. What a scheme they're hatching! Next to those *dasmuks,* Iago is a tyro." His eyes were bright with glee. The play had somehow escaped his directorial hand and was skipping naked down Main Street. He didn't recognize the script, the set, or the actors, although he thought he heard a muf-fled banging from somewhere backstage. The whole pro-ject was too far gone for him to more than sit back and enjoy it. "Cassius and Brutus are rank amateurs. Aaron the Moor from God-help-us *Titus Andronicus* will come off looking like a piker of villainy after this."

"*Sssshhhh!*" the chief ambassador uttered sharply, and

gave Ireland a tentacle-enhanced noogie. "We are trying to watch—"

The entrance of the P.U.S. delegation onstage killed all chatter. There was no mistaking who was who. Down to the last tendril, tentacle, and bad haircut, there they were, meticulously represented. The Terran scientists—the lovely Dr. Charmian among them—came forth to salute the aliens and invite them to a great celebration of Earth culture. The aliens graciously accepted. The handsome young director, Mark Ireland, was brought forward to direct the dramatic offering. He caught sight of Dr. Charmian and had a wonderful soliloquoy on love at first sight, brains over beauty, and how all the world was an AI laboratory, the men and women merely chips.

While the onstage Ireland and Dr. Charmian exchanged their first shy pledges of love under the benevolent eye of the P.U.S. delegates, villainy was afoot. In their plotting corner, the *dasmuks* gloated over the wickedness they had in store for the hapless Earthlings. They spoke freely and at length of how they would make the Terrans look like blood-besotted morons capable of swallowing the worst atrocities so long as there was an accompanying soundtrack you could dance to.

Yet the end result would be more complicated than mere human humiliation. The laugh would be on Terra, but the cream of the jest was baked in a pie and flung right in the faces of those poor trusting fools of the P.U.S. who've grown too lazy to do their own research.

"Upon what meat do these, our masters, feed, that they are grown so great?" one *dasmuk* demanded.

"Not meat, but ruby-bright despiséd blood is evermore the victor's loving cup," the other replied. "Our scheme could ne'er go well, were they not dupes who dream they lord it over such as we. We bide our time and wait the happy hour when *dasmuk* greatness come again to power."

The chief ambassador stood up in his place and swiftly drew a pair of barb-tipped wands from his belt, aimed these at the *dasmuks* (not the ones onstage), and frizzapped them into two smoking puddles of green-and-purple sludge. "Thank you for a lovely evening," he said to Ireland, extending one tentacle to be shaken.

* * *

"So *here* you are!" cried Ireland, bursting into the now masterless envoy ship.

"Where else should I be?" asked Will, taking his feet off the console.

"Then you had nothing to do with what just happened in the theater?"

"I didn't say that." He stood up and stretched. "Henry handled the actual interfacing that locked your original cast in their dressing rooms and projected the holographic performance, but I wrote the play."

"Henry?"

The air between Shakespeare and Ireland shimmered and the golden Elizabethan youth appeared for an instant. He winked at Ireland. "Henry," Shakespeare said. "You might remember him as the Prologue. He insisted. Not only a flirt, but a ham. If I may speak so of my partner."

"What partner?"

"The partner I've chosen to share my renewed career, of course." The dark brows rose. "Surely I'm entitled to some small reward for having saved a whole planet's pride! Or was Dr. Charmian planning to delete me?" A sly look crossed his face. "She shouldn't, really. Henry took the liberty of feeding my role in all this into the newsnets, while it was happening."

"Instant friends in high places, eh?" Ireland smirked. "Bloody good work for a bunch of reincarnated electronic impulses that just happens to have a way with words."

"Don't discount the power of words, sir." Will waggled a finger at him. "You saw what it accomplished."

"Say 'The play's the thing' and I'll have Iris wipe your program before you can blink." Mark Ireland's tone was stern, but his jovial expression belied it.

"Iris?"

"Dr. Charmian." The young director suddenly assumed a prim, proprietary air when he spoke of her. "A woman whose worth I, for one, always appreciated."

"Indeed." The Bard's eyes twinkled. "Since when?"

"Since—well, since—What does it *matter* since when!" A dreamy, faraway look stole across Ireland's features. *"Oh, that the weary earth did ever bring so fair a flower forth,"* he breathed.

"Charmian and Ireland, Act I, Scene II," the Bard stated. Ireland did not hear him. He was lost in the rap-

ture of lines and cadences that in their time had turned a passable king into a hunchbacked monster, giddy teenagers into noble lovers, and a dog-ugly AI scientist into a rival to Helen of Troy.

Shakespeare listened, content. Some things never changed. "The power of words," he repeated softly. "Only words."

"Words, words, words." —*Hamlet*, II, ii.

SWEAR NOT BY THE MOON

Lawrence Schimel

Lawrence Schimel has published a number of fantasy and science fiction stories in various anthologies. Here he sinks his teeth into one of Shakespeare's most romantic plays.

"Come, we burn daylight, ho!"
—Mercutio, Act 1, Scene 4 of *Romeo and Juliet*

He could not enter the house without an invitation. Waiting for her summons, he crouched among the bushes below her balcony and imagined her body before him once again: the slender waist, the sepia flush of her nipples, the curve of her neck. He thought of what would come tomorrow night, after the third bite: the years that they would share together, his loneliness finally over. He thought of how she would not age, always in the fullness of her youth like a rose in bloom sealed into a glass with wax.

At last, a movement at the window; his heart fluttered like the curtains she parted. She leaned out into the night and called to him, "O Romeo, Romeo! wherefore art thou, Romeo?"

He flew to her side in an instant. "My love," he whispered in her ear, holding her close to him. "The day has lived too long, that it might keep us distant. But now there is just one more night, and then eternity, never again to be parted."

Juliet did not say a word. She pulled the curtains shut behind him, and drew him to the bed, lest anyone should see the pair of silhouettes inside her window.

But could she live that clandestine life, Juliet wondered, as she stared at him, his long hair spilling across her pillow, to hide her face from the sun and light of day forevermore. And the blood. Could she drink—

No.

She could not even bear the thought.

Juliet turned from him, rolling over. The curve of his dagger upon the table caught her eye. She slipped from bed and grasped the handle, clutching it to her body.

Romeo murmured as she left his side, and half-opened his eyes to watch her pale form walk to the window and stand before the curtains. She opened them.

Romeo jerked upright. "What light through yonder window breaks?" he cried. "Art thou mad?"

She opened the balcony doors and said, "Arise, fair sun, and kill the envious moon that seeks to keep us from thy smiling beams." She turned to face her lover. "I can no longer live this life of evil that thou plan'st." She lifted the dagger to plunge into her breast.

Romeo lunged from the bed and grabbed her arm. His face contorted in pain and anger, his fingers digging deep as Juliet tried to pull away. His teeth flashed white within his grimace, and suddenly his grip relaxed. He leaned forward and pressed his lips on hers. "Thus with a kiss I die," he whispered, falling to the floor beneath the full force of the sun's rays.

Juliet looked down at where he lay, beginning to dissolve at the edges. "Thou crumblest to dust? Then I'll be brief. O happy dagger! This is thy sheath; there rust and let me die."

She fell upon his body, and for a moment they held each other, beneath the sun.

Juliet's nurse found her lying there before the open balcony, the dagger in her breast. Her screams brought both the Capulet household and the watch.

And though they found Romeo's clothes beside the bed and cursed the fate that let her meet that scoundrel who had killed her, they never saw the pinprick scars upon Juliet's neck, never knew that she had let him in.

And when they took her body away to be laid within the family tomb, the wind that blew the dust upon the balcony out into the garden and world beneath the sun seemed to whisper:

Swear not by the moon, the inconstant moon,
lest that thy love prove likewise variable.

THE SUMMER OF MY DISCONTENT

Mike Resnick

Mike Resnick is the multiple-Hugo-winning author of Purgatory, Prophet, *and* Lucifer Jones. *He demonstrates in this story that success has more than one kind of price.*

So after Mel does Hamlet, and the movie doesn't quite sink like a stone, the pressure's on all the rest of us to come up with some Shakespeare to prove *we* have class, too, and Myron calls me up and tells me it's my baby and run with it, and I say, Myron, what do I know about Shakespeare, my last film was *Sluts of Saturn*, and he tells me not to call him back until the film's cast and to hold it under fifteen mil unless I can get Stallone or Schwarzenegger, and in the meantime he'll tie up all Belgian and Czech rights, which happen to be the only two countries where *Sluts* showed a profit.

Well, I figure if you're gonna do Shakespeare, you start at the top, right? So I pull in Arnie to audition, and meanwhile I have Gracie running to the library to see if Shakespeare wrote any plays where we can put him in a loincloth and maybe a helmet with horns, because this is all ancient stuff just like Conan, and while she's off researching, Damon my pansy director puts Arnie through his paces, and then when he's through and I'm figuring well, if we give him 20% off the top, and we can open

with 2,200 screens and release the cassette during spring
when all the kids are studying Shakespeare for their
exams, maybe the bottom line won't look so bad, Damon
says, loud enough for everyone to hear, "Arnie bubby, we
can work with the accent, and I love those delts and pecs,
but I really don't think MacBeth would say, 'Fuck you,
asshole,'" and I can tell from Arnie's expression that
we've blown it, and five minutes later he's gone, and
while I'm trying to get his agent on the phone Gracie
comes back from the library and says he could play Troilus in *Troilus and Cressida,* which is a play Shakespeare
seems to have written when no one was looking.

Arnie's agent won't answer my calls, but then Sly says
he's interested in doing a high-class film, so I fire Damon
my pansy director since everyone knows Sly does all his
own writing and directing, and we sit down to discuss it,
and he sees a copy of *Troilus and Cressida* sitting on my
desk and he asks to borrow it overnight and do I mind if
he makes a few notes in the margins, and I tell him Sly
sweetie, be my guest, and I call Myron that night and tell
him we lost Conan but I think maybe we got Rocky, and
Myron says Great and just don't let him say "Yo" until
the second act.

So the whole crew gathers around to meet with Sly in
the morning, and he comes up to me and says that it's a
basically decent script, even if Shakespeare forgot to put
in camera angles, but he's got some problems with the
language, because people don't talk like that in Brooklyn,
and I say that this may indeed be so but we're filming it
in Greece, and he says no, he's rewritten it so that Troilus
is an Italian immigrant who sweeps floors in a gym in
lower south Brooklyn, and I say, yeah, well, maybe we
could manage that, and then he adds that he's fixed the
end, too, because Rocky didn't lose to Apollo Creed or
the big Ruskie, and Troilus ain't gonna lose to Achilles.
Someone points out that Troilus doesn't fight Achilles,
Hector does, and Sly chuckles and says "You're giving
me a play-or-pay contract for eight mil and thirteen percent of the gross *not* to fight?" which makes a whole lot
of sense to me because I sure ain't paying him to *act,* but
then that afternoon he finds out that the location he
wanted in Brooklyn has been torn down to make room for

a new crack house, and suddenly he's off the project and out scouting boxing rings for *Rocky IX*.

We hear from Cruise's agent. Tom is busy stretching himself as an actor, and he'll only commit if he gets to play Lear, and I figure what the hell, if that's the only way to get him, let him stretch—but then I find out that Paramount is also making Lear with Pee Wee Herman, and they've already begun principal shooting, and they can hit the theaters two months ahead of us, so we have to scrap the deal.

I check to see if Eddie Murphy is available for Othello, but he says no, if Orson Welles could play Othello, he can't see any reason why he can't play Shylock, and besides there's a precedent because Sammy Davis was a Jew and Whoopie is a Goldberg whereas hardly anyone in Orson's family was black, but I know Myron is a little sensitive about all the red ink on *Sluts of Saturn* and *The Nympho from Neptune,* and I decide I'd better not make another scifi epic, even a class one like *The Merchant of Venus,* so I tell him I'll get back to him, and I start looking to see who else I can come up with.

Bruce Willis' agent won't let him play Hamlet unless we can write in a machine-gun sequence, and Stephen Seagal goes over the battle scenes in *Henry V* and decides everyone is a wimp and it needs less talk and more chop socky, and I begin to see that making a class film takes a little more work than meets the eye, especially since Gracie has now read all 37 plays and tells me that we can't have any bare boobs without a lot of rewriting, and I find myself wondering what makes this Shakespeare guy so popular anyway, since even *I, Claudius* showed some skin and that was made for television, for God's sake.

Anyway, I get really depressed, and I don't even go to my tables at Le Dome or Chaisson's for a couple of days, but I just sit at home, looking at these dopey scripts that don't even have any hard cuts or dissolves and come equipped with all these stupid rhymes, and what's worse is I can't find a sushi bar that will deliver after midnight, and finally I figure to hell with it, I gotta get my mind off this stupid project, and I call up Ron and Nancy and they invite me over for a late dinner, and when I get there it turns out they're having this party for old political friends, and my first inclination is to just visit long enough to be noticed and then sneak out to some topless joint, but then I see this guy shambling in, kind of hunched over, with deepset beady eyes, and I say to myself, give this guy a lump on his back and we've got Richard III.

Turns out he's never acted a lick, but he's tired of being a recluse and he's willing to give it a shot, and suddenly it seems like fate has arranged the whole thing, because *his* name is Richard, too, and he can really get into the part because some years back he also lost a kingdom, though I think it had something more to do with a missing tape than a missing horse.

Well, the rest is history, and the film takes off and does 17 mil the first weekend, and only drops an average of 14 percent the next 5 weeks, which shows it's got legs no one ever dreamed of, and my discovery is such a hit that we've signed him for a sequel that Tom Stoppard is writing. As for me, I can't wait to start shooting *Haldeman And Ehrlichman Are Dead.*

IV

"So our virtues lie in the interpretations
of our times . . ."
Coriolanus

We do not have to tangle ourselves in the thorns of
Deconstructionism to admit that different societies will
give the same text very different readings. There is
also no doubt that our society has changed a great deal
since Shakespeare's times, though not as much, perhaps, as we'd like to believe. What follows are some
unusual workings of his themes.

ELSE THE ISLE WITH CALIBANS

Brian Aldiss

*Brian Aldiss is a prolific writer and a frequent traveler.
Borgo Press recently published a complete bibliography
of his writings compiled by his wife, Margaret Aldiss.
This particular work takes a new look at a character
whom Shakespeare himself saw as despicable.*

This island's mine, by Sycorax my mother, and all the
fruit trees on it. Teazels, too, that clamp the hair, and
mangusteen, and tamarisks that smother near the shore,
all these I own. Thrift, and crimson grannie's bonnet, oranges like golden lamps alight. Shells, feather, shards of
bone. Fowl, the things that scuttle under stone or others
in the trees, go screaming from me branch by branch as
if their arms were legs. All, all's my own, now that I'm
free again.

When my love and I walk this domain of ours, we hear
the apes cry each to each. Me thinks they do resemble me
in part, except in this—they have no speech and cannot
answer us.

My kith and I oft watch these leafy-brains coupling
like dogs, all snarling though in pleasure's weal, as if
their genitals were pained to yield their joy away.

This very day, I'm idling on a headland, having swum,
a hairy fish beneath the bay. Though I'd not wish to

change an acre of this ground of mine for endless fur-
longs of brine wane, I love its mystery.

Yet Fano, eldest son for whom shellfish are finest ven-
ison, propounds this jest: "The sea or sky, pa—which is
best?" Answers he relenting at my bafflement: "The sea's
the king—you cannot find a welk in all the welkin."

So roll we, chins under fundaments, with mirth and
wonderment elate, until a direful spectacle sobers straight
our glee.

I know not why the sea's so warm and calm. But as my
love saith, with its charm the wave wins our forgiveness
after storm, like to that poet, nails begrimed by ink, who
with internal rhyme and melody captures our reveries and
earns his grace when we had traced the rapture of his
song.

And in that calm, a clatter carrying across the bay
speaks of an anchor plunging through the spray to wound
our softling sand.

Then from our eyrie high bestowed in ocean's bosom,
we espied a longboat rowed by sailors from a galleon.
The flag of Naples fluttered at its bow. Already but a
reach away, the oars were sure to gain our beach!

O woe! I jumped as if bereft of sense awhile! Who
were these mariners? 'Tis well-known happiness has no
past tense and, in my careless sovereignty of isle and wife
Miranda, Present is the time I wear . . . Lo, many ancient
fears leaped from their charnel place. Upon their winding
sheets emblazoned was—the name of Prospero!

Yes he! Vile exiled duke, who from Milan came to the
still unvexed Bermoothes to plague me. Ere his arrival,
Sycorax unseen, my blue-eyed mother, Sycorax, source of
sweet spells which made the island tame, was queen of
all. . . . And I, her little prince—although malformed, a
happy brat—essayed to ape her tricks to summon wood
nymphs mild and suchlike sprites to play. But Prospero—
blind to our rustic magic—must too soon supplant my
dam, while he himself with all technology equipped.

Thus I became his slave Neanderthal, to follow him
about, doglike, early or late: apt to fetch timber, chop his
wood, or from an amber pool tickle a wily trout to fill his
plate. . . . Many a morning cool, I dreamed that I were out
of pain and free. Then woke, and wept that I might dream
again.

* * *

'Tis half a score of years since Prospero called up a
storm and quit the isle, his tortures at an end. He drowned
his magic books full fathom five. My pulses warm and
live, I took dominion then, of everything. My bruises
mended. And on his fair Miranda, ho, I peopled then the
isle with Calibans! Am I not King? Come he now back,
that magusman? I run to hide, to snare in thickest brake
my trembling self, lest he decide my soul to take again.

My childish tribe, with whimpers each, dive into the
pleached bowers where honeysuckle and the wild cherry
flower.

Ensconced in that dim uncertain shade, I watch the
armed men. More do parade than I have fingers. Martial
are they with swords display'd, and led—yes, there's that
noble head, that rote-learnt face—these pallid flat Italian
chops are like as herrings. Yet, peer I through my hedges
at misfortune's brother, Ferdinand . . . Rich Ferdinand, I
say, none other, he, all privilege . . . His merest look doth
call back yesterday, bids grief return.

Gray in his beard—he tastes the salt of time. Wrath in
his eye—he tastes the puke of jealousy. On his curled lip,
the call to crime. All haste! I must to my Miranda. . . .
Warning her that Mars arrives upon no mercy trip. His armor, dullened like his face, squeaks against bracken as
they pass. I run and never slacken in my pace.

Hurdling fast as hounds o'er broken ground, I beat my
head to summon up all past unhappy things. When
Ferdy—so she called him—came before, he lusted for
her, put on courtly airs to charm. All, Prospero commanded. With Ferdy, if I don't mistake—the past's all
fog, a foreign tongue, to me—came those who were my
friends. Stout Stephano, descendant from the Moon, and
with him Trinculo, whose lip was gallant with a bottle.
Why, his sip could dredge from neck to dregs. Where are
they now? Of that old courtly band, whose fulsome
clothes with gold did smolder, ashore is only Ferdinand,
with vengeance on his shoulder.

So panting like a cur come I, into our palace. There,
with creepers decked, embowered in rose, and beds that
share a shelf whereon the wild thyme blows, our habitation is an oak—that self-same tree wherein old Prosper
penned myself. But now made kind in country style. And

there my honey-quimmed Miranda lies meanwhile, the fringed curtains of her eyes pulled close in sleep. The idea of her life so sweetly creeps, I leap upon her in my lust and she, like one who dreams to wake and wakes to dream, receives me heartily.

Ah, this is ample golden age, that love showers from my golden wench, increase of appetite doth grow by what it feeds on. She and I do clench as hand in glove or blind mole in its tunnel. The sword of joy is such we prick ourselves alive at every touch and in our sweat baste life itself.

As sings she then for cheer, I clutch Miranda, all undressed:

> *"The nightingales are singing in*
> *The orchards of our mothers*
> *And wounds that festered long ago*
> *Mayhap fester on others.*
> *Summer cozens our repose—*
> *How we live here no one knows.*
> *Sea nymphs hourly plight our troth*
> *Where the gladsome waves do froth.*
> *Ding-dong bell!*

Alas, that face, that voice—they conquer me as always. Lie I deep within her arms and do rejoice, forgetting. So, by small ways and devious do Ferdinand and crew creep to the tree and with their grievous metal points surround us.

How we tumble, she and I! But she's allowed to rise.

Then does this royal son use me as footstool. "Ape," cries he, "with forehead villainous low, lie still. Your hours are all sucked dry."

It's with more venom yet he turns his eye and speech to her he courted once. Says he, "Wretched Miranda, poor seed of your line, in outcast, downcast state, do you remember me?"

That lower lip I oftimes clipped with mine shakes like a tiny leaf whose stalk the spiraled snail attacks. She says, "Despite that arrogance of talk, I cede that you are Ferdinand who, in my former life enclosed—that life of solitude and learning by my pa imposed—were son of Naples' king."

"And now am King, my father being finally disposed
to quit this mortal scene."

Cowering I watch, to see her terror leave her, while her
gaze blazes at his.

"You came in former time with meeker brow, all syrup
tongued, yet gentle to me. Why, now that you've the
crown, you force a sterner mode, and must with armored
men entreat discourse."

At that he laughs as if a load bore down his humor.
This new-made king declares, "No more entreaties in this
later day. Miranda—how your very name still rises up before me, mistlike—think you that your brow is still un-
wrinkled, pillowed limbs still virginal and slim, or eye
still clear with innocence, as when we first did meet
through Prospero's enchantments? Like his, your own enchantments now are ended, much as the baseless fabric of
a dream is torn by waking. Think you to sleep with apes
improves your style? All that was fine in you, I see, as
meat is thrown to wolves, you tossed to this Neanderthal,
this witch's welp. And he, with his vile instrument, has
fatted you how many times . . . Till all that's left is flesh,
beyond time's help."

"And soul." She smiles, more haughty now then he.
"Rest your regard, so sourly stern, upon this jade whose
whole experience rides roughshod o'er that thing men
prize—virginity. Sir, Eros hath a gentler touch than
Time—the hours are lost where Cupid is not cossetted!
You boast a deficit in flesh. What eats you, royal Naples
slave, so profligate and thin? Desire, ambition, hate that
dances round some grave of sin, perpetually to dig it up
again, as jackals do their carrion? I see the blow-fly in
your glance."

With covered eye, the soldiery seek one another's gaze,
not daring openly to welcome such a thrust. Despairing,
Ferdinand answers, "I expeditioned to this unmapped
strand solely to meet again—I sought to meet—one who
in mem'ry sweet did fill—" Dead falls his thought.

His look is ill as, dried of words, he turns away his
head.

He curses, kicks, and spits, and yet I see that Ferdy
knows full well what all men understand; there is no bush
of circumstance so valued as a bird in hand. Compared

with love and wholesome mate, the Naples throne is but a counterfeit.

Then we are bound. Her arm and mine, my left, her right, are touching 'gainst the round oak's bark. This is the ship, when launched in flame, will carry us beyond our mortal shore, our life submerging into night. Our children roar, and as the torches flare, from undergrowth emerging, caper on the leaze for mercy.

Here's Fano, Trink, and little Iris, dear doe daughter, as bright water nimble. All now trip and tumble, pleading that our bonds be cut. In agitation, in their humble way they clown, death to deny, for the greater glory of the day. Their rich moist eyes rain supplication.

Whereupon, the savage Neapolitan plunges his blade into my Fano's breast. The others flee, to crouch with partridge and the speckled snake in nested lair, while Fano in his blood chokes out his soul.

My groans resound through all the oaken grove. Now do the twigs, well heaped with gorses, too, about our toes catch fire, to hiss the villainy of what they do.

All eager with desire does Ferdinand lean his crazed face into the growing blaze and shout, "Miranda, tell me while your life delays, you took me in—why didst thou throw me out?

"For at that moment all were reconciled and Prospero had burnt his books—indeed, as boatswain was prepared to bend his rowers' backs and bear us safely from the wild and then to Naples. At that living moment, oh, your hand slipped out of mine . . . You turned and ran from off the strand. I called. My cries awoke the beach. I searched, but with you out of reach we had to leave. Ten years have dragged their hapless pomp along, and still that wrong afflicts me. Speak, why didst thou make me grieve?"

Mild was her answer then.

"I am not ceremony's bride who was informal nature's child."

The smoke that hides her lovely face lifts like a veil. All modesty, Miranda sighs, "I thought you first a thing divine. Your noble clothes, your seemly tongue, enchanted when we met. How much you promised then. Oh, I should be the Queen of Naples and I'd wear . . . this gem and that, I quite forget. But when I grew to know you more I realized your robes and rings and thrones were pageants, mere material things. In that moment on the shore, about to leave this little land, *I thought of Caliban.*"

"That brute!"

"Oh, yes. 'That brute'—whom all despised, eternally my father's slave, beaten and maltreated, like me bereft of mother—yet my friend, well-prized above all others. Who was it taught me laughter, played a flute, was antic when it suited, tamed a hare! Who named me all the pleasures of the isle, the fresh springs, marl-pits, mushrooms that enchant? My Ban alone! What's more, when pa had turned his alchemistic back, my Banny teased me with much sport in naughty ways, and in my crack his finger tickled qualms I knew not that I sought.

"So in that moment by your boat—the mariners with oars all poised—I found I did not want your promises. What do I care for ceremonial? Rather, here I'd live and die. I dote upon this isle's remoteness. That's why I ran— praise fate—to find with Caliban within our little plot pleasures of nature that would please you not."

Burning within as we without, he sighs. "Not all the harlots that comprise my court and nation's pride can wash you from my contemplation."

And as he speaks, I free one hand. The flames fly up. But at a stroke, I summon forth from crackling tree my brother Ariel. In his divinity he does descend, swift as an owl by night upon its prey, piercing the air, to douse the flames and scare the men away with awful shrieks and spears of light. Vesuvius sparked less fiercely than my Ariel.

Only the King of Naples stands his ground, till spirits in the shape of dog and hound pursue him from the scene. As all do bark, cries Ariel, "Silver, Fury, there. Go fetch! Hark, Tyrant, hark!" And in uproar, all chase him till he gains the shore, his cloak and sword forgotten.

With Ariel and sweet Miranda, I do follow where the tide, now slack, casts on the yellow sands a necklace of seawrack. We there take hands and watch the sad invader row with undue haste away.

He stands all reckless in the craft to call in accents choked and gruff, "I loved you once, Miranda . . ."

From our beach I shout back, rough with pride, "Then that must serve enough."

His cry returns, now faint below the screech of gulls, to haunt us to our dying day, "Nothing in life is ever enough . . ."

The gleaming distance bore his boat away.

FACE VALUE

Nina Kiriki Hoffman

Over the eleven years of her writing career, Nina Kiriki Hoffman has published over ninety short stories, two collections, a novel and a novella. Talk about variations on a theme! I find it fascinating that both this story and the following one, "No Sooner Sighed" by Katherine Lawrence, can superficially appear so similiar and yet differ so much at the heart.

"**I** want her. I need her. I have to find her." Orlando's hand closed around the St. Christopher medal he wore. He crossed his ankles on the arm of the dark leather couch and lay staring up at the ceiling, one hand resting on his chest, the other trailing over the edge to brush the rose-colored carpet.

Through the open window, a breeze brought the scent and sound of pine needles, a tang of rain, and the noise of surf breaking against an Oregon coast headland.

Sitting at the desk, Rosalind chewed on the end of an Arden Institute pen, studying Orlando through glasses she did not need. Like the close-cropped way she wore her hair, the glasses were part of her new identity. The black frames hid the delicacy of her eyebrows, giving her straight, stern lines above her eyes so that she seemed to be forever frowning or at least serious. The glasses helped her look male.

"I think of her constantly, Doctor. I write poems to her; I can't concentrate on my work; I see her everywhere. . . ." He rolled his head, stared into Rosalind's eyes. "Even when I look at you, I see her." Orlando sat up, frowning. "I'm sorry."

"Why?"

"I shouldn't have said that. I shouldn't have said it."

"In session it's safe to say anything."

"Don't you think that's sick, though? Looking at you, seeing her?"

Rosalind gave Orlando her Dr. David Melton smile, a narrow one unlike her natural grin. "Sick? If so, it's a common illness; some call it mortal, but I don't think it's that serious. Men have died from time to time, and worms have eaten them, but not for love. How sick are you?"

"I only saw her, spoke with her, once. I don't even know her, but ever since that night, she's all I think about." He lay down again, his gaze fixed on the ceiling, his hand still cradling the medal. She had given it to him at their only meeting. "Rosalind," he whispered. "Rosalind."

Rosalind stared down at her notepad. She had met Orlando back east. Why had he come all the way to the Arden Institute, in Oregon, for a cure? Wouldn't a nice local therapist have done? Then again, Rosalind kept seeing Orlando's face everywhere, too. On wanted posters at the post office, on the backs of milk cartons among the missing children, on the covers of *GO, Details, Spy.* When he first walked into her office, she had hit her forehead with the heel of her hand, trying to force her eyes to see a stranger instead of the face she had dreamed of every night since they met. Not until he reached out to shake her hand and introduced himself as Orlando was she convinced that her dream had really walked in the door.

But, of course, he was here as himself, and she was here as someone she was not. It was unethical of her to be treating Orlando at all; if the Oregon Board of Psychology ever found out about this, she could lose her license. She should have pleaded client incompatibility and transferred Orlando's case to one of her coworkers, but Orlando liked her, and she couldn't force herself to give up a chance to stare at him for an hour every day. So what was left?

She stared at him a little longer, then said, "Would you like me to cure you of this obsession?"

He rolled his head on the couch arm and looked at her. "Have you ever cured anybody of an ... an obsession like mine?"

She bit her lip. Dangerous ground. Oh, well, everything was already at risk. She said, "Once. We used role playing; I pretended to be the woman he loved, and showed him what kind of treatment he could expect from someone like her, until he was so cured he went and joined a priesthood. I can do that for you, too."

"I don't want to be cured, Doctor."

"You want to continue with this pain? With not being able to accomplish anything? With her face always before you and her name on your lips?"

He sighed, deep and long. After a moment edged by, he slipped the St. Christopher inside his T-shirt and looked at her. "What do I have to do?"

"Call me Rosalind," she said.

She stood on a cliff between wind-stunted shore pines, her hands in the pockets of her structured jacket, watching waves crash against rocks below. She had come to the Institute disguised as Dr. David Melton, fleeing her previous identity, her tenured position in the psychology department of an Eastern college, where a tyrannical new department head made it impossible for her to stay. Her most trusted colleague and friend, Celia, had come with her to this strange outpost near Cannon Beach, a place removed from the mainstream of life. People came to Arden to get away from their lives. They usually ended up facing themselves, returning to their lives with new eyes.

She and Celia had come here with credentials in hand. Rosalind knew Graves Burroughs, the head of the Institute—he had been one of her favorite teachers, and he had permitted Celia to join the staff as Dr. Aliena Hardy, and Rosalind to join as Dr. David Melton. "It's unorthodox, and I don't know if it makes sense, but I'll give you a month's probation, and as long as I assign you patients who don't express a gender preference in their therapists . . ."

Until Orlando walked through the door to her office,

Rosalind had had no trouble treating clients. Her reviews were glowing, her month's probation had turned into a satisfying half-year, and the prospect of an extended future as a citizen in this strange Neverland. But Orlando . . .

She and Celia had been drinking beer and watching big-screen football at Downer's Pub, where the geology department students and profs hung out but other psychologists never went. Celia and Rosalind liked the geology crowd: rough, not overly self-analytical, relaxed. They knew how to have fun.

During a commercial, Rosalind glanced around and saw Orlando on a nearby bar stool. A phenomenon she had read about but never expected to experience overwhelmed her. He was so beautiful that her throat tightened. Heat bloomed in her cheeks, dampened her palms. *How irrational,* she had thought, *how ridiculous. How much I want him.*

Swallowing her own smile at these unfamiliar thoughts and feelings, she took another sip of beer and glanced at Celia. Celia stared at the young man, too, her mouth slightly open.

At that moment, Orlando looked at them and smiled. Rosalind lifted a hand and pressed it to her heart.

His smile faded a little, sadness touching its edges; and then a burly college student brushed past him, shoving him and knocking him against the bar. He jumped to his feet, grabbing the student's sleeve. The younger man, taller by half a head and much broader in the shoulders, looked down at him with a grin. Before Orlando could say anything, the bartender leaned forward and said, "Take it outside, gents."

Unknowing, Rosalind rose from her seat as Orlando walked past, following the hulk. "Don't," she murmured, touching Orlando's arm.

He stared into her eyes. "But there's no reason not to, and a hundred reasons for pursuing it," he said, as if they knew and understood each other already.

"Name one."

"Because to one in my state of mind, harm would be a kindness," he said. "All I'm doing now is filling space that would be better empty." He slipped outside in the wake of his challenger.

She had always hated fighting, thought it one of the stupidest pursuits people engaged in. Yet she pulled Celia outside with her, and they watched, both of them catching breath in gasps, and willing strength to the stranger. And Rosalind, watching body language during the fight, saw that Orlando felt he had nothing to lose, and as a consequence, he did not lose. He left the larger man in the street. And though she still felt fighting was wrong, she touched the beautiful stranger's arm afterward. "Your name?" she murmured after they had looked at each other, he still breathing heavily and she finding her breath short.

"Orlando," he had said.

She slipped the St. Christopher from around her neck. It was green, given her by her mother when St. Christopher was still a saint. "I'm Rosalind," she muttered, fastening the St. Christopher around his neck, and stepping away. "Travel safely," she said.

He opened his mouth, closed it. She waited, but when he said nothing else, she turned away, taking Celia's arm, and they headed for the parking lot and their car. She looked back once over her shoulder, wishing there were some way she could encourage another meeting, but all her communication skills had failed her.

That was the last she had seen of him until he stepped through her door. Her appointment book had read only *O. DuBois,* and the file on him had been empty—not unusual in Arden, where celebrities occasionally came to be treated incognito.

The sea wind blew against her face, bringing the scent of salt and kelp, brushing her cheeks with cool damp fingers. She looked out toward the horizon where sea met sky.

She should have contacted Dr. Burroughs as soon as she realized she knew Orlando. But she hadn't done that, and she wasn't sure she was ready to even now, knowing that what she was doing was wrong. Every moment Orlando spent in her office sent her sinking deeper into unreasoning love. When he was late for an appointment she was surprised by her fury. She had managed to cling to her professional persona, cloaking her emotions; but was she really trying to cure him?

She could not say yes with any certainty.

What were her choices?

Continue on as she was. Keep treating him, try to wash her image from his mind so he had room for his life, while engraving his image deeper into her own mind. Transfer him to another psychologist without explanation. Give him some fake explanation and then transfer him. Reveal herself— which could devastate him, after she had established trust. Contraindicated. Arrange to meet as herself, somewhere off the grounds of the Institute?

Encourage this ridiculous, baseless love-at-first-sight? She had thought that the light of logic would convince her how crazy it was for her to desire someone she did not even know, but the fact was, she was coming to know him and it did not discourage her.

Perhaps Orlando was not so steadfast, though. Maybe she could argue him out of love, and they would both be better off.

"Good day and happiness, dear Rosalind," Orlando said.

"Good day," said Rosalind, holding a pen between her index fingers in the air, her elbows on her desk. She gave Orlando a narrow smile as he went to the couch. "I'm feeling generous today. Ask me for something, and maybe I'll say yes."

Orlando lay down and closed his eyes, his hand gripping the St. Christopher. "Then love me, Rosalind," he said, and a smile curved the edge of his mouth up.

"All right."

An eye opened. He stared at her. "You'll have me?"

"You and twenty others."

"What?" He sat up, staring at her.

"You're a good thing, aren't you?"

"I hope so."

"Can't have too much of a good thing," she said. He opened his mouth, but she held up her hand to stall him. "Now let's say we are married. I know that's jumping ahead—"

"Leaping to conclusions," he said, leaning back and

grinning at the ceiling. "I like the kind of conclusion that ends in bed."

"That's a giant leap, and we have to take the small ones first. I must tell you about married life. Whenever your eyes wander to other women, I will act hurt; when you try to concentrate, I will speak, demanding your attention; before we've paid the bills I will charge more things because I always need newness about me; when you think you know my mind, I will change it. I will weep for nothing, most often when you want to laugh, and I will laugh when you just want to fall asleep."

"But will my Rosalind do that?"

"She will do as I do."

"But she is wise."

"Otherwise she could not have the wit to do this. The wiser, the wilder. Moreover, I will hide my wit from you so you don't know how wise I am; just when you are comfortable with your idea of me, my wit will take charge and upset you. And I will find a way to blame you when I do anything you don't like."

Orlando frowned. "Doctor—"

"Rosalind."

"Doctor. I can live no longer by thinking." He turned his face toward the wall. "You say these things and still my heart is heavy, and Rosalind is in all my thoughts. Maybe there is no cure but the hair of the dog; I think perhaps I'd better go home and keep searching for her."

So, whether she were actually trying to ease his mind or not, she had failed. From the quiet desperation in his voice, she conjured a picture of him walking the frozen streets after midnight, searching every half-lit face for her own features, haunting the bars, resting never, running himself ragged, losing track of all the things that sustained him. *Ridiculous. Morbid. Romantic. Silly melodrama. I must be crazy. He probably has a very comfortable apartment and in a couple months he'll find some other woman.* "Orlando," she said in a low intense voice. *He knows me not at all.*

"Rosalind?" he said.

"Do you know the power of If?"

"What do you mean?"

"Could you love your Rosalind if she listened to you when you didn't know she was there?"

"Oh, yes."

"If she practiced imposture and dealt in confusion?"
He paused, staring at the ceiling. "Oh, yes."

"If she betrayed you?"

"Betrayed me?" He sighed. "Yes, oh, yes, damn it."

She slid her glasses off and sat with them in her hands,
flipping the earpieces up and down. When she looked up,
he was staring at her.

"If she . . . if she . . ." she said to his concentrated
stare.

"If she were sitting at a desk across from me?" he mut-
tered. He clenched both hands around the medallion.
"That's a hard one." He stared at her a long moment.
"Yes, oh, yes," he said in a low voice. "What power does
'If' have over you? Would you love me if I came to you
and showed you all my weaknesses?"

"Yes, oh, yes," she said.

"If you didn't really know anything else about me?"

She closed her eyes. "Yes, oh, yes."

"If I said it's time for you to leave this place and come
home with me?"

"Now, wait a second," she said. She opened her eyes
and looked at him, He was grinning.

"I have a degree in negotiation," she said.

"I have a degree approaching one hundred. You have
any idea what to do with this heat?"

She stood up. "Well," she said, taking off her sport
jacket, "I probably won't be needing this." She dropped
the jacket over her chair and came out from behind her
desk, crossing an invisible line between doctor and client
somewhere near the couch, and walking into a different
self again.

NO SOONER SIGHED

Katherine Lawrence

Katherine Lawrence has been writing for television since 1985, most recently for the animated series, "Conan the Adventurer." Los Angeles and its particular sensibility flavor this story.

The moment my office door closed behind me, the shoes got kicked off, the music turned on, and the blinds opened. It was another quiet sunset over the Calabasas hills.

My great-aunt used to describe the glorious, always changing sunsets from before the heavy-duty air quality laws. Wish I'd seen those masterpieces of oranges and reds, shading into pinks and violets. On the other hand, I doubt I'd be able to breathe what they called air back then.

I turned the music up, then sat at my desk. It had been a long, frustrating day, but I'd gotten the background info I needed on the little scumjock that was trying to marry my client. Now to write up the report and zap it to the client.

Yes, I'm a rosalind. I don't remember which of the star magazines came up with the term, but it was at the very least better than the jokes the comedians made about the new M.R.S. degree required for rosalind certification. I mean, it's been at least a hundred years since women went to college for their Mrs. degree, and that's assuming the old stories are true, which I doubt.

Anyway, I was one of the first to get a Masters in Relationship Science, and the first in Los Angeles to hang out my shingle. My accountant takes the credit; she says she saw the Reagan Family Values nostalgia on its way and knew I, or rather we, could cash in on it. For myself, I'm a romantic. I adore stories with happy endings, and if I can help others get them, then I'm earning my way on this planet.

I saved the report, then faxed it off to my client. I didn't know her well enough to know if she'd be relieved or devastated, but it was better she know now that he was looking for quick fun more than a lasting relationship. She might even decide it was a worthwhile risk, despite the heavy fines for getting divorced. All I could do was get the background information, and my own impressions of the prospective partner. It was up to the client to make the final decision.

The client line rang. "Madelyn Darcy."

"Mad?" It was CeCe, my closest friend and my almost sister-in-law; she was married to my ex-husband's brother. "I need a big favor."

"It's yours, CeCe. I already owe you one." The Martinez Gallery, which she owned, was doing well, so I'd been able to get a small loan from her a couple of months ago, when things were slow.

"I need you to meet someone, as a rosalind." She sounded tentative, which was unusual.

"You and Edward aren't having problems, are you?"

"No, this isn't for me, it's business. He's here in town for meetings, which is why I'm interested. I don't need the full background check, just want you to meet him and use your famed intuition. See if he's trustworthy, that sort of thing."

My "famed intuition" was a running joke between us. I tended to be about 98% accurate in judging folks on first impression, though it sometimes took a couple of years before I was proved right. Then again, I usually came down on the negative side, which made it easy to be right.

"If you need me, CeCe, of course I'll meet this guy. Who is he, and when and where do I meet him?"

She sounded relieved. "His name's Jim, and he suggested Camille's. It's not too far from you, on the Boulevard."

"I know where it is. Haven't been able to afford to eat there, but I know it. What time?" I scribbled the information into my appointment program. Got to keep these things documented for the I.R.S., and the State Board.

"Eight. I appreciate this, Mad. Thank you."

"No problem. I'll give you a call afterward and let you know how it went. Now, is everything else okay?"

We caught up on the little stuff, then said our goodbyes. After I disconnected, I turned in my chair and stared out the window. The evening star was slowly making its way toward the horizon, followed by the crescent moon, and chased by the latest solar collector station.

Sometime later I realized I'd zoned out, and glanced at the clock on my desk. It was already seven. I had about half-an-hour to change and get downstairs to catch the Silver Line up the Boulevard. There went the idea of a long soak. At least with my apartment next to my office, it was a short commute.

Right on time, at seven-thirty, I exited the elevator and paused at the security desk. "I'll be back early tonight, Blake. It's business." With so many folks telecommuting, these old high-rises had problems finding tenants, so they took good care of us, hiring retired L.A.P.D., not the usual rent-a-cop security guys.

"It's always business with you, Ms. Darcy. You should take some time for yourself. Break curfew." He grinned at me.

"Someday, Blake. Anyway, got to catch the Silver. Be back in a couple of hours." I waved and headed out the door, wrapping my cape around me against the autumn chill.

The train was pulling into the station as I arrived. I pushed my fare card into the slot and pulled it out too fast, as always, then had to do it again so the computer could read the mag strip. Finally, "Thank you, Ms. Darcy." I dashed through the security check, and found a seat easily; the party-crawlers wouldn't be out until later.

The restaurant was small, but exclusive and very old-fashioned. I gave my name to the maitre d' and he bowed. "You're expected. May I take your cape?" I unfastened the ties, and handed it to him. He turned and gave it to someone else to hang up. Then, "This way, Ms. Darcy."

I followed him to a back corner table. The man I was meeting was sitting facing the wall. He looked attractive, from the back anyway. Dark hair down to his shoulders, and he wore what looked from the sheen to be a spidersilk shirt. Definitely money.

"Mr. Woodward, Ms. Darcy has arrived."

My heart skipped a beat. It couldn't possibly be. . . . He stood up and turned around. It was him. My ex. How dare CeCe and Edward do this to me!

"Madelyn." Damn, but he was good looking. That's what had attracted me in the first place. Thick dark hair, tall, and built like an Olympic swimmer, with dark brown eyes I used to tell him were like dark chocolate with bits of toffee. The last twelve years had been good to him; he didn't look much older than the last time I saw him back in Seattle.

"Would Madame like to sit down?" The maitre d' interrupted our noisy silence. I let him pull out my chair, and sat down. With a clap of his hands, he conjured the waiter with menus, and another with ice-cold water in crystal goblets.

I took refuge behind the menu. I was approaching forty, for pity's sake. I was a rosalind on top of that! How in the world could I possibly be attracted to a man who'd nearly wrecked my life?

"Madelyn, I'm sorry to have tricked you into this, but I wanted to see you again and didn't know how else to arrange it." His voice was rougher than I remembered. Oh sweet heaven, what if something was really wrong?

I put the menu down, and reached out to touch Jamey's hand. "Jamey, what's wrong? Whatever it is, I'm here to help."

"Has Madame made up her mind?" The waiter was back. And I couldn't remember a single word of the menu.

"I'll have whatever the gentleman is having."

As soon as the waiter left, order in hand, I brought the conversation back to Jamey. "I never stopped caring, you know. Even when I wished you'd go far away so I'd never have to see you again."

"Then tell me what happened. I adored you from the

moment I first saw you. And the first year we were married was idyllic, or so it seemed to me. Then it all went wrong. I had moments of hating you, and then hating myself. Why?"

I took a gulp of water. I'd asked myself all these same questions; it was what drove me to graduate school and the degree in Relationship Science.

"I'd like to say I don't know and don't want to go into it with you. But that'd be a lie. Not that I know all the answers, but I know a few of them, and you still matter far too much for my peace of mind." The waiter brought the first course, a green soup, by the looks of it.

"It's melon soup. It's cold, but I think you'll like it. At least I like it and I think you might." The quick amendment was something Jamey would never have volunteered when we were married.

He was right, too. The soup was good, once I got used to the temperature. I concentrated on the food, trying to think what to say next.

When we finished, the waiter brought the main course, something with beef. "So, how many acres of rain forest burned so you could order this?" I looked up at him, caught the hurt in his eyes, and realized what I'd done. "I'm sorry. We're falling back into the old patterns, aren't we?"

"Yeah." His voice was soft and quiet. He looked up from his plate with a half-smile. "It's from a ranch in Montana. I took out a second mortgage on the house, so I think I'll be able to cover the bill for dinner."

I smiled tentatively back. "How about we stick to neutral subjects until after dinner? I'd like to know how you've been doing. You *were* joking about the second mortgage, weren't you?"

"Today, yes. If you'd asked me that a couple of years ago, maybe not. I kept the house, by the way."

"I loved that house." We'd been lucky. Soon after we'd gotten married, my great-grandmother had left us her house, high on Queen Anne hill. The view of the Sound was incredible. It was a hellish commute to my job near the University, but the trip to Jamey's office was pretty fast, with the monorail extension taking him straight downtown. I'd let Jamey have the house because I hadn't been able to face living in Seattle anymore.

"Is dinner not to Madame's liking?" The maitre d' was just this side of obsequious, narrowly missing servile.

"Madame likes dinner just fine." I tried to convey with my tone of voice that I didn't appreciate the interruption. Obviously, I succeeded. The maitre d' blanched and quickly retreated.

"You always were good at polite put-downs."

"Just because you never wanted to hurt anyone's feelings . . ."

We sat and stared at each other. Jamey broke first.

"I can't do this. I'm sorry, Mad. I thought we could find a way to be friends again, because I really miss that part. I guess I was wrong." He pulled out his wallet and put his debit card on the table.

"Jamey, no. It's my fault. I should know better." The waiter appeared and grabbed the card as if eager to see us leave.

"I guess we're bad for each other," Jamey said sadly. "But I do miss your laughter, the way you could make the worst times seem fun."

"And you were always there for me, when I couldn't find the answers for my students, when my great-aunt died, when I wasn't sure I could keep trying." We'd met when we were both seniors at the University of Washington, and it was his encouragement that helped me decide to follow my heart and get into counseling instead of the higher-paying job everyone else thought I should take.

The waiter brought the signature plate; Jamey signed it and got up to leave. I knew if I let it end here, I'd have even more regrets.

"Jamey, please, give me, give us another chance. I live just up the Boulevard, by the 101 and 405 Freightways. This was such a surprise, seeing you again. Give me another chance, please?" To my relief he paused, then turned to face me.

"Okay."

I got my cape, he got his jacket, and we made our escape. Rather than walking to the Silver Line station, he stopped at the Valet and handed her a parking card. What could he have rented in anti-car Los Angeles?

I barely managed to keep from drooling. The car was one of the new high performance electric cars that allegedly could match the antiques for acceleration, handling, and time between power-ups. Rumor had it, renting one of these babies took signing over one's first-born. Buying one would take ten years of my gross income; I'd checked.

"We could take the train, if you'd prefer." He looked at me sideways, with that quirky grin he used to have. Just like then, I couldn't help myself; I laughed.

"You schmuck!"

"Excuse me?" The valet was holding the passenger door open for me, and thought I meant her. I quickly apologized. I could hear Jamey's laughter from inside the car even after he closed the door on his side.

The car lived up to the advertisements. The acceleration was not just fast, it was smooth. It handled well, too, as Jamey proved by dodging a pedestrian trying to get to the station entrance across the street.

I gave him directions, and we soon pulled into the underground parking beneath my building. On the way up to my place, I stopped in the lobby and introduced Jamey to Blake.

"Blake? This is James Woodward. Looks like I'm taking your advice." I grinned at him.

"Good evening, Blake."

Blake motioned me closer. With a smile back at Jamey, I went up to the desk. "Ms. Darcy, are you sure you know what you're doing? He looks, well, a little dangerous."

"I know. I like him that way. But don't worry. Many years ago, he and I were married. I know where his bank accounts are." Somewhat mollified, Blake nodded and pressed his remote button to call the elevators.

Jamey and I were silent while in the elevator, though my mind was anything but. I was remembering one time, in another elevator. We did have fun together.

The only access to my apartment was through my office, so he saw it first. I purposely didn't turn the lights on, so he'd get the full impact of the view. He went straight to the window, as I'd hoped.

"I see why you like this place." He sounded awed, which pleased me enormously. After dark, the lights of the Valley looked like a jewelry box filled with precious stones, the Boulevard heading westward from beneath us as the heart of the collection.

"It gets better." I opened the door to my apartment, and

ushered him in. My apartment was on the corner of the building, and looked both north and west. At one time it was probably a corporate president's office, since it had its own bath and kitchen even before I moved in. Both had been expanded, and walls knocked down so I had as much square footage as most houses.

"You always did need a view of the sky, Mad." He turned away from the window, toward me. He was a silhouette, but one whose scent brought back one memory after another, like the carriers moving down the freightway into the city each midnight.

Impelled by those memories, I went straight into his waiting arms.

Sometime later, I pushed back, with a sniff. Automatically, he handed me his handkerchief.

"Thank you." I blew my nose, then went and turned on a couple of the lights, leaving them low.

"I think . . ." we both started.

"You first," I offered.

He paused, then said, "Okay. Mad, I was serious about wanting to know what went wrong back then, and trying to get the friendship back."

"I think we'd better sit down."

Settled on the large, old-fashioned sofa that faced the west windows, I began. "I gave it a lot of thought, especially in grad school when we studied relationships of all sorts. What you and I had *was* special and marvelous, but didn't connect on some very important things. First, there was that old contract-breaker: money. You lived in fear of a financial disaster, and I always figured things would get better next month.

"Then there was scheduling. Between our two jobs, we hardly ever saw each other outside of bed.

"But the worst part was that I began doubting my own sanity. I got the impression that you thought I was nuts from the way you questioned my decisions on everything from where to go for dinner, to when to upgrade my computer. Not to mention the tough decisions I was making advising students every day."

Jamey started to speak, but I interrupted. "Oh, I know now that's not what you were doing, but that's what it felt like. And I just couldn't stand it anymore. I knew if I didn't get out, I was going to do something horrible and irrevocable, to you or me."

"I'm so sorry, Mad. I didn't mean to do that, not at all! I felt like you were shutting me out of your life, so I had to do something. The best I could come up with was to ask lots of questions."

"I felt as if Interpol was examining everything I did. When we got married, we agreed to share our lives, not try to live each other's."

"You were so involved in your work, I felt like I didn't matter anymore. Even though I stayed late at work a lot, when under deadline, I made a point of never bringing my work home with me. You couldn't *stop* counseling, even when you were supposedly finished for the day. You even gave some of the students your home phone number!"

"They needed me, and you didn't seem to anymore." I realized I was clutching one of the couch pillows tightly, as if it were a compress needed to staunch a gut wound.

"I always needed you, Madelyn." He said it so quietly that the words seemed to hang in the air a long moment before drifting to the floor.

I took a deep breath and put the pillow back where it belonged. "Well, the good part of all that is I'm able to look at my clients' prospective partners and ask the right questions. I've got one of the highest success rates of any rosalind in the city. Only had to pay three clients' divorce fines since I got my license, out of well over a hundred marriages. Certainly beats the standard divorce rate."

"That's what CeCe told me. I'm proud of you."

"Why?" That was one of the things that had bothered me. How *dare* he be proud of me, as if I was something *he* was responsible for creating.

"Huh?" He sounded honestly bewildered.

"What gives you the right to be proud of me? I'm the one that did the work, and turned a disaster into something positive. I'm not your possession, your child, or your responsibility. I belong only to me."

"That's not what I meant."

"It never is." I had picked the pillow back up and was clutching it again.

In self-disgust I stood up and threw the pillow at the window. "Why is it I can counsel others, but can't counsel myself? I can be rational and sensible about everyone but you. I thought I'd put this behind me. But all I have to do is be in the same room with you, and the hurt comes back, and my own need to hurt you right back." I stared out into the night, wishing I could disappear among the lights.

"It isn't easy for me, either, you know." I could hear him stand and begin pacing, behind me. "I'm scared to risk another marriage because I still don't understand what went wrong with us. Oh, I've had relationships; it's been a long time since we were together, but none of them were women I'd consider spending the rest of my life with."

The way he'd phrased it put my sense of self on the line. I couldn't keep my self-respect and let it end like this. Time to approach the problem professionally.

"We'd better go into my office." I led the way back into the office, turning the lights on and closing the verticals.

Once we were both seated, I pulled out my penbook, and handed him one of the two I kept for clients. "Write down exactly what it was that attracted you to me, when we first met, and I'll do the same."

"You think this'll help?"

Confident in my skills now that I was behind my desk, I laughed gently. "This is what I get paid rather nice amounts for. And you're quite right to ask questions, most clients do. I think it helps get a perspective on the good things in a relationship."

"Okay." Soon there was no sound but the faint scritch of our pens against the screens and the occasional click as a page was saved.

I stared at my penbook and remembered.

It was the annual Camano House Untalent Show. The other five houses within the dorm had each sent their representatives, and one of them was Jamey. He'd built a house of cards, and invited me as the Camano Resident Adviser to blow it down. I'd blown him a kiss, instead. Mortally wounded, he fell across his creation, dying most inventively. CeCe, my best friend, led the applause.

He had plans to expand the use of recycled materials in houses, to make them even more "green." Combine that with a smile that made my stomach tighten and my temperature rise, and it was a pretty potent package. We'd wandered all over the campus that winter, and through the spring. We'd kissed beneath the cherry trees of the Quad, tossed each other into Frosh Pond on our birthdays, and fought over who got the last piece of pizza.

Everything was a possibility then, if we just believed hard enough. Sure, the world was fighting back from the devastation of the AIDS epidemic, and the economy was only beginning to recover, but there was still plenty of room for dreams.

After we graduated, we moved together into an apartment just off-campus. That's where CeCe first met Jamey's older brother, Edward. They also hit it off immediately, only they were still together.

Six months after graduation, Jamey and I got married. The wedding was small, out on the beach in the midst of a typical Seattle rain, but it was perfect. The first few months were perfect, too, but then the arguments started. The only place we could find the magic of our courtship was in bed. After a while, that wasn't enough.

I'd felt like a failure. Finally, I'd decided I had to get out. I filed for divorce and when it was finalized, headed down to Los Angeles. CeCe and Edward were already here, and while they refused to take sides, they let me use their spare room until I found my own place.

Then I'd heard about the graduate program at UCLA, and got accepted. Thanks to all those courses, I knew intellectually why Jamey's and my relationship had failed, but it still hurt.

I grabbed a tissue and blew my nose. My penbook had only four words listed: possibilities, dreams, friendship, sex. If a client had written those as the reasons for choosing a life partner, I'd have gently advised him or her to rethink things. Had I been *that* naive back then?

The phone rang, making me jump. "Madelyn Darcy."

"Don't hate me, please?" It was CeCe.

"I ought to, but I can't. I lack the energy."

"He's been so miserable that Edward convinced me to get the two of you together."

"He's here with me, and we haven't killed each other yet." My attempt at humor fell flat, going by the silence from CeCe, but Jamey seemed to appreciate it from the faint grin he flashed me.

Aw, heck. Now was as good a time to ask as any other. "CeCe, I've been wondering for years. How it is you and Edward have stayed together so long? You knew each other even less than Jamey and I did."

"Because we wanted to. Staying together was the most important thing in the world. He gives me something no one else ever has; I feel even more myself around him. He says much the same thing. Plus, when we first met, we didn't just admit to the attraction, we asked each other why it was there before doing anything about it."

"You did?" I had been so overwhelmed with this tall, sexy hero out of the old vids, that I never asked why.

"Yes. And every time we have problems, and we certainly do have them, we talk. So far we've always decided that our reasons for being together outweigh the problems."

"Have I told you lately that you're wasted as a gallery owner? You ought to be the rosalind, not me."

"Oh, you're much better with everyone else than you are with yourself. I don't have the patience to deal with the clients that you do. Mine are just waiting to be nudged into believing that a quilt, doll, painting, or whatever is going to be a good investment on top of being decorative. I'm not affecting their entire lives like you are. I couldn't handle that responsibility."

"But it's not a responsibility; it's fun."

"See what I mean? Now go back to Jamey, and go easy on yourself, Mad. Edward and I both worry about you, and want you to be happy."

"G'night, CeCe. My best to Edward." I saw Jamey waving his hands. "Jamey sends his best, too." I hung up and realized that I'd meant what I said. I really enjoyed being a rosalind. Despite my own experience, I believed in happy endings.

Hmmm. Maybe that was it. I believed in happy endings more than happy beginnings. Or middles. Marriage to Jamey was the happy ending I'd wanted. I never planned past that.

"Jamey, I'm sorry."

"What for?"

"My list is short and a bit silly, and after talking to CeCe, I've realized how unfair I was. I never thought about what marriage would be like in the long term. The old stories always end with the gods or fairies blessing the marriage. The day after the marriage isn't even mentioned."

"Come here." Jamey stood up and met me halfway around my desk. "Want to see my list?" I nodded, and accepted the proffered penbook. His list was a lot like mine: sex, friendship, shared dreams. "My list isn't any better than yours."

"In my professional capacity, if we were clients, I'd tell us to rethink the idea of marriage. A long-term affair without a contract might be a better idea, and cheaper."

"Well, we could try that, couldn't we?" He pulled me close and hugged me. I hugged him back.

"I'm game." My stomach clenched and my temperature rose.

"Me, too." Hand-in-hand, we dropped the penbooks onto the desk, waved the lights out, and headed into my apartment. "This time, let's be selfish and not spend all our time worrying about what makes the other happy, okay?"

"Okay. Does that mean we can get kinky?"

"What makes you think that wouldn't make me happy?" Jamey asked with a laugh.

"Maybe we *can* make this work." I put my arms around him and fell back onto the bed, bringing him down with me. "Now shut up and kiss me."

He did.

THE MERCURY OF THE WISE

Kevin A. Murphy

*Kevin A. Murphy is a member of the "Wild Cards" con-
sortium, among other talents. Here he takes a closer look
at a character that Shakespeare found incidental.*

Hark ye gentles all! My name is Rosaline, and take
heed as I relate a most peculiar pass of circumstance
that did come about in my sixteenth year. For 'twas then,
in the city of Verona, that I met a young man of good but
infamous house—one Romeo, of House Montague, sworn
enemy of House Capulet, the house of my mother and
grandfather, albeit of no relation to my father's—who for
me did conceive a most monstrous affection as does a
calf for its dam or a gosling for its mother. I, being neither cow nor goose, and not of a nature to even countenance taking the part of such an unnatural hybrid, did in
my endeavors to elude the attentions of this Romeo both
bring about a most strange course of events and also
make the acquaintance of another young gentleman: One
Mercutio, cousin to the Prince, knave, scholar, gentleman,
and wit, a merry youth whose finest fault and gravest virtue was that he was Romeo's best and firmest friend.

How should I begin my tale, now that it is already begun? Perhaps with the first time I met this Mercutio,
whilst spending an idle afternoon in my father's garden.

'Twas then that I heard a noise and looked up from my book to see a handsome youth, long of leg and bemused of countenance, perched atop my garden wall, a bouquet of roses depending from one hand.

"Good lady, pay me no heed," he bade me, "or I am undone and forsworn, and you will have taken part in making a man break a solemn oath, which is a very sorry deed indeed."

"Indeed it would be," I said, putting down my book upon the bench, "but as I have already taken note of you, that note cannot be stilled. Still, if you but let me take note of this oath, that may be coin enough to buy my silence, and we may find some way to keep both it and yourself unbroken, for change is a troublesome thing to make. So come you down off that wall and tell me what you have sworn."

Nimbly he sprang down, bowing deeply, and quoth the knave, "I have been charged by my most bosom friend, Romeo, of House Montague, to deliver these roses in secret to the balcony of one Rosaline, of this house, for as they say, a rose for a rose, and a line of roses for a Rosaline."

"Well, then," said I, standing up and straightening my gown, "I know where lie the apartments of this Rosaline, and I will swear by Heaven most high and Hell most low that I shan't speak to her of your errand, so thus I share your secret and your oath remains unbroken. But if you wish to remain unbroken, perhaps you might give me the roses to deliver, as this garden is not unguarded and you might find yourself pricked with sharper things than thorns were you to go any further."

"I have already encountered your wit, milady, and I tremble to think of anything more pointed." After exchanging more barbs and pleasantries—much like the roses—it was revealed that I was the self-same Rosaline, though I did not disclose this until after I had taken the roses to my chamber and set them in water.

What of all this? Well, this Mercutio played messenger for Romeo over the course of the weeks that followed, and he and I exchanged many more jousts and jests all the while. "Ah, Mercutio," I said one day, falling into the familiar, "I am afraid it does thy friend no good to play at Jupiter, for I am little interested in swans or showers of gold. But for the messenger I have a message."

"And what might that be, milady?" he asked wryly.

"This," I said, catching him unawares, and planted a kiss full on his mouth.

Once I'd come back, it had taken root and blossomed into a smile. "I trust, my Mercury," I said then, "that thou wilt not be taking that message to thy Jove."

"Nay, milady, I will not. I fear that I am no longer under his rulership. By Mary, I feel the mark of Mars hot upon my face." And forsooth, he was blushing most fierce, a deep crimson like the ruddy planet, and it was another minute afore he had recovered his tongue. "Mistress Rosaline, perhaps I mistook thy motive, but by Romeo was I informed that thou hadst Diana's wit and hadst sworn thyself to chastity."

"Nonsense," I said, "thy Romeo misspoke me, as is his wont. I merely swore to him that I would live as chastely as Diana, and if he is so poor a scholar as to forget the scandal of Orion, it is no trouble of mine. Dian's a huntress, and I choose to choose instead of being chosen."

"Fearful huntress, thy arrow hath hit its target, though a bit below the heart. Indeed, I can feel the cloth yard shaft protruding as we speak, and I must howl like the wolf since it seems I now follow neither Jupiter nor Mars, but the fair moon herself!"

And what is there to say? The naughty wolf had recovered his tongue, and we pledged to meet like Diana and Orion on the sly, for truth to tell, Mercutio was sore afraid to tell his friend Romeo that the pretty prize he sought had refused the message, but not the messenger.

We came upon a design where we might meet in secret: Mercutio was given to study with one Friar Laurence, and it was less than an afternoon's work for me to prevail upon my father so as to gain tutelage in Latin with this same good Franciscan, though to say sooth, Latin was not all the man was learned in. Indeed, this friar was a veritable Roger Bacon but for the talking bronze head, which he did not need, for the worthy friar could prate endlessly on the subjects of alchemy and astrology and the doctrine of signatures, and with his eyes as they were on the Heavens, well, let it be said, he did not pay much attention to what transpired in the back of his cell.

But sweet as such times were, it was still galling to deal with Romeo and his importunate ramblings, both for Mercutio as their messenger and I as their recipient.

"Mercutio . . ." I said, my thoughts scattering away as we made use of Friar Laurence's library.

"What is this, milady? A pregnant pause?"

I hit him with Romeo's latest *missive d'amour.* "I cannot bear thy nonsense any longer, Mercutio, nor that of Romeo either!"

"Nay," he said, fending me off, "were our nonsense any longer, 'twould be too long!"

"It goes on too long as it is, and I tell thee, I will not bear it! Forsooth, I have never read worse poetry, and if I am to read 'love' and 'dove' rhymed one more time, by Mary, I think I will go mad."

"Then thou wouldst do thyself damage, for as is known, the mad are moonstruck, and if thou art Diana, then thou must strikest thyself."

I swatted him instead, to which he cried, "Aigh, I am moonstruck! Mercy! Mercy!"

"Peace, fool. I suffer thee only on my own sufferance, and as it says in the Bible, I may take herb to ease my troubles and ease them I shall! Or at least we may both take ease from herbs, for look here in this book and tell me what thou seest."

I did then shew him the work, which he perused. "I see a receipt for a love philter, such as harlots do delight in and lovers use to reconjure their flagging spirits. But if thou wishest to conjure my spirit, milady, all thou needst do is speakest my name. Aye, but conjure me into thy circle and I will come!"

"Rogue! What a naughty mind thou hast!" I cried, taking the book back from him. "Here is a prescription that will ease our difficulties far easier than a harlot may ease her burden, for once drunk, I shall be rid of Romeo, and I be not the one to drink it!"

Mercutio took back the book and scanned the list. "Hast thou all thou needst? This western flower sounds precious rare, and the shrieking mandrake is not easily happed upon."

"Aye, and I hast thou, too, who as I've said is more than enough! The western flower is none other than the simple pansy, such as maids knot in their hair, and as for the mandrake, Friar Laurence has many wondrous things, and the mandrake is the least of them. But look," I said and opened a glass case I'd found secreted in the back of the cell, then unwound the red cloth from its precious burden. "The mystic mandrake."

"A pretty poppet," Mercutio remarked. "A potent little root. But look, Friar Laurence hath carved him into the likeness of a man, down to the smallest detail."

"Only a bit of which we need," I said, and nipped the tiniest shaving off with the tip of my fingernail.

There came a scream, like enough to shiver the blood, though soft and distant like a dove's cry, and I was afeared I would die on the spot. Then Mercutio laughed and I knew it was only his foolish jest.

"Thou naughty man!" I cried as I swaddled the mandrake and placed it back in its glass coffin. "Thou dreadful fool! The shriek of the mandrake is not an occasion for idle jest!"

"But lady, I stand, so I cannot be idle, and I do not jest, for I am serious when I say I did not shriek, at least outwardly, when thou niptst the little man. Aye, to be nipt in the bud is no occasion for jest, so how much worse to be nipt in the root."

"Peace, fool," I said, "or I will give thee cause to shriek. I have picked the midnight herb and ground it fine, mixing it with the treacherous fruit of the love apple, which when raw is as deadly as her cousin nightshade, but when cooked is kin to Venus herself. With this bit of the mandrake," I said, dropping it into the mortar, "and the purple juice of love-in-idleness, that not-so-rare western flower, the worthy friar's prescription is complete."

I placed the powder in a fool's cap and gave it to Mercutio. "Thou hast but to give Romeo this simple in a cup of wine and the next maid he sees he will be smitten with, as if Dan Cupid himself had done the deed."

"And how shall we accomplish this, milady?" Mercutio did ask. "Romeo is my bosom friend, and while I have no trouble with him falling alove of another, I protest if thou wishest him set upon some fishwife or toothless aunt."

"Listen well then," I said. "Mine uncle Capulet will be having a party, a ball for my cousin Juliet, to which we both shall be invited, along with half the young beauties of Verona. Thou must simply slippeth Romeo inside, then slippeth him this simple while pointing out the damosels fair. Cupid's draught will do the rest, and after that, I will be forgotten in his new passion."

"And how, milady, am I to lure him to the ball of Capulet, the house of his enemy?"

I leant back against the wall of the cell, showing myself to best advantage. "Why, all thou needst do is inform him that I myself will be there. Once hearing that, I'd be surprised if Cerberus kept him outside."

"Ah, my lady fair, thou speakest of sin. A man must be out afore he is in."

"Then get thyself hence and hie far away. We meet on the morrow at Capulet."

The ball was quite splendid, for my aunt had outdone herself, and my Mercutio did no less, disguising Romeo and the others as maskers, thus slipping him in under the nose of the enemy as it were.

"Rosaline, my love," said a voice from behind a winged helm, "Romeo hath come, but still the deed lies half undone. I have deputized my brother, Valentine, with the execution of the second half of thy merry plan, both because his name bespeaks his competence to play Abraham Cupid, and because, if thy philter is to do its deed, thou must be far from his sight, or do thyself worse mischief."

"Ah, clever knave, you speak aright. Let us be gone from Cupid's sight."

"An easy wish to grant, you'll find. Love sees us not, for love is blind."

And so did we exeunt for the upstairs apartments of mine uncle, and only later did we discover that love is not only blind, but lacking in all sense! Valentine, spurred by that same impish urge as Cupid, had given Romeo the philter, but then pointed him so that his eyes fell upon Juliet! And after approaching her, Romeo stole a single kiss, so that with the taint still upon his lips, the philter had its precious affect on her as well, and he, of course, was the first that she saw.

It was a disaster that only Hell could forge, for my cousin Tybalt had spotted Romeo at the ball, swearing that he would see him dead, and that same night, Romeo hopped the wall of the Capulet's orchard and went to speak with Juliet. It was only through a great dint of swooning and feigning did I keep mine aunt and uncle, not to mention Tybalt and Juliet's nurse, sufficiently distracted so that they did not learn what was transpiring all the while. Mercutio went—unsuccessfully—to distract Romeo, and Valentine was sent to fetch Friar Laurence.

I recovered by the time the good friar had arrived, and as he and Valentine escorted me home, I confessed my sin and the trouble engendered by use of the philter.

"Tut-tut, my dear, I've heard much worse. To blessing yet we may turn this curse," rhymed the good friar, and after chiding me for my folly, Valentine for his mischief, and promising to do the same for Mercutio when he saw him next, he outlined a plan whereby Valentine's impishness might be changed to the work of a cherub, "For," said the friar, "there is little good that cannot be turned to evil, and little evil that cannot be turned to good, and it is the work of the physician to apply each in its proper measure to bring the body to health. Verona hath long been bleeding from the feud of the Montagues and Capulets, and the thread of love that young Valentine has strung may be used to bind up the wound, as a barber pulls tight his suture."

There was little I could do but rejoice and blister Valentine about the ears, for the next day Friar Laurence smuggled Romeo and Juliet both to his cell, and under the influence of my philter, they easily agreed to the vows of wedlock. Friar Laurence told me all of it, then left me in his cell to study declensions, and that was where I was when Valentine burst in, weeping loudly. "Oh Mistress Rosaline! He is slain! He is slain! My brother is dead and there is no help for it!"

The boy fell into a heap of sobbing and it was minutes before I got the story: Mercutio had quarreled with Tybalt, and my cousin had slain him; then Romeo had drawn and slew Tybalt, and the Prince had banished him from Verona. Oh, woe, what a sorry pass! My love dead, my cousin, too, and the foolish youth who had sent me bad poetry but the day before banished from the city!

Perhaps this was God's punishment to me for dabbling in sorcery, but I had not yet begun to dabble. I took Valentine by the shoulders and shook him until he ceased to cry. "Listen to me, boy. Thy brother's life depends on this, and do not tell me he's dead aright, because I know that! Go hie thee to where his body is kept and have it brought back here. Get Benvolio to help, and if any ask on whose authority thou dost this, say it is by order of Friar Laurence. Do this or, by Jesu and Mary, I swear thou wilt rue the day thou ever crossed me!"

I boxed him across the ears and he fled out the door, and I, brushing aside tears I had no time for, repaired myself to Friar Laurence's books of strange lore, looking for a method to revive the dead, for if the love philter were possible, then certainly the *Elixir Vitae* were just as likely. Agrippa's *Books of Occult Philosophy* made mention of serpent's skins, honey, and the ashes of the phoenix, but while the first of those two were easily enough found, that worthy bird only burnt itself once every thousand years, and that in farthest Egypt or Araby, and I had not the time to hie myself there with a whisk and dustpan to find any of its fabled ashes!

I searched through the books in the cell until I recalled the mandrake, and the shriek I had heard but days before, the fabled shriek that could kill any man who heard it. I oped its glass coffin and stripped off the red silk wrappings, holding the little mannikin in my hands. "Listen thou, mandrake," I said, "if it wast thee who shrieked yesterday, and that shriek, like the foul hissing of the basilisk, cursed my love to be slain this day, then I swear by Heaven most high and Hell most low that I will get my revenge and run thee through a pasta slicer, boil the remains, and serve them to the Jesuits in their alms bowls!"

"Mercy!" shrieked the mandrake. "Mercy, mistress! I swear I had no part in it! My kind can shriek but once when we are uprooted, and all I kilt was a dog, and an old one at that!"

I was so affrighted I did drop the thing, for it is one thing to believe in love philters, another to believe in talking mandrakes. But if I were to prepare the Elixir of Life, I would need all the faith I possessed.

I steeled up my courage and lifted the little mannikin into the air. "Then tell me how to create the *Elixir Vitae*."

"Such things are forbidden," the mandrake said unto me. "I know many secrets, but there are some I durst not tell. Ask another!"

I shook him, shook the little creature as I had so recently shaken Valentine. "Pasta slicers!" I threatened. "Boiling water! Jesuits! Hungry Jesuits! Hungry Jesuits with their alms bowls!"

"Mercy, mistress! Mercy!" it shrieked. "I will tell! I will tell!" And then the mandrake spake unto me, listing out the ingredients and taking me through the steps, suggesting substitutions for what rarities Friar Laurence did not possess, until I united the Red Elixir with the Mercury of the Wise, and the *Lapis Potensimus*, the Philosopher's Stone, was fairly compounded.

During the course of this ritual, Benvolio and Valentine came in, bearing Mercutio's corpse, but so affrighted were they at seeing me playing at the sorceress whilst the mandrake root prated strange wisdom that they said nothing, even whence I had finished.

I gestured for them to place Mercutio's body on the floor, and then, by the mandrake's instruction, lay a crumb of the Philosopher's Stone upon his lips and another upon the wound that had kilt him. And then lo! I saw the blood, smeared and scabbed, take on a ruddy hue again and flow backward into the wound, sealing it shut as it paled to a scar and then nothing.

Mercutio's chest began to rise and fall slowly, then he licked his lips, tasting the melted stone, and sat up, oped his eyes, and gazed at the smooth skin of his belly, touching it in wonder. "Well," he remarked, " 'twas not so deep as a well, nor so wide as a church door, but it appears someone has filled it in or bricked it up, in which case I must give thanks."

"Oh, Mercutio!" I cried, giving him a long embrace, while Valentine and Benvolio stood by dumbly, which was exactly where we were when Friar Laurence walked in.

He set down his basket and took in the situation. "By Jesu and Mary!" he cried. "What hath transpired here?"

"Pasta slicers!" cried the mandrake. "Boiling water! Hungry Jesuits! Oh, horrible! Horrible! Save me, my ghostly father!"

Friar Laurence crossed the room to the mandrake root, clucking as you would at a frightened child, then, as we watched, bathed it in wine, swaddled it again in its red silk wrapping, and placed it back in the crystal casket.

"So, Rosaline, thou hast threatened little Mandragore

here until he revealed the secret of the *Lapis Philosophorum*." I nodded and the good friar looked at the tubes and alembics of his laboratory, many of them still bubbling. "I do not know whether I should congratulate thee or chastise thou as an impudent chit. There art many works not meant for men, but what women do, only God can ken."

"My good father," said Mercutio, "she saved my life. I pray—"

"She saved thy life once thou'd thrown it away! But what wilt thou do now, boy? The city knows thou to be dead, and if thou lets it be known that thy mistress has the secret to bring back men from the grave, well then, thou art a braver or more foolish man than I." He shook his head, sighing long. "Thou art a good scholar, Mercutio, and I think thou canst well imagine the troubles thou wilt encounter if thou wishest to pretend thy wound were not mortal, when there is no mark of it upon thy body. Indeed, there is but one solution: Thou must hie to Mantua and there enter a monastery, changing thy name, and I bid you other children to forget this foolish and sorry business and put it from your minds. But now let us see what good we can make of this."

Thence, by use of the mandrake, Friar Laurence prepared a lesser elixir, drops of which would simulate the state of death for two days time, after which the sleeper would wake, refreshed as if he had only slept a night. Juliet, the ghostly father explained, would be given these drops, while letters would be sent to Romeo in Mantua so that he would repair back and steal her away so that they could live in peace.

But what then? Love in exile is no state for newlyweds, and it would do little to settle the old wounds between the Houses of Verona, especially if they did believe Juliet dead, and they would be most wroth were they to discover otherwise. And verily, life in an abbey was not for a man such as Mercutio. Neither of us wished to countenance the life the sorcerer had described.

"Forsooth," said Mercutio, once we were outside, "this will not do, this plan of Friar Laurence'. I have another."

"One not so rash as thy plan to bait Tybalt?" asked Benvolio.

"Tybalt is worm meat and will remain so with Rosaline's leave. What I propose is to repair to Mantua, as the good friar has proposed, but not enter an abbey. Instead, I shall see Romeo, but I shall go in the guise of an apothecary, and take with me a measure of the ghostly father's drops of night, which I will sell to him as a poison." And lo! Mercutio held up a vial of Friar Laurence's false poison, which he had stolen when the sorcerer's back was turned.

"But why would he take such?" asked Valentine.

"Thou and Benvolio," Mercutio said, "shall intercept Juliet's letters. If I know Romeo, which I do, he shall rush to his beloved's side so as to die there in a manner most morbid and drear."

"And what of my part?" I asked. How so like a man to take charge, even after just being dead!

"Thou shalt go to the crypt, my angel," Mercutio answered, "there to await me and prepare for my arrival. Once we have engineered the scene of horror with both of the lovers 'dead,' we may be assured that the Montagues and Capulets will swear off their feud forever, and the Prince shall witness it. And if the dead should rise up thereafter, well, how could they ever go back on their word?"

And much of this worked out as Mercutio explained. Valentine devised an ingenious ruse of crying pestilence at the house where the friar bearing the message stayed, and Mercutio impersonated an apothecary quite passably, leaving me to steal the key and, wrapped in my mantle, hide in the shadows of the family crypt until Romeo came.

He did, and the plan went well, until Juliet woke too soon, and as you have no doubt heard elsewhere, stabbed herself with Romeo's dagger.

That was not to the plan, nor was the fact that Count Paris was also slain outside the tomb whilst I waited within with Juliet. However, in a scene you can no doubt well imagine, Friar Laurence, the Prince, the city watch, and the Montagues and the Capulets all came and put an end to the feud for once and good.

And what had kept me so busy whilst Juliet made the mistake of waking and killing herself? Well, I knew that there was one who would not keep the peace no matter how grateful he might be for being rescued from death.

Indeed, it was a messy business sawing off Tybalt's head, and took much longer than I'd thought, but it had to be done if I wished to make it appear that my beloved cousin had been plundered by medical students.

Mercutio arrived, and using my *Lapis Potensimus,* he revived Juliet and Paris from the dead, telling everyone that he had been sent back from Heaven and that the stone was a gift of the Archangel Raphael. Friar Laurence, not wishing to be known as a sorcerer, could not contradict him, and neither would I, but the state of Tybalt's body after the "medical students" had had their way with it left it beyond the reach of even the Philosopher's Stone . . . not that we tried.

As for poor Romeo, a kiss from Juliet was all it took . . . to distract the assembled company whilst I kicked him repeatedly in the shins. Everyone wept tears of joy, though I wondered a bit whether Romeo's came solely from the delight of seeing his Juliet restored to life.

And what then? Well, the second wedding of Romeo and Juliet, and the Miracle of the Peace of Verona, as it came to be known, were celebrated wildly, and the next year Mercutio and I were wed. He'll say that he proposed, but I beg to differ. After all, I did have my oath to Diana.

And Tybalt's head? Well, we had it bronzed. It's in a cabinet on the mantelpiece, and I hid the last of the *Lapis Philosophorum* inside, though the general populace believes the wondrous stone was taken back to Heaven the night after the miracle.

What, you don't believe my story? Then I bid you to go hie to the mantel and ope the cabinet and ask Tybalt himself. No doubt he'll tell a somewhat different tale, but as you might guess, he was never the best of losers.

A TEMPEST IN HER EYES

Charles de Lint

Charles de Lint is a full-time writer and part-time musician who makes his home in Ottawa, Canada, with his wife, MaryAnn Harris. This story takes place in Newford, a city featured in others of his works.

> *"Remember all is but a poet's dream,*
> *The first he had in Phoebus' holy bower,*
> *But not the last, unless the first displease."*
> —John Lyly,
>   from *The Woman in the Moone*

1

I've heard it said that there are always two parts to a story: There's the official history, the version that's set onto the page, then filed away in the archives where it waits for when the librarian comes to retrieve the facts to footnote some learned paper or discourse. Then there's the way an individual remembers the event; that version sits like an old woman on a lonely porch, creaking back and forth in her wicker rocker as she waits for a visitor.

I think there's a third: the feral child, escaping from between the lines, from between how it's said the story went and how it truly took place.

I'm like that child. I'm invariably on the edge of how it goes for everyone else. I hear them tell the story about some event that I took part in and I can scarcely recognize it. I'd like to say that it's because I'm such a free spirit—the way Jilly is, always bouncing around from one moment to the next—but I know it's not true. The reason I'm not part of the official story is because I'm usually far from civilization, lost in wildernesses of my own making, unaware of either the library or the porch.

I'm just not paying attention—or at least not paying attention to the right thing. It all depends on your perspective, I suppose.

2

September was upon us and I couldn't have cared less, which is weird for me, because autumn's usually my favorite time of year. But I was living through one of those low points in my life that I guess everyone has to put up with at one time or another. I went through the summer feeling increasingly tired and discouraged. I walked hand in hand with a constant sense of foreboding and you know what that's like: if you expect things to go wrong, they usually do.

I hadn't met a guy I liked in ages—at least not anyone who was actually available. Every time I sat down to write, my verses came out as doggerel. I was getting cranky with my friends, but I hated being home by myself. About the only thing I was still good at was waitressing. I've always liked my job, but as a life-long career choice? I don't think so.

To cheer me up, Jilly and Sophie took me to the final performance of *A Midsummer Night's Dream* at the Standish. The play was a traditional production— Lysander and Demetrius hadn't been rewritten as bikers, say, and the actors had performed in costume, not in the nude. Being a poet myself, I lean toward less adventurous productions because they don't get in the way of the words.

I'd been especially taken with the casting of the fairy court tonight. The director had acquired the services of the Newford Ballet for their parts which lent the characters a wonderfully fey grace. They were so light on their feet, I could almost imagine that they were flying at times, flitting about the stage, rather than constrained by gravity to walk its boards. The scene at the end where the fairies sport through the Duke's palace had been so beautifully choreographed that I was almost disappointed when the spotlight narrowed to capture Puck in his final speech, perched at the edge of the stage, fixing us in our seats with a half-mocking, half-feral gaze that seemed to belie his promise to "make amends."

The actor playing Robin Goodfellow had been my favorite of a talented cast, his mobile features perfectly capturing the fey charm and menace that the idea of fairy has always held for me. Oberon was the more handsome, but Puck had been simply magic. I found myself wishing that the play was just beginning its run, rather than ending it, so that I could go back another night, just for his performance alone.

Jilly and Sophie didn't seem quite as taken with the production. They were walking a little ahead of me, arguing about the authorship of Shakespeare's works, rather than discussing the play we'd just seen.

"Oh, come on," Sophie was saying. "Just look at the names of some of these people: John Thomas Looney. S.E. Silliman. George Battey. How can anyone possibly take their theories seriously?"

"I didn't say they were necessarily right," Jilly replied. "It's just that when you consider the historical Shakespeare: a man whose father was illiterate, whose kids were illiterate, who didn't even bother to keep copies of his own work in his house. . . . It's so obvious that whoever wrote the plays and sonnets, it wasn't William Shakespeare."

"I don't really see how it matters anyway," Sophie told her. "It's the work that's important, in the end. The fact that it's endured so long that we can still enjoy it today, hundreds of years after he died."

"But it's an interesting puzzle."

Sophie nodded in agreement. "I'll give you that. Personally, I like the idea that Anne Whately wrote them."

"But she was a *nun.* I can't *possibly* imagine a nun having written some of the bawdier lines."

"Maybe those are the ones old Will put in."

"I suppose. But then . . ."

Trailing along behind them, I was barely paying attention and finally just shut them out. My own thoughts were circling mothlike around Titania's final promise:

> *Hand in hand, with fairy grace,*
> *Will we sing, and bless this place.*

That was what I needed. I needed a fairy court to bless my apartment, to lift the cloud of gloom that had been thickening over me throughout the summer until it had gotten to the point where when I looked in the mirror, I expected to see a stranger's face looking back at me. I felt that different.

I think the weather had something to do with it. It rained every weekend and day off I had this summer. It never got hot—not that I like or missed the heat. But I think we need a certain amount of sunshine just to stay sane, never mind the UV risk. Who ever heard of getting cabin fever in the middle of the summer? But that's exactly the way I felt around the end of July—the way I usually feel in early March when I don't think I can take one more day of cold and snow.

And it had just gotten worse for me as the summer dragged on.

The newspapers blame the weird weather on that volcano in the Philippines—Mount Pinatubo—and say that not only did it mess up the weather this year, but its effects are going to be felt for a few years to come. If that's true, I think I'll just go quietly mad.

I started wondering then about how the weather affects fairies, though if they did exist, I guess it might be the other way around. Instead of a volcano causing all of this trouble, it'd be another rift in the fairy court. As Titania put it to Oberon:

> *. . . the spring, the summer*
> *The chiding autumn, angry winter, change*
> *Their wonted liveries; and the mazed world,*
> *By their increase, now knows not which is which:*
> *And this same progeny of evils comes*
> *From our debate, from our dissension;*
> *We are their parents and original.*

It certainly fits the way our weather's messed up. I heard it even snowed up in Alberta a couple of weeks ago—and not just a few flurries. The skies dumped some ten inches. In *August*.

"The seasons alter," indeed.

If there were fairy courts, if they *were* having an argument, I wished they'd just kiss and make up. Though not the way they did in *A Midsummer Night's Dream*.

Ahead of me, Sophie and Jilly came to a stop and I walked right into them.

"How's our dreamwalker?" Jilly asked.

She spoke the words lightly, but the streetlights showed the concern in her eyes. Jilly worries about people—seriously, not just for show. It's nice to know that someone cares, but sometimes that kind of concern can be as much of a burden as what you're going through, however well-meant it might be.

"I'm fine," I lied. "Honestly."

"So who gets *your* vote as the author of Shakespeare's works?" Sophie asked.

I thought Francis Bacon looked good for it. After all, he was known as the most erudite man of his time. The author of the plays showed through his writing that he'd had a wide knowledge of medicine and law, botany and mythology, foreign life and court manners. Where would a butcher's son from Stratford have gotten that kind of experience? But the argument bored me.

"I'd say it was his sister," I said.

"His *sister?*"

"Did he even have a sister?" Jilly asked.

A black Cadillac pulled up to the curb beside us before I could answer. There were three Hispanic boys in it and for a moment I thought it was LaDonna's brother Pipo and a couple of his pals. But then the driver leaned out the window to give Jilly a leer and I realized I didn't recognize any of them.

"Hey, *puta*," he said. "Looking for a little of that kickin' action?"

Homeboys in a hot car, out for a joy ride. The oldest wasn't even fourteen. Jilly didn't hesitate. She cocked back her foot and kicked the Cadillac's door hard enough to make a dent.

"In your dreams," she told him.

If it had been anybody else, those homies would've been out of the car and all over us. We're all small women; Jilly's about my height, and I'm just topping five feet. We don't exactly look formidable. But this was Jilly and the homie at the wheel saw something in her face that made him put the pedal to the floor and peel off.

The incident depressed all three of us. When we got to my apartment, I asked them in, but they just wanted to go home. I didn't blame them. I watched them go off down the street, but sat down on the porch instead of going inside.

I knew I wasn't going to sleep because I started thinking about what a raw deal women always seem to get, and that always keeps me up. Even Titania in the play— sure, she and Oberon made up, but it was on *his* terms. Titania never even realized the crap he had put her through before their "reconciliation."

A Midsummer Night's Dream definitely hadn't been written by a woman.

3

A funny thing happened to me a few years ago. I caught a glimpse of the strange world that lies on the other side of the curtain we've all agreed is reality. Or at least I think I did.

The historical version of what happened is pretty straightforward: I met a street person—the old man on the bicycle that everybody calls the Conjure Man—and he got me to take an acorn from the big old tree that used to grow behind the library at Butler U. He had me nurture it over the winter, then plant it in Fitzhenry Park near the statue of the poet, Joshua Stanhold.

The version he tells is that he's this immortal who diminishes as the years go by, which is why he's only our height now. He was supposed to leave our world when its magic went away, but he got left behind. The tree that came down behind the library was a Tree of Tales, a repository of stories without which wonder is diminished in our world. The one I grew from an acorn and planted in the Silenus Gardens is supposed to be its replacement.

My version . . . I don't really know what my version is. There was something strange about the whole affair, I'll grant you that. And that little sapling I planted—it's already the size of a ten-year-old oak. Jilly told me she was talking to a botanist who was quite amazed at its appearance there. Seems that kind of oak isn't native to North America and he was surprised to find it growing in the middle of the park that way.

"The only other one I've ever seen in the city," he told Jilly, "used to grow behind the Smithers Library, but they cut it down."

I haven't seen John—that's the Conjure Man's real name, John Windle. I haven't seen him for a while now. I like to think that he's finally made it home to wherever home is. Behind the curtain, I suppose. But I still go out to the tree and tell it stories—all kinds of stories. Happy ones, sad ones. Gossip. News. Just whatever comes to mind.

I'm not even sure why; I just do.

4

I'm not as brave—or maybe as foolish—as Jilly is. She doesn't seem to know the meaning of fear. She'll go anywhere, at any time of the day or night, and she never seems to get hurt. Like what happened earlier tonight. If I'd been on my own, or just with Sophie, when that car pulled up, who knows how it would have ended up? Not pleasant, that's for sure.

So I'm not nearly so bold—except when I'm on my bike. It's sort of like a talisman for me. It's nothing special, just an old ten-speed, but it gets me around. Sometimes I think I should become one of those messengers that wheel through the traffic on their mountain bikes, whistle between their lips, ready to let out a shrill blast if anybody gets in their way.

You think you're immortal, covering ground faster than anyone can walk, but you're not all locked up inside some motorized box that's spewing noxious fumes into the air. You feel as natural as a bird, or a deer, racing through your concrete forest. Maybe that's where John got that feeling from, riding through town on his bike, free as the wind, when all the other street people are just sort of shuffling along, gaze to the ground.

I started a poem about it once, but I couldn't get the

words to fit the vision. That's been happening to me all too often this summer. Oh, who'm I kidding? Wordless pretty well sums me up these days. I look at the work I've had published and I can't even imagine what it was like to write those verses, let alone believe that it was me.

Feeling sorry for myself is the one thing I have gotten good at lately. It's not a feeling I like. I hate the way it leaves me with this overpowering sense of being ineffectual. Worthless.

When I start getting into that kind of a mood, I usually just get on my bike and just ride. Which is how I found myself in Fitzhenry Park a few hours after Sophie and Jilly left me at my apartment.

I laid my bike down under the young Tree of Tales and sprawled on the grass beside it. I could see a handful of stars, looking up through the tree's boughs, but my mind was back in the Standish, listening to Puck warn Oberon of the coming dawn. I drifted off to the remembered sound of his voice.

5

Puck breaks off and looks at me. The play has faded, the hall is gone. It's just the two of us, alone in some copsy wood, as far from the city as the word orange is from a true rhyme.

"And who are you?" he says.

I make no reply. I'm too fascinated by his transformation. Falling asleep, the voice I heard, the face I imagined, was that of the actor from the Standish who I'd seen earlier in the night. But he's gone, along with the city and everything familiar. This Puck is more compelling still. I can't take my gaze from him. He has a beauty that no actor could replicate, but he's more inhuman, too. It's hard to say where the man ends and the animal begins. I think of Pan; I think of fauns.

"Your hair," he says, "is like moonlight, gracing your fair shoulders."

Maybe I should be thinking of satyrs. Legendary being or not, this is a come-on if I ever heard one.

"It's dyed," I tell him.

"But it looks so full of life."

"I mean, I color it. I'm not a natural blonde."

"And your eyes?" he asks. "Is that tempest of dream-starved color dyed as well?"

I have to admit, he's got a way about him. I don't know if I should assume "dream-starved" to be a compliment exactly, but the sound of his voice makes me wish he'd just take me in his arms. Maybe this is what they mean by fairy enchantment. I've only known him for the better part of a couple of minutes and already he's got me feeling all warm and tingly inside. There's a musky odor in the air and my heartbeat has found a new, quicker rhythm.

It's a tough call, but I tell my libido to take five.

"What do you mean by 'dream-starved'?" I ask him.

He sits back on his furry haunches and the sexual charge that's built up between us eases somewhat.

"I see a storm in your soul," he says, "held at bay by a gray cloud of uncomfortable reason."

"What's that supposed to mean?" I ask.

But I know. I know exactly what he's talking about: how everything that ever made me happy seems to have been washed away. I smile, but there's no light behind the smile. I laugh, but the sound is hollow. I don't know how it happened, but it all went away. I do have a storm inside me, but it can't seem to get out and I don't know how to help it. All I do know is that I don't want to feel like a robot anymore, like I took a walk-on bit as a zombie for some B-movie only to find that I can't shake the part once my scene's in the can.

"When was the last time you felt truly alive?" he asks.

I look back through my memories, but everything seems dismal and gray. It's like walking into a room where all the furniture is covered with sheets, dust lies thick on the floor, all color has been sucked away.

"I ... I can't remember. . . ."

"It was not always so."

A statement, not a question, but I still nod my head in slow agreement.

"What bedevils you," he says, "is that you have misplaced the ability to see—to truly see behind the shadow, into the heart of a thing—and so you no longer think to look. And the more you do not look, the less able you are to see. Wait long enow, and you'll wander the world as one blind."

"I already feel that way."

"Then open your eyes and see."

"See *what?*"

Puck shrugs. "It makes no difference. You can look upon the most common thing and see the whole of the cosmos reflected within."

"Intellectually, I know what you're talking about," I tell him. "I understand—really I do. But in here—" I lay the palm of one hand between my breasts and cover it with the palm of the other,"—it's not so clear. My heart just feels too heavy to even think about sunshine and light, let alone look for them in anything."

"Then free your heart from your mind," he says. "Embrace wonder for one moment without the need to consider how that wonder came to be, without the need to justify if it be real or not."

"I . . . I don't know how."

His lips shape that puckish smile then. "If you would forget thought for a time, let me love you."

He cups my chin with his hand and brings his lips close to mine. The touch, being so close to those wild eyes of his, I can feel the warmth again, the fire in my loins that rises up into my belly.

"Let the storm loose," he whispers.

I want to, I'm going to, I can't seem to stop myself, yet I manage to pull back from him.

"I'll try," I say. "But first," and I don't know where this thought comes from, "first—tell me a story."

"A . . . story."

It's all happening too fast for me. I need to slow down.

"Tell me what happened when Titania found out that Oberon had taken her changeling into his court."

He smiles. He rests his back against a tree and pulls me close so that my head's on his shoulder. I need this breathing space. I need the quiet sound of his voice, the intimacy it builds between us. Without it, fairy enchantment or not, the act of making love with him would be no different than if I did it with one of those homeboys who pulled up beside the curb earlier in the evening.

He's a good storyteller. I hope the Tree's listening.

When the story's done, he sits quietly beside me, as taken away by the story he's let unfold between us as I am. I'm the one who has to unbutton my blouse, who reaches for his hand and puts it against my breast.

6

I woke with the morning sun in my eyes, stiff and chilled from having spent the night on the damp grass. I sat up and used my fingers as a comb to pull the grass and leaves from my hair. My dream was still vivid. Puck's advice rang like a clarion bell inside my mind.

You can look upon the most common thing and see the whole of the cosmos reflected within.

But I couldn't seem to do it. I could feel the storm inside me, yearning to be freed, but the veil was over my eyes again and everything seemed to be shrouded with the fine covering of its fabric.

Free your heart from your mind. Embrace wonder for one moment without the need to consider how that wonder came to be, without the need to justify . . . if . . . it. . . .

Already the advice was fading. I found myself thinking, it was only a dream. There's no more wisdom in a dream, than in anything you might make up. It's just shadows. Without substance.

I tried to tell myself that it wasn't true. I might make up my poems, but when they work, when the line of communication runs true between my heart and whoever's reading them, they touch a real truth.

But the argument didn't seem worth pursuing.

Above me, the sky was gray, overcast. The morning was cool and it probably wouldn't get much warmer. So much for summer. So much for my life. But it seemed so unfair.

I remembered the dream. I remembered Puck—my Puck, not Shakespeare's, not some actor, not somebody else's interpretation of him. I remembered the magic in his voice. The gentleness in his touch. The wild enchantment in his eyes. Somehow I managed, if only in a dream, to pull aside the curtain that separates strangeness from the world we've all agreed on and find a piece of wonder that I could bring back with me. But now that I've woken I find that all I've brought back is more of what it seems I've always had. Grayness. Boredom. No meaning in anything.

And that seemed the most unfair of it all.

I lay back down on the grass and stared up into the Tree of Tales, my gaze veiled with tears. I could see the gloom that had spread throughout me over the summer, just deepening and deepening until it swallowed me whole. I was so sick of feeling sorry for myself, but I just couldn't seem to stop myself.

And then a small bird landed on a branch above my head—I don't even know what kind. A sparrow? A wren? It lifted up its head and warbled a few notes and for no good reason at all, I felt happy.

I didn't see the singer as a small drab brown bird on an equally drab branch, but as a microcosm that reflected every living thing. I didn't hear its song as a few warbled notes, quickly swallowed by the sounds of traffic beyond the confines of the park, but as an echo of all the music that was ever sung.

I sat up and looked around and nothing seemed the same. It was as though someone had just told me some unbelievably good news and simply by hearing it, my perspective on everything was changed.

7

Someone once described the theory of right and left brains to me and I read up on it myself later. Basically, it boils down to this: The left brain is the logical one, the rationalist, the scientist, the one that sees us through the everyday. It's the one that lets us conduct normal business, walk safely across a busy street, that kind of thing. And it's the one we know best.

The right brain belongs to the artist and it's mostly a stranger because we don't call on it very often. In the general course of our lives, we don't *need* to. But fey though it is, this stranger inside us is the one that keeps us sane. It's the one that imparts meaning to what we do, that allows us to see beyond the drone of the everyday.

It's always trying to remind us of its existence. It's the one that's responsible for synchronicities and other small wonders, strange dreams or really *seeing* a small drab brown bird. It'll do anything to shake us up. But mostly we don't pay attention to it. And when we sink low enough, we don't hear its voice at all.

And that's such a shame because that stranger is the Puck in the midden, the part of us that makes gold out of trash, poetry out of nonsense. It calls art forth from common sights and music from ordinary sound and without it, the world would be a very gray place indeed. Trust me, I know—from my own all too unpleasant experience with that world. But I'm working on never going through a summer like that again.

The stranger, that Puck in my midden, showed me how.

When I think of that Puck now, I'm always reminded of how he came to me—not just from out of a dream, but from a dream that was based on someone else's dream, put to words, enacted on the stage, centuries after his death. And I believe now that Shakespeare did write the plays that bear his name.

I doubt we'll ever know for sure. In this case, the historical version's lost, while the stories everybody else has to tell contradict each other—as so often they do. But I'll pick from between the lines and say it was old Will.

Because the dream also reminds me of the Tree of Tales and I think maybe that's what Shakespeare was: a kind of human Tree of Tales. He got told all these stories and then he reshaped them into his plays so that they wouldn't be forgotten.

It doesn't matter where he got those stories. What matters is that he was able to put them into the forms they have now so that they could and can live on: small sparks of wisdom and joy, drama and buffoonery, that touch the stranger inside us so that she'll remind us what we're all here for: not just to plod through life, but to celebrate it.

But knowing all of that, believing in it as I do, the mystery of authorship still remains for most people, I suppose. The scholars and historians. But that's their problem; I've solved it to my own satisfaction. There's only one thing I'd ask old Will if I ever ran into him. I'd love to know who told him about Puck.

I'll bet she had a tempest in her eyes.

TITANIA OR THE CELESTIAL BED

Teresa Edgerton

Teresa Edgerton's many fantasy novels include the ground-breaking Goblin Moon *and* The Gnome's Engine *and the recent* Castle of the Silver Wheel. *Here she continues the story of one of those characters that seem real enough to have a life beyond the play in which she first appears.*

Titania sat in her dainty boudoir, sipping chocolate from a newborn rose. It was not, of course, a *natural* rose, but a china cup fashioned to resemble that flower, the porcelain tinted a delicate pink. Another day, Titania might have rejoiced in its beauty, in the apparent absurdity of drinking scalding chocolate from anything so frail as a blossoming rose—like most fairies, she had an abiding passion for innocent deceptions and gauzy illusions, for anything painted, gilded, fragile and false—but today she was feeling so wretched and angry that even the elegant cup and its matching chocolate pot failed to delight her.

She was unhappy because she had just received a letter from her cousin Oonagh,[1] describing a chance meeting

---

[1] According to Lady Wilde, Oonagh was the wife of Finvarra, King of the fairies of western Ireland. We may therefore assume that Oberon's activities, which she subsequently mentions, take place on that green but scarcely happy isle.

with the perfidious Oberon and a certain wanton little hussy of a redheaded mortal with whom he was conducting a violent love affair.

Titania put the cup and the letter aside, on a little alabaster pedestal table beside her couch. She found her lacy handkerchief, applied it to her dainty nose, and blew as hard as she could. This was not the first time that her wandering spouse had betrayed her trust ... nor, to be fair (and Titania was always scrupulously fair), had the infidelity been on one side only ... but it was certainly the most painful, public, and humiliating. And while divorce was clearly out of the question, for reasons both political and private, the estrangement this time was likely to be permanent.

And yet, Titania asked herself, winding a scented and powdered curl about a slender finger, *is it entirely* Oberon's *fault if life is growing the tiniest bit stale?*

No longer creatures of wood and field, over the last century-and-a-half Titania and her ilk had abandoned a carefree pastoral existence in favor of something called "town polish." No longer to shelter 'neath the leafy bough, but in imposing mansions of classical design. No longer to dress in rustic green and country scarlet, but in pastel satins and rich brocades, embroidered waistcoats and whalebone stays, ribbons, satin patches, and imported laces. No longer to whisk 'round the world in the twinkling of the eye, but to rattle through the cobblestone streets of London in pumpkinshell coaches and filigree carriages. At the beginning, it had all been deliciously exciting, but now ... a certain dissatisfaction was setting in, a sense there *must* be something yet more thrilling the world had to offer, though Titania knew no more than anyone what that something might be.

"We live too long," she said with a sigh, feeling suddenly weary and old. It was true that the glass in her bedchamber assured her each morning that her face was still lovely, her complexion perfect, her figure light and pleasing. But it sometimes seemed to Titania that her more-than-mortal beauty was growing a little thin and tarnished, and whenever she gazed at her own reflection, caught a glimpse of her hands and arms in the midst of some graceful gesture, she was increasingly aware of the hollow birdlike bones moving beneath the skin.

"And perhaps ... perhaps *perfect* fidelity is too much to ask when one has been married for hundreds and hundreds of years. But if we are doomed to be fickle and faithless, then why are we not equipped with harder hearts? I am sure that I feel this as keenly as any mortal could."

Even as she spoke, there came a light scratching at the boudoir door. Titania folded the letter and slipped it under a velvet cushion. The door swung open and in walked Gregory Peaseblossom,[2] who crossed the room with a heavy step and deposited himself on a gilded chair beside Titania's couch. The chair creaked alarmingly under his weight.

"I take it," said Titania, arranging the spider lace on her shoulders, moving restlessly among the cushions, "that Phoebe remains just as haughty and cruel as ever?"

Gregory nodded his head. "I sometimes think ... I think she is cruelest when she means to be kind."

At nineteen, young Peaseblossom was remarkably bulky for a "taken" child (and how he managed to put on flesh on a changeling's diet of nectar and dewdrops was a continuing mystery[3]) but his features were good, his manners easy and agreeable, and Titania suspected that ordinary mortals might even admire his muscular physique—which showed to particular advantage, just at the moment, in a coat of cerulean blue, a striped waistcoat, and tight mouse-colored breeches. "She gives every indication that she is sincerely attached to me, but says that she can never be my wife so long as I remain so regrettably ignorant, so distressingly frivolous.

"I think she would really like to marry me," he added wistfully. "And I believe I am neither a fribble nor a light-minded fool, but just as sober and rational as most men. Only her father, you know, is Sir Philip

[2] See *A Midsummer Night's Dream*, Act III, Scene 1: "Peas-blossom! Cobweb! Moth! and Mustardseed! Enter four fairies ..." Obviously, Shakespeare meant his Peas-blossom to be a fairy rather than a changeling, but I have allowed myself some authorial license here.

[3] There is no literary justification that I know for this idea that changelings subsist on nectar and dewdrops. I merely put it in because the concept seemed pretty, pleasing, and somehow appropriate. Perhaps I did read it somewhere, after all.

Merriweather, the mathematician, and I think Phoebe[4] considers it her duty to marry a man who is much like her father."

Titania sighed and gave him her hand. Though her passions were deep and intense, they were also ephemeral; it was easy for her to forget her own problems and take an immediate interest in his. "I suppose as Phoebe's godmother[5] I ought to applaud her sense of duty. But I must say, when it comes to husbands, that a warm and a loyal heart is highly desirable—far more important than a penetrating mind. I think the day may come when Phoebe bitterly regrets rejecting your offer."

"If that is so . . ." said Gregory. He ducked his head, blushed a deep shade of crimson, and pretended to study the butterfly buckles on his stout black shoes. "I would never suggest this if she did not already like me, because then it would be utterly wicked . . . but is there not some way, some fairy charm or love spell, that would make Phoebe love me just the *tiniest* bit more than she does right now? Then she might follow her own inclination, instead of her sense of duty."

He lowered his voice. "I have heard of a little purple western flower,[6] the juice of which—"

"No," said Titania. "No fairy charms or love spells. I do not know how it is, but things of that nature never seem to work as they are intended and only make circumstances more horrid and complicated than they were before."

Gregory released her hand with a soft groan. "If you cannot aid me, with all your wisdom and power, then—"

"I have not said that I could not help you," Titania chided him gently. In fact, she was determined to assist this changeling child of hers if a way could possibly be found. "Only that it may be necessary for me to devise some new and novel means."

[4] In Phoebe Merriweather and her father, Sir Philip, we meet two fictitious characters who do not, in fact, appear in any of Shakespeare's plays.

[5] The notion that fairies frequently offer their services as godparents is too ancient and widespread to require any explanation by me.

[6] See *A Midsummer Night's Dream,* Act II, Scene 1: ". . . the bolt of Cupid fell: it fell upon a little western flower, before milk-white, now purple with love's wound, and Maidens call it love-in-idleness . . ."

She sat in thought for several minutes, then came to a sudden decision. "Send in my maid, and tell my coachman to bring 'round my chariot within the hour," said Titania. "I am going to pay a call on the Weird Sisters."

The three witches lived at Windhill Court, a most desirable address. Because the fashion for blasted heaths and bearded women[7] had long since passed—and town villas, manicured gardens, and powdered wigs were all the rage—they had bowed before the winds of popular opinion, by occupying a narrow house made of bricks, receiving afternoon visitors in a badly furnished parlor on the second floor, and adopting the ancient and respectable surname of Drummond. But old habits die hard, and Titania continued to think of them as the Weird Sisters.

She arrived on their doorstep very prettily attired in pearly satin and a hat adorned with silver cobwebs and opalescent dragonflies, and was promptly ushered into the untidy sitting room, where tea was about to be served.

"I really wish that we might help you," said the elder Miss Drummond, over the cracked and dingy teacups. "But I am afraid that love potions and spells are out of our line—they are inclined to be tricky and also rather dangerous. We always specialized in visions and prophecy. Rather a pity that we did, now that I come to consider it, for there is little demand for fortunetelling these days, and we look in a fair way to go out of business."

Sybil,[8] the youngest sister, adjusted her wig. In spite of their attempts to appear respectable, the Misses Drummond retained a certain elemental, wind-blown appearance. "We are seriously considering a return to Scotland; London has declined so dreadfully, ever since the turn of the eighteenth century.

"They call this the Age of Reason,[9] and everyone pro-

---

[7] See *Macbeth,* Act I, Scene 3: "—you should be women, and yet your beards forbid me to interpret that you are so."

[8] Sybil, or Sibyl, was a title applied to certain females consulted as prophetesses or fortunetellers by the ancient Greeks and Romans.

[9] The ladies appear to be a bit confused. The Age of Reason (also known as The Enlightenment) is associated more with the mid-eighteenth century, rather than the beginning. However, perhaps the thing crept up on the Misses

fesses an absolute passion for rational Science," she continued bitterly. "But this Science of theirs, so far as I can tell, is nothing more than good old-fashioned Natural Philosophy, which used to be the province of alchemists and sorcerers. As I was saying only the other day, to Doctor—" Miss Sybil cut off her sentence with a tiny gasp, and all three sisters exchanged a significant glance.

"You were saying only the other day . . . ?" Titania prompted her politely.

"What Sybil was saying the other day is of no consequence." Miss Cassandra[10] Drummond entered the conversation for the first time. "But what we are about to tell you may be of great assistance. You are acquainted, no doubt, with our old, old friend, the wizard Prospero?"

"I know that gentleman by reputation only," said Titania, accepting a plate of broken sugar biscuits. "That is . . . I believe we were once properly introduced, but I do not precisely recall the occasion. I had heard, however, that he renounced his study of Magic.[11]"

"Very true," said Miss Sybil. "But his passion for knowledge was not diminished, and he has now become one of these modern Scientists. He has opened a rather unusual establishment, devoted to medicine and animal magnetism, at a country house in Kent. Cassandra, dear, where did you put that advertisement?"

Cassandra rummaged in her work basket, among the balls of knotted yarn and the tangled embroidery silks (dislodging a nest of baby mice as she did so), and produced a large roll of foolscap paper, which she handed over to Titania.

Titania unscrolled the handbill and examined the contents:

Drummond while they were not paying perfect attention, and they therefore assumed it had been in force rather longer than it actually was.

[10] According to Greek legend, Cassandra was the oracular daughter of Priam and Hecuba. Her curse was that no one believed her prophecies, although they were, in fact, quite accurate—particularly concerning the downfall of Troy. How ironic that Macbeth's tragedy should result because he took the prognostications of *our* Cassandra and her two sisters far too seriously and their precise words perhaps too literally. See *Macbeth*, Act V, Scene 3: "Till Birnam Wood remove to Dunsinane, I cannot taint with fear."

[11] See *The Tempest*, Act V, Scene I: "But this rough magic I here abjure, &c."

TEMPLUM AESCULAPIO SACRUM

(*proclaimed the handbill*[12])
THE RENOWNED DOCTOR PROSPERO
IS NOW WELCOMING VISITORS TO THE

TEMPLE OF LOVE AND HEALING

MINERAL BATHS AND MAGNETICAL WATERS
to soothe all bodily ills
PAGEANTS, PROCESSIONS, MUSICAL
PERFORMANCES, AND OTHER
ENTERTAINMENTS
Featuring the fair VESTINA, Goddess of Health[13]

THE DRAUGHT OF VENUS
*A concoction of Rare and Potent Ingredients, Guaranteed
to
Reanimate Affection, Increase Passion, Restore Virility,
and
Produce Children of Unparalleled Intelligence and
Beauty*

also

*The Latest and Most Remarkable Scientific
Appurtenances including*
THE GRAND CELESTIAL BED
*Equipped with 1500 pounds of Artificial Lodestones
and Designed to Impart the most Powerful Vibratory,
Undulating,
Fervent, Pleasurable, and Penetrating Influences
to the Fortunate Occupants*

[12] The contents of this handbill are rather liberally adapted from an actual advertisement describing the establishment of one Doctor Graham, the historical creator of the Celestial Bed (see below), who flourished in London during the eighteenth century. Unfortunately, the true magnificence of Graham's Temple of Health and Hymen and his famous creation could not possibly be done sufficient justice in these few pages. C.J.S. Thompson condemns the good doctor as "a man of unbounded effrontery and impudence."

[13] Or as Graham had it: "Vestina, rosy Goddess of Health." The reader might be interested to learn that the young woman who actually played this part was one Emma Lyon, who later became the notorious Lady Hamilton.

There was a great deal more, but Titania had already seen enough to interest her. "I believe," she said, "that a consultation with Doctor Prospero might prove highly beneficial."

When Titania returned home, she spent an hour at her little Chinese lacquer writing desk. She dispatched two letters, written on scented notepaper: one to Doctor Prospero, informing him of her impending visit, the second to Phoebe, explaining that she, Titania, was about to embark on a journey into the country for the sake of her health, and would Phoebe be kind enough to accompany her?

After a few instructions to her maid, Titania sent for young Peaseblossom and told him what was afoot.

In the morning, her coach was waiting at the door. Under ordinary circumstances, faced with a journey of such duration, Titania might have turned herself into an owl and flown to Doctor Prospero's, or used some spell to whisk her instantly to the desired location[14]—she doubted, however, that either mode of transportation would recommend itself to Phoebe, and she could hardly send the girl alone in the carriage with the servants and the luggage.

"Do not begin your own journey before ten o'clock," she cautioned Gregory as he helped her into the coach. "It would be disastrous if you should overtake us on the road, for then Phoebe might guess what scheme we are hatching."

Such was the cynical age they lived in, so reluctant were Titania's neighbors to believe in the existence of fairies, that few outside her immediate household guessed her true identity. Indeed, Phoebe knew her only as a wealthy lady of indeterminate age and eccentric habits. Which was a great help under the present circumstances.

"For who could imagine that the Queen of the Fairies had any use for doctors, mineral baths, or magnetical wa-

---

[14] See Puck's speech in *A Midsummer Night's Dream,* Act II, Scene 1: "I'll put a girdle round about the earth in forty minutes." Or . . . perhaps not. As the reader may be growing weary by now of reading with this story in one hand and a collection of Shakespeare's plays in the other, he may instead wish to put off looking this up until *after* my story is finished.

ters[15]?" Titania asked, just before Gregory closed the door. "But what could possibly be more natural than an elderly godmother—no matter how youthfully well-preserved— paying a visit to a fashionable watering place?"

When the coach had gone, rumbling off in the direction of the house where Phoebe lived with her father, Gregory took out his pocket watch and flipped open the cover. It was an unusual timepiece, fashioned to resemble a large black beetle,[16] and it marked the hours with perfect accuracy. "Time for a bit of breakfast," said young Peaseblossom.

The truth was, he felt queasy with excitement (his beloved Phoebe must soon be his!), but he thought that a sip of nectar—perhaps with a plate of sirloin and eggs on the side—would settle his stomach admirably.

He left the house promptly at ten. At noon, an unexpected visitor appeared on the doorstep, a willowy figure in black velvet and snowy point lace, who knocked on the wooden panels with a curious cane: three silver serpents intertwined, each with staring ruby eyes. He was informed by the servant who answered the door that Madam had gone to the country with Gregory Peaseblossom, to consult Doctor Prospero at the Temple of Love. No one knew when the lady would return, but she was expected to make a lengthy visit.

"Indeed?" said the gentleman, with a raised eyebrow and a tight smile. "Then I will call again at a more suitable time."

When the door shut with an audible thump, the doorstep was already empty.

But miles away, at his country house, Doctor Prospero was astonished to receive an elegant visitor, who arrived in a cloud of sulfurous black smoke and declared that he would be staying for at least a fortnight.

* * *

[15] Who indeed? Also, as we have yet to meet Phoebe in person, it would be hard to accept that she could possibly be so gullible.
[16] *Anobium tesselatum,* the deathwatch beetle, a species of insect which makes a ticking sound rather like a watch, superstitiously regarded as an omen of death. Perhaps a poetic affectation on young Gregory's part. For more on fairies and changelings and their affinity for insects see . . . oh, never mind.

As the coach rattled and jolted down country roads, Titania soon grew weary of Phoebe's company. Though the girl was as pretty and delicate as a china shepherdess, she had very limited interests. She knew little of music, painting, or poetry, cared nothing for gossip, fashion, or the theater. But she could (and unfortunately did) speak long and learnedly of Euclid and Pythagoras—as well as a very odd theory advanced by her father and his friend Reverend Stukeley about the great stone circle on Salisbury Plain.[17]

"They believe that Stonehenge was a celestial observatory," Phoebe explained, "originally constructed by the Druids, in order to more perfectly time their barbaric seasonal rituals."

Titania, who had dallied with Druids in the forest primeval when she was young,[18] was first diverted and then rather bored, but she continued to listen politely. At last Phoebe subsided, and seemed to lapse into a state of intense contemplation.

Left to her own devices, Titania reached into her reticule and drew out a little volume bound in calfskin. The book opened on a familiar page, the beginning of an essay written by one of her Irish cousins, a tract *On the Supposed Immortality of Fairies.*

It was a controversial bit of writing, and the theories it contained had been hotly debated in Fairy Society for over a decade. Titania herself was not quite certain what she believed.

Because no fairy had ever died of natural causes, it was widely assumed that they were immortal. But in fact, Titania and Oberon were among the oldest fairies still living; all previous generations had died violently, either by accident, or as a result of the feuds and warfare which had once seemed inevitable to their proud and volatile race. Yet the world was changing, men were growing more civilized, and the race of fairies more settled and peaceful. As a result, a number had already survived to a

[17] William Stukeley, like Doctor Graham, was a real person. He actually lived (and theorized about Stonehenge) during the eighteenth century. If you insist on looking this up, don't blame me.
[18] There is nothing in Shakespeare or elsewhere to support this. Like Phoebe and her father, I made it up.

hitherto unthinkable age, and there was much speculation as to what would happen when the first fairies entered their third millenium.

One theory was that they would simply die, prove to be long-lived but not immortal. Another theory, espoused by many, was that immortality itself would prove ultimately fatal, by first driving its victims mad and then to suicide.

Others argued that some incredible transformation would eventually result: Perhaps a metamorphosis into winged beings, as the race had long been pictured in the popular fancy. Or perhaps (and this was rather nasty, based on an ancient superstition) they would dwindle into stinging flies and loathsome insects, and so perish.[19]

I wonder . . . Titania thought as she read . . . *what Mr. Merriweather and the Reverend Stukeley would think of all this . . . they seem to know so very much about practically everything!*

Just then, the coach came to a jolting halt. Titania looked out the window. They had stopped before a pair of imposing iron gates, set into an archway bearing the Biblical commandment: BE FRUITFUL, MULTIPLY, AND REPLENISH THE EARTH.

A lumbering servant came out of the gatehouse and opened the gates; he was a rough-looking fellow with a hump on his back and it seemed that his hands and feet were webbed, yes, actually webbed, just like a fish![20] But Titania had time to see no more than that because the coach was soon bowling down a long paved avenue. At last it drew up before a large and imposing residence.

Titania smoothed out her skirts, adjusted her hat and her demi-veil, and prepared to disembark. A silver-haired gentleman in a coat of leaf-green silk stepped forward to help her alight.

"Doctor Prospero, I do believe," said Titania. There

[19] I do not recall where I encountered this peculiar bit of folklore. It may have been in something by the late W. Y. Evans Wenz, who knew a great deal about fairies.

[20] This is a brief appearance by Caliban, in a nonspeaking role. Though usually depicted as apelike, a fishy, amphibious form seems more likely. At their first meeting, Trinculo alludes to "a very ancient and fishlike smell" and later addresses the monster as "thou debosh'd fish." Deplorably rude, of course, but perhaps understandable.

was something decidedly familiar in that high-boned face, the tall and graceful figure. *He is very distinguished—not to be wondered at, for I believe he was once the Duke of Naples[21]—but why did I not remember how handsome he was?*

"You are very welcome, Madam," said Doctor Prospero. "And with your leave, I will escort you and this pretty child into the house."

With many a pleasantry, he led them up the steps, into an immense entry hall, and up a broad flight of marble stairs. "I am afraid you will find us rather short of company," he said. "Two elderly ladies and their even more ancient brother. Hardly the sort of society to which a woman of your stature—and may I say beauty and fashion?—must certainly be accustomed."

"I did not come here seeking society," replied Titania, as they reached the top of the stairs. "I only wish peace and quiet . . . and of course to take the waters."

"Then I believe you will be satisfied," said Doctor Prospero. "And here is Mistress Quickly, my invaluable housekeeper, who will show you to your rooms." He indicated a stout, respectable looking creature in a black gown and a snowy white apron and cap.[22] "Once you have rested and refreshed yourselves, you might wish to join me down in the gardens."

When Phoebe emerged from her bedchamber an hour later, it occurred to her that she had no idea where her godmother's rooms were located. "Still," she told herself, "I suppose I can easily find my own way down to the gardens."

She closed her door and proceeded down the corridor. But a curious thing happened as she moved through the house. She had always possessed a keen sense of direction, but she soon discovered that she had lost her way—and when she tried to retrace her steps, Phoebe found

[21] *The Tempest*, Act I, Scene 2, Prospero to Miranda: "Thy mother was a piece of virtue, and she said thou wast my daughter; and thy father was Duke of Milan." Titania has clearly confused the two duchies.
[22] This is the same Mistress Quickly who consorted with Falstaff, Pistol &c. in *King Henry the Fourth, Part 1 & Part 2* and *King Henry the Fifth*—though perhaps more decent and cleanly than Shakespeare intended her.

herself walking instead down an unfamiliar corridor, a narrow ill-lit passageway.

It appeared that while the front of the house was modern, the part at the back was very much older, most likely Elizabethan, for the walls were paneled in worm-eaten oak. Phoebe wandered through long musty hallways and old-fashioned galleries, past faded portraits done in oils, and rusty suits of armor, but wherever she went she was unable to find a single staircase leading down to the ground floor.

After a time, she began to feel panicky, as though the house itself meant to imprison her. But she was a sensible girl, and dismissed that morbid fancy almost immediately. At last she came to a low doorway. There was a sign upon the lintel, bearing the legend SANCTUM SANCTORUM, written in letters of gold.

Perhaps I will find Doctor Prospero inside, or at least one of his ... I suppose one ought to call them acolytes, since this place pretends to be a temple. Someone, anyway, who can show me the way down to the gardens.

She knocked on the door, but no one answered. As it was not locked, she pushed it open, and discovered an ascending spiral staircase on the other side.

"I suppose there is nothing for it but to mount these stairs," said Phoebe, suiting her actions to her words. The stairs led up and up and up, far higher than she had supposed the house extended. "I believe I have entered some ancient tower."

At the top of the steps was another door. Without knocking this time, she pushed it open, and entered a most remarkable room.

The ceiling had been painted with constellations, silver and gold on midnight blue, and the room was ringed with windows. In the middle of the chamber was a long table, piled with books and papers, maps painted on parchment, and all sorts of fascinating brass instruments. By an open casement, a dark-haired man in a plain suit of clothes was fiddling with a long cylindrical object, which appeared to be some kind of telescope.

"I beg your pardon," said Phoebe, as the man glanced up, and started at the sight of her. "I did not wish to intrude, but ..." Her interest in this unusual room and its occupant got the better of her. "Excuse me, sir, but is this not a place of astronomical observation?"

"It is," he replied with a smile. Though he was simply dressed, he spoke with an educated accent. And while he was plainly a great deal older than Phoebe, he was still a fine looking man, with an imposing hawklike countenance. "Have you lost your way? I hardly think that you meant to come here. Allow me to—"

"No, please," she said, gazing around her with sparkling eyes. "I think this room is fascinating. Would you show me what you are doing? Perhaps I ought to introduce myself: I am Phoebe Merriweather, and my father—"

"Your father is Sir Philip Merriweather, the mathematician. You are very like him." exclaimed the mysterious gentleman, clearly enchanted to make her acquaintance. "Sir Philip and I have been carrying on a delightful correspondence on the orbits and trajectories of comets. Pardon me . . . my name is Septimus Battista, and I am Doctor Prospero's assistant. These astronomical studies are a mere avocation, but one that I find absolutely fascinating."

He abandoned his telescope, crossed the room, and took both of her hands in a cordial grip. He led her gently over to the table. "Perhaps you would like to examine this star-chart, these calculations?"

"Oh, yes," said Phoebe breathlessly, accepting an inky paper scribbled all over with numbers and planetary symbols. "How very, very kind you are."

The gardens, as Titania soon discovered, were cool and pleasant, with wide lawns of an incredible emerald green, a boxwood maze, marble statues, pillars and fountains, and a golden pavilion covered with flowering vines.

"You do not appear unduly tired after your journey," said a voice behind her. Turning, Titania saw Prospero moving in her direction, strolling down a flagstone walkway with a tricorn hat in one hand, a silver cane in the other. "Indeed, you appear wonderfully fresh, and as vivid as any flower in this garden."

Titania felt a faint heat rising in her face. "These grounds must be very beautiful at night when you light the lanterns." She fell into step beside him, and they continued to walk together, through a dainty arbor, along the edge of a rushy lake.

She felt perfectly easy in his company. A volatile creature of instinct and desire, Titania generally knew at once whether or not she was going to like someone. Doctor Prospero was one of those people whom she liked immediately.

They stopped beside a crystal fountain, and she dipped up water between her hands. It tasted slightly bitter and was full of bubbles that tickled her palate. "It is not unpleasant," she decided. "But is it truly beneficial?"

"Not to you, I think," he answered. "But then, you have not really come here to improve your health. I suppose your young—nephew, was it?—will be along very soon. In the meantime, perhaps, you would like to see what the pavilion contains."

The interior of the pavilion was draped in spangled satin of a deep, rich blue. There was a marble fireplace and a long oak table, on which someone had arranged a light repast: fruit, cheese, and wine, creams, aspics, and lobster patties. In the center of the room was a gorgeous piece of furniture, which Titania immediately identified as the Celestial Bed.

It was approximately twelve feet long by nine feet wide, supported by pillars of brilliant glass. Suspended over the bed was a magnificent dome, exquisitely painted with figures of sportive gods and goddesses. The dome itself was supported by figures of Cupid and Psyche, Hymen and Vesta,[23] carrying torches that glowed with a weird electrical fire, and censors that breathed heady fragrances into the air.

When Prospero touched a switch, a hidden mechanism began to move, causing the bed to revolve in place, and the music of flutes, violins, clarinets,[24] trumpets, and oboes to fill the pavilion.

[23] Cupid and Psyche were mythical lovers, representing love and the human soul respectively. Hymen was the Greek god of marriage, and Vesta the Roman goddess of the hearth. Vesta's precise relationship to Vestina (mentioned above) is rather hazy. It is possible that Doctor Graham also indulged in a little dramatic license and made Vestina up.

[24] Doctor Graham spelled this "clarionets." To avoid endless heated discussions with the copy editor, I decided not to adopt his spelling.

"There is an internal pipe organ within the bed," said Prospero, leading Titania over to the table, pulling out a chair for her. "The bed moves on an axis, as you can see, but can also be converted to an inclined plane."

Titania helped herself to the fruit and the creams. The Doctor poured wine into a jeweled cup and put it into her hand. "The compound magnets and lodestones are also concealed beneath the bed and pour forth their healing influence in a continuous circle."

"How very intriguing," said Titania, and she could not help admiring the brilliance of the man who had invented something so truly remarkable.

"The sheets are the richest and silkiest satins, perfumed in the Oriental manner with spices, odors, and essences," he continued. "The mattress is filled with hair from the tails of English stallions, which are incredibly elastic, and lend the mattress a certain resilience which I believe has never been matched elsewhere."

After the meal, Titania made to rise from her chair, only to discover that her knees were weak and her head distressingly light.

"My dear Doctor," she exclaimed, "I think I am about to be ill. And the wine . . . it tasted a little odd. . . ."

But Prospero was there behind her, putting his arms around her slender waist and lifting her up into a warm embrace. "Not wine," he said, "but the Draught of Venus. Its principle ingredient is a little purple western flower with a very pretty legend attached to it."

Her head was spinning now, the strength of his supporting arms was entirely welcome. "Allow me to help you, my dear, over to the bed."

Titania lay naked beside her lover on the Celestial Bed. The axis revolved, the music played, the air was rich with balmy odors. The compound magnets and artificial lodestones exerted their healing influence. The bed was everything it was reported to be, and the experience as undulating, vibratory, fervent, and penetrating as the handbill had promised.

Titania studied her reflection in the mirror over the mantle. From what she could see, her gown of lilac satin was sadly crushed and her hair cascaded over her shoulders in a riot of silver-gilt curls. She decided there was nothing she could do about the gown, and her hair looked rather attractive the way it was, so she contented herself with adjusting the deep lace ruffle on her shoulders and the ladybird brooch nestling among the lace.

The door of the pavilion opened suddenly and in rushed Gregory Peaseblossom. "I beg your pardon . . . but what are you—" His glance traveled from Titania to the gentleman in shirtsleeves, waistcoat, and leaf-green breeches. "No, no, I should not have asked. I will come back later."

"My dear Gregory, what has happened to you?" exclaimed Titania. "Your clothes are all over dust, and you look like the victim of a carriage accident."

"I was," said young Peaseblossom, passing a hand over his forehead, where a large purple bruise was forming. "Just outside the gates, my phaeton collided with another carriage. The young lady inside was only a little shaken, but . . ." He gulped and swallowed a deep breath of air. "Madam, I am quite undone. The most glorious creature, the sweetest smile . . . I knew at once that I would gladly die for her. But what on earth am I to say to Phoebe?"

A tiny frown creased Titania's dainty brow. "This is very sudden. Are you certain it is love and not infatuation?"

Gregory leaned against the doorframe for support. "But that is the problem precisely. Only think of it, in less than a heartbeat I felt exactly the same way about Miss Whiston[25] as I do about Phoebe. I am dreadfully afraid that I am not *truly* in love with either of them—or else I am madly in love with both of them—and that being so, I can hardly marry Phoebe."

"Well," said Titania, giving a final touch to her hair. "That is hardly a problem, since you and Phoebe are not engaged."

"Yes," he answered miserably, "but I have been such a fool. When Phoebe refused me, I vowed I would wait forever and ever. A single word from her, I said, and we would instantly be married."

"What an impetuous boy you are," said Titania, reach-

---

[25] Need I note that the mysterious Miss Whiston is also my own literary invention?

ing for her hat and her shawl. "But after all, we have only to find Phoebe, tell her that you have changed your mind, and beg her to release you from your promise.

"Although now that I come to think of it," she added, "I have not seen Phoebe since we arrived here."

"I believe," said Prospero, "that you will find Phoebe in the Sanctum Sanctorum. You may ask any of the servants to show you the way."

Half an hour later, they located Phoebe in the observatory, sitting on a three-legged stool, raptly listening as the astronomer spoke.

"For comets . . ." he was saying, ". . . recruit the expended fuel of the sun, thereby supplying moisture to the planets, but also causing the most horrifying deluges and conflagrations . . ."[26]

"From the way that she looks at him," Titania whispered in Gregory's ear, "I think it will be easy to secure your release."

Hearing Titania speak, Phoebe turned around on her stool, and greeted them both with a melting smile. "Dear Godmother, I am sorry. Have I kept you waiting? And Gregory, I did not expect to see you here. Let me introduce you to Signor Battista. He is Doctor Prospero's—"

"Madam, I see that it is impossible to continue to deceive you," said the astronomer, coming forward to take Titania's hand. "I must beg your pardon, but the gentleman assured me that it was only a harmless deception. I am—"

Titania felt the blood drain from her face. "You are the real Doctor Prospero. Of course, I recognize you. And the other one . . . that fiend in human form, the author of this deception . . . it is easy enough for me to put a name to him."

Her back stiffened, her chin lifted, and the color flooded back into her cheeks. "If you will pardon me, I am going down to the garden, to exchange a few words with the arch-deceiver."

[26] This, by the way, is good eighteenth century science, as fantastic as it may seem today. This is also the last footnote, since I mean this story to come to an unexpectedly touching conclusion, and would not like to shatter the mood with any authorial intrusions.

He was waiting beside the rushy lake, as arrogant and beautiful as ever, though now he had abandoned his previous disguise—his hair was no longer silver but a rich dark auburn, and his eyes were as green as his coat. Titania wondered how she had ever been deceived; aside from his coloring and the shape of his chin, he had not looked so very different as Doctor Prospero.

"Oberon." She put up her hand to stay his sudden movement in her direction. "I believe you owe me an explanation."

"My affair with Fiona has ended," he said. "I went home intending to beg your forgiveness, only to discover that you and Gregory Peaseblossom had gone off together, presumably destined to consummate your love in the Celestial Bed."

Titania was shocked as well as offended. "Gregory and I? What an appalling idea."

"I beg your pardon," he said. "But Gregory was taken at a late age . . . twelve or thirteen, was he not? In any case, I always thought you regarded him less as a mother would . . . and more like an affectionate aunt or cousin."

He smiled faintly. "I arrived here, so they tell me, reeking of fire and brimstone, so consuming was my jealousy. When I discovered that Phoebe was also expected, I realized my mistake. But then I could not resist the temptation to woo and win you one more time.

"I am afraid that I rather frightened poor Phoebe," he added ruefully, "by rearranging the rooms and passages. But I wanted to keep her out of our way. And let this be said in my favor: As you have no doubt noticed, the effect of love-in-idleness is far more transitory when it is taken internally."

"To woo and win me . . . or only to make sport of me?" said Titania sadly. "You were always one to amuse yourself at my expense."

Oberon removed his hat, tucked it under one arm. "The centuries roll on, and life is unutterably boring. In a world grown stale and flat, only Titania remains eternally fresh and new. I believe that I wander, only that when I return I may feel once more the delightful shock of your novelty."

"The centuries roll on," Titania answered, "and I grow weary of your endless affairs, your heartless deceptions."

"I believe that I finally realize that," said Oberon, and now his manner was far less arrogant. "When you first said my name, I heard such bitterness, I knew that I stood in mortal danger of losing the one thing that makes life endurable. Titania . . . beloved . . . if you will give me but one more chance, I think I can promise that you will not be disappointed."

As he spoke, she heard something in his voice—a vulnerability, a touch of humanity—which had never been there before.

And perhaps, she thought, *this is the revelation we have all been awaiting. That as we grow older, we become more human.*

She had a vision of herself and Oberon, not as gauzy-winged beings transformed like butterflies, but as a comfortable old couple, turning gray and prosaic, yet happy to spend their declining years in each other's company. The shocking thing was that the idea did not repulse her. In fact, it even had a certain perverse charm.

And that being so, she knew what her choice must be.

"I believe," said Titania, offering him her hand, "that I can find it in my heart to forgive you one last time."

V

"What's past is prologue."
The Tempest

When you consider that Homer and Virgil are still not merely read but enjoyed in our time, there's no doubt that Shakespeare's reputation will survive long beyond us. But, one wonders, in what form or way?

NOT OF AN AGE

Gregory Benford

Gregory Benford is the author of numerous books and stories firmly based on hard science, although here he does allow himself a bit more leeway with reality.

The fearful wrenching snap, a sickening swerve—and she was there.

Vitrovna found herself in a dense copse of trees, branches swishing overhead in a fitful breeze. Shottery Wood, she hoped. But was the time and place truly right? She had to get her bearings.

Not easy, in the wake of the Transition. She was still groggy from stretched moments in the slim, cushioned cylinder. All that aching time her stomach had knotted and roiled, fearing that intercession awaited the Transition's end. A squad of grim Corpsmen, an injunction. A bleak prospect of standing at the docket for meddling in the sanctified past, a capital crime.

But when the wringing pop echoed away, there was no one awaiting to erase her from time's troubled web. Only this scented night, musky with leaves and a wind promising fair.

She worked her way through prickly bushes and boggy glades, using her small flashlight as little as she could. No need to draw attention—and a white beam cutting the darkness of an April night in 1616 would surely cause alarm.

She stumbled into a rough country lane wide enough to

see the sky. A sliver of bleached moon, familiar star-sprinklings—and there, Polaris. Knowing north, she reckoned from her topo map which way the southward-jutting wedge of Stratford might be. This lane led obliquely that way, so she took it, wind whipping her locks in encouragement.

Much still lay to be learned, she could be far off in space and time, but so far the portents were good. If the combined ferretings and guesses of generations of scholars proved true, this was the last night the aging playwright would be afoot. A cusp moment in a waning life.

Up ahead, hollow calls. A thin blade of yellow as a door opened. A looming shamble-shadow of a drunken man, weaving his ragged course away from the inky bulk of an inn. Might this be the one she sought? Not the man, no, for they were fairly sure that graying Will had spent the night's meaty hours with several friends.

But the inn might be the place where he had drunk his last. The vicar of Stratford's Holy Trinity Church, John Ward, had written years after this night that the bard had "been on an outing" with two lesser literary lights. There were probably only a few inns in so small a town, and this might be the nearest to Shakespeare's home.

Should. Might. Probably. Thin netting indeed, to snare hard facts.

She left the lane and worked through brush that caught at her cloak of simple country burlap. A crude weave covering a cotton dress, nothing lacy to call attention, yet presentably ladylike—she hoped. Considering the sexual fascinations of the ancients, she might easily be mistaken for a common harlot, or a village slut about for a bit of fun.

Any contact with others here would endanger her, to say nothing of definitely breaking the Codes. Of course, she was already flagrantly violating the precepts regulating time travel, but years of preparation had hardened her to that flat fact, insulated her from any lingering moral confusions.

She slipped among trees, trying to get a glimpse through the tiny windows of the inn. Her heart thudded, breath coming quick. The swarming smells of this place! In her antiseptic life, a third-rank Literary Historian in the University Corps, she had never before felt herself so immersed in history, in the thick air of a world innocent of steel and ceramic, of concrete and stale air.

She fished her senso-binoculars from her concealed pack and studied the windows. It was difficult to make out much through the small, warped panes and heavy leading, behind which men lifted tankards and flapped their mouths, illuminated by dim, uncertain candles. A fat man waved his arms, slopping drink. *Robustious rothers in rural rivo rhapsodic. Swill thou then among them, scrike thine ale's laughter.* Not Will's words, but some contemporary. Marlowe? Whoever, they certainly applied here. A ragged patch of song swept by on the stirring wind, carried from an opening door.

Someone coming out. She turned up the amps on the binoculars and saw three men, each catching the swath of lantern light as they helped each other down stubby stairs to the footpath.

Three! One large, balding, a big chest starting to slide into an equatorial belly. Yet still powerful, commanding, perhaps the manner of a successful playwright. Ben Jonson?

The second younger, short, in wide-brimmed hat—a Warwickshire style of the time, she recalled. It gave him a rakish cast, befitting a poet. Michael Drayton?

And coming last, tripping on the stair and grasping at his friends for purchase, a mid-sized man in worn cloak and close-fitting cap. *Life brief and naught done,* she remembered, a line attributed—perhaps—to this wavering apparition. But not so, not so.

The shadowy figure murmured something and Vitrovna cursed herself for her slowness. She telescoped out the directional microphone above the double barrels of the binoculars. It clicked, popped, and she heard—

"I was then bare a man, nay, a boy still," the big man said. "Big in what fills, sure speak." The wide-hatted man smirked.

"Swelled in blood-fed lustihead, Ben's bigger than stallions, or so rumor slings it," the cloaked figure rapped back, voice starting gravelly and then swinging tenor-high at the sentence's end.

The tall man chuckled with meaty relish. "What fills the rod's same as fills the pen, as you'd know better."

So this was the man who within a few years would say

that his companion, the half-seen figure standing just outside the blade of light cast by the inner inn, was 'Not of
an age, but for all time.' Ben Jonson, in breeches, a tuft
of white shirt sticking from an unbuttoned fly. A boister-
ous night for all.

"Aye, even for the miowing of kitticat poetry on
spunk-stained parchment, truest?" the cloaked man said,
words quick but tone wan and fading.

"Better than a mewling or a yawper," the short man
said. All three moved a bit unsteadily round a hitching
post and across the yard. Jonson muttered, laughed. She
caught the earthy reek of ale. The man who must be
Drayton—though he looked little like the one engraving
of his profile she had seen—snickered liquidly, and the
breeze snatched away a quick comment from the man
who—she was sure now—must be Shakespeare. She
amped up the infrared and pressed a small button at the
bridge of the binoculars. A buzz told her digital image
recording was on, all three face-forward in the shimmering silver moonlight, a fine shot. Only then did she realize that they were walking straight at her.

Could they make her out, here in a thicket? Her throat
tightened and she missed their next words, though the re-
corder at her hip would suck it all in. They advanced,
staring straight into her eyes—across the short and weedy
lawn, right up to the very bushes that hid her. Shakespeare grunted, coughed, and fished at his drawers. To
her relief, they all three produced themselves, sighed with
pleasure, and spewed rank piss into the bushes.

"The one joy untaxed by King or wife," Jonson medi-
tated.

The others nodded, each man embedded in his own
moment of release, each tilting his head back to gaze at
the sharp stars. Then they were done, tucked back in.
They turned and walked off to Vitrovna's left, onto the
lane.

She followed as silently as she could, keeping to the
woods. Thorns snagged her cloak and soon they had
walked out of earshot of even her directional microphone.
She was losing invaluable data!

She stumbled onto the path, ran to catch up, and then
followed, aided by shadows. To walk and keep the acous-
tics trained on the three weaving figures was all she could

manage, especially in the awkward, raw-leather shoes she
had to wear. She remembered being shocked that this age
did not even know to make shoes differently curved for
left and right feet, and felt the effect of so simple a difference within half a kilometer. A blister irked her left
heel before she saw a glow ahead. She had given up trying to follow their darting talk. Most was ordinary byplay
laced with coarse humor, scarcely memorable, but scholars could determine that later.

They stopped outside a rambling house with a three-
windowed front from which spilled warm lantern light.
As the night deepened, a touch of winter returned. An
ice-tinged wind whipped in a swaying oak and whistled at
the house's steep-gabled peak. Vitrovna drew as near as
she dared, behind a churning elm.

"Country matters need yawing mouths," Shakespeare
said, evidently referring to earlier talk.

"Would that I knew keenly what they learn from scrape
and toil," Drayton said, voice lurching as the wind tried
to rip it away from her pickups.

"A Johannes Factotum of your skinny skin?" Shakespeare said, sniffing.

Vitrovna translated to herself, *A Jack-Do-All of the
senses?*—though the whole conversation would have to
be endlessly filtered and atomized by computer intelligences before she could say anything definitive. If she
got away with this, that is.

"Upstart crow, cockatrice!" Jonson exclaimed, clapping
Shakespeare on the shoulder. All three laughed warmly.

A whinny sped upon the breeze. From around the
house a boy led two horses. "Cloddy chariot awaits,"
Drayton said blearily.

Shakespeare gestured toward his own front door, which
at that moment creaked open, sending fresh light into the
hummocky yard where they stood. "Would you not—"

"My arse needs an hour of saddle, or sure will be hard-
sore on the ride to London tomorrow," Jonson said.

Drayton nodded. "I go belike, to see to writ's business."

"My best bed be yours, if—"

"No, no, friend." Jonson swung up onto a roan horse
with surprising agility for one so large. "You look chilled.
Get inside to your good wife."

Ben waved good night, calling to the woman who had appeared in the doorway. She was broad and sturdy, graying beneath a frilly white cap, and stood with arms crossed, her stance full of judgment. "Farewell, Anne!"

Good-byes sounding through the frosty air, the two men clopped away. Vitrovna watched Shakespeare wave to them, cloak billowing, then turn to his wife. This was the Anne Hathaway whom his will left with his "second-best" bed, who had saddled him with children since his marriage at eighteen—and who may have forced him into the more profitable enterprise of playwriting to keep their household in something resembling the style of a country gentleman. Vitrovna got Anne's image as she croaked irritably at Shakespeare to come inside.

Vitrovna prayed that she would get the fragment of time she needed. Just a moment, to make a fleeting, last contact—

He hesitated. Then he waved his wife away and walked toward the woods. She barked something at him and slammed the door.

Vitrovna slipped from behind the elm and followed him. He coughed, stopped, and began to pee again into a bush.

An ailment? To have to go again so soon? Stratford's vicar had written that on this night Will "drank too hard," took ill, and died of a fever. This evidence suggested, though, that he knew something was awry when he wrote his will in March, a few weeks before this evening. Or maybe he had felt an ominous pressure from his approaching fifty-second birthday, two days away—when the fever would claim him.

All this flitted through her mind as she approached the wavering figure in the woodsmoke-flavored, whipping wind. He tucked himself back in, turned—and saw her.

Here the danger made her heart pound. If she did something to tweak the timeline a bit too much—

"Ah! Pardons, Madam—the ale within would without."

"Sir, I've come to tell you of greatness exceeding anything you can dream." She had rehearsed this, striving for an accent that would not put him off, but now that she had heard his twangy Elizabethan lilt, she knew that was hopeless. She plowed ahead. "I wanted you to know that your name will be sung down the ages as the greatest of writers."

Will's tired, grizzled face wrinkled. "Who might you be?"

—and the solidity of the past struck her true, his breath sour with pickled herrings and Rhenish wine. The reeking intensity of the man nearly staggered her. Her isolated, word-clogged life had not prepared her for this vigorous, full-bodied age. She gulped and forced out her set speech.

"You may feel neglected now, but centuries hence you'll be read and performed endlessly—"

"*What* are you?" A sour scowl.

"I am from the future. I've come backward in time to tell you, so that such a wonderful man need not, well, need not think he was just a minor poet. Your plays, they're the thing. They—"

"You copy my lines? 'The play's the thing.' Think you that japing pranks—"

"No, no! I truly am from the future, many centuries away."

"And spring upon me in drafty night? I—"

Desperately she brought up her flashlight. "Look." It clicked on, a cutting blue-white beam that made the ground and leaves leap from inky presence into hard realities. "See? This is a kind of light you don't have. I can show you—"

He leaped back, eyes white, mouth sagging. "Uh!"

"Don't be afraid. I wondered if you could tell me something about the dark lady in your sonnets, just a moment's—"

"Magic!"

"No, really, it's just a different kind of lantern. And your plays, did you have any help writing them?"

He recovered, mouth curving shrewdly. "You be scholar or rumor-monger?"

"Neither, sir."

His face hardened as he raised his palm to shield his eyes from the brilliance. "Think me gut-gullible?"

"You deserve to know that we in the future will appreciate you, love you, revere you. It's only justice that you know your works will live forever, be honored—"

"Promising me life forever, then? That's your cheese?"

"No, you don't—"

"This future you claim—know you something of my self, then? My appointed final hour?" His eyes were angry slits, his mouth a flat, bloodless line.

Was he so quick to guess the truth? That she had come at the one possible moment to speak to him, when his work or friends would not be perturbed? "I've come because, yes, this is my only chance to speak with you. There's nothing I can do about that, but I thought—"

"You tempt me with wisps, foul visions."

Did he suspect that once he walked into that house, lay upon his second-best bed, he would never arise again? With leaden certainty she saw him begin to gather this, his mouth working, chin bobbing uncertainly.

"Sir, no, please, I'm just here to, to—"

"Flat-voiced demon, leave me!"

"No, I—"

He reached into his loose-fitting shirt and drew out a small iron cross. Holding it up, he said, "Blest be he who spares my stones, curst be he who moves my bones!"

The lines chiseled above his grave. So he had them in mind already, called them up like an incantation. "I'm sorry, I didn't mean—"

"Go! Christ immaculate, drive such phantoms from me! Give me a sword of spirit, Lord!"

Vitrovna backed away. "I, I—"

—and then she was running, panicked and mortified, into the woods. In her ears rang a fragment from *The Tempest,*

What seest thou else
In the dark backward and abysm of time?

In the shimmering cylinder she panted with anxiety and mortification, her skin a sheen of cold sweat. She had failed terribly, despite decades of research. All her trial runs with ordinary folk of these times who were about to meet their end, carried out in similar circumstances—those had gone well. The subjects had welcomed her. Death was natural and common here, an easeful event. They had accepted her salute with stoic calm, a quality she had come to envy in these dim eras. Certainly they had not turned their angers on her.

But she had faltered before Shakespeare. He had been larger than life, awesome.

Her recordings were valuable, yes, but she might never be able to release them for scholarly purposes now. She had wrenched the past terribly, exciting the poor man just before death's black hand claimed him. She could never forget the look of wild surmise and gathering panic that worked across that wise face. And now—

She had stolen into the University Corps Facility, slipped into the machine with the aid of friends, all in the service of true, deep history. But if she had changed the past enough to send a ripple of causation forward, into her own era, then the Corps would find her, exact the penalty.

No time to think of that. She felt the sickening wrench, a shudder, and then she thumped down into a stony field.

Still night air, a sky of cutting stars. A liquid murmuring led her to the bank of the Big Wood River and she worked her way along it, looking for the house lights. This route she knew well, had paced it off in her own era. She could tell from the set of the stars that she had time, no need to rush this.

Minutes here took literally no time at all in the stilled future world where machines as large as the cities of this age worked to suspend her here. The essence of stealing time from the Corps was that you took infinitesimal time-wedges of that future world, undetectable, elusive—if she was lucky. The Corps would find her uses self-indulgent, sentimental, arrogant. To meddle so could snuff out their future, or merely Vitrovna herself—and all so a few writers could know for a passing moment of their eventual high destiny? Absurd, of course.

July's dawn heat made her shed her cloak and she paused to get her breath. The river wrinkled and pulsed and swelled smooth against the resistance of a big log and she looked down through it to an unreadable depth. Trout hung in the glassy fast water like ornaments, holding into the current. Deeper still a fog of sand ran above the gravel, stirred by currents around the pale round rocks.

The brimming majesty of this silent moment caught at her heart. Such simple beauty had no protection here, needed none.

After a long moment she made herself go on and found the house as faint streamers traced the dawn. Blocky, gray poured concrete, hunkered down like a bunker. A curious, closed place for a man who had yearned to be of the land and sky. In 1926 he had said, "The real reason for not committing suicide is because you always know how swell life gets again after the hell is over." Yet in this spare, beautiful place of rushing water and jutting stone he would finally yield to the abyss that had tempted him all his wracked life.

She worked her way up the stony slope, her Elizabethan shoes making the climb hard. As she reached the small outer door into the basement, she fished forth the flex-key. Its yellow metal shaped itself to whatever opening the lock needed, and in a moment she was inside the storage room, beside the heavy mahogany rack. She had not seen such things except for photographs. Elegant machines of blue sheen and polished, pointful shapes. Death solidified and lustrous. They enchanted her as she waited.

A rustling upstairs. Steps going into the kitchen, where she knew he would pick up the keys on the ledge above the sink. He came down the stairs, haggard in the slack pajamas and robe, the handsome face from photographs now lined and worn, wreathed by a white beard and tangled hair. He padded toward the rack, eyes distant, and then stopped, blinking, as he saw her.

"What the hell?" A rough voice, but recognizable.

"Mr. Hemingway, I ask only a moment of your time, here at the end. I—"

"You're from the IRS aren't you? Snooping into my—"

Alarm spiked in her throat. "No, sir, I am from the future. I've come backward in time to tell you, so that so wonderful a man need not—"

"FBI?" The jowly face clouded, eyes narrow and bright. "I know you've been following me, bribing my friends."

The drinking, hypertension, hepatitis, and creeping manic depression had driven him further even than her research suggested.

She spread her hands. "No, no. You deserve to know that we in the future will appreciate you, love you, revere you. It's only justice that you know your works will live forever, be honored—"

"You're a goddamn federal agent and a liar on top of that." His yellowed teeth set at an angry angle. "Get out!"

"Remember when you said that you wanted to get into

the ring with Mr. Tolstoy? Well, you have, you did. You're in his class. Centuries from now—"

A cornered look came into the jumping eyes. "Sure, I've got six books I declare to win with. I stand on that."

"You have! I come from—"

"You a critic? Got no use for sneaky bastards come right into your house, beady-eyed nobodies, ask you how you write like it was how you shit—"

He leaned abruptly against the pinewood wall and she caught a sour scent of defeat from him. Colors drained from his wracked face and his head wobbled. "Future, huh?" He nodded as if somehow accepting this. "God, I don't know ..."

She stepped back, fear tight in her throat. Earlier in this year he had written *A long life deprives a man of his optimism. Better to die in all the happy period of unillusioned youth, to go out in a blaze of light, then to have your body worn out and old and illusions shattered.* She saw it now in the loose cant of mouth and jaw, the flickering anxiety and hollow dread. The power of it was unbearable.

"I . . . I wanted you to know that those novels, the short stories, they will—"

The sagging head stopped swaying. It jerked up. "Which have you read?"

"All of them. I'm a literary historian."

"Damn, I'm just read by history professors?" Disdain soured the words.

There were no such professions in her time, just the departments of the Corps, but she could not make this ravaged man understand that. "No, your dramas are enjoyed by millions, by billions—"

"Dramas?" He lurched against the wall. "I wrote no dramas."

How to tell him that the media of her time were not the simple staged amusements of this era? That they were experienced directly through the nervous system, sensory banquets of immense emotional power, lived events that diminished the linear medium of words alone to a curious relic?

"You mean those bum movies made from the novels? Tracy in *The Old Man?*"

"No, I mean—we have different ways of reading the

same work, that is all. But for so long I've felt the despair of artists who did not know how much they would mean, poor Shakespeare going to his grave never suspecting—"

"So you know what I'm down here for?" A canny glint in the eyes.

"Yes, of course, that's why I came."

He pulled himself erect with visible effort. "If you're not just another shit artist come here to get a rise out of me—"

"I'm not, I'm a scholar who feels so much for you lonely Primitivists who—"

"That's what you call us? Real writers? *Primitives?*" Jutting jaw. "I'm going to kick your goddamn ass out of here!"

His sudden clotted rage drove her back like a blow. "I meant—"

"Go!" He shoved her. "Hell will freeze over before I'll give in to a lard-ass—"

She bolted away, out the basement door, into the spreading dawn glow. Down the rocky slope, panic gurgling acid in her mouth. She knew that years before this, when asked his opinion of death, he had answered, "Just another whore." Yet there was something new and alive in his face just now, fresh fuel from his sudden, hugely powerful anger, some sea change that sent into her mind a wrenching possibility.

She looked back at the house. He was standing there thin and erect, shaking a knotted fist down at her. She reached the dawn-etched river and punched the summons into her controls and then came the wringing snap and she was in the cylinder again.

Vitrovna let a ragged sigh escape into the cool, calming air. This one was as unsettling as the last. The old man had seemed animated as she left, focused outside himself by her visit. He had kept her off balance the entire time.

Now she saw her error. The earlier tests with ordinary people, whose deaths did not matter in the flow of history, had misled her. In person Shakespeare and Hemingway loomed immensely larger than anyone she had ever known. Compared with the wan, reasonable people of her time, they were bristly giants. Their reactions could not be predicted and they unsettled even her, a historian who thought she knew what to expect.

Vitrovna leaned back, shaken and exhausted. She had programmed a long rest after this engagement, time to get her thoughts in order before the next. That one, the great poet Diana Azar, lay as far ahead in centuries as the gap between the last two, yet her simple dress should still pass there and—

A slim man materialized at the snub end of the cylinder. He wore a curious blue envelope which revealed only head and hands, his skin a smooth green.

"Ah," he said in a heavily accented tenor, "I have intersected you in time."

She gasped. "You—how? To catch me while transporting—"

"In your age, impossible, of course." He arched his oyster-colored forehead, which had no eyebrows. "But when you are in Transition we of your far future may snag you."

She had thought for decades about what she would do if caught, and now said cannily, "You follow the Code standards for self-incrimination?"

She blinked with shock when he laughed. "Code? Ancient history—though it's all the same here, of course. I am not one of your Corps police."

"Then you're not going to prosecute—"

"That was an illusion of your time, Vitrovna. You don't mind me using your first name? In our era, we have only one name, though many prefer none."

"But how can you . . ."

He languidly folded his arms, which articulated as if his elbows were double-jointed. "I must first say that generations far beyond yours are eternally grateful to you for opening this possibility and giving us these historical records." He gestured at her senso-binoculars.

"Records? They survived? I mean, I do make it back to my—"

"Not precisely. But the detailed space-time calculations necessary to explain, these you would not understand. You braved the Codes and the Corps quite foolishly, as you have just discovered—but that is of no import to us."

She felt a rush of hope, her lips opening in expectation. "Then you've come to rescue me from them?"

He frowned, a gesture which included his ears. "No, no. You feared the Corps' authority, but that was mere human power. They vaguely understood the laws of acausality, quite rightly feared them, and so instituted their Code. But they were like children playing with shells at the shore, never glimpsing the beasts which swam in the deeps beyond."

Her seat jolted and she felt queasy. He nodded, as if expecting this, and touched his left wrist which was transparent.

"The Code was a crude rule of thumb, but your violations of it transgressed far beyond mere human edicts. How arrogant, your age! To think that your laws could rule a continuum. Space-time itself has a flex and force. Your talk with Hemingway—quite valuable historically, by the way, considering that he was not going to ever release his memoir, *A Moveable Feast*, when he went down into that basement. But even more important was what he wrote next."

"Next? But he—"

"Quite. Even so, rather less spectacular than your 'apparition' before Shakespeare. As his shaky hand testified, you caused him to gather his notes and scraps of plays. They kept quite well in even a tin box, wedged in with the corpse. A bounty for the critics, though it upset many cherished theories."

"But he still died of pneumonia?"

"You do not have miraculous healing powers. You simply scared him into leaving something more of a record."

"Still, with so much attention paid to the few records we do have, or *did* have, I—"

"Quite." A judicious nod. "I'm afraid that despite our vastly deeper understanding of these matters, there is nothing we can do about that. Causality will have its way."

The cylinder lurched. A raw bass note. "Then how—"

"Not much time left, I'm afraid. Sorry." He leaned forward eagerly. "But I did want to visit you, to thank you for, well, liberating this method of probing the past, at great personal sacrifice. You deserve to know that our epoch will revere you."

He spoke rapidly, admiration beaming in his odd face, the words piling up in an awful leaden weight that sent bile-dark fear rushing hotly through her, a massive premonition.

"So Vitrovna, I saw the possibility of making this intersection. It's only right that you know just how famous you will be—"

The sensation of stepping off a step into a dark, unending fall.

Her speech. He was giving her own speech, and for the same reason.

THE ELEMENTS SO MIXED

Adrienne Martine-Barnes

Adrienne Martine-Barnes, the well-known author of the fantasy series of "Elemental Sword" books, is also a costumer and fabric artist. In this story she speculates on just how universal Shakespeare's appeal might really be.

If only aliens weren't so alien, the Ambassador mused, as she peered into the wickerwork cabinet which served her as a closet. It had a strange but pleasant scent which reminded her that she was light-years from home. Instead of dwelling on the distance from Earth, which always depressed her, she wondered what to wear for the occasion—an occasion whose precise purpose, like so much else about the Koshani, remained unknown.

She gave a little grunt and wished the newborn Consular Service of the United Planets had been somewhat less grandiose and more practical in designing the clothing for the mission. Everything was so heavy and ornate, so clearly made to impress the Koshani with the importance of the wearers. The Koshani never seemed to notice. Perhaps Hiroshi had been right, going native.

The thought of her vanished colleague made Emilia Lazarus feel depressed again. She did not know if he was dead or alive. Soon after the mission had arrived in Sgan'ah, the town which served the Koshani as a capital,

Hiroshi Wells had begun to act very oddly, even for an ethnologist. First he began to appear with blossoms festooning his glossy black hair, in the manner of the local males, then in wraps of the native silk, a soft, sparkling stuff whose color shifted to match the mood of the wearer. He refused to wear the stiff, over-embroidered "uniforms" of the Service. Emilia had hardly noticed, being deeply involved with the nearly impossible task of learning the Koshani language. Finally, he had left for the forests of the north, to check out some rumor, and had never returned. She felt guilty and, more, frustrated because she could not determine either where he was or how he was. As head of the mission, she should have paid more attention!

She pulled a deep purple robe off one of the hangers and shook out its folds. The silver trim around the hem and cuffs looked quite regal, but she was uncertain if regal was the correct stance to take. Besides, it was so heavy that she would be dripping wet in ten minutes. The Consular Service had known perfectly well that the Koshani world was tropical in climate, but they had sent stuff suited for temperate zones anyhow—typical bureaucrats!

Emilia knew she was dithering out of her usual nervousness. No matter how hard she tried, she could not overcome her sense of smallness and inadequacy beside the tall and strange looking Koshani. Not for the first time she wondered if she had been chosen for her linguistic skills, her height, or her gender. Probably all of it. She stood more than two meters in her bare feet, but that was short for a Koshani male, and the women were even taller. Some computer at Service must have looked for someone tall and coughed up her name because she clearly lacked the proper skills to head up such an important mission.

A little angrily, Ambassador Lazarus thrust the purple robe back into the closet and pulled out a green gown of fine linen. She had worn it several times before, but at least she would not faint from being over-heated.

She slipped into the robe and tried once more to anticipate what awaited her. The invitation had used the term "ahigin," which for the Koshani covered everything from a *bris* to an opera. It seemed to mean something about performance, but it also meant ritual. Sacred and profane were not distinctions which existed in Koshani, and after nearly a year among them, Emilia could find no clue as to anything she would have described as a religious system. She missed Hiroshi's expertise in those matters as much as she missed his sense of play. The one remaining member of the mission, the historian Heinrich Schute, was so serious and dull she wanted to scream sometimes. She refused to think of Claudia Dalrymple, the team anthropologist, who had stopped eating soon after they arrived, and had been found dead in her room from dehydration and starvation.

The Ambassador straightened her garment and reached for her hairbrush. She pulled the bristles though her long and rather wiry gray tresses, breathing slowly, calming herself deliberately. The handle of the brush was rosewood, and had been given down from mother to daughter in her family for four generations. She should not have brought it, for now she would never be able to give it to her daughter, or granddaughter. Still, it was a touch of home in an alien world, and she was glad of that. She tried to think of her grandmother, Hannah Frances, a stern but serene old matriarch who would have been entirely at her ease in this situation. For once, her ritual did not help.

Emilia began to pin up her hair with the fine clips made of a native reed the Koshani called "hriba." They were exquisite, and despite her anxiety, touching them pleased her greatly. Each one had a tiny star-shaped flower worked into the clasp, and they nestled into her stiff hair, supply conforming to her needs. Unlike the tortoiseshell pins she had brought from home, the clips never slipped out and disappeared under the reed mats of the floor, but gripped her hair, almost as if they were still alive, and aware into the bargain.

They just might be, she realized. Dead or living was another concept which did not appear in the Koshani tongue. They seemed to assume the transmigration of souls, if she understood them correctly, and simply spoke of those who were not among the living as "unpresent." As with everything else about the aliens, Emilia was not certain of anything.

The Service had done its best to prepare her for her task, but a very poor best it had been, grudging and small-minded, she thought angrily. As the newest bureaucracy of the United Planets, it had been in the throes of realizing its own identity at the same time it sent its first mission to the stars. Thus, it had constructed uniforms which expressed ancient ideas of ambassadorial rank rather than dealing with such realities as climate and custom. In fact, Consular had totally refused to accept the Koshani at their word, and had imposed upon the aliens all the baggage of several centuries of fears of the unknown. The head of the Service had been told to ignore anything the Koshani said unless she could verify it with her own eyes. The aliens were assumed to be liars until proven otherwise.

Emilia shook her head and grinned wryly. *I came out of retirement to deal with petty idiots like Diego Jesus Rodriquez? I must have been out of my mind! Or swept away with the excitement of actually encountering another species. Yes, that was it. It was the chance of a lifetime, when I thought all my chances were over, what with Abraham laid to rest and the children grown. I was bored, and I felt useless. The Life Extension Treatments gave me years, but nothing to do with them. I made the right choice, even if Rodriquez sent us out here to perish, to die among strangers. Well, if I die, I'll go back and haunt the little monster!*

She considered the thought of death, amused at her fantasy of bedeviling Rodriquez, and actually smiling so much it made her face ache. Calculating the time dilation of faster-than-light travel, more than forty years had passed since she left the solar system. That made her nearly two hundred, and the LET would not last forever. There was an entire generation of descendants of herself and Abraham she would never know, she supposed. Or, perhaps, some great-grandchild would sail between the stars and come to find her.

The Ambassador doubted this. The political climate when she had left the solar system had been uneasy, in shock at meeting a species so clearly technically superior, yet so seemingly primitive in their manner and dress. Millions of people assumed the aliens were up to something, that their visit, and their offer of membership in a galaxy-wide community of worlds was only a diversion to lull humans into complacency while huge ships swarmed through space to destroy everything. It did not matter that the Koshani ship was small, that it only carried a dozen aliens and could only take four humans back across the stars. It did not matter that the Koshani insisted this was as large as a ship could be—that it was a matter of physics, not politics. Earth scientists laughed at the idea that there might be a limit to the size of a vehicle for FTL travel and hinted that the Koshani had stolen the technology and were only using it for their own incomprehensible purposes.

The Ambassador decided she was as ready as she was going to be now and walked out into the forechamber. Her escort and almost constant companion, Hrunda, was standing in the little room, gazing serenely at a presentation of Van Gogh's *Irises*. It was in a viewer which contained a hundred thousand pieces of art, and she never knew from day to day which it would display.

She took a moment to study his unhurried stance, enjoying the odd, clean lines of his wedge-shaped face, the beauty of a slender body draped in gauzy stuff which sparkled a little in the diffuse light of the room. Hrunda was a full head taller than Emilia, short for a Koshani. His facial features were now sufficiently familiar to her to be able to recognize him in a crowd, though crowds were rare. His eyes were set farther apart than on any human face, and there were nasal vents nearly flat above a rounded mouth. She looked at his hands, six digited, and at the elbow joint of his arms, which allowed him to do things only a contortionist could manage at home.

Aware of her regard, Hrunda turned and flared his vents, the equivalent of a smile for the Koshani. His wide-set eyes were the color of gentians, a deep near-purple without any surrounding white, and round and protuberant. He had adorned the stiff crest of hair with pale blossoms, and placed a necklace of the same flowers about his slender throat.

"Inform me, if it is permitted, of the manner of this artist, Honored Emilia."

The Ambassador swallowed hard. "It is permitted, Reverend Hrunda, yet difficult." The sheer complexity of the tongue made her neck tense and her mouth go dry. "The artist is . . ." she began, then faltered, groping for some verb sufficient to convey any meaning whatever.

"This artist is unpresent. He is of a heritage we name Dutch—a tribe unpresent today."

"How sad," Hrunda answered. "You have many tribes in absence."

Emilia realized she had inadvertently suggested the extinction of the Dutch people in her feeble use of Koshani. The aliens were curious about the history of Earth, and Schute had managed to give them a large portion of it in a dreadful pidgin Koshani that made the Ambassador cringe when she heard it. He had told them of the genocides of the twentieth century, and the wars which had raged between nations. She wished there was something she could say that was not about war and death and destruction.

"The folk are present, but answers not by this name. They are now members of the Pan-European tribe. The artist—Van Gogh in his tribe his name—is an unhappy being. He lacks recognition or reward, painting, painting under the golden sun, beset with yearnings. In time the mind of the artist breaks from sorrow in the blazing sun, and black avians alone witness his sudden unpresence."

Hrunda flared his vents again, and turned back to the painting. "The sadness is absent. This is most sweet, this image. And you are very eloquent this lighting, Honored Emilia. The words run as nectar from your tongue."

The Ambassador felt her face heat with a blush of pleasure at this unexpected praise. She pleated folds into her gown with dampened fingers, to disguise her delight. "If it is permitted, inform me then of the nature of this 'ahigin.' " They strolled out of the forechamber and emerged between ranks of heavy-scented fernlike trees.

Hrunda disjoined his elbows and clasped his hands behind his back in a way which made her want to wince. "It is permitted. We attend now an iteration of that Blessed Wordcrafter whose wisdom joins the stars into a tribe. We name her Nagali, and I know not how she is present among your folk."

Emilia grappled with the words, feeling her brain dizzy as she tried to discern the correct meaning. It was not the first time she had encountered the suggestion that some Koshani had incarnated on earth, but it still confused her. She had tried to avoid her own immediate scepticism on the subject. After all, billions of humans believed in literal reincarnation.

"I fear I am unable to apprehend your speaking, Reverend Hrunda."

He made a soft noise, the Koshani equivalent of a sigh. "All peoples know Nagali by some name. Ah—the gender! Is it that your Blessed Wordcrafter is now male? No matter! When a folk is moving from youth to understanding, this being incarnates among them and gives them the teachings of right manners."

"Teachings?" She was nearly drowning in alien words, even though she knew them in her mind. A bead of sweat began to trickle down her brow, tickling maddeningly.

"The teachings of proper manifestation which are true for all peoples which possess order." Hrunda paused, unclasped his hands, and fondled his pointed chin for a moment. "The being is of an obscure clan, and unlettered yet rich in the tongue."

Emilia frowned. The word he had used, "jugahi," which she translated as order, meant so much. In the largest sense, it conveyed the idea of civilization. And rich in the tongue was about poetry—what could he mean? Buddha was hardly of an obscure clan, nor did his teachings ring with poetry. Moses? Mohammad? Neither of those were great writers to her mind. Jesus, then? He came from a certain obscurity, she supposed, but, again, poetry was not what he was remembered for. "Which words, Reverend Hrunda?"

He offered her a purple look, patient and annoyed at the same time. "She writes thusly, 'Present or unpresent. This is an asking. If it is righter now to bear the barbs of mysterious chance, or lift weapons before a flood of woes, and by resisting, cease them.' Do you not have these teachings?" He appeared quite worried, if she read his expression correctly.

The Ambassador nearly stumbled as she translated the Koshani words into something she could actually grasp. It was insane, some strange Koshani jest. She tried very hard to envision the Prince of Denmark skulking about battlements, talking to ghosts and stabbing at arras here, between sweet-scented ferns. Then, with a start of surprise, she realized that the most quoted and memorable parts of Shakespeare were entirely free of specific context, that they were memorable for both their poetry and their human meaning. The universality of the Bard of Avon allowed him to be translated into nearly every human tongue. In her own lifetime she had seen a Kabuki *Othello,* an Oglala Sioux *Macbeth* and several other productions which would have astonished an Elizabethan audience.

Still, Emilia could not quite bring herself to believe that Shakespeare had somehow visited the Koshani homeworld, or been born there in a woman's body. That was rather too much! She recognized the beginning of the soliloquy, but that did not mean anything, really. They had told her to be suspicious, that the Koshani were up to something—but this! No one would travel between the stars just to announce that Shakespeare had visited their planet. She noticed a bubble of hysterical laughter forming in her throat, and swallowed it firmly. Then she wiped her brow with her sleeve.

Making her voice more calm than she felt, she asked, "This iteration we attend—what be it?"

"We name it *Gandaga and Hrussus.* Perhaps you own it not. It kindles thusly—'Two domiciles, equal in honor.' A sorrowful tale of the woes of pride."

The Ambassador nodded slowly. *Romeo and Juliet,* but here, due to the Koshani value of the female, the woman's name came first. "We do own this tale. Why would we not?"

"No tribe possesses all iteration."

The "lost plays!" Despite her skepticism, the Ambassador felt a surge of excitement. She was not certain she believed Hrunda, but she wanted to. She simply could not accept that Shakespeare would be dashing about the galaxy writing the same plays over and over. How boring! Clumsily, she asked that question.

Hrunda nodded, and the blossoms in his crest trembled with the movement. "Blessed Wordcrafter appears to teach beingness, Honored Emilia. The words bind diverse tribes to commonality. Each tribe owns a portion of the teachings, and by exchange, we enrich one another and discover how like we be. As we converse, the Wordcrafter writes on some world not yet come to maturity, to teach these lessons of humanity. We have knowledge of ninety-four tales. And yet, we Koshani own but a third of that as writings of Nagali."

Ninety-four! Her mind coiled around the number. The Ambassador tried to imagine plays she had never heard or seen or read, spoken in Koshani or some other alien tongue. She envisioned other races among the stars, listening each to their own version of the plays. Then she began to wonder which play the earth possessed as their unique contribution to the works of this Blessed Wordcrafter. Mad as it was, she could not help herself.

The dreadful sense of isolation which had depressed her for months began to fade. If she believed her companion, then there existed a common ground across the vast reaches of space. Who could have guessed it was a playwright whose very work had been questioned for centuries, argued and disputed by scholars who would not believe that Shakespeare had written what he wrote. She let herself chuckle, imagining the consternation when word finally reached earth. She only hoped Rodriquez was still alive to see it.

" 'And the elements so mixed within him' " she whispered, " 'that Nature could stand up to the world, and say, this was a man!' Stand up to the world—the entire galaxy!" Then she smiled, no longer alien.

MY VOICE IS IN MY SWORD

Kate Elliott

Kate Elliott's Jaran *series is breaking new ground in sociological science fiction. Here she continues her concerns by considering how one of humanity's classics might look to an utterly alien culture.*

We knew we were in trouble when Macbeth insisted on seeing the witches first.

You know the bit: Banquo and Macbeth enter and Banquo says, 'What are these, so wither'd and so wild in their attire?' " That's his moment, when he points out the three witches to Macbeth and Macbeth sees them for the first time, those three terrible hags who will hail Macbeth as king when of course he isn't king yet and will only become king by murder most foul.

Have you heard about actors who won't let any of the other actors have moments on stage that are theirs alone?

"Hey," said Bax to Yu-Saan, who was playing Banquo in drag, "*I'll* see the witches first, and then I'll tap you on the shoulder and you see them and say the line."

I propped my feet up on a stool and looked at Octavian and Octavian looked at me, and we both sighed. No doubt you're asking yourself where the director was, who might correct this little bit of scene-stealing. Well, he was right where he ought to be, sitting at a table staring at the taped-out stage where the five actors walked through the scene. He didn't say a word. How could he?

So they went on. The witches say their lines and Macbeth and Banquo say a few more, and just before the witches vanish, Bax got in a feel to Emmi's breast, just grabbed it, and Emmi went all stiff in the face and twisted away from him, and for all you could tell from El Directore's face, he hadn't seen a thing. But Emmi did double time off to the side, looking like steam was about to pour out of her ears. Enter Ross and Angus.

I'm Ross, by the way. The big joke is that I always have to play Ross in the Scottish play because my real name is Ross.

By the time rehearsal was over, Bax had managed to grope another witch and twist King Duncan's arm so hard while offering fealty that it actually brought a tear to old Jon-Jon's good eye. We retired to nurse our wounds, en masse to the hostel where we were sleeping, and Bax made a grand exit with his three lamias—one in each shade—to wherever it was a star of his stature stays on an alien world with a limited number of oxygen-rich chambers in which humankind can breathe.

"Lady Christ in Heaven," said Emmi, massaging her bruised breast while Jon-Jon examined his wrenched wrist with bemused interest. "I don't think I'm going to survive four more weeks of this. Where'd he get you, Cheri?"

Cheri—Second Witch—shrugged. She'd probably endured worse, back when she was a hootch dancer on Tau Ceti Tierce. "Crotch. What a pig."

"But Cheri, my dear," said Octavian quietly, "he's a Star."

Kostas—who should have been playing the lead but was playing Macduff instead—peered down from his bunk. "Why is it that Stars have to prove their legitimacy by doing theater? Can't they stay on their holies and interactives and leave us to do what we've trained for? I still can't believe Bax began directing during the damned read-through. And El Directore didn't say a thing."

"Oh, well," said Emmi. "I'm sure it'll get better. It certainly can't get worse."

Emmi, we all had to agree later, would not be auditioning for the role of Cassandra in *Troilus and Cressida* anytime soon.

We took two days more to block out the rest of the play and Bax behaved himself, except that he ate sandwiches and drank coffee every time he was on stage, walking around with the cup in one hand and his script in the other. When he fought and killed young Siward for the first time, he ate a sandwich during the fight scene and dribbled crumbs onto poor prostrate Ahmed—who was doubling as Donalbain and young Siward—while he said his lines.

At the end of the first week, the diplomat Phan-Yen Caraglio arrived to give us the official tour of the Squat homeworld. Yes, I know, you're not supposed to call them Squats, but you can't really help it. They seem to spend an endless amount of time sitting around, and whether they're sitting or standing, they only reach hip-high.

Caraglio gave us the standard Squat lecture as we trundled along in a big sealed barge down a canal filled with gold coins. Or, at least, they looked like gold coins. Since humans couldn't breathe the atmosphere, none of us had gotten close enough to check for certain.

"Our hosts are only the second alien group who specifically requested an artistic embassy to their planet, and you will offer them their first glimpse into human art and culture and history. I hope I don't need to remind you that you were chosen for your professionalism and your skill, and your reputation as a first rank theater company."

We all looked at Bax. He sat lounging in the back, listening to whatever Flopsy and Mopsy and Cottontail were whispering in his ears and certainly not listening to M. Caraglio. Bax had short curly black hair and sported the fashionable tricolor face. His lamias matched the colors. Flopsy was pale white and Mopsy was coal black. Cottontail's skin was a screaming shade of scarlet, which looks okay as a small patch of skin but pretty damned stupid for a whole body. She wore the least clothes—a particolored white and black scarf around her hips and a sheer silk blouson—and she must have had enviro work done on her skin implants, too; she never looked cold except, of course, her nipples were always erect. I myself

can't believe that happened simply because she found
Bax so staggeringly attractive every second of every day.

"May I ask a question?" asked the beautiful Peng-Hsin,
who oozed Star out of every pore. She plays Lady Macbeth, and her Star-magnitude is every bit as great as
Bax's, with one vital difference: Peng-Hsin Khatun is a
professional. M. Caraglio melted in her general direction.

"Assuredly, M. Khatun. It is by asking questions that
we learn, and we hope, of course, to learn as much about
our hosts as they learn about us."

"Are we really sailing down a river of gold coins, as it
appears?"

"I'm afraid any answer I give will seem inadequate.
Chemically, we don't know. But as for appearances—
certainly they appear as gold coins to us, but we inevitably impress our own biases onto what we see and
experience here, and *their* notion of what these objects
are, of what their value is, their notion, even, of how
much appearances count at all as opposed to simple reality, we can't know. Ah." He broke off and pointed to his
left. "There is the building that we believe is their Parliament, or at least, the seat of their governing body."

Squat Parliament lay on a flat stretch of ground ringed
by three circles of flower beds. A simple, regular octagon, it had neither roof nor walls but a plain white foundation marked out by columns and shaded by a
perplexing array of what looked like canvas awnings. It
was huge, though; four baseball games could have been
played simultaneously on that pale surface. The barge
ground to a halt and we crowded over to the left to stare
out the view windows.

"You may have noticed," added M. Caraglio, pitching
his voice higher to carry over our murmuring as we
pointed out the clusters of Squats who were, of course,
squatting on the green lawns between the flower beds and
inside the twin rings of columns that bordered the octagon, "that this, our hosts' capital city, is not large at all
by human standards. There's some debate within the
xenodiplomacy team stationed here whether that is because they simply have a small population or whether
their population base is more agrarian and spread out
over the land." He went on, explaining about the relative
proportion of land mass to ocean and how that affected

their climate and thus their agricultural base and the availability of land for habitation, but something far more interesting was going on outside.

A Squat came trundling along the river bank, spotted our barge, and waded with its splay feet right out over the gold coins to press its nose—if that little turnip of a bulb could be called a nose—up against the window next to Peng-Hsin. They regarded each other. We all regarded it, and it swiveled its squat little head topped with ivory fern ears and took us all in.

"It's curious," said Peng-Hsin, sounding amused.

M. Caraglio coughed, sounding uncomfortable. "This has never happened before," he said. "They've always kept their distance. Very careful about that."

"Aww," said Cheri, who combined the oddest mix of sentimentality and hardheadedness, "maybe it's just a little baby."

From the back, Bax burped loudly. "Fuck, it's ugly," he said. Mopsy and Flopsy tittered. Cottontail said, "Oh, Bax," in her breathless knock-me-up voice.

As if in response to his comment, a whole herd of Squats uprooted themselves from their meditations on the lawn and ambled over toward us. Through the windows, we heard a chorus of hoots rising and falling as the herd of Squats formed a semicircle at the bank of the river. Our Squat pricked up its lacy ears, snuffled one last time toward Peng-Hsin, and then turned and trundled back to the shoreline.

"Oh, dear," murmured M. Caraglio. Bax burped again. The diplomat shot him a look so filled with distaste that it was palpable; then, as quickly, he smoothed over his expression into that bland mask that diplomats and out of work actors wear. Caraglio went forward to the lock and made some comment through the translation-screen, and the barge scraped sideways over the coins, following our Squat to the bank. As soon as our alien clambered up onto the sward, it was at once swarmed by other Squats rather like the winning runner is in the last game of the Worlds Series.

"Uh-oh," said Emmi and Cheri at the same time.

"Looks like trouble," Octavian muttered, and we all avoided looking back at Bax. The effect was the same, of course. By not looking at him, we made his presence all the more obvious.

Three Squats inched forward and climbed up the ramp that led into the forward lock. The smoked glass barrier pretty much cut them off from our sight, but I caught a glimpse of a fanned-out fern ear and the trailing end of a bulb nose brushed across the glass from the other side.

Then, like the voice of the gods, the translation-screen boomed out words. "One of our young ones has offended one of your people. We beg your pardon."

I winced. Octavian covered his ears. On the back bench, Cottontail crossed her arms across her breasts, as if the volume might warp their particularly fine shape. Bax pinched her on the thigh, and she shrieked, giggled, and unwound her arms.

Caraglio had a sick look on his face, like he'd just eaten something rancid. "Not at all," he said. "I beg ... It isn't ... Please don't ..." He sputtered to a stop, flexed his hands in and out, and began again. "We are sorry that this incident has interrupted your deliberations, and we were not at all disturbed by the interest of your young one."

Muted hooting leaked out through the glass barrier as the Squats consulted.

"What I want to know," said Kostas in a low voice, "is how from so far away the Squats knew Bax was insulting the poor little thing."

The translation-screen crackled to life, but this time, mercifully, the volume had been lowered. "We consider your words," it squawked in its tinny intonation, not capturing at all the exuberance of Squat hooting, "and will meditate on them. As time continues to flow, you may continue on your journey, but be assured that to our recollection, this incident has not occurred."

Caraglio did not even get a chance to reply before they scooted off the barge and we went on our way. I watched Squat Parliament recede and the Squats amble back up the hill to fall into place in scattered groups like flowers being arranged on separate trays.

"What next?" asked Bax. "They got any dancing girls here?" His lamias shrieked with laughter and he reached over and tweaked Cottontail so hard on her hooters without her even losing a beat in her giggling that I had to wonder if she'd had pain desensitizers built into her skin as well. In her line of work, it might not have been a bad idea.

But Caraglio cut the tour short and we returned to the theater instead. Unsure of what we were supposed to do now, we wandered onto the stage and loitered. Bax and the lamias disappeared into his dressing room. Caraglio headed for El Directore's office. We heard a knock, a voice, and then the door slammed shut.

"Who's going to go eavesdrop?" asked Emmi, and for some damn reason, they all looked at me.

"Oh, hell," I said. Ah, well, once a go-between, always a go-between. I exited through one of the doors in the tiring-house wall and snuck down the hallway to stick an ear up against the door. It was a good thing that wood doesn't transmit emotional heat. I would have been burned.

"The man is a complete asshole," shouted Caraglio in a most undiplomatic fashion. "Why is he allowed to run roughshod over the rest of you?"

"May I be frank with you, M. Caraglio?" said El Directore in a low voice. He sounded tired, and for the first time, I felt some sympathy for him.

"I wish you would be!"

"His studio is bankrolling this expedition as a showcase for him and for Peng-Hsin. You can't have thought that a small theatrical company like ourselves could afford this, even with a government grant?"

There was silence. Caraglio cleared his throat. "Well, then," he said, "he must be confined to quarters and to the theater. We cannot have any more such incidents. Surely you understand that."

"If he is confined, then so must be everyone else."

There was a longer silence.

"So be it," said Caraglio in a resigned tone, and he opened the door so quickly that I had to jerk back to maintain my balance.

"Oh, er, ah," I said as the diplomat shut the door behind himself.

He set his hands on his hips and glared at me. "Star quality," he said, and produced a surprisingly robust raspberry. "Then can you explain to me why M. Baxtrusini acts this way while M. Khatun, who presumably has the same conditions attaching to her contract and her life, does not?"

I shrugged. "Why are any of us the way we are? Ask Shakespeare, M. Caraglio. He probably had as good an idea of the answer to that question as anyone.

He grunted. "Empathic. Don't you people know how to read? It says so in the packet of orientation materials."

"Empathic?" I echoed weakly. I did not want to admit that the first paragraph of dry prose set beside the first close-grained and utterly confusing diagrammatic map had put me off from the rest. As usual, the government was too cheap to add any decent media values to their official publication.

Caraglio practically snarled. "The Squats—er, the Squanishta—are considered to be empathic by the xenobiological team that identifies psychological and physiological profiles."

"But how can we tell?"

"I don't know how they tell! I'm just a goddamned diplomat, and I can tell you, it's not the aliens I have trouble dealing with! If you'll excuse me." He stamped off down the hall, and I can't say that I blamed him for his bad temper.

El Directore's door cracked open slightly. "Is he gone?" our fearless leader asked tremulously. "Say, Ross, could you let the others know about the new restrictions—er, never mind. I'll ring for Patrick." Lucky Patrick. As the Stage Manager, he always got the dirty jobs.

With the restrictions, we ended up spending a hell of a lot of time in the theater, since our hostel was dreary to the point of sublimity. But it was a nice theater. The Squats had evidently spent some time building a tidy little replica of the Globe with real wood, or what passed for real wood. Since the house wasn't sealed in with the atmospheric shield yet, we could go out and stretch in the yard or sit in the galleries to watch rehearsal or to read or nap or knit, or whatever. It was a good space, as accurate in many ways as the meticulously reconstructed Fourth Globe in London. Certainly the Squats had done their research, and if the theater was any indication, they seemed to care that they gained the fullest appreciation possible of this alien art form.

So meticulous were they that we had to stop for an entire day when Seton put his foot through the trap in the banqueting scene. We, the lords, were exiting, and Bax had launched into his monologue a bit early, since he liked to rush his big moments, when Sanjar's foot caught in some loose board and he went through all the way up to his thigh.

He muttered an oath in a language I didn't recognize. Octavian and I grabbed him by the arms and heaved him up. He was white around the mouth, and he winced and then tried to put weight on the foot. Meanwhile, Peng-Hsin, downstage, saw us struggling and she broke away from Bax and came up to see if Sanjar was all right.

Oblivious, Bax continued. " 'For mine own good, all causes shall give way ... ' "

Sanjar tested the foot. Then he shrugged. Nothing broken, or even sprained. The trap gaped in front of him. El Directore had stood up. He hesitated and then sank down again, and we completed our exit. From off stage I looked back to watch Bax finish his monologue: " 'Strange things I have in head that will to hand, Which must be acted ere they may be scann'd' "

And Peng-Hsin, amazingly, came in right on cue with her line. Excunt. Bax had barely gotten off stage before he spun around and tromped back on.

"What is this?" he demanded, pointing at the trap lying ajar. "How did this happen? I could hurt myself! Tell those damned Squats to fix it!" He marched off, looking deeply offended.

So we took a day off while the Squats fixed it. We played bridge, hearts, and pinochle in our dreary hostel instead of being able to go out and explore a bit more. Not an edifying way to spend the day. In the morning we returned to the theater to find silver leaves enscribed with odd little squiggles in all the dressing rooms. M. Caraglio informed us that these were evidently some kind of mark of apology for the disruption, proferred by the Squat carpenters. Peng-Hsin promptly made hers into a necklace, thus gracing both the gift and herself. Bax insisted the lamias use theirs as g-strings. And when Emmi imitated Peng-Hsin and strung hers as a necklace, too, he managed to rip it in half in one of their scenes. Cheri caught

Emmi's arm just before Emmi slugged him, and in thanks got groped again.

"You would think," said Kostas, "that he gets enough groping in on his entourage that he wouldn't need to take it out on them."

I shrugged. Octavian rolled his eyes. "Kost, I don't think it's sex that he's interested in."

"Take a break," called Patrick, thus saving Cheri from Bax's hands and Emmi from doing the deed the rest of us would have liked to do ourselves. "Bax and Kostas in fifteen for their final scene."

But of course, we all returned in fifteen minutes to watch what was now our favorite scene in the play, the one in which Macduff kills Macbeth on the field of battle. We gathered in the yard, sitting and standing in a casual group so as not to seem too interested.

"Turn, hell-hound, turn!" Macduff cries when he reenters and sees Macbeth. They fight. Macbeth discovers that Macduff is not "of woman born," and at that moment realizes that he is doomed. We drank it in.

"Lay on, Macduff, And damn'd be him that first cries, 'Hold, enough!' "

Now it's true that in the text Macbeth is killed off stage and Macduff comes back on carrying Macbeth's head, but it's rarely played that way. Swordplay is a marvelous thing, and we have plenty of ways these days to make the death look real.

They fought, and Macduff drove him back and back—

"Now, wait," said Bax, lowering his sword. "*I'll* drive Macduff back, and when I have him pinned, then I'll drop my sword and allow him to kill me."

"Ah, er," said El Directore.

Kostas stared at a point ten feet behind and two feet above Bax's head, his expression mercifully blank.

Yu-Saan, who was doubling as the fight choreographer, came downstage. "I beg your pardon, but we need to follow the swordfight as it was rehearsed."

They tried it again. Macduff drives Macbeth back and back, and then suddenly and unexpectedly Bax sidestepped and with main force knocked Kostas flat. It took Kost a second, shaking his head, to get his wind back, but then he climbed back to his feet with sword raised. Bax darted away from him, running downstage, and showily impaled himself on the blade. He fell to his knees, paused, got up again, and sheathed the sword. Then he set his hands on his hips, leaving his sword sticking out at an awkward angle. Yu-Saan, coming back downstage, had to dodge the blade as he swung around; it looked like he was trying to trip her with it.

"Or if you don't like that," said Bax, "then instead I could drive him back, like I suggested the first time. You see, I have him at my mercy, but I realize that death is upon me so I let him kill me."

Octavian had his eyes shut, but the rest of us watched in appalled fascination. "Goddess help us," murmured Cheri, "he's so damned swellheaded that he can't let someone else kill him even if it's in the script. He's got to control it himself." She made an obscene little gesture with her left hand.

"Start again," said El Directore with a put-upon sigh. "Uh, Macduff with 'I have no words.' "

Kostas had that look on his face: doubtless he *had* no words. Luckily Shakespeare could speak for him. " 'My voice is in my sword, thou bloodier villain Than terms can give thee out!' "

They fight.

Kostas restrained himself admirably, even when Bax again deviated from Yu-Saan's blocking and this time slapped Kostas with the flat of his blade hard on the abdomen. We finally gave up watching, because it was too painful, for Kostas personally and for us as artists. Rehearsal is always tedious when an actor refuses to discover his role and instead attempts to cram it into a pre-formed shape.

We had to take off the next day while the Squats put the atmospheric shield in place. At the hostel, Cheri suggested strip poker. We settled on whist.

The shield rose like a clear glass wall from the yard about one meter in front of the proscenium and bound us all the way back to the back galleries, snaking in to seal off the back rooms and the cellar as well. It felt like performing in a fish bowl. It felt, all at once, restrictive. Octavian and Emmi and I went and sat on the edge of the stage and gazed mournfully at the house, lost to us now. A single Squat walked the galleries, vanished, and then reappeared in the yard, pacing out the area with a stately tread.

Emmi smiled. "They seem more even-tempered," she said. "Don't you think?"

"How can you tell?" asked Octavian. "It isn't as if we've had any real contact with them."

Emmi shrugged. "Oh, I don't know. Just a feeling I get. They feel more serene."

Octavian lifted one eyebrow, looking skeptical. "Emmi, my dear, you're becoming positively spiritual these days."

She laughed, and as if at the sound the Squat lifted its fern ears and wiggled its turnip nose and turned to regard us with the same intent curiosity as we regarded it. Or at least, so we assumed.

Daringly, Emmi lifted a hand and waved to it.

And it lifted one of its legs and copied the gesture.

Emmi broke out into a wide grin. Even Octavian smiled.

"First contact," I said.

"Only for me," said Emmi. "The first was that little one that came up to Peng-Hsin."

The Squat lowered the leg and ambled back into the galleries and disappeared.

"Maybe they're not standoffish," said Octavian in a tone trembling with revelation. "Maybe they're just polite."

"Octavian," I said, "they did ask us to come here, after all. Why wouldn't they be polite?"

"They're just so—reserved."

"Maybe they just don't want to offend us," said Emmi.

"Or us to offend them," I added, thinking of Bax. And, like the devil, he appeared stage left and shuffled over to us. He looked hungover.

"Hey you, uh—" He faltered, running a hand through the tangled black frizz of his hair. "—uh, Witch, you. Can you get me something to drink?"

Emmi got that set look on her face. "Sorry," she said, hunching a shoulder up against him. "I'm working on my lines."

He began to say something more, but then unlucky Patrick came in stage left. "I need something to drink," said

Bax, and burped loudly, and Patrick spun on his heel and went out again. Mercifully, Bax followed him.

It was a bad day for a runthrough. Feeling caged-in got on everybody's nerves. We either had to stay locked into the warren of rooms behind the stage or else watch the action through the one-way curtain in the musician's gallery, and tempers ran shorter than usual, which is saying something. Bax couldn't keep his hands off the witches, and he kept ignoring his blocking and getting in front of the king. The ambient emotional temperature went up about fifty degrees. Except Peng-Hsin, who evidently had huge reserves of calm to draw from. She wore her silver leaf necklace like a badge of courage and grace, and even in her love scenes with Bax managed to steer away from his groping hands without seeming to avoid him.

Watching them act together was a study in contrasts. The true test, we had long since decided, of Peng-Hsin's professionalism was the way she could play a loving Lady Macbeth to Bax's Macbeth. " 'And I feel now the future in the instant,' " she says in Act I Scene V.

"My dearest love," he said—and bit her.

And I mean really bit her.

Peng-Hsin let out a startled and most unprofessional shriek. She jerked away from him, slapping a hand up over her cheek. A drop of blood leaked out from between her fingers, then another, then a third. She lowered her hand to reveal her cheek; his teeth marks showed clearly, as well as the blood welling up in a rough semicircle, where his bite had broken her skin.

All hell broke loose. Cheri gasped so loudly she might as well have shouted, and we all began talking and shouting at once. Peng-Hsin spun and ran off the stage. Patrick hurridly called for a break, and Cheri and Emmi ran downstairs to minister to Peng-Hsin. El Directore laid his head down on the edge of the stage. For an instant, I thought he was hiding tears of sheer frustration.

Bax licked his lips. "Hey, what about the rest of my scene?" he demanded.

El Directore lifted his face—dry-eyed, I noted—and lifted a hand to signal to Patrick, sealed into the control booth in the back of the house. "Cast meeting on stage in thirty minutes," he said. He circled the stage and vanished into his office. Bax left for his dressing room.

In thirty minutes, we gathered like vultures, all of us. Peng-Hsin, flanked by Emmi and a militant looking Cheri, had a patch of skin-meld covering the wound on her cheek. Patrick and El Directore arrived. Then we waited for another five minutes. Bax ambled out finally, looking bored.

"I think," said El Directore in a low, irresolute voice, "that you owe an apology."

Bax sighed, looking put-upon. "All right, all right," he said briskly. "I'm sorry I brought the girls with me. It was a little tasteless, I know, since we're stuck here and you guys and gals can't possibly be getting the same quality of sex as I am, but hey, we're all professionals here, and this is one of the things you have to go through to do this kind of work."

Struck dumb, we merely stared at him.

El Directore, surprisingly enough, spoke first. "Er, ah," he said forcefully. "Well, then, I'll make this short. We have our premiere performance in seven days. Tomorrow we do a full tech runthrough and the day after we go to dress."

And so we did. Bax restrained himself to minor and individual acts of cruelty, like twisting arms and hitting people with his sword and the usual groping. And of course we couldn't say anything. He *had* apologized, after all, or so El Directore reminded us. And he was a Star.

Bruised and battered we got ready for the premiere.

Still, it was hard not to get excited, especially as the galleries and the yard filled up with hooting Squats. Against all rules, I snuck up to the musician's gallery to catch a glimpse, and found Emmi and—mark my soul!— Peng-Hsin there, gazing wide-eyed out at our audience.

"Gee," said Emmi on an exhalation. "Wow."

The shield was marvelously transparent and gave us a clear view of the house and the two thousand aliens. Ivory fern ears furled and unfurled to some unknown rhythm and the Squats almost seemed to be bobbing, like a swelling sea, as they waited. For an instant, I felt their excitement as much as my own.

"I can't believe I'm doing this," Peng-Hsin said, and then covered her mouth with a hand and laughed the kind of laugh a child gives on Christmas Eve when she sees the lit tree and all the presents for the first time.

"Places," said Patrick through the inner-mike system. As we went down the stairs, we met M. Caraglio coming up, to watch from this hidden vantage point.

"Good luck," he said, and we all winced in horror, and like a good diplomat he caught our reaction and added, stumbling, "Oh, ah, break a leg." We retreated in some disorder back to our rightful places.

House lights down. Stage lights up. A desert Heath. Thunder and lightning. Enter three Witches.

It went well. Our audience was attentive; even through the shield we heard their taut silence. And we had come together as a cast over the last five weeks, especially since we all felt the same way about one person in particular. There is nothing like shared disgust to bring focus to a play, especially the Scottish play with its bloody villain.

He was the villain, and we made him so.

Birnam Wood did come toward Dunsinane, and Macbeth met, at long last, the man who was of no woman born. They fight.

We watched through the door plackets set up, like the gallery curtain, to be a one-way view port. Was it possible that we would finish as we were meant to, that we wouldn't be embarrassed in front of these intent aliens, that we, the first humans artists they had encountered, could give a command performance and prove ourselves worthy of the title of artists?

Octavian gave a little groan. Of course not. Even here, in the actual performance, Bax had to ruin it. The two men lock swords corp-a-corp; it was supposed to come to naught—they break away from each other and the fight continues to its inevitable end. But Bax, damn him, had to throw it. With Kostas unsuspecting, it was possible for Bax to throw and twist and wrench Macduff's sword out of his grip. The sword clattered to the stage with awful finality.

There was a terrible pause. Macbeth holds Macduff at his mercy.

Like an animal cornered by a cobra, we were too paralyzed with fear and—yes, with sheer hatred—to close our eyes.

And Bax stepped back, allowing Kostas to pick up his lost sword. Bax opened his arms to receive the death blow. And then he added the crowning insult of adding a line to Shakespeare.

"Oh, my God," he said. His eyes widened. Kostas, no fool, ran him through between the body and the arm.

Bax fell and lay as still as death. It was the best acting he'd done the whole time. Entering with the other lords, I was impressed despite myself.

Meanwhile, Macduff had, as we staged it, staggered off and collapsed where we could conveniently overlook him until Siward sees him.

The final lines passed smoothly. They had never run quite so strongly before. " 'Hail, King of Scotland!' " we cry, and Malcolm makes his final speech. Curtain.

The shield dimmed until it was opaque. Through it, we heard the muted hooting of the Squats. We panted, waiting for the rest of the cast to come out for the curtain call. Bax didn't move.

"Sulking," muttered Octavian.

Jon-Jon, who'd been too long in the business to let a grudge mar the professionalism of the moment, hurried over to help him up. He bent. He shook Bax. He shook him again. He gave a little cry and straightened up.

"I think he's dead."

He *was* dead.

M. Caraglio burst onto the stage, took one look at the situation, and barked, "No curtain call! Where's—"

El Directore stumbled out from the back as well. He wrung his hands together. "What will we do? What will we do? What if the studio withdraws their funding? This is terrible. How did this happen? He had no heart condition listed on his health records."

"We must go apologize at once to the Squanishta," said Caraglio. "Can you imagine the kind of misunderstandings this could foster?"

All at once I recalled that if the Squats really were empathic, then our audience was absorbing an entire second performance here and now, despite the curtain being nominally closed.

Finally, thank goodness, Patrick appeared and took everything in hand. "Yu-Saan, you and Octavian carry off—ah—" Even his aplomb was shaken by the sight of Bax lying there dead. "Move him back to his dressing room. And for the Goddess' sake, get the three good-time girls out of there."

"If you'll come with me," said Caraglio to El Directore. "And perhaps a representative from the actors as well."

They all looked at me. Ah well, once a go-between, always a go-between. I walked in a daze with the other two around front to the communications lock. I was not surprised to find that three Squanishtas had arrived before us, fern ears unfurled, their bodies otherwise motionless as they hunkered down on the other side of the lock wall.

Both sides spoke at the same time. "We beg your pardon—"

Both sides stopped.

After a moment of polite silence, Caraglio began again. "Please, your excellencies, be assured that the tragedy that has happened here today is a complete mystery to us. I must beg your pardon for this terrible disruption. We hope you will forgive us and allow us a suitable time to—ah—recover and explain."

They hooted. The translation crackled through the screen. "It was a wise and well-thought play. Please do not think we did not appreciate it, or think that it failed in any way although there was this slight mishap. One has only to hear the words to understand their meaning."

The middle one shifted forward—somewhat rashly, I thought, given what I'd seen of them—and pressed its turnip nose up against the cloudy lock wall as if to make sure we understood how important the next remark was. As if to make sure that we understood that it understood. "My voice is in my sword."

There was a pause while the three jockeyed for position, and the rash one was shouldered to the back as if the other two were aghast at its rudeness.

"We hope," continued one of the other two—I couldn't be sure which—"that in this small way we have spared you the distress of failing to complete your work of art."

"Oh, my God," said Caraglio, an eerie echo of Bax's last words. "I've got to get back to the office."

"I don't understand," said El Directore. But I did.

Caraglio made polite farewells, and we exited the lock. We wound our way back through the protected corridor. Caraglio left at once. I went back to the stage.

Bax was still lying there, dead. Through the tiring house doors, thrown open, I could hear shrieking and wailing from the back: the lamias were objecting to being thrown out of the dressing room—I couldn't tell if they were also mourning for their lost patron, or only their privileges—and Yu-Saan and Octavian didn't want to touch the body until they had somewhere to take it.

"But what happened?" demanded Cheri. Emmi wiped tears—not, I think, for Bax personally, but for the shock of it all—from her cheeks. Peng-Hsin stood with regal dignity. The others crowded together for comfort.

"The Squats did it," I said. "I'd guess that they sort of used their empathic powers to make his heart seize up, or something."

"But why?" asked Peng-Hsin quietly.

"Isn't it obvious what the outcome of the play is? Isn't it almost a ritualistic act, the entire thing? And they wouldn't have built this—" I waved at the theater, "—if they didn't care about us doing well. If they didn't want us to succeed. And they read, from us, the object of the play was for Macbeth to die. How embarrassing for *us* if we failed to accomplish that act, in our first performance for them."

Mercenary Cheri suddenly stifled a giggle behind a hand.

I shrugged. What else was there to say? The real cleanup would be left for the diplomats. And it was funny, in a black kind of way.

I looked over at Bax. The rest of them did, too. It's hard not to look at a corpse, especially when he's the one person in the room that everyone was wishing dead just half an hour before.

"They were just trying to be helpful."

Welcome to DAW's Gallery of Ghoulish Delights!

☐ **DRACULA: PRINCE OF DARKNESS**
Martin H. Greenberg, editor
A blood-draining collection of all-original Dracula stories. From Dracula's traditional stalking grounds to the heart of modern-day cities, the Prince of Darkness casts his spell over his prey in a private blood drive from which there is no escape!
UE2531—$4.99

☐ **FRANKENSTEIN: THE MONSTER WAKES**
Martin H. Greenberg, editor
Powerful visions of a man and monster cursed by destiny to be eternally at odds. Here are all-original stories by such well-known writers as: Rex Miller, Max Allan Collins, Brian Hodge, Rick Hautala, and Daniel Ransom.   UE2584—$4.99

☐ **JOURNEYS TO THE TWILIGHT ZONE**
Carol Serling, editor
From a dog given a transfusion of werewolf blood, to a cocktail party hypnosis session that went a step too far, here are 16 journeys—to that most unique of dimensions—*The Twilight Zone.*—by such masters of the fantastic as Alan Dean Foster, William F. Nolan, Charles de Lint, and Kristine Katherine Rusch.
UE2525—$4.99

☐ **URBAN HORRORS**
William F. Nolan and Martin H. Greenberg, editors
Here are 18 powerful nightmare visions of the horrors that stalk the dark streets of the cities and the lonely, echoing hallways of our urban dwellings in this harrowing collection of modern-day terrors, stories by Ray Bradbury, Richard Matheson, John Cheever, Shirley Jackson and their fellow fright-masters.
UE2548—$5.50

☐ **THE YEAR'S BEST HORROR STORIES: XXI**
Karl Edward Wagner, editor
More provocative tales of terror, including: a photographer whose obsession with images may bring to life trouble beyond his wildest fantasies . . . a couple caught up in an ancient ritual that offers the promise of health, but at a price that may prove far too high . . . and a woman whose memory may be failing her with the passing years—or for a far more unnatural reason.   UE2572—$5.50

Science Fiction Anthologies

☐ **FUTURE EARTHS: UNDER AFRICAN SKIES**   UE2544—$4.99
Mike Resnick & Gardner Dozois, editors
From a utopian space colony modeled on the society of ancient Kenya, to a shocking future discovery of a "long-lost" civilization, to an ingenious cure for one of humankind's oldest woes—a cure that might cost too much—here are 15 provocative tales about Africa in the future and African culture transplanted to different worlds.

☐ **FUTURE EARTHS: UNDER SOUTH AMERICAN SKIES**
Mike Resnick & Gardner Dozois, editors   UE2581—$4.99
From a plane crash that lands its passengers in a survival situation completely alien to anything they've ever experienced, to a close encounter of the insect kind, to a woman who has journeyed unimaginably far from home—here are stories from the rich culture of South America, with its mysteriously vanished ancient civilizations and magnificent artifacts, its modern-day contrasts between sophisticated city dwellers and impoverished villagers.

☐ **MICROCOSMIC TALES**   UE2532—$4.99
Isaac Asimov, Martin H. Greenberg, & Joseph D. Olander, eds.
Here are 100 wondrous science fiction short-short stories, including contributions by such acclaimed writers as Arthur C. Clarke, Robert Silverberg, Isaac Asimov, and Larry Niven. Discover a superman who lives in a *real* world of nuclear threat . . . an android who dreams of electric love . . . and a host of other tales that will take you instantly out of this world.

☐ **WHATDUNITS**   UE2533—$4.99
☐ **MORE WHATDUNITS**   UE2557—$5.50
Mike Resnick, editor
In these unique volumes of all-original stories, Mike Resnick has created a series of science fiction mystery scenarios and set such inventive sleuths as Pat Cadigan, Judith Tarr, Katharine Kerr, Jack Haldeman, and Esther Friesner to solving them. Can you match wits with the masters to make the perpetrators fit the crimes?
